A DETECTIVE  VEL

KILLING THE MUSIC

JACK GATLAND

Hooded Man MEDIA
INSPIRATION • PRODUCTION • PUBLICATION

Published by Hooded Man Media.

First Edition: October 2021

PRAISE FOR JACK GATLAND

'This is one of those books that will keep you up past your bedtime, as each chapter lures you into reading just one more.'

'This book was excellent! A great plot which kept you guessing until the end.'

'Couldn't put it down, fast paced with twists and turns.'

'The story was captivating, good plot, twists you never saw and really likeable characters. Can't wait for the next one!'

'I got sucked into this book from the very first page, thoroughly enjoyed it, can't wait for the next one.'

'Totally addictive. Thoroughly recommend.'

'Moves at a fast pace and carries you along with it.'

'Just couldn't put this book down, from the first page to the last one it kept you wondering what would happen next.'

Before LETTER FROM THE DEAD...
There was

Learn the story of what *really* happened to DI Declan Walsh,
while at Mile End!

An EXCLUSIVE PREQUEL, completely free to anyone who
joins the Declan Walsh Reader's Club!

Join at www.subscribepage.com/jackgatland

For Mum, who inspired me to write.

For Tracy, who inspires me to write.

CONTENTS

PROLOGUE

From the moment that he arrived at the venue, Dave Manford knew that this had been a *terrible* mistake.

The venue itself was fine; *Eastcheap Albums,* a corner bar in the heart of the City of London at the junction of Eastcheap and Lovat Lane was a structure amid a strange mish-mash of Gothic style buildings and steel and chrome monstrosities, where international corporations rubbed shoulders with hipster coffee bars and juice lounges.

Eastcheap Albums was part of a chain of music-themed bars that leaned into the aesthetic, with vinyl albums racked up in shelves behind the ornate, golden-lit bar on the left of the room. Here you could sit in luxurious red velvet high chairs and stare up at Prince, David Bowie, the cast of Grease and Bob Marley among others, all immortalised on album covers with even *more* albums, apparently several thousand in total interspersed among the various tables, chairs and loungers in the venue.

To the right of the bar and against the back wall a small stage had been set, so that customers, dining on what looked to be expensive cocktails and stone-baked pizzas, could be entertained by some of the best upcoming acts in the industry, now rocketing up the ladder of fame.

Or, as Dave mused, staring around the bar, *tumbling haphazardly down it.*

It hadn't been his idea to start his comeback tour here. He'd wanted to start at the *O2 Arena* in Greenwich, or more likely, the *Indigo Lounge* there. He'd seen a few other eighties bands re-invent themselves at the Lounge, and they always said good things about it. And, more importantly, it was on the Jubilee Line, so it was easy to get home from.

Or maybe somewhere like the *100 Club* on Oxford Street would have been good, even an intimate gig at the *Roundhouse* off Primrose Hill but no, Lydia had explained slowly to him that *this was a great place;* not only was it swish and trendy, but they could hire it out completely, so that every person there tonight was hand-invited for the return of *Dave Manford's Alternator.*

Dave originally wanted to call the new group *Alternate Tour*, a play on words of the title of the band that he and his brother had started decades ago; *Alternator*, a five-piece indie rock band that hit the charts and even broke America with their second album, *Secrets and Lies* back in 1987. But, after his brother Nick had disappeared right before Christmas 1998, believed to have committed suicide after finally becoming sick of the fame that his band gave him, Dave found himself ousted by his own band.

Apparently this was because of some contractual morality clause he'd broken, although it was more likely that Benny Simpson was a bitter old queen who should have been fired as manager years earlier, The clause he'd allegedly broken by giving his brother means to defend himself, and the items he also needed to function on a day-to-day basis meant he could no longer be part of *Alternator*, couldn't *call* himself part of *Alternator* or even sing any of the *Alternator* songs, as pretty much all of them had been written by Nick and guitarist Andy Mears, who'd continued writing solo for the band after Nick disappeared.

Well, that was bollocks.

He might not have written them, but he'd certainly contributed to them, especially the ones on *Secrets and Lies*. By then Nick was whacked out on coke and painkillers every night and unable to focus, let alone create on a daily basis, and Dave had been the one to hunt him down, clean him up, give him shiny new pills to bring him back to coherence and drag him to the studio every morning. Sure, Andy had done the heavy lifting, the smug little prick, but it'd been Dave that cared for his brother, that kept him coping, no matter what it took, and what rules he had to break in the process.

That *Hollies'* song *'It ain't heavy, he's my brother'* could literally have been written for him.

And so, just over twenty years ago, Dave Manford had found himself without a band. His band.

And, more importantly, was no longer a shareholder in *Secrets and Lies, n*o longer gaining the yearly royalties, while still silenced by the NDAs he'd signed when agreeing the deal.

But that was fine as he had money, he absolutely detested the bag of dicks he laughingly called his old *bandmates*, and he had plenty to do with nothing *Alternator*-related cluttering up his valuable time. He'd always talked about his planned solo work, especially a musical he wanted to write about *Jack The Ripper,* but over the years he'd failed at both; the solo album, although critically acclaimed by several niche magazines had failed to chart when it came out in 2007, resulting in the label dropping him before he could complete his agreed subsequent two albums, and his *Ripper* musical was considered by everyone to be a clever meta joke because of some throwaway line in a rock parody called *This Is Spinal Tap,* where two band members, seeing their band breaking up, decide to write a *Jack The Ripper* musical.

A sketch that haunted Dave at every meeting he tried to pitch it at.

In the end, Dave had gone into record producing; when the band had been big in the early nineties, and with the album royalties he made from *Secrets and Lies,* he'd bought an old church in Shoreditch and renovated it into a recording studio. The acoustics were great, and he'd built in some sound-proofed booths for when the tracks needed to feel more closed in and personal. He'd also built a state-of-the-art production booth with the control room stolen piecemeal from the Islington *Britannia Row studio* when they moved to Fulham. As such, he had the same equipment that had recorded parts of *Pink Floyd's The Wall,* a far better album than anything that *Alternator* had released for years, and over the last two decades he'd enjoyed a healthy income from that side of the business, producing for a varied collection of artists, many of whom didn't even know who *Alternator* were.

Which always made him warm and cosy inside.

A couple of years ago, though, things moved again. For a start, Marna, the bitch of a wife that married Nick a few years before his disappearance had pushed to have him declared legally dead, most likely to gain whatever was left by him she hadn't already stolen. Then Lydia, probably hearing this through Marna had heard news that *Alternator,* still touring the regional theatre routes with *Greatest Hits* shows were planning on recording a new album, their first studio recording for over a decade and the first with singer Peter Suffolk, who'd joined the band around nine years earlier. Digging deeper, and pushing hard on her family connection, Lydia had heard that *Alternator's* back catalogue was gaining interest with some serious hedge fund investors, especially after *Dog Tired,* the biggest selling single from *Secrets and Lies* had charted again after being used in some Marvel superhero movie. Buying back catalogues had become big money of late; Bob Dylan had sold his to Universal for three hundred million dollars, while the rumour mill claimed Stevie Nicks gained about a hundred million for eighty percent of her *Fleetwood Mac* rights.

Lydia was convinced that despite the fact that they hadn't had a hit in years, with the new fans coming in through streaming platforms due to *Dog Tired* being a bona fide hit again, they could be looking at *eight figures* for the rights to the back catalogue.

Money that *Alternator* would get.

Money that Dave should have a legal right for a percentage, kicked out of the band or not.

Money, more importantly, that couldn't be made until Marna controlled Nick's estate, which explained why she was so desperate to have him classed as *deceased,* after decades sponging off his name.

And if they didn't class Nick as dead, then there'd be some lengthy court battles, because even though Smug Andy co-wrote the songs, he wasn't a founding member of *Alternator.* And couldn't do anything.

But Dave could.

So, with the notoriety gained from *Dog Tired* and *Secrets and Lies,* Dave had put together a comeback tour, half his own solo work and half classic *Alternator* songs that he had a hand in creating. He knew they wouldn't come after him; there was every chance that to get the sale through they'd need him, and as such he was currently untouchable.

Which brought him to *Eastcheap Albums* on a Tuesday night, with a session musician band he'd only played with twice before for an audience of City moneymen, the point being to gain an interest in the songs from people who could truly put together a solid counter-deal. People who'd be interested in backing Dave Manford's right to gain money from the band he'd created with his younger brother when they were teenagers.

It was, however, the first live gig he'd played in almost fifteen years. And the stage fright had hit him the moment he'd stepped onto the tiny wooden dais they laughingly called a stage.

He was sweating; he could smell it. But he was wearing a black shirt, so hopefully it wasn't too noticeable. And the session was only forty minutes, so as long as he stayed hydrated, he'd be fine

His main worry was his heart; he'd had a murmur a couple of years back, not a full-blown cardiac issue, but enough to scare the living hell out of him, and he'd worried about overloading himself tonight. Lydia had given him a ring to wear; it felt uncomfortable on his right hand, the coolness of the silver plating mixing with the slickness of his sweat. She'd called it *wearable tech,* explaining that it was some kind of heart rate monitor, body temperature gauge and a dozen other things that told her in real time how he was doing physically, all given to her through bluetooth by three small prongs in the base of the band that touched his skin, but all he cared about was that if his heart rate or temperature spiked, she'd call the event off, which could kill everything here.

So deep breaths then, Davey.

Nodding to the other band members—although to call this rag-tag bundle of musicians a 'band' was frankly insulting, he moved to the microphone as the lights turned on, momentarily blinding him.

'Um, hi, everyone,' he said, unable to see anyone now. The middle area of the bar, usually filled with tall tables and chairs, had been emptied to provide a 'gig experience', and around thirty people were standing there, only slightly lower than Dave because of the stage's lack of height.

Not exactly Glastonbury, he thought to himself. At the back of the small crowd there was a familiar face; his nephew, watching silently, expressionless. A sudden, irrational fear came over Dave, that he might be asked tonight to repay a substantial loan he'd borrowed three years back.

To hell with that, he thought bitterly. *The little shit can afford it. Maybe he's here to buy the whole bloody catalogue? Maybe I should try to be nice to him. Maybe I can get another large loan off the gullible fool.*

The audience was still silent, and Dave realised he'd been drifting. Forcing a smile, he glanced at Lydia to the side, beside the bar, giving a thumbs up signal.

Dave had expected a slow start, but he hadn't expected *apathy.* However, he remembered these weren't *Alternator* fans; these were invited city stooges. Leaning back, he grabbed a bottle of water, taking a large mouthful. He hadn't been the lead singer back in the day. That was Nick.

But whatever Nick could do, Dave could do better.

'Well, that was shit,' he said, tossing the bottle aside. 'I said *hello everyone!*'

This time, spurred on by his own enthusiasm, the crowd reacted with a few half-hearted whoops and cheers.

Good enough, Dave smiled to himself.

'I'm Dave Manford, and with my brother Nick I created the rock band *Alternator,*' he said, warming to the moment, feeling the mic stand in his hand, the coldness of his ring resting against it. 'My brother disappeared over twenty years ago, but I'm still going strong.'

A louder cheer now, and Dave was feeling the audience. He was winning them over and he hadn't even sung a single note. Maybe he didn't need to. Maybe those singing lessons Lydia had sorted were for nothing.

No, he had to give them a show.

'So how about we start with the big one, eh?' he asked. 'The one you've all come to hear me sing?'

He paused for dramatic effect.

'How about *Dog Tired!!*' he yelled.

With a song that they actually knew, the audience went wild. Instantly, Dave Manford was transported back to one of their first gigs in London, at the long-gone *Marquee Club* on Wardour Street. They hadn't known who *Alternator* was there either, mainly because for years Nick had been playing the wrong music. But by the end of *that* gig, one that showed the *new* side to the band, one suggested by Dave, they had a three-record deal with EMI, and within a year they recorded *Jester's Childhood.*

By the end of this one, I'll start something that'll ensure that I'm more famous than Nick had ever been.

Nodding to Mickey, the fat, bald drummer who was squeezed tightly into his drum kit at the back of the small stage, Dave looked out into the crowd as Mickey clacked the rhythm on his drumsticks for a count of four before starting the beat of *Dog Tired*. The guitars began gently and the base would kick in before Dave, lead-singing here, would join in around the eighth bar.

However, Dave wasn't counting.

Dave was staring out into the crowd, his mouth half-open as he looked at the figure in the middle of the hand-picked audience; a hoodie up over their head and round, *John Lennon*-style shades over their eyes, nodding in time with the beat, mobile phone in their hand. However, unlike the others, holding up their phones and filming the performance, this one was held loose, with the figure holding a finger over the screen as they stared back at Dave.

'*Dave!*' hissed Mickey, and returning to the moment, Dave realised the band was replaying the first eight bars again, allowing him to recover. He nodded and looked back into the audience.

The figure was still there.

'You shouldn't be here,' he whispered, but the words fed through the microphone and the audience, all invited, wondered what the hell the old guy on stage was talking about, or whether this was a new version of the song they hadn't heard before. 'You're not real.'

The only person who didn't wonder what Dave meant looked up at him with a smile, the light catching a face under the hoodie as, while keeping Dave's gaze, they tapped the screen of their phone, activating some kind of app on it.

It didn't hurt at first; Dave hardly even felt the electricity as it ran from his hand, currently gripping the microphone and up his right arm. In fact, there was a split second where he wondered if this would blow up the bio-ring. Instinctively he grabbed at his wrist, trying to pull it away, but managed to somehow fuse his hands together, with the electricity now flooding up his right arm, through his shoulders and now back down his left arm, only to start the journey again. Dave was sure that he could even see the electric currents moving through his body like a sine wave. It would have been fascinating if the screaming hadn't been so distracting.

No, wait. You're the one screaming.

The screaming stopped as the bar plunged into darkness, the main fuse now shorted and Dave Manford, founder member of *Alternator,* fell backwards into the drum kit, his eyes wide open and glazed over in death. The energy that pulsed through the microphone stand had terribly burned his hands, and around him was a sickly barbecue smell.

The audience stood confused for a moment, unsure whether this was part of the show, whether Dave Manford was trying to be a new *Alice Cooper* or something, but as the lights came back on, they saw the hideous truth of Dave Manford's tragic end.

In fact, the only person who *didn't* see was the stranger in the hoodie who, using the darkness and lack of power to their advantage had left *Eastcheap Albums* the moment the shock to Dave had started, heading south down Lovat Lane at a leisurely pace, their phone now back in their pocket.

Dave Manford would get none of the hedge fund *Alternator* money. But he had been correct about one thing.

Dave Manford was about to become more famous than his brother *ever* was.

1

JAILHOUSE ROCK

Declan Walsh was effectively blind, but that didn't bother him.

The last time he'd traveled with Tom Marlowe he'd been unconscious and, on awaking endured a rather musty smelling black cloth bag over his head, both to ensure that he didn't work out where the mysterious Whitehall offices of Emilia Wintergreen's *Section D* was located; at the time they didn't know whether he would be friend or foe, and so the cloak and dagger activities were probably necessary. However he'd been allowed to leave the premises without a hood on, now effectively accepted as a trustworthy asset, and the bag and sedatives had been retired.

This time however, he was going somewhere that *Section D* didn't fully control, and while Tom drove Declan's Audi to wherever it was they were going to, Declan sat in the passenger seat again, the same musty smelling hood over his head.

He didn't mind Tom driving, he didn't mind the hood. The only thing he minded was going to wherever they were driving to in the first place, because this journey was one that he didn't really want to make.

Section D had a history with *The Last Chance Saloon*; for a start, when Declan was recently on the run from the police and accused of terrorism, it emerged that Trix, the onetime office intern of the department and now part of *Section D* had used her role there to assist him in his escape from custody. After he was cleared, he'd been brought to meet Emily Wintergreen, herself a onetime member of Patrick Walsh's Command Unit, and the ex-wife of Alexander Monroe, Declan's now-DCI mentor. It was a marriage that caused Monroe discomfort when discussing, mainly because on accepting the role in *Section D*, Wintergreen had effectively wiped all evidence of her past life, turning herself into a myth, in the process annulling the marriage without even saying goodbye.

Yeah, Monroe probably dodged a bullet there. Wintergreen wasn't really a people person.

Wintergreen had nonetheless honoured her past complicated connections; she'd made sure Declan had help in clearing his name, she'd passed him the details of the *Red Reaper* serial killer, allowing him to solve his dad's last case and avenge his parents murder, even sending her best agent, Tom Marlowe—who was also her kind-of nephew, which made him *Monroe's* kind-of nephew—in the same van to pick up Karl Schnitter, onetime friend of Declan's, now revealed to be an East German Hauptmann during the Berlin Wall years with a list of bodies behind him, and place him somewhere deep and hidden before the CIA tried to pull him out.

Even *thinking* about all this gave Declan a headache.

Then last month she'd sent Tom to assist in an investigation involving secret nuclear reactors under Greenwich Park, and after they'd finished the investigation, Trix had appeared in St Anne's Church graveyard after the funeral of Lucy Shrimpton like a millennial ghost, quietly pulling Declan aside and explaining that *Section D* would need a favour from him. Karl Schnitter had spent years working with the Russians while moving up the East German ranks and still had contacts who were once in the *Stasi*, information still relevant, even today. This was why the CIA had wanted to keep him close, but this was also why his requests were listened to. And Trix had explained that they'd learnt Karl had some information they needed to gather, but his fee for this exchange was to have ten minutes with Declan, alone.

Declan really didn't want to do this. But Declan had a morbid fascination for how the last few months had treated Karl, a man who had been known as a simple mechanic by Declan for almost all of his life.

A man whose daughter had tried to kill Jess.

And so now Declan sat patiently in his car, the tracker turned off before they left, listening to Tom Marlowe discuss football results as they passed the time on the journey, while quietly wondering whether he'd listen to Karl Schnitter—or try to kill him.

KARL WASN'T IN A STANDARD PRISON; THAT WOULD BE TOO easy, too public for him. Instead, he was in an MI6 black site, a terrorist prison that not only didn't exist on paper, but was more likely to be destroyed, with all inhabitants inside than be revealed to the public. And, as Declan walked through the various security sections that took him, layer by layer deeper into the building, he couldn't help but wonder whether this would have been the final place for him if Malcolm Gladwell and DI Frost had gotten their way, and Declan hadn't been able to prove that he wasn't an extremist terrorist earlier that year.

The thought troubled him. He'd been innocent of his crime but had been so close to being thrown to the wolves. *How many others in here were similar, suffering the same injustices?*

Tom had wandered off to get a coffee, tossing Declan his car keys back, but he'd had to relinquish these to the building's grim looking security guards, along with his wallet, house keys and any small change he had in his pockets, passing Tom his phone in case anything important happened while he was inside the—well, whatever this building was officially called, although Declan assumed quite correctly that it didn't really have an official title. Eventually, he entered a small, barren room; the only furniture in it were two seats and a table, made of metal and welded together, while the base was bolted to the floor. Not a single part of it was moveable. Which probably meant there wasn't a single part there that could be turned into a weapon.

Sitting at the closest seat, Declan waited. And, after a moment, the other door opened and Karl Schnitter, aka Karl Müller, was brought into the room.

He was slimmer than when Declan had last seen him, but not by much. His hair was whiter and slightly longer, and he'd grown out a beard, most likely because he hadn't been allowed access to razors. He was paler, but this was probably due to lack of sunlight, and he wore a red one-piece overall as a uniform.

As he entered the room and saw Declan, his eyes lit up.

'Declan!' he exclaimed as he walked to the other seat. 'I did not think you would come.'

Declan looked to the guard who'd brought Karl in; he stood by the door, as if waiting for a command to leave. And although it was minuscule, the slightest nod by Karl gave the guard leave to exit the room, closing the door behind him. It wouldn't have been noticeable unless you were looking for it, and Declan had been.

Karl has control over some guards here.

'I came because it helps others,' Declan replied stiffly. 'I don't know what sick idea you have here, but we're never going to chat like we used to.'

'Oh, I know,' Karl smiled warmly. 'But I am not the one you once knew.'

'I never knew you,' Declan snapped. 'That became clear the day I learnt you killed my parents and tried to kill Jess.'

'How is Jess, anyway?' Karl ignored Declan's tone. 'Finished her GCSEs?'

'You don't get to ask questions like that,' Declan leaned back on the seat, forcing his anger back down. All he wanted to do right now was lean across the table and strangle him.

'I get that,' Karl nodded. 'I heard she did well though.'

Declan looked to the wall, smiling. He knew that this was just an attempt to get a rise out of him.

'Even I don't know how she did,' he replied. 'The results aren't until August. Nice try.'

Karl leaned closer. 'You should be a better father,' he whispered. 'She started slowly, and almost walked out, but then she settled down and really shone, so I have been told.'

Declan looked back at his onetime friend. There were too many details here that could be checked up on; Karl was never someone who would embellish something without having extra up his sleeve.

He knew.

Declan didn't know how he'd managed it, but until he spoke to Jess, there was no way to confirm. But one thing was evident; this was a power play on Karl's part. And if it got him out of the room, Declan was happy to let the German have it.

'You look well,' he muttered. 'That's disappointing.'

'You look tired,' Karl nodded. 'Your suit looks worn and your hair is unkempt, as usual. I would think nightmares the cause of your lack of sleep?'

'I sleep fine,' Declan protested. Karl laughed, and for a moment Declan saw the old Karl Schnitter in front of him. He shook his head, casting that memory aside.

'Perhaps your housemate is too loud at night?' Karl smiled. 'Or perhaps the two of you...' he let the suggestion hang in the air, and Declan chose not to reply, noting silently that Karl Schnitter also knew that for the last month Declan had a tenant, a housemate in the form of DS Anjli Kapoor. It wasn't romantic, and Declan resented the accusation.

'Why am I here?' he asked irritably. 'You've had four minutes of your ten already. I can't believe you just wanted to talk exams.'

Karl nodded.

'Did you find my Mark?' he asked, and Declan knew he was talking about the East German Mark that he used to judge his victims with as the *Red Reaper,* a doctored and double-sided Mark that Declan had swapped out at the last minute.

A Mark that, as it flipped in the air, Declan had attacked Karl before it hit the ground.

'Yeah, I did.'

Karl's smile widened.

'How did it land?'

'Why am I here?' Declan asked again, tiring of this game.

As if expecting this, Karl nodded.

'I want you to pass a message through to Ilse,' he said, straightening in the seat, now all business. 'I think they are going to be moving me on soon, and I might not get another chance to say goodbye to her.'

'Since when did you become father of the year?' Declan shook his head. 'I don't know what your plan is, but there's no way I'm going to see her.'

'I understand that,' Karl nodded. 'That is why I wrote a note. All you have to do is pass it to her.'

'Yeah, that's not going to happen,' Declan laughed. But before he could continue, Karl held up a hand.

'I would expect you to examine the contents,' he said. 'And your friends in *Section D* can also check it. There is no underhand plan here, just a genuine attempt to apologise to a woman who spent her whole life not knowing who her father truly was.'

Declan stared at the man across the table for a long moment. As much as he hated this man, he really wanted to believe him.

'Fine,' he replied eventually. 'You sort out the message and I'll pass it on.'

'I have it on a USB drive,' Karl nodded. 'They would not let me send it as just paper, in case I doctored it somehow. I had to photograph it. I will get someone to pass it on.'

Declan didn't like the casual way that he'd commented; to have someone pass it on meant that he had someone happy to help him do so. And Declan remembered the way the guard had waited for Karl's say so before leaving.

Rising from the chair, he nodded curtly.

'You do that,' he said. 'Unless there's anything else here, we're done.'

'I also want to make a promise,' Karl added. 'I know things are not good between us right now—'

'Is that what you call this?' Declan wanted to laugh, but Karl was straight-faced.

'No matter what happens, Declan, I would never hurt your family—'

'No, just kill my parents.'

Karl looked pained. 'That was different. Daughters are different. They are sacred, untouchable in this business.'

'And what business is that?'

Karl Schnitter ignore the question as he continued.

'Ilse made a mistake, and she is paying for it.'

He rose to meet Declan.

'My issues are with you and you alone,' he continued.

'That sounds remarkably like a threat,' Declan hissed. Karl smiled.

'Not at all,' he replied. 'I am always here for you, even when you do not know that you need me. And because of this, Jess does not need to fear me. No matter what.'

Declan was about to reply to this when, behind him, the door opened. As Declan glanced over, the guard that had left earlier returned and, at a second, almost imperceptible nod from Karl, pulled a USB drive from his pocket and passed it over.

'Been holding that long?' Declan smiled sweetly as he took the drive. The guard didn't reply, simply stepping backwards and walking to the back door. Shrugging, Declan turned and walked to the opposite door, deliberately ignoring the German serial killer standing in the middle of the room.

But, as he reached the door, rapping to open it, he looked back to Karl.

'It landed heads,' he said. 'I won.'

'Yes you did,' Karl smiled as Declan left through the now open door. 'Yes, you did.'

———

ONCE OUT, DECLAN WAS TAKEN THROUGH THE CORRIDORS, returned his items and escorted outside, back to the waiting Tom Marlowe, who passed him one of the two *to-go* coffees in his hand.

'Did he have his chat?' Tom asked. Declan in return passed across the USB drive.

'Message for Ilse,' he said. 'I'd suggest you get Trix to look at it first, and then fire the guards, because at least one of them is working for Karl.'

'Good to know,' Tom stared down at the USB drive. 'I'm guessing you'd like a copy sent to Billy?'

'Please, and by a more analogue route, as I don't trust you guys and networks,' Declan nodded. 'Bike courier is fine.'

Walking to the Audi, Tom pulled out Declan's phone as Declan passed over the car keys once more.

'Uncle Alex has been calling,' he said as Declan noticed the four missed calls. 'I took the fifth one. I hope you don't mind.'

'What's the problem?' Declan checked his texts, but nothing new was there.

'Some singer, a onetime rock star fried himself on stage,' Tom was already climbing into the van. 'What am I, your message service?'

Declan dropped a quick text to Monroe, telling him he'd

be back in London within the hour, and climbed into the Audi, placing the musty hood back onto his head while finishing his luke-warm coffee. Then, with a sudden shiver, he pulled the phone out and texted Jess before pulling it fully on.

Quick question, how did your exam go? Any problems?

After a minute, a reply came through.

I thought we already talked about the exams?

I know, but I heard you almost left or something, but stayed?

There was a long wait for a reply. And then

How did you know that, dad? I never told you.

Declan felt a solid shiver run down his spine.

If Jess hadn't even told him about this, how the hell did Karl Schnitter know about it?

2

SCENE OF THE CRIME

IT WAS ANOTHER HOUR BEFORE DECLAN ARRIVED AT *EASTCHEAP Albums*, Tom pulling the Audi to the side and then driving off the moment Declan's feet touched the pavement. He'd promised to leave the car back at Temple Inn, but Declan reckoned that Tom simply didn't want to have another uncomfortable conversation with Monroe.

Monroe, meanwhile was waiting for him at the door, stroking his white goatee.

'Interesting little jaunt?' he asked, half amused, yet at the same time half annoyed. Declan understood why his boss would feel this way, what with his personal connection to both Wintergreen and Marlowe, so steered the conversation away by shaking his head.

'Karl Schnitter says hi,' he replied, peering past Monroe and into the bar itself. Forensics officers were already working through the venue, and Declan could see Doctor Rosanna Marcos in her custom grey PPE suit crouching down by the stage at the back of the room, the spotlights on, helping the examination.

'Booties and gloves first,' Monroe said as they entered, pulling on a new set of blue plastic boot covers over his shoes. 'There's no point putting the whole shebang on, as the place was filled with people running around like headless bloody chickens when they realised he was dead.'

'He?' Declan asked. 'You're going to have to get me up to speed, Guv. All I heard was it was some one-time rock star or something.'

'Ah, that'll be Tom Marlowe's incredible deductive powers then,' Monroe shook his head. 'How we entrust the fate of the nation in his hands is a bloody mystery to me.'

They entered the building and carefully made their way over to the stage, Declan scanning the inside of the building as he did so. He could see DC Joanne Davey, also in full PPE gear, her frizzy red hair half-hidden under the hood working near the bar and shining a penlight torch into what looked like a power socket, with PC Morten De'Geer, the tall, strapping Viking of an officer in gloves and mask helping her. To the right, by a window to the street stood DS Anjli Kapoor, as immaculately dressed as ever, taking a statement from what looked to be bar staff, and by the stage, Doctor Marcos was examining a microphone stand.

'Dave Manford,' Monroe explained, as they stopped beside Doctor Marcos. 'One-time founding member of the British indie band *Alternator.*'

Declan nodded. 'I had a couple of albums as a kid,' he replied. 'Didn't they have a guy die at sea or something?'

'More the something,' Monroe nodded. 'Nick Manford, Dave's brother. Finished a gig on a Thursday night in Brighton back in 1998, Friday morning they found his car beside the entrance to a clifftop beach, some of his clothes on the stones.'

'What, so he just walked in and drowned himself?'

'Well, that's what we're supposed to believe,' Monroe shrugged. 'Apparently he had legal issues connected to possession of multiple class-A drugs and an illegal firearm, and if he hadn't, well, *disappeared*, he'd have likely been locked up.'

'And that's worse than death?'

'That's what we know so far, laddie. Chances are there was a ton of larger shite waiting to fall on him too,' Monroe nodded to the microphone stand. 'Anyway, last night ol' Davey boy decides to launch a comeback tour, hires a few session musicians and then plays an evening gig here for an invited audience of city investors.'

'Funding for a tour?'

'Funding for something,' Monroe agreed. 'He starts his concert and then somehow electrocutes himself live on stage, thanks to faulty wiring on the microphone.'

'I thought that sort of thing was nothing but an urban legend?' Declan backed away from the stand, as if expecting it to attack him.

Monroe smiled.

'Don't worry laddie, it's disconnected now,' he said soothingly. 'The audience got to see, up close and personal, Dave Manford fry himself to death.'

'Okay,' Declan looked around the bar again. 'I'm guessing we don't think it's an accident?'

'Oh, we *know* it's not an accident,' Doctor Marcos rose now, pulling her hood away from her curly brown hair and removing her mask. 'We found a connector, spliced into the amp at the back that links to a device.'

'What sort of device?'

'One we don't recognise,' Doctor Marcos admitted. 'But it

looks like something deliberately made to not only short the supply to the amplifier, but send the electricity directly through the mains and up the mic stand, into the microphone itself.'

'Murder.'

'*Bluetooth* murder,' Doctor Marcos nodded to Davey, who picked up a small clear bag from the ground beside her, bringing it over. In it was a small phone-shaped device, the casing cracked and burned, as if thrown on a barbecue for five minutes.

'They connected this to the amp. I think someone sent it a Bluetooth message, setting it off. A more modern equivalent of the terrorist who sends a phone call to a second phone, triggering a detonator.'

'So whoever this was not only wanted to kill Dave Manford, but wanted to do it at a specific time,' Declan nodded. 'What's the range?'

'Unsure yet,' Doctor Marcos passed the burned plastic back to Davey, who left. 'However, the more traditional *call the phone* route meant you could be anywhere with phone service to do it. This? The killer had to be nearby, maybe even here in this room.'

Declan looked around the stage area. 'Up close and in his face,' he mused. 'That's someone making it personal. Do we have CCTV?'

'Anjli's getting that now,' Monroe said, looking over at her. 'Detective Sergeant, how are we doing?'

Anjli Kapoor nodded to the staff member, and closing her notebook, walked over to Declan and Monroe. Like them, she only wore booties and gloves over a navy blue suit with pastel pink blouse, her black hair pulled back behind her head in a matching scrunchie.

'CCTV is on a cloud server, and they're sending Billy the login details,' she said, nodding at Declan. 'You okay, Guv?'

'Tell you all about it later,' Declan nodded at the stage. 'What else do we have?'

'Manford was disliked by his session band, claiming he was a bit of a prick to them during rehearsals, quick to charge and slow to pay, that sort of thing and his manager? Agent? Whatever she was left the building the moment they declared him dead, rather than deal with any of the shit that followed.'

'We have a name?'

'Lydia Cornwall,' Anjli replied. 'Apparently her late husband was Ray Cornwall, big PR guy for Britpop bands in the nineties, and she's always known Dave Manford. Got the impression though that this was more a favour than a business arrangement.'

'Why do a comeback gig for city investors?' Monroe shook his head. 'I mean, barely any of them would have heard of him or *Alternator*. Surely doing a gig for some fans would have been the best starting point?'

'They gained notoriety again after some big-budget action film used a 1987 song called *Dog Tired*,' Anjli smiled. 'Apparently it's in the top ten streaming chart on Spotify.'

'You seem scarily well informed on that,' Declan raised an eyebrow. 'Are you a fan?'

'No, I'm not the fan,' Anjli's grin grew wider. 'But we have one in the department.'

'Detective Superintendent Bullman is a bit of an expert,' Monroe continued. 'DS Kapoor finds this funny.'

Declan smiled. Bullman had mocked him mercilessly during the *Magpie* case once she learnt he was a fan of the books as a child. The possibility of returning the favour was too good to pass up.

'Any other witnesses to chat to?' he asked, and was rewarded with a nod to the bar area, where a lone man stood. He was in black shirt and trousers with a little name tag on his shirt. Declan assumed that this was the bar manager, or someone similar.

'And he's...?' Declan asked. Monroe shrugged.

'No idea, laddie, but he turned up for work first thing when nobody else did, even though he was here last night.'

'Perhaps he's just really diligent at his job.'

'Or perhaps he's trying to get an idea of what we've found,' Monroe replied. 'It's not the first time some bugger's tried to get the scoop on us, just to pull the wool over our eyes.'

Declan nodded at this; over the last few cases, they'd had their share of suspects that wormed their way into the case before being outed as connected to the crime. Whether it was Lucy Shrimpton, Tessa Martinez or even DI Frost, there was a list of people who thought that, if they appeared eager to help, they'd gain information.

Or, Declan mused, *maybe the guy was just really good at his job.*

Wandering over, he pulled out his notebook and pen, giving his most disarming smile to the man as he approached.

'Not the best day to come to work,' he commented.

The man, in his late twenties, and with a trendy haircut that involved having everything beneath the tips of the ears shaved off gave a weak smile in response.

'I had to come in,' he explained. 'I'm the duty manager for

last night, but I also deal with the stage acts and the, well, the equipment.'

Declan now understood why the man was in that morning.

'You set up the wires and amps for the gig,' he commented.

The man nodded, his face paling.

'Did I kill him?' he asked. 'Nobody will tell me. I've worried myself sick about it all night.'

'I can't tell you anything, as this is an active investigation,' Declan commented, looking around. 'But what I can say is that this wasn't an accident. So, if you saw anyone suspicious around the equipment...?'

The man shook his head dumbly as the enormity of the situation hit him.

'I didn't do it,' he said, spoken more as a term of relief than a statement.

Declan nodded.

'It looks that way,' he replied, still trying to stay impartial. 'However, if you have any clues that can help us, or anything that could give us a lead to look at, we'd appreciate it. What's your name?'

'Dan,' the man replied. 'Daniel. Wooten. And I was around from six yesterday, so I saw everyone.'

'Anything stand out?' Declan noted this down. 'Any people there who looked out of place?'

'It was a private event,' Dan nodded. 'Everyone looked out of place. But there were a couple that come to mind.'

'Oh yes?' Declan looked up. Dan nodded, as if eager to prove his worth, now he knew he wasn't a killer.

'Well, everyone was from the City, yeah? Like bankers and stuff?' Dan tried to explain. 'Lots of expensive suits, old school ties, that sort of thing. Young money too. It was like they'd walked into an office building, the band that is, said 'hey everyone, free drinks' and then left.'

'Was it free drinks?'

'No, I mean it felt like an office had emptied and come in here,' Dan struggled to explain. 'Hedge fund bros and City wankers. You know? One-percenters.'

Declan very much knew what Dan was insinuating.

'But there were people who stood out?'

'Yeah,' Dan was warming to his role now. 'The manager, she was twitchy as hell at the bar all night, but that was probably because of the row.'

'Row?'

'Yeah, she had a bit of a barney with some bloke around fifteen minutes before the show started. He was a bit lairy, you know? I assumed she owed him money.'

'Why would you think this?' Declan was writing again in the notebook. Dan shrugged.

'At one point she was telling him he only deserved half the fee, and he was pissed as hell when she gave him a package.'

'Can you describe him to me?' Declan asked. Dan pointed to a CCTV camera beside the back of the bar.

'No need,' he said. 'When you check the CCTV, you'll see them on that camera. Front and centre.'

Declan noted the camera's location. 'And the other one?'

Dan considered this. 'He was an odd one,' he continued. 'Couldn't see his face well, as he was wearing a hoodie for most of the evening. He was alone, too, not really talking to anyone. But he was money, you know? *Nike Vapormax* trainers, and I mean the new ones, not last year's with the pull strings. *Ralph Lauren* joggers and a *Raf Simons* hooded sweater.'

'And that's money?' Declan asked, amused.

'Dude, that sweater alone costs more than your suit,' Dan replied. 'Easily a grand to buy.'

Declan whistled as he wrote this down. That sweater was worth more than his entire *wardrobe* of suits. Although, when you found them covered in blood half the time, it was better to keep to the cheaper, off-the-rack styles.

'So he was rich,' Declan looked up. Dan nodded.

'Rolex on the wrist, expensive leather bag on his shoulder, he wasn't the usual visitor we get, and he stood out here like a sore thumb,' he replied. 'He was around before the show started though and disappeared when the craziness happened.'

'Did you see when?'

Dan shook his head.

'We were more focused on the body by that point,' he said.

Declan thanked Dan for his time and passed a business card with his number on to him, telling him to contact him by text if he remembered anything else from the night. This done, he walked over to Anjli and Monroe, now moving to the main entrance, pulling off their gloves and booties.

'Back to the office?' he asked. Monroe nodded.

'Aye, we won't know anything else until Rosanna and her team find something new, or Billy gains us a hit from his little computer fortress,' he said, looking over at Dan, now cleaning glasses on the bar. 'Anything from your man there?'

'Super rich man in a hoodie hanging around and another bloke having a row with the manager before the event start-ed,' Declan pulled off his blue booties, placing them in a bag held out for him by a suited Forensics Tech. 'I'll have a chat with Billy, see if we can get an image of him. Maybe—'

'No need,' Anjli smiled, pulling out her phone. 'The woman I was talking to over there? Probably the only fan at the event, by pure chance. Saw the fight and clocked him immediately. Apparently she was going to ask for his autograph before he got intense with Lydia Cornwall.'

'Autograph?' Declan was thrown by this. 'Who was it then?'

Anjli opened her phone to show a webpage, an image of a man on it. He was in his fifties, his brown hair longer than most but still stylised, a pale jacket over a blue shirt as he played his acoustic guitar in what looked like a church nave.

'This man,' she said. 'Peter Suffolk. Lead singer of *Alternator*.'

'So perhaps he was here to wish Dave well?' Monroe suggested, but Anjli shook her head.

'Chances are, they never met,' glancing around the bar, Anjli was still taking in the scene. 'Suffolk took over the lead singer role when the previous lead, Jesse Morrison, was injured in a bike accident, retiring afterwards.'

'Bike accidents stop you singing?' this surprised Declan.

'Bike accidents stop you prancing around on stage,' Anjli replied. '*Alternator* was primarily a touring band back then. Still is, really. Anyway, Peter Suffolk joined the band almost fourteen years after they kicked Dave out, so unless they met at some outside event, it's unlikely they knew each other, and Peter didn't really have a reason to be here.'

'He did if his reason was to remove Dave Manford,' Declan muttered. 'He did if something that Dave was doing here, in front of these big money city folk, was going to affect the band.'

'Get on that,' Monroe nodded. 'Let's regroup, see what Billy has and then go find this singer and the runaway manager who disappeared last night.'

Declan took one look back at the stage as he left the bar.

Dying on stage was far easier than he'd realised.

3

TAKING CARE OF BUSINESS

BILLY WAS WORKING AT HIS CYBER-CRIME STATION WHEN Declan arrived at the office. As ever, he was in a bespoke suit and waistcoat ensemble, a dark blue wool-blend which, considering they were approaching June, seemed a little warm. That said, Billy spent most of his time in an air-conditioned office, so a wool-blend waistcoat over a shirt and pastel yellow tie was probably a good idea.

'Morning Guv,' he said as he turned to face Declan, Anjli following him into the room, but heading upstairs. 'Sarge. How was your visit?'

'Not as much fun as I wanted it to be,' Declan took his own jacket off, hanging it on the back of his chair as he turned back to Billy. 'He's doing better than I'd hoped.'

'Always the case,' Billy nodded. 'Did you find out what he wanted?'

Declan nodded. 'A message to his daughter,' he replied. 'It was on a USB stick, and Tom said he'd courier a copy over to you, so you could have a look at it.'

Billy returned to his monitors.

'I'll use an air-gapped laptop for it,' he said. 'It's a laptop that's not connected in any way to the network. Last thing I want is him playing virus games.'

'Good thinking,' Declan ran a hand through his hair, looking around the office. 'Let me know when you get it.'

'Anything else?' Billy asked. Declan thought for a moment before nodding.

'He knew about Jess,' he explained. 'Her results. He knew she had a panic attack in the exam room when even I didn't know.'

'So he's having someone watch her.'

'In an exam room?' Declan shook his head. 'Even I don't know how—'

'CCTV,' Billy replied. 'Most schools use them now. If there's a camera there, he could have had someone hacking into it.'

Declan didn't like this, but it still felt marginally better than an actual physical person being there. He spent a long moment weighing up his next move; he didn't want to waste police time, but this was his *daughter*.

'Could you—' he started, but Billy was already typing.

'If someone hacked the feed, I should be able to trace them,' he said. 'You can get a time and date of the exam, right?'

Declan nodded.

'I'll come back to you on that,' he said as Anjli walked down the stairs from the upper floor, two mugs of coffee in her hand.

'One for you,' she said, passing it to Declan, who stared at her suspiciously.

'You don't usually make me coffee,' he replied.

Anjli shrugged.

'I over-made,' she replied. 'Thought I'd be nice, what with you having a rubbish morning.'

Declan warily took the coffee mug and sipped at it.

'It's good,' he said, placing it onto the desk, looking back at Billy. 'Perhaps—'

'How good?' Anjli asked, her own mug on the desk as well, her arms crossed as she watched him.

Oh no, Declan thought to himself. *I've fallen into a trap here.*

'Very good?' he offered. Anjli nodded at this, as if expecting more from him.

'You'd drink this?' she asked again. 'Like, in the morning?'

And finally Declan understood.

'This is about the coffee machine, isn't it?'

'You said I could get one when I moved in.'

'And you can.'

'It's been a month,' Anjli shifted position, becoming more confrontational now. 'Every time I've suggested it, you've changed the subject.'

'I didn't want you to waste money on something that wasn't appreciated,' Declan glanced helplessly at Billy, trying to dig himself out of the hole he'd obviously dug.

'Did you appreciate that?' Anjli showed the coffee on the table. Declan picked it up again, taking a sip. He couldn't argue the point; it was excellent coffee.

'Yes,' he replied. 'It's a good cup.'

'Great,' Anjli smiled again. 'We have the same machine arriving at the house tomorrow.'

With this, she turned and walked to her own desk, sipping at her mug as she did so. Billy, trying his best to hide a smile, looked at Declan.

'You know people think you're secretly married, don't you?' he whispered.

'Keep up with that and you might find the rest of this on your head,' Declan deadpanned.

'She's just trying to take your mind off things,' Billy moved back to his desk, in case Declan made good on his threats.

'Why?' Declan asked. 'It's not like I've been worried about seeing Karl Schnitter. And it's not my first time in a prison.'

'I didn't mean that,' Billy replied cautiously, realising that Declan didn't know what he was talking about. 'I meant about Francine Pearce.'

Declan stopped drinking his coffee, the mug half reaching his lips as he spoke.

'What about her?'

Billy looked across the office at Anjli now, as if silently willing her to reply for him. However Anjli, wisely kept to her own work.

'I thought you knew they released her yesterday,' Billy explained. 'They dropped the case against her.'

If Declan could have, he would have screamed loudly, even hurled the mug across the office. However, instead, he simply nodded at this.

'She called in some favours.'

Billy nodded. 'I reckon so,' he said. 'Probably doesn't hurt that one of the people connected to her is about to become Prime Minister.'

Declan hissed under his breath at this. Charles Baker had been in debt to Francine Pearce for most of his political career, and at the end she'd threatened him with a gun on the roof of Devonshire House before being arrested. She'd also attempted to shoot Declan with the same gun, before realising the gun was firing blanks. Declan assumed that the fact she'd tried to shoot a police officer would be enough alone to place her in prison for a very long time, but then when he'd been on the run and charged with being a terrorist, Declan had visited her to gain information on who could have killed Kendis Taylor, only to find her living a relaxed life in witness protection while waiting for her trial.

She ratted him out to the police that night.

The chances were that this act alone gained her favour and showed that she was happy to cooperate. And when Malcolm Gladwell and *Rattlestone* were taken down, she had offered every piece of information on them she had as currency for her freedom.

And now she was free.

'Well, she'll have an issue returning to her old life,' Declan muttered. 'They wound down *Pearce Associates*.'

'True, but she was probably moving everything around while in custody,' Billy said before pausing. 'That's not helping, is it?'

'No, not really,' Declan smiled. 'Still, she knows better not to mess with us right now, and I can't see Baker defending her any time soon.'

He leaned back against the table, stretching his arms, loosening his back muscles. He hadn't realised quite how tense he was.

'Still, we'd better monitor her,' he finished. 'In the meantime, let's keep on with the current problem. Do you have anything yet?'

Billy turned back to the screens, nodding as he did so. 'They sent me the cloud details about half an hour ago, and so I've been trying to see what happened that evening.'

'Trying?' now Anjli returned to the conversation as she left her desk and walked over. Billy nodded.

'The CCTV's a bit shit,' he replied. 'They angle it at the door, the bar and the exits. There are no cameras aimed at the stage.'

'I'm guessing that's because nobody's likely to be stealing anything from there,' Declan muttered. 'Though that's annoying.'

He opened his notebook, flicking through the notes he'd made while in the bar. 'The barman claimed there was a fight with the manager?' he asked.

Anjli nodded.

'One woman there said it was Peter Suffolk,' she added.

Billy scrolled through the footage from the camera at the back of the bar. The foreground was lit up, and they could see the bar, while in the far background, the stage was slightly visible. People were moving around the bar at speed, but one figure, a woman, was standing at it for most of the speed-through.

'I'm guessing that's the manager?' Declan asked.

Billy nodded.

'Lydia Cornwall,' he stopped the tape, showing the woman; dressed in jeans, leather jacket and with her shoulder-length, bottle-blonde hair crimped and loose, she looked irritated, like she'd been stood up for a date. The quality wasn't great, but she looked to be in her fifties.

'She seems a little pissed off,' Declan mused. Billy nodded, scanning again through the footage.

'She's waiting for someone,' he replied. 'And not Dave Manford. As you said, Peter Suffolk was there, and it wasn't an accidental meeting.'

On the screen, now slowed down again, a man appeared.

The biggest problem here, though, was that with the CCTV being in black and white, it was hard to work out what colours the man was wearing. As far as Declan could work out he was also in his fifties, with what looked like brown, flowing hair with either blond highlights or grey streaks, a black T-shirt over what were most likely blue jeans and a black suit jacket over it all. Around his neck was a small scarf, cravat, or something similar, and he wore a messenger bag over his right shoulder.

'What's that around his neck?' Anjli asked.

'I think it's a buff, or a snood,' Billy replied. 'It keeps your neck warm. Which, as this is Peter and he's the current lead singer of *Alternator*, he probably wants to ensure his throat stays at peak condition.'

'Or he just wants to look like an archaeologist,' Declan shrugged. 'I'm guessing there's no sound?'

Billy shook his head.

'However, you can see by the body language that she's angry, and he's almost apologetic. It's reminiscent of a schoolboy being torn a new one by his teacher.'

'Happen a lot, did it?' Anjli glanced at Billy with a slight smile.

'More times than you can imagine,' Billy grinned.

On the screen, they saw Lydia pulling a package out of her leather jacket, slamming it against Peter's chest. Peter then reluctantly took it, placing it into his own jacket's inner pocket.

'There,' Declan said. 'Rewind and pause.'

Billy did so, and the three detectives stared at the image on the screen and the package that Lydia held.

'It's small, an envelope,' Anjli squinted at the screen. 'It's about half an inch thick. Maybe banknotes?'

'Why would Lydia Cornwall be giving Peter Suffolk money?' Declan mused. 'Does she even know him?'

'I'll look into that,' Billy let the footage continue. Declan, watching it, leaned back.

'Now that's interesting,' he said, absentmindedly sipping at the coffee. 'Peter Suffolk walks in, as if expecting a bollocking. Lydia gives him one, and he sheepishly takes it. Then she gives him something, maybe money, and then look at his face. Look at the way the conversation changes.'

Declan was right. On the screen Peter was angry, waving his arms as Lydia patiently waited to speak. Then, pulling out a small package from his own pocket, he slammed it on the counter before storming off.

'Maybe she didn't give him enough money?' Anjli suggested.

'We need to find out,' Declan nodded. 'And work out what he left, too. Anything else?'

'Yes,' Billy opened another screen on the monitor, a long shot of the bar from the door. Far in the distance, they could see Dave Manford on the stage, preparing to start. In the foreground, however, talking to someone off screen, most likely the doorman was a man in an expensive-looking hoodie.

'This man isn't the usual city investor,' Billy explained. 'He's—'

Declan leaned in, cutting him off.

'Yeah, I see what you mean,' he replied. 'Those look like *Nike Vapormax* trainers, the new ones, not last year's with the pull strings. I can't be sure, but I think he's wearing *Ralph Lauren* joggers, and that's definitely a *Raf Simons* hooded sweater.'

Billy looked at Declan in utter shock.

'That's amazing,' he said. 'I was going to say the same

about the hooded sweater, but I hadn't even clocked the trainers.'

'There's a Rolex on his wrist, too,' Declan leaned back.

Billy frowned at this.

'You can't see his wrist,' he argued, then leaned back in his chair as he realised. 'So, which witness gave you all that?'

'The barman,' Declan grinned. 'Said that the guy was definitely money, didn't talk to anyone the whole time he was there and left pretty much at the beginning of the gig.'

'So why was he there?' Anjli asked. 'And, more importantly, who is he?'

'That's easy to work out,' Billy zoomed through the footage, stopping. In the background, Dave Manford seemed to talk to the crowd as, in the foreground, the hooded man was leaving, his face visible on the screen. At seeing it, Billy whistled, leaning back once more, as if to get a better look at the person on the screen.

'Meet Eden Storm,' Billy said, almost in awe. 'Producer, entrepreneur, activist, you name it. Grandaddy invented toothpaste or something like that and Eden there is worth billions.'

'Why would a billionaire attend this?'

'Maybe he's a fan?'

'Not of a nobody trying to restart his career,' Declan muttered.

'Shh, don't let Bullman hear you say that,' Anjli replied softly. "She's in mourning.'

Declan shook his head. 'Well, we need to look into him as well.'

On the screen the footage continued as, in the background, Dave fell backwards into the drum kit. There was a moment of stillness, as everyone there stopped to see what was going on.

'Why's the footage stopped?' Declan asked.

Billy shrugged.

'That's all we have,' he replied. 'The electrical shock tripped the power and everything ended. The CCTV simply turned off, as well as the lights, the music, everything.'

Declan looked around the office.

'So currently we have a device designed to kill a man at close range, a murderer that had to be in the room, a hooded billionaire and the lead singer of the band that kicked Dave out, meeting with his current manager, taking what looks like a bribe.'

He turned to Anjli.

'Did I miss anything?'

Anjli shook her head.

'Why do I feel we're only at the entrance to this rabbit hole?' she asked.

Declan shrugged.

'Because nothing's ever easy for us,' he replied, looking down at his mug. 'Hey, any chance of a refill? You make great coffee.'

He ducked as she threw the stapler across the office. It clattered to the floor beside the door, stopping at Monroe's feet as he entered.

'You were a second too early to hit me,' he replied caustically, looking at the now embarrassed Anjli. 'Something you want to share with the class, lassie?'

'Thought I saw a rat,' Anjli lied. 'Was a shadow.'

'Well, let's not chase shadows today, eh?' Monroe was already walking to his office, gently tossing the stapler back to Anjli. 'Briefing, fifteen minutes.'

He stopped at the doorway, looking back with a grin.

'And could you make me a coffee, lassie?' he asked innocently. 'I hear you make a great coffee.'

As Monroe entered his office, Anjli glared at Declan, hiding his own smile.

'I'm going to drink the machine coffee,' she hissed. 'You can stick to your terrible instant coffee.'

Declan nodded, admonished.

'You're right,' he replied. 'I was childish. But there's one thing you need to remember.'

'And what's that?' Anjli sullenly replied, remembering to add 'Guv?'

'Monroe likes two sugars these days,' Declan said, almost running from the office before Anjli could throw the rest of her desk items at him.

4

DIRECT ACTION BRIEFING

'RIGHT THEN, SETTLE DOWN, YOU MISCREANT REPROBATES,' Monroe commanded as Declan and the others filed into the briefing room. At the back, against the glass wall was PC De'Geer, talking quietly to DC Davey, while to the right as Declan approached his usual chair was Billy, already connecting the laptop to the plasma screen on the wall. Anjli had sat down in her usual seat too, notepad already out and on the desk, while Doctor Marcos and Monroe stood at the front, Bullman hovering around the door like a ghost with ADHD.

Billy smiled as he gave a thumbs up to Monroe, the screen behind the DCI now coming to life.

'You're remarkably bloody chipper,' Declan muttered. Billy looked over at him.

'I might have something on this,' he replied, tapping his nose. 'Waiting for my source to confirm it.'

'And by source, you mean another tech nerd who lives in his parents' house, right?' Anjli grinned before looking over to Declan. 'Sorry.'

'Why are you apologising to me?' Declan was confused.

Anjli shrugged.

'Well, you're technically doing the same.'

'I don't think it's the same when the parents are dead, lassie,' Monroe added, bringing the attention back to the front of the briefing room. 'Aye, we all set? Good. So, let's get started.'

He looked at Bullman.

'You want in on this?' he asked.

Bullman shook her head.

'I'll advise from the side.'

'You sure, Ma'am?' Declan piped up. 'I hear you're a bit of an expert on *Alternator*. Bet you're really good at pub quizzes.'

Bullman fixed Declan with a murderous gaze, but he simply smiled back innocently. He'd waited months to get his revenge on Bullman, word for word, after she mocked his fandom of the *Magpies* books, and turnaround was fair play.

'What do we have so far?' Monroe asked. Doctor Marcos nodded to Billy, and on the plasma screen an image of Dave Manford, half strewn over the drum kit and obviously dead, appeared on the screen.

'David Manford, sixty-seven years old, died last night when a microphone failed to ground correctly and electrocuted him live on stage.'

'I thought you said that it was a supply shortage?' Declan looked up from his own notes now. Doctor Marcos nodded.

'It's more complicated than that,' she explained. 'I was giving you a layman's term explanation. The more complex one is that someone connected the microphone incorrectly. You see, the metal capsule of the microphone itself shouldn't have any kind of current running through it. It's not a power cable. Also, neither should the metal case of a mixer or power amplifier. However, if you touch the microphone while touching another piece of metal connected to the same sound equipment, you effectively become part of the circuit.'

'Electrical current is a bit like water,' Billy added from the side. 'It always follows the path of least resistance.'

Doctor Marcos nodded.

'There're tons of examples of this happening,' she said. 'Keith Richards was shocked on stage, even Grimes had a shock through her earphones.'

'I know who Keith Richards is, but I don't have a clue who or what a Grimes is,' Monroe interrupted.

'That's because you're a hundred and two and only listen to dead singers,' Doctor Marcos snapped back quickly. 'Ooh. You can add Dave Manford to your playlist now.'

She looked back at the briefing room.

'Now, here's the catch,' she continued. 'Usually, it's guitar players who shock themselves. The mic isn't plugged into the right amp, and then the metal guitar strings tap the mic stand and connect the circuit. And if it's not grounded correctly, you get a major shock. Happened to Leslie Harvey of *Stone The Crows* in the seventies, and he died from his injuries.'

'Dave Manford doesn't have a guitar,' Declan pointed at the screen. 'So how did he manage this?'

Doctor Marcos tapped the plasma screen, and a photo appeared of a small, burned phone-like device.

'Someone spliced this into the amp,' she explained. 'In an everyday setting, a band would plug everything in before a gig and assume that their equipment is properly grounded, but in fact the power mains can often have different ground potentials. By this I mean the transient over-voltage that enters the earth as current.'

Declan glanced around and noted that only Billy seemed to understand this. Undaunted, Doctor Marcos continued.

'Basically, if any of the plug sockets are wired with different ground potentials, there's a very strong likelihood you'll get a shock hazard with the audio equipment.'

'Like what happened to Mister Manford,' De'Geer nodded as he wrote this down.

'In these situations, electricity flows from higher potential to lower potential,' Doctor Marcos nodded back to the Viking police officer, glad for at least one other person in the room understanding this. 'Therefore, if the plugs have a difference in potential, electricity flows to whichever is the lower ground. If we have a microphone plugged into a grounded mixing console, connected to a wall to the side, while we *also* have a grounded guitar amp plugged into a wall at the back but *also* plugged into the console, then if we touched the guitar strings and microphone simultaneously, we could make the electrical connection.'

'And the voltage would flow to the lower ground potential,' Billy nodded, as if this was the easiest solution in the world.

'And therefore result in a shock,' Doctor Marcos looked back at the image. 'Now, Manford wasn't using a guitar, so he couldn't make that electrical connection. So this device, spliced into the amp, artificially creates a difference in potential and makes the electrical connection at the same time.'

'And Dave Manford dies on stage,' Declan shook his head. 'This is all incredibly complicated.'

'No, in a way, it's genuinely not,' Doctor Marcos replied. 'It's simple, and more importantly, it's happened enough times to class it as an accepted problem with live gigs. Anyone could have plugged this in, nobody would have realised, and then *boom!* Dave Manford's jamming with Prince and Jimi Hendrix in the sky. Although the connection alone would have just jolted him, blasted him backwards. We're still working out why his hands stayed glued to the stand throughout the shock.'

'You mentioned it was bluetooth?' Declan continued. Doctor Marcos looked to DC Davey, who rose now.

'The device is fried, but we think there was a jury-rigged app on it that, when turned on, made the connection, in the process burning it out. This isn't as simple as a call, it would have had to have had a command bluetoothed to it, or even airdropped. Either way, you can't do this from a mile away. This was done by someone in the room.'

'We have a list of the invited guests,' Monroe added. 'We're going through them right now. So, now we know how he was killed, let's look into who killed him and why?'

He looked to Bullman in the doorway.

'Can you tell us a little about the band?'

'Sure,' Bullman replied, entering the room and standing at the front. 'But it won't be that relevant. He was out of it over twenty years ago. After Nick died, they didn't want him in the band.'

'Nick was Nick Manford, his brother and co-founder?' Anjli asked. Bullman nodded.

'They were brothers from Rotherham, just off Sheffield,' she explained. 'There's a ton of bands created around there. *Pulp, Def Leppard, Arctic Monkeys, Human League*, the list goes on. Anyway, Nick did Art History at Hull University, came out with a second and decided he wanted to start a band instead. Dragged his brother Dave into it, who at this point was working as a carpet fitter, and they created *Alternator* in the late seventies. Very Prog Rock back in the day, and they were likened to bands like *The Alan Parsons Project* and *Renaissance,* very twiddly keyboard based, with Nick doing the primary playing—' she stopped, looking around the briefing room.

'What, so Rosanna there talks about the joys of *lower ground potentials* and *alternating currents* and that's headline news, but I talk about bands and you fall asleep?'

'No, Ma'am,' Declan said carefully. 'It's just that apart from maybe DCI Monroe, none of us were alive back then.'

Bullman went to reply to this but then simply stopped, sighing.

'Children,' she muttered. 'I'm surrounded by bloody children.'

'I like how you didn't label me in that,' Doctor Marcos winked.

Declan shrugged.

'You're not a day over twenty-seven, Doc,' he replied with a smile.

Bullman sighed theatrically before continuing.

'Anyway, so they toured the UK for a couple of years,' she said. 'Over that time, Dave and Nick gained a band, Dave playing bass with Martin Reilly on drums, Graham Hagen on keyboard, mainly replacing Nick as he moved more into a lead singer role and Bruce Baker on guitar. They got notoriety in the business, but they were a new band in an old genre, and their only album, *Deviation One* was through a very small distributor. If they sold more than a hundred copies I'd be impressed.'

'So they weren't great then?'

'There were better bands out there,' Bullman explained. 'However they weren't stupid, and knew they needed to change with the times. They changed their style, and in 1981 played demos of their new songs on Tommy Vance's Radio

One *Friday Rock Show* and even did a slot on the *Peel Sessions*. This got them a deal with EMI Records, and their debut album, *Jester's Childhood,* came out in 1983.'

'Were you a fan then?' Declan asked.

Bullman nodded.

'I was at Uni when they were starting,' she replied. 'They played my student union around then. The band was in the same wheelhouse as *Marillion, Magnum, Little Angels,* even *Thunder*, playing a very commercial rock style. They moved down to West London and in 1984 their first single, *Kathleen* reached number four in the chart, sending *Jester's Childhood* into the top ten, and *Alternator* onto a year long European tour.'

Declan glanced at his own notes.

'I don't have Bruce Baker in the band,' he said. 'I have Andy Mears.'

Bullman nodded. 'So after the tour, in early 1986, they went straight into the recording studio to work on their second album, *Secrets and Lies*. They were burned out from the tour, and there were rumours that Nick had gathered himself a major drug habit by then, dabbling mainly in pain killers, mescaline and cocaine. It took them close to a year to finish *Secrets and Lies,* eventually moving from the EMI-approved studios in Kentish Town where they fought daily and staying at a residential studio in West London. After the Kentish Town part of the recording, Baker quit, saying he'd had enough, and they brought in Andy Mears to take over. This saved them because Andy was fresh, and he could get them going again. The album came out, *Dog Tired* became a number one success around the world in 1987 and suddenly they were at superstar level, touring America and supporting bands like *Whitesnake*.'

'We might need to speak to Baker,' Monroe mused. 'If there was bad blood then, there could be worse now.'

'Baker died three years back,' Bullman replied sadly. 'Pretty much fell from the wagon, and drank himself unconscious while driving his car off a cliff.'

There was a moment of silence as everyone took this in.

'So they became super famous,' Anjli was writing. 'Then what?'

'By the early nineties, they'd changed their musical style again,' Bullman continued. 'Andy was more an Indie Rock guy, and he was leading them towards what would eventually become *Britpop*, trying to mimic the early success of *Oasis* and the *Manic Street Preachers,* that style of music. But by then, Nick had pretty much checked out. He wasn't happy there, they'd had issues with their manager, Benny Simpson, who they'd had since the EMI days, Nick was caught firing an unlicenced firearm in a London club and was one court case away from doing time for it, and he'd married a groupie, Marna Valkenburg, who wanted him to go solo.'

'Were you heartbroken when he married?' Declan smiled. Bullman looked back at him.

'Distraught,' she replied coldly and Declan decided that even though she'd mercilessly ripped him apart during the *Magpies* case, this was probably not the time to gain revenge.

Seeing him deflate in front of her eyes, Bullman nodded and looked at the others.

'The marriage didn't last long, though,' she added. 'Because in 1998 he drove home after a gig in Brighton and never arrived.'

'This was where he committed suicide, Ma'am?' De'Geer, writing his own notes, asked. Bullman nodded.

'Marna was worried and called the police the next day,

and they found his car near Birling Gap in East Sussex, some of his clothes on the beach itself. The police checked into it but with no body couldn't conclusively state that Nick had committed suicide. After that, with Nick missing, Marna and Benny took control and within a couple of months Dave was ousted from the band, pretty much because nobody really liked him, but officially due to breaking a moral clause in his contract because he'd provided the weapon that the police arrested Nick with, and had been supplying most of his drugs for the previous decade. Why he'd found the gun, or why Nick needed one, was never explained. He'd been doing his own thing for years by then, mainly producing for other bands, so he was solvent, but he never gained another penny from *Alternator*, and never toured again.'

'Until now,' Monroe replied. 'Why is now different?'

'The staff at the venue mentioned to me that the whole thing was Dave's way to get in on some hedge fund action,' Anjli spoke now, reading from her notes. 'That the band is being looked at for a back catalogue buyout, possibly in the millions. But with Nick still not legally dead, there's no way to finish the deal without Dave being involved, as even though he was kicked out, on the early documents he's co-founder and blood relative.'

'And now, with him dead?' Monroe asked. Anjli shrugged.

'Back in the air again,' she said. 'Probably being discussed by some bankers right now.'

There was a beep, and Billy glanced at his laptop.

'I might have something a little off-kilter,' he said as he looked back at the room. 'I've been talking to some *Alternator* groups, and there's a theory already on the net.'

'You don't mean the curse, do you?' Bullman shook her head. 'It's pointless.'

'Curse?' Declan asked. 'We're not on bloody curses again, are we?'

Billy brought up an image on the screen, the *Secrets and Lies* album cover.

'There's a legend among fans that this album is cursed, in the same way that *Macbeth* isn't named backstage in theatres and is called the *Scottish Play,*' he said. 'Apparently, there have been five deaths since the album, all mysterious, and all people connected to the recording. There's a conspiracy—'

'That something happened during the recording, and a pact was made to cover it up,' Bullman interrupted irritably. 'We all know about it, and it's bollocks.'

'This was your big thing?' Monroe tutted at Billy, shaking his head. 'And I had such high hopes for you.'

'But if there are related deaths, it's worth looking into it,' Declan glanced at Monroe. 'Look at the *Magpies* case. That was people dying to ensure the survivors had a bigger payout.'

'Conspiracies are kind of our thing, I suppose,' Monroe nodded. 'We might as well keep it on the board for the moment.'

He looked at Bullman.

'I know you keep out of cases, but we could use you on this,' he suggested.

Bullman nodded agreement.

'I can't promise I'll be able to help that much,' she replied.

Monroe looked back at the group.

'Right then,' he started. 'Lines of enquiry are this rich bloke who was there, Eden Storm—we need to know why he was at the gig and why he left early. Peter Suffolk too, I want to know why a new member of *Alternator* is gaining little envelopes from Dave Manford's manager. And, at the same time I want the manager in here too. She must know more about what's going on.'

'I can take Suffolk,' Declan suggested.

'I'll speak to Eden Storm,' Anjli offered.

'That leaves me and the Guv talking to the manager,' Monroe looked at Bullman. 'Unless you have anyone else we should talk to?'

Bullman nodded.

'Interview the band, see if any of them have had run-ins with Dave recently. And find Benny Simpson, their manager. He retired twenty years back but I'm sure he's still around somewhere.'

'I have him already,' Billy said and on the plasma screen an image appeared; it was one of those newspaper *WHERE ARE THEY NOW* pieces, and Benny, in his trademark chunky glasses could be seen in a wheelchair in a nursing home. 'He was admitted into *Steadfast Nursing Home* in Surrey two, maybe three years ago. He's wheelchair bound and suffering from early stage dementia, according to the piece, written a year ago.'

'Check into it,' Bullman added. 'I want confirmation that's more than the tabloid press talking shit.'

'Doctor Marcos, DC Davey, keep on with the forensics, let's see if we can gain anything else from the device,' Monroe looked at De'Geer. 'You go back to the bar and see if anyone else remembers anything. Be imposing and scary.'

Finally, he looked over at Billy.

'You? Keep hunting these conspiracy groups down,' he smiled. 'Let's see what stones we can overturn. Could find some tidbits we can throw at some of the others.'

The room burst into action as everyone rose at once. Declan nodded at Anjli as he exited, walking to his desk.

His phone, left on it when he walked into the briefing room, was glowing, showing that a message had just been received. Picking the phone up, he looked at the text on the screen.

Watch your back. She's gunning for you.

Confused, Declan checked the number to see there was none. Was this a message from Trix or Tom? Who was gunning for him? The only woman Declan knew with an issue with him was probably Francine Pearce.

Who'd been released the previous day.

Sighing, Declan placed the phone in his jacket pocket and sat back at his desk, searching the database for Peter Suffolk's address. It was already looking to be a long, incredibly annoying day. The last thing he wanted to be doing was looking over his shoulder.

Maybe you should just head it off at the pass, the voice in his head whispered. *Meet with Pearce and nip that problem in the bud.*

The screen flashed up an address for Peter Suffolk and, writing it down, Declan nodded to himself.

If he got a chance that day, Declan and Francine would have a little heart-to-heart.

5

ABNEY PARK

FOR A MAN WHO HAD SPENT THE BETTER PART OF FORTY YEARS playing drums, an activity that spent a lot of energy and was an arm workout more brutal than most bench press exercises, Martin Reilly was surprisingly slight. In fact, by looking at his bald head and narrow face you might even assume that Martin Reilly was, in fact, very ill.

Martin wasn't. In fact, he was in better shape than he'd been for years.

After the last *Alternator* tour, he'd gone on a bit of a detox bender—he wasn't married, and his last girlfriend had left over a year back, citing that his touring lifestyle had destroyed their relationship, in the process pouring out every bottle of whisky he owned into a sink and throwing his expensive cigars into the rubbish, allowing the bin men to take away hundreds of pounds of expensive *Monte Cristo* cigars and, more importantly, half a humidor of the *Arturo Fuente Opus X 10th anniversary edition* cigar; forty cigars that, if sold now, would cost over ten grand to buy.

Ten grand tossed on the tip.

She'd been gone by the time he'd gotten back from the tour, which was good, because if she'd been in the house, he'd have killed her.

But, after this, he'd used it as a healing event, cutting out the cigars and the whisky, and taking up Keto and CrossFit. A man in his sixties would never excel at this the way others did, but it'd done wonders for him, and he was now one of those born-again CrossFit zealots that he used to absolutely hate, hanging around the Keto-friendly café bars of Windsor, trying to pick up women half his age.

Graham Hagan was *jealous* of him.

Graham had instead embraced the other direction; he was easily three stone heavier than he was ten years ago, and he found touring to be a pain, mainly because the backstage food was always so bloody healthy. Graham was a savant of fat, fried foods. He was bordering on obese, likely pre-diabetic and one cream cake away from a heart attack. But in his own way, he was still living the rock-and-roll lifestyle, having grown his greying, ginger hair into a frizzy ponytail.

With sunglasses on, he looked like a fat Mick Hucknall.

Like Martin, Graham had never married, but this was more because of choice. He'd been asexual for a long time now; maybe even since the eighties.

Maybe even since that night.

And now Graham was meeting Martin in Windsor Great Park, walking along the path in silence, like two Cold War spies.

'You think it was an accident?' Martin asked.

'The prick's not been on stage for twenty years,' Graham almost laughed. 'And Lydia organised it, so she probably found an electrician off *Craigslist*.'

'We don't have *Craigslist* in the UK,' Martin replied. 'You've been in California for too long.'

'Not bloody long enough,' Graham muttered. 'The moment this is signed and sealed? I'm off back to LA.'

'What if it isn't?' Martin asked, and Graham could hear a tremor of nervousness in the tone. 'What if something happens, and it *can't* be sold? What if they look into the album royalties?'

'The story's been out there for thirty years,' Graham stopped walking, turning Martin to face him. 'We stick to it.'

'What if we didn't?' Martin was looking around the park now, as if expecting assassins to leap out from behind trees at any moment. 'What if we finally came clean?'

'About what?' Graham snapped. 'We don't know what happened that night. We've never known.'

'Before that, then,' Martin almost pleaded. 'The girls. The party—'

Martin was healthier than he'd ever been, but even he didn't spot the slap before Graham backhanded him across the cheek, sending him stumbling backwards, off the path and onto the grass. Graham was larger than Martin was, and his blow had weight behind it.

'Now you listen here,' Graham hissed. 'You might have had your *come to Jesus* moment, but I haven't. We tell the police, we go to jail. Or worse—maybe you forgot what happened to Bruce?'

'Bruce was an accident,' Martin rubbed at his cheek resentfully. 'He was sozzled.'

'And Dave was *sizzled* last night,' Graham leaned in. 'It's the curse.'

Martin laughed, backing away as Graham went to slap him again.

'Jesus, Graham, I really thought you were serious for a moment,' he said. 'The curse is—'

'The police will look into this,' Graham hissed. 'They'll look into *Alternator*. They'll look into the girls, into *Lorraine*.'

'*Shut up!*' Martin grabbed Graham now, pushing him backwards until he backed up against a tree. 'Never say that name. *Never!*'

'Nick, Dave, Bruce, Clive, all dead,' Graham snarled back. 'Which of us is next, eh? You or me? Which of us is going to die first?'

'You don't know what you're saying,' Martin walked away, but Graham grabbed him by the arm.

'Do you still have that holiday caravan in Chertsey?' he asked, and for the first time, Martin saw the fear in Graham Hagen's face.

'I do,' he replied. 'Why?'

'I think we need to go off grid,' Graham whispered. 'Just for a couple of days. Don't tell anyone where we are. Just escape, lie low and wait it out.'

'But what do we do about the contracts?' Martin asked, shaking his head. 'We need to stay in the loop.'

Graham thought for a moment.

'We'll get one of the sessions to keep us in the loop,' he said with a smile. 'Chris Joseph or Peter Suffolk. Neither of them were around then, and neither of them have any say in the contract signing. We'll get them to be our eyes and ears.'

Martin thought about this.

'Dude, someone killed Dave,' Graham urged. 'That weren't no accident. There's only a handful of us who were there that night, and once the police work back to that, they'll work back to why it happened. They'll work back to *us*.'

Reluctantly, Martin nodded.

'I'm guessing your bags are already packed?' he asked.

Graham smiled; a dark, sad one.

'Have been since Bruce died,' he said.

Martin took a deep breath, looking around the park. He loved Windsor, and the thought of being cooped up for two days, or even longer with Graham bloody Hagen in a static caravan was horrifying.

'Meet me there this afternoon,' he said. 'I'll pass the message to one of the newbs and get them to keep us updated.'

Suddenly remembering, Graham passed Martin a phone.

'Use this,' he said. 'It's a burner.'

'Since when did you start carrying around burner phones?' Martin was incredulous.

'Since someone electrocuted Davey bloody Manford,' Graham muttered as he walked off, heading back towards the car park.

———

LYDIA CORNWALL HADN'T INTENDED TO LEAVE HER APARTMENT that day; the whole horror show of the previous night still weighed heavily on her head.

She wasn't even sure how she made it home that night, as from the moment Dave was electrocuted on stage until the moment she woke up in her bed, she felt as if she was in a dream, a haze, where she'd simply sleepwalked back to Hackney. She'd been emotionless, numb... until she arrived home.

And then everything hit her at once. She hadn't cried; she still hadn't cried yet, but the memories, the confusions, the late-night brain worms were all there in force, pulling her from pillar to post, revisiting every bad moment in her life, as nearly all of them involved the Manfords and *Alternator*.

It was an accident. It had to be.

Who'd want to kill Dave Manford? They had years to do it when he was alone in his recording studio, and nobody would have cared. He wouldn't have even made the news. To kill him at the start of his show, in front of so many witnesses, that wasn't a personal vendetta, that was a statement made to the others on the list. Reminding them what would happen if they spoke out.

Lydia knew too well what would happen if you spoke out, as she stared down at the gravestone in front of her.

RAYMOND CORNWALL
LOVING HUSBAND

Abney Park had once been a magnificent parkland, but in the 1800's, it had been repurposed as one of the 'Magnificent Seven' garden cemeteries of London. It was also a woodland memorial park and local nature reserve site and so aside from being a onetime cemetery, with over two hundred thousand people buried inside, it was also filled with tourists. On a good day it was a pleasant thirty-minute walk from Lydia's apartment. On a bad day like this, it took a good deal longer, primarily because her gated community had reporters standing outside, desperate for a statement about what happened the previous night.

She wasn't even Dave's manager; she'd organised this as a favour, partly because of their history, but also because of the friendship Raymond and Dave had had in the years they knew each other. Raymond had helped Dave's recording studio get off the ground, and in return Dave had passed him a secret, late one night, one that changed Raymond and Lydia's relationship forever, and sent him to Bruce Baker, and his death.

She hadn't known about this latter part until last night when Dave, filled with nervous energy, had told her, unaware of what damage that one conversation had done eight years earlier.

Lydia wiped away a tear.

'Happy anniversary, my love,' she said sadly. 'I didn't forget you. No matter what's happened so far today.'

There was a rustling of leaves and Lydia spun around angrily, expecting to find a reporter standing there, notebook in hand. Instead, it was a man, tall, over six feet and slim with it. His hair was still thick for his age, which was now in his early sixties, but had been left to grow out into a shaggy, curled mop, and dyed cherry red. He wore a leather aviation jacket and glasses over a sweater and jeans, his white *Nikes* now spattered with mud as he walked towards her.

'Lydia,' he whispered. 'My condolences.'

'Which one,' Lydia snapped. 'Ray or Dave? You've made no secret you hated both of them.'

'That's not fair,' Andy Mears replied, staring down at the gravestone. 'I never hated Raymond. I just felt he was misguided.'

'Misguided?' Lydia laughed, but it came out as a coarse rattle. 'That's rare, coming from you. Who misguided him?'

Andy now looked up at Lydia.

'You know damn well who did.'

'Careful now,' Lydia moved close, looking up at the *Alternator* guitarist. 'You're sounding like you believe Bruce was killed.'

'Bruce was a drunk who couldn't stay sober,' Andy replied

calmly. 'He screamed conspiracy to every corner, while happily taking album royalties and sucking up to Tamara. If he wanted to be the hero he claimed to be, he could have gone to the police with what he believed.'

'You know he couldn't,' Lydia snapped. 'We both signed the contract. We all did.'

'And some of us have dealt better with it than others,' Andy looked up across the graveyard. 'You have a plot here?'

Lydia shook her head.

'People don't get buried here anymore,' she said.

'Raymond did,' Andy commented.

'Raymond was a long-time trustee of the *Abney Park Trust*,' Lydia replied. 'And his parents were two of the last people buried here. He had heritage to claim on.'

'And a truckload of money donated to some worthy cause, I'm guessing?'

Lydia stayed silent for a moment.

'It was always Ray's dream,' she eventually said. 'I couldn't let them take it away from him. I did whatever it needed to ensure it happened.'

'And paid for with your money,' Andy noted casually. '*Alternator* money.'

'*Hush* money.'

'Still the money you used to pay for it. Just like how you funded his dying business over the years, too.'

'It's what husbands and wives do,' Lydia replied caustically. 'You wouldn't know, judging by what you did to yours.'

She looked around.

'Is *she* here?' she asked, half-joking. 'Watching me through the trees, too scared to come and talk to me?'

'No,' Andy shook his head. 'She's at home, watching the news.'

'Probably dancing,' Lydia crouched, pulling a weed from the gravesite. 'Soon she'll be able to do it on Dave's grave too.'

'You sound like a victim,' Andy muttered. 'That you've lost people, that you're hard done by. Is that how you feel?'

'Shouldn't I?' Lydia snapped back. 'I watched a friend die last night.'

Andy laughed at this.

'Dave was never a friend,' he replied. 'Maybe he was a *shag* back in the day, but the only reason you helped him was to help yourself. Like you always do. Or had you forgotten the girls?

Lydia glared at Andy Mears. If looks could kill, he would already have joined Dave Manford.

'I only gave advice,' she said flatly.

'You told them that if they started spouting off about what happened that night, trying to cash in on the feeding frenzy that followed Nick's disappearance—'

'Death.'

'—that you'd destroy their entire lives,' Andy finished.

'I never said anything to them,' Lydia straightened. 'I never even contacted them.'

'You didn't need to,' Andy scoffed in reply. 'That's the joy of having a massive PR Svengali as a husband. It's always easier to let the hired help make the threats.'

He took in a breath, looking around the cemetery as he breathed in the air.

'You told them to back off when it happened,' he said, matter-of-factly. 'You told them that was what groupies did. That they could make money off it. You suggested they could whore themselves—'

'I did no such thing!' Lydia interrupted, reddening.

'Whore themselves like you did,' Andy finished. 'You

paint yourself the victim, but you told them what to do. You told Ray what to do. You both told Bruce what to do and last night you were telling Dave what to do.'

Lydia stared furiously at Andy, tears of anger running down her face.

'Tell me,' he continued. 'Who will you get to do things now that all your lovers are dead?'

His message given, Andy nodded briefly before turning and walking off.

'Wait,' Lydia called out. 'Why are you here, anyway? This isn't anywhere near your stomping grounds.'

'I felt a little nostalgic,' Andy replied. 'What with all the buy-out paperwork and the song being popular again, it made me think of the good old days.'

'There were no good old days,' Lydia sighed. 'Not after *Bear Studios.*'

Andy nodded again.

'That's my next stop,' he said. 'I haven't been there since... well, *since.*'

'You sure about that?' Lydia smiled, the first she'd made in a while; a vicious, vendetta-fuelled one. 'A little birdie told me you've been trying to buy it for years.'

Andy laughed.

'That little bird is just as misguided as Raymond was,' he said as he walked off, back towards the west entrance and Stoke Newington.

Lydia stood alone in Abney Park cemetery, next to the grave of her husband, a grave that she knew she would never be allowed to be placed next to when she died.

Always the victim.

No, not the victim. Because she knew that deep down, Andy Mears was right.

She'd stopped being a victim the day she'd help gaslight two teenage girls into believing they were nothing more than drunken whores. The day she'd set Lorraine Warner on the path to her own death.

And finally, Lydia Cornwall cried.

6

CROSS-EYED MARY

PETER SUFFOLK LIVED IN A RATHER NICE LOOKING TWO-bedroom terraced Georgian house a couple of minutes north of Hampstead Underground station, a location in which Declan felt too poor to even walk around the moment he pulled up in his police-issued, battered Audi. He didn't know how much the houses around here cost, but for Suffolk to own anything around here, meant that he had to be paying a low to mid-seven figure mortgage.

The road to the house was on a hill, so not only was it a steep climb to the gate, but the house itself had a small, several-levelled garden to the side, the back of which showed off a white-walled basement window which caused Declan to reassess the house's value. The neighbours around here included people like Ricky Gervais, Helena Bonham-Carter and Liam Gallagher, although Liam probably knew Peter Suffolk well, them both being singers and all that.

Declan didn't really know if singers bonded, but he'd seen on the report Bullman made before he left that *Alternator* had been on the same bill as *Oasis* at a couple of festivals early in the latter band's career, so it made sense they knew each other, if only from fights at the bar.

Knocking on the door, Declan wasn't sure what to expect, but the one thing he didn't was to find the door opened by a man in his mid-fifties wearing nothing but a bathrobe, his hair slicked back and wet.

'Your timing's bloody impeccable,' Peter Suffolk said, his voice giving away a slight northern twang. 'Whatever you're selling, come back later.'

'I can wait if that helps?' Declan showed his warrant card, and the man froze, as if realising this was more than some door-to-door sales selling.

'This is about Davey, isn't it?' Peter shook his head. 'I haven't spoken to him for years.'

'Still want to talk to you.'

Peter sighed.

'Give me five minutes, yeah?' he asked, moving back into the hallway so Declan could enter. 'Wait in the main room. Back there.'

He pointed at a white walled living room that Declan could see at the end of the hallway, with patio doors leading out to a small, concealed garden. Nodding, Declan made his way through as Peter ran off to dry himself off and put on some clothes.

In the living room, Declan faced a wall of books and photo frames, while opposite, in alcoves either side of the mantlepiece, were hundreds of twelve-inch vinyl records. The wall to the left had an expensive-looking turntable on a wooden sideboard, but no speakers beside it. There was a sofa and an armchair in the centre, placed around a glass coffee table and Declan noted that there was no TV in the room; this was most likely the music room, as he could see a sound bar on the mantlepiece.

Walking to the photos, Declan saw that these were primarily professional. There were a couple of scattered images of Peter Suffolk in group shots, and another blonde woman, most likely his partner was visible in a couple of these, but the others were from events and concerts he was on stage at. Pulling out his phone, he took a couple of quick snaps, in case any of these helped with the case. There was Peter with *Alternator*, live on stage. A couple of group shots, probably from PR teams. There were also images of Peter on stage dressed as other singers, most likely tribute performances, and a couple of backstage photos from what looked like award shows; one had him with David Bowie, another showed a far younger Peter next to Elton John. There were others, but Declan didn't recognise any of them.

'Admiring my scrapbook?' the voice came from behind him, and Declan turned to see Peter Suffolk, now in jogging bottoms and a gym hoodie, slippers on his feet. His hair was hastily blow-dried, and still had that slight static fuzz to it.

'Peter Suffolk?' Declan asked.

'I'd bloody hope so, you're standing in his sunroom,' Peter smiled. 'Sorry, a joke. I do it when I'm nervous.'

'Why would you be nervous?' Declan asked.

'Sorry, what was your name again?' the request was natural; Declan hadn't given his identity but at the same time Declan felt this was a delaying tactic to give Peter more time to think.

'Detective Inspector Walsh, Temple Inn Command Unit,' he replied. 'We're investigating—'

'Davey, yes, I thought so,' Peter sat on the armchair, indicating for Declan to sit on the sofa. 'I'm nervous, you see, because if it gets out I was there, it could cost me my job.'

'How so?' Declan pulled out his notebook as Peter shrugged.

'Because *Alternator* and Davey bloody hated each other,' he replied simply. 'Like absolutely detested each other. Andy wouldn't even piss on Davey if he was on the ground and on fire.' He thought about this for a moment.

'Well, he'd probably piss on the bits that weren't on fire, that is.'

'That would be Andy Mears, the guitarist?'

'Andy Mears the whole damn show,' Peter smiled. 'He pretty much *is Alternator*. Him and Marna.'

'You don't sound like a fan,' Declan noted. At this, Peter shrugged.

'I'm a work-for-hire session musician, nothing more,' he explained. 'I sing the songs on tour. We haven't recorded an album with new stuff since I arrived in the band.'

Declan nodded at this, writing it down. 'How long have you been with the band?'

'Since 2011,' Peter replied. 'Their previous singer, Jesse Morrison, left when he broke his leg, or hip, I can't remember the details, but it meant he couldn't keep up with the tour schedule. They dumped him while he was still in a cast.'

'Harsh.'

'Business,' Peter shrugged. 'I'd known them for a couple of years on the circuit, I'd been in a band that supported them a few times and so we chatted, I quit my old band and started on tour the next month.'

'Why the name change?' Declan asked. 'Your driving license says your name is Andrew...' he peered at the name in his notebook. 'Knight?'

Peter smiled.

'It's pronounced *nut*, actually,' he explained. 'But my surname's spelt K-N-Y-T-T-E with a silent K. I've had people all my life call me *Kanute, Kanette, Knight, Nit*, a whole variation.'

'And I'm guessing the last thing you want as an actor is a name that doesn't work first time?' Declan replied.

'Exactly,' Peter nodded. 'My dad came from Suffolk, and as there's already an Andy Suffolk in Equity, I used my middle name, which I've used most of my life anyway. And to be frank, it would have been a massive pain if there'd been two Andys in the band.'

Declan nodded.

'Besides,' Peter grinned. 'Nobody gave two shits when they called David Bowie, Freddie Mercury or even Elton John by their stage names. Social media's shown us that names can be whatever they want. What you're given at birth isn't who you are.'

'And this is your only job?' Declan looked around the room. 'I'll be honest, Mister Suffolk, I didn't realise that being the lead singer in a band that's only toured for the last fifteen years gave such an extravagant lifestyle.'

Peter laughed at this.

'Christ no,' he shook his head. 'I do solo stuff as well, mainly cruise liners. I'll do a three-week cruise in between *Alternator* tours. I even have a four-person series of gigs with other lead singers. And when I'm not doing that, I'll tour in productions as Roy Orbison or Buddy Holly, you know the type of thing. I've gotten pretty fast on the makeup side for those gigs. And, if you put me next to Roy when in makeup? You wouldn't tell us apart.'

'Well, apart from the fact that Roy Orbison's been dead for years.'

'It was hypothetical,' Peter almost sulked back in reply.

Declan kept writing.

'So you keep yourself busy,' he said.

'That's only the tip,' Peter continued. 'I converted my loft into a recording studio and I produce a few smaller bands, and that brings in almost the same as I make singing.'

'I thought recording studios were enormous spaces with glass windows?' Declan was surprised at this, as the house didn't seem large enough to have an expansive loft space. Peter leaned back in the chair.

'All you need is a booth and a MacBook these days,' he explained. 'Half the bands out there create a studio in a back room or even under the stairs. Somewhere without an echo. The days of the residential studios like *Rockfield* are pretty much over, or they've massively downsized.'

Declan looked up from his notes.

'So if you're making this money, and you're scared of losing the *Alternator* gig, why turn up to Dave Manford's show last night, and why take what looked like an envelope of money from his manager?'

Peter stopped, considering this before leaning forward and lowering his voice.

'This is like a doctor-patient, right?' he asked. 'Anything I tell you won't be divulged publicly?'

'First off, there's no need to lower your voice, unless you're the one recording this,' Declan deliberately leaned back. 'And second, I will pass your information to whomever it seems reasonable to do so. But if you're worried, we're not likely to be giving it to the local papers soon.'

Peter thought for a moment and then sighed.

'I was getting an envelope of money because Lydia was paying me for services rendered,' he replied. 'For the last two months, I've been building Dave's singing voice back up.'

'I thought you said the band hated him?'

'They do,' Peter replied. 'Well, Andy does. The rest don't give a shit.'

'And you said you hadn't spoken to him for years.'

Peter nodded. 'And I was telling the truth about that,' he replied. 'I didn't want to be caught in the same room as him, it'd end my career with *Alternator*. So I recorded a series of videos for her, going through warm-up exercises, the straw technique, all that sort of thing.'

'The straw technique?' Declan looked up in interest at this. 'I'm hoping this isn't drug related.'

'Far from it,' Peter shook his head. 'It's actually called *straw phonation.* You take a straw, stick it into your mouth and make a seal around it with your lips, so you're partially blocking your vocal tract.'

'Why exactly?' Declan was finding himself strangely fascinated by this.

'You make high-pitched sounds, humming through it as you expel air through the straw,' Peter continued. 'It strengthens your vocal cords, rebalancing and re-coordinating the vocal mechanism, the muscles that work with the breath to give your voice resonance. Which strengthens your voice and makes it less likely to fail.'

He smiled.

'I learnt it on cruise ships,' he said. 'You're spending weeks in air-conditioned rooms, and that plays merry hell with your throat, I can tell you. I even have a stainless steel one I take everywhere with me.'

'Why?' Declan asked, confused at this.

Peter looked horrified for a moment.

'Plastic straws are destroying our planet,' he replied sincerely.

Declan nodded at this, writing it down. To be honest, Peter Suffolk struck him as the kind of man that would have his own, specially made straw in its own wooden, felt-lined case.

And probably a spare one, just in case one broke during the re-coordinating of his vocal mechanism.

'We saw the CCTV of last night, and on one of the cameras, you seemed angry when you received the payment,' he continued.

Peter's face darkened, and he nodded.

'Yeah, Lydia screwed me,' he replied. 'I came to pick up my money, and she started having a go at me, saying I hadn't done half the work because I was supposed to sit with him and work on the voice together rather than literally video-phone it in. And, when she gave me my fee, she'd discounted a chunk of it, without ever having mentioned this during the sessions.'

He stared out of the window, anger pouring off him.

'I then kicked off because, not only was I risking my future with the band by helping her in the first place, I was doing the same by even turning up. I'd noticed the paparazzi out the front, and I knew she'd set it up not for the gig, but so she could get a photo of me leaving. That's the kind of sneaky shit the bitch did.'

'Sounds like you know her well,' Declan noted. Peter, in reply, shrugged.

'She's been around for years, and I've heard the stories,' he replied. 'In professional wrestling, there's a term, *ring rat*. These are the women who don't really care about wrestling, but they really want to shag the wrestlers. In music, you have groupies, who are similar, but they at least stay fans of the music too. Lydia? She just wanted to sleep her way through the band.'

'And did she?' Declan didn't mean to sound as if he wanted salacious gossip, but the question hung in the air for a moment.

'No idea,' Peter eventually replied. 'Before my time. This is back in the eighties. I don't even know if she was legal when she started screwing around.'

'You left her with something too,' Declan continued. 'What was it?'

'A USB drive with all the videos I'd made on it,' Peter replied casually. 'She already had them through email, but I wanted to make sure she got what she paid for. I never named Dave in them, so I could claim I made them for anyone.'

Declan watched Peter for a moment.

'Does the band know Dave's dead yet?' he asked. 'I mean, I'm sure they've seen the news, but have you spoken to them?'

Peter nodded.

'Marna called half an hour ago, ecstatic,' he said. 'Not at the death, even if she was happy about that, she's still clever enough not to show it publicly, but the fact that the royalties are rocketing. Everyone's downloading the songs again. For some reason, when someone dies, the fans always download the songs to listen to. And the news organisations are using snippets, and that brings in money. Andy's talking to people about the back catalogue, and Dave's death probably adds another million to the asking price.'

'Do you get any of that?' Declan asked. Peter shook his head.

'I told you, I'm only a session musician,' he said. 'I don't get royalties. And besides, the only album doing anything is *Secrets and Lies,* and that has a weird payment structure, anyway.'

Declan stopped writing. 'How so?'

Peter shifted in his seat as he worked out how to explain this.

'The first album didn't do gangbusters, even with a top ten single, and the second one, *Secrets and Lies* wasn't even named, just *Album Two* on the books. EMI gave them a nice location to work with in Kentish Town, but they couldn't get together on the same page. Nick was whacked out on Scooby snacks—'

'Scooby snacks?'

'Drugs,' Peter smiled.

'Which ones?'

'*All* of them, from what I've been told,' Peter continued. 'Anyway, Nick was in no state to work, Dave was spending most of his time keeping Nick happy with buckets of drugs and hookers, they'd got post-tour burn out and they were fighting. Bruce, the guitarist, left the band around here, realising they were tanking and EMI were trying to get out of the contract.'

'You're still not explaining how the weird payment structure came about,' Declan replied.

'Andy Mears turned up,' Peter carried on. 'Now, remember this is all second-hand information, stuff I've picked up in dressing rooms over the years, but he knew them from the circuit similarly to how I did years later and, when things were really falling apart, he suggested they move studios, finding a residential place in West London for them. But EMI wouldn't pay for it, saying they'd paid for the studio already. All that was available was literally enough to cover rent and studio space. So Nick came up with an idea. That they wouldn't take any salaries from the budget, but would instead profit share.'

'The band?'

'Everyone,' Peter replied. 'The band, the producer, the guys who sound engineered, everyone who was in the studio, whatever their role, weren't paid a salary, but got an equal percentage. Top to bottom. And over the years, it's made more money for everyone than the wages they'd have earned doing it would have been. Andy came on as a full-time guitarist and wrote half the songs.'

Declan thought for a moment.

'So, if this back catalogue was sold, how would that affect this deal?'

Peter shrugged.

'They'd have to buy out everyone,' he explained. 'Well, everyone left, anyway.'

'You mean the curse?' Declan raised an eyebrow, and Peter laughed at this.

'There's no bloody curse,' he replied. 'They recorded the album thirty-five plus years ago. People working on it were in their thirties and forties. Now they're in their seventies and eighties. People die. It's a simple fact. And the deal made back then didn't grandfather the rights to descendants or spouses, so once dead? Poof! The rights revert to the original group and the payout gets bigger each quarter.'

'But with five people dead, including Dave, that amount must rocket up right now.'

'Technically, it's four, as Nick isn't legally dead,' Peter corrected. 'That said, I don't know the ins and outs, as—'

'You're just the session musician,' Declan nodded as he wrote in the notebook. 'How did you bypass the paparazzi?'

'Sorry?' Peter was thrown by the sudden change in direction here. Declan looked up.

'You left before the gig started, but you didn't go out the front,' he continued. 'How did you get out?'

'Back door leads out halfway down Lovat Lane, behind the bar,' Peter said, looking a little uncomfortable. 'There was one pap there, taking shots, but I paid him twenty quid and deleted the images from his camera. Far cheaper than trying to do that to all of them.'

Declan nodded, closing the notebook and rising.

'I'll need to speak to the other band members,' he said as Peter rose to meet him. 'Any idea the best way to do that?'

'Go through Marna,' Peter nodded. 'But don't mention Lydia when you do.'

'They know each other?' Declan considered this. *Rival managers probably would,* he supposed.

Peter grinned.

'I'd bloody hope so,' he said as he led Declan to the front door.

'They're half-sisters.'

7

MONEY, MONEY, MONEY

ANJLI HAD EXPECTED TO BE FORCED TO JUMP THROUGH HOOPS to gain an audience with Eden Storm, what with him being an American citizen and a billionaire, but it had been surprisingly simple. After explaining who she was, and why she was calling, emphasising that Eden being found at the scene of a murder wasn't exactly great PR, and that a quick chat to clear up everything would ensure this went away quickly, she was given a time and location to meet with him in Central London.

Although LA-based, Eden had been working in the UK for around four months, creating a new line of electric cars named *Edison* based around three competing British giga factories. Business wise, he looked to be the bastard child of *Elon Musk* and *Jeff Bezos,* although Eden had made his money the old-fashioned way; he'd inherited it from his mother, Tamara Rothstead-Page when she died, and his mother had inherited it from her grandfather, who'd helped create one of the largest pharmaceutical companies in America, literally bringing toothpaste to the masses.

Eden however hadn't wanted to work in toothpaste, and as a teen had sold half his shares, moving most of his billion-dollar fortune into film and TV in LA, while working as an activist against climate change, acting as a spokesperson for zero emission technology, a belief that had led him to his series of state-of-the-art electric vehicles.

The reception area was in a building in the heart of Mayfair, on Upper Grosvenor Street. It was on the third floor of a beautiful white-brick Georgian townhouse, and had marble floors, with gold panelled walls leading to a marble and wood reception desk with a plant on the end. Two leather sofas faced a leather chair in a U-shape, a glass coffee table in the middle. On one wall was a picture of Eden, printed on canvas; but to anyone walking in, there was nothing else to state what this reception was even for.

Anjli felt self-conscious in her charcoal grey suit as she waited for someone to come and collect her; the place felt more like a cool retreat than an office entrance, and Anjli whiled away the minutes playing games on her phone until the door opened beside the reception desk and a burly man, his black hair trimmed to a buzz cut, wearing an expensive looking black suit entered and nodded to the receptionist. He looked like someone had shaved a bear, but he was obviously in charge, as the moment he arrived and gave confirmation, the receptionist looked up to Anjli.

'You can go in now, Detective Sergeant,' she said. Anjli placed her phone away and rose, stretching out her spine as she straightened. She wasn't going to rush after being made to wait. And, having given it a good few seconds of simply standing, she walked through the door that the shaved bear had emerged from.

There was a corridor ahead, and a glass walled boardroom to the side. It held a large, walnut-patterned desk, with a giant TV to one end and a view of Mayfair through full-length windows on the other. Sitting at the desk in a blue corduroy bomber jacket over a green and white rugby shirt was Eden Storm.

He was young, maybe in his early thirties, his dyed white hair spiked out, each tip styled immaculately. Anjli wondered for a moment whether Eden had hairdressers do that every morning, but pushed the thought aside as he stood, showing with a hand for Anjli to sit facing him.

'Please,' he said as he sat back down. 'Can I get you anything? Tea, coffee, water?'

'Coffee would be fine,' Anjli replied and noted the shaved bear nodding to Eden before leaving. 'Interesting place.'

Eden looked around the room.

'I don't really know if I've ever been here before,' he replied. 'I own offices like this all over the world. Boltholes to take last-minute meetings in.'

'This is a hell of a bolthole,' Anjli responded as she pulled out her notebook. 'I know companies that would kill for a postcode like this.'

Eden shrugged, and Anjli could see that the business aspect really wasn't that important to him.

'I suppose,' he said. 'I mean, I don't rent them. My board takes care of all that.'

'Your board,' Anjli nodded as she noted this down. 'They control a lot of what you do?'

'God no,' Eden laughed. 'They just pick up the pieces after I come up with a brilliant plan. Or make my insane visions work. I'm building a UK-based electric car company right now to rival *Tesla*, and I think I've given three of them heart attacks this year already.'

'Is this *Edison?*' she asked. 'I've seen this mentioned in the news.'

Eden smiled. 'I named it that for the obvious reasons, mainly Thomas Edison verses Nikola Tesla being one of the most famous rivalries of all time. But the press got it wrong. It's actually *Edisun*. With a 'u', for sun.'

'Why?'

Eden leaned closer.

'Because my cars will change the world,' he said. 'Currently, an electric car needs to be charged at a charging point. Half a dozen different companies offer this, but it means anyone with an electric car has about five different membership cards to use them. Apart from *Tesla*, who has their own charging infrastructure.'

'So what, yours won't need to be charged?' Anjli asked. 'I guess the sun means solar powered?'

'Exactly,' Eden nodded. 'Now, van-lifers that use solar can only power items in their vehicles and have massive, traditional photovoltaic solar panels on the roof. If we did this with the cars, we'd need to do the same thing.'

'Solar panels all over a car.'

Eden nodded.

'We've gone to the next level,' he whispered. '*Solar paint.* Well, two types of it. Quantum dot solar cells, otherwise known as *photovoltaic paint,* and the more usable *perovskite solar paint,* known alternatively as spray-on solar cells. Perovskite solar cells can take on liquid form, making them the ideal candidate for solar paint, and in fact were spray painted onto a surface at the *University of Sheffield* back in 2014. It's why I've made a substantial donation to the research department.'

'And is this possible?'

Eden shrugged.

'Who knows,' he replied. 'At best? I change the world. Houses without power can paint their outsides. Cars can run forever in sunny climates. And if it doesn't? I'll have pushed forward the research, and I'll still have a car that rivals Musk's.'

Anjli stopped writing and observed Eden silently for a few moments.

'Let's cut to the chase,' she said, leaning back in the chair as she watched Eden. 'Why were you in *Eastcheap Albums* last night?'

'I was invited,' Eden replied lazily.

'No, you weren't,' Anjli shook her head. 'We've checked the guest list on the door. You weren't on it.'

She stopped as the door opened, and the shaved bear walked in, placing a coffee on the desk.

'White, no sugar, right?' Eden smiled, and it was the smile of a man who was sending a message. *He'd taken the time to find out how Anjli took her coffee. What could he find out if he really tried?*

'I prefer it black,' Anjli picked up the cup, sipping it. 'But we all make mistakes.'

It was wonderful coffee. Great, even. And even though she did indeed take it like this, the last thing she was going to do was let Eden Storm think he had the last word. Eden sat with an unreadable expression on his face, although Anjli felt frustration emanating from him.

Probably wasn't used to people disagreeing with him.

'As I said, we don't have you on the list,' she placed the cup back on the table, folding her arms. Eden pursed his lips together for a moment, as if contemplating his response.

'Someone like me, we, well, we don't go on lists,' he said.

'I know, God, it makes me sound such a dick, but I haven't needed to be on a list in years.'

'We also don't have you on CCTV entering the building,' Anjli added. 'Although we do have you talking to the doorman before people entered, and we have you leave seconds before Dave Manford died of an electrical shock.'

'Just lucky, I guess.'

'Oh, please, cut this *disillusioned millionaire* shit out,' Anjli snapped, finally tired of the act. 'I so don't have time for it.'

For the first time, Eden Storm seemed to take interest, leaning forward on the chair and placing his elbows on the boardroom table.

'First off, I'm a billionaire,' he said.

Anjli shrugged.

'Couldn't give a damn, Mister Storm,' she replied. 'I just want to catch a killer.'

'Second,' Eden continued, ignoring Anjli's jibe, 'I was there because I'm a friend of the family. Well, sort of.'

'Sort of?' Anjli pressed. 'Go on.'

'I knew Dave and Lydia in passing,' Eden carried on. 'I'd bumped into them all my life, here and there. Always grafting, always looking for a payout.'

'Why would these two be in your life?' Anjli had opened the notebook again as Eden looked around the room as if deciding whether or not to answer.

Eventually, he did.

'Nick Manford was my biological father,' he replied, looking back from the Mayfair skyline. 'Mom and Nick had a fling when he was in London. She was engaged at the time, and it was never formally stated, but there are enough sites out there who claim to have the scoop.'

'Why isn't this public knowledge?' Anjli asked. 'You're his only heir, and now surviving blood relative.'

'Look around,' Eden almost laughed. 'I'm worth billions. Why would I worry about a few song royalties owed to me? Let the others fight it out. I went there last night because I was in town, my uncle was playing my father's songs and I was feeling nostalgic.'

'In that case, why did you leave?'

'Because once I was there I realised it was a mistake,' Eden shook his head. 'I didn't realise how far Dave had fallen. I didn't want him to see me because I knew that if he did, he'd hit me up for another loan.'

Anjli leaned back in the chair.

'We're under the assumption that Dave Manford has been quite successful as a producer,' she said. 'Unless you know something we don't?'

'The money he's pissed away in that studio was money I gave him,' Eden replied, a little too calmly, as if forcing himself to stay relaxed. 'Money he promised to pay back years ago but never found time to do so.'

'So you weren't there to consider buying the back catalogue?' Anjli shifted in her seat. 'You were debt collecting?'

Eden's reply to this, however, was more laughter.

'I'm Nick Manford's son,' he said. 'I wouldn't have to bid millions for the back catalogue, as I could simply start proceedings to state him as dead, get my lawyers to settle with Marna and inherit them anyway.'

'Why don't you?' Anjli was writing again, considering Eden's testimony.

'As I said, I don't need it.' Eden looked at his watch. 'I'm sorry, but I really need to go. I have a flight waiting.'

'Leaving the country?' Anjli rose, placing her notebook

back into her inside pocket. Eden joined her in rising, shaking his head.

'Just to Manchester,' he said. 'Private jet, checking a new factory. You could come along if you want. We'd be back by dinner.'

He smiled.

'Maybe even have some together after?'

Anjli felt herself blush. Eden Storm was about her age, and he was incredibly good looking.

'I'm sorry, but I'm on duty,' she replied with a curt nod. 'Enjoy your trip though.'

Enjoy your trip? What the hell, woman?

Anjli looked over to the shaved bear, who showed an open door for his employer. Eden, however, had walked around the desk and stood to her right.

'I'm sorry Dave died, but it was expected,' he said. 'The guy was a walking heart attack. Never bothered looking after himself, because he was too busy blaming everyone else for his health issues But if you're looking for someone who may have wanted him dead, I'd check the band.'

'*Alternator*?' Anjli asked. Eden nodded.

'I saw a lot of them over the years, even though I wasn't legitimate,' he said. 'And all of them hated each other. It was only a matter of time before they started offing one another.'

He looked at his watch.

'And I really must fly, Anjli,' he said. 'Enjoy the coffee. I'll have it placed in a to-go cup.'

Before Anjli could say anything, Eden left the boardroom, the shaved bear following him. Now alone, Anjli considered what she'd learnt.

Eden was possibly Nick Manford's son. Could that have

given him a reason to kill Dave? Some revenge vendetta that needed to be looked into and discussed?

Over dinner?

Anjli shook her head and turned to leave, but faced the receptionist from outside, a takeout coffee cup, complete with lid in her hand.

'For you,' she said, passing it to Anjli, who sipped at it.

It was *wonderful* coffee.

ANDY MEARS HAD MADE GOOD TIME FROM ABNEY PARK AND now stood outside *Bear Studios*, ignoring the light rain that was falling onto him.

The building was a one storey barn, effectively, built on land that had been unused after the *de Salis* family had sold it off, piece by piece hundreds of years ago after buying the land, demolishing it in the 1800s and turning the once beautiful gardens, created originally by Viscount Bollingbroke, and then added to decades later by the Earl of Uxbridge, into brickfields.

That's some serious revenge going on there, he thought to himself. *To take a beautiful Manor House, only built for fifty years and demolish it? That's a spiteful person ensuring that nobody wins.*

He chuckled to himself. This was very much what was happening with *Alternator* right now, with people looking to take the back catalogue, buying it up and splitting the successful songs out, discarding the ones that nobody cared about.

But Andy cared about them.

Walking back to the main gate, Andy stroked the old

brick wall that surrounded the building. When he'd first arrived at the studios in the eighties, he'd been told it was a wall built to keep plague victims out of Dawley, with a large grave for them built the other side, one that had been unearthed when the nearby Stockley Park Industrial Estate had been built. There had been long nights spent at the studios during the recording and creation of *Secrets and Lies*, and Peanut, one of the recording engineers had been convinced that he could hear the cries of the dead out there while on a massive LSD comedown.

Andy had since learnt that the wall *had* been built to keep plague victims out, but it was a different plague; in 1755, Henry, Earl of Uxbridge had owned Dawley House and built this wall, a mile-long one, around Dawley House and its lands to keep out smallpox, or rather any unwanted visitors who might have been carrying it, from entering. There were no plague pits that were known of. No ghosts of the dead, buried on unconsecrated ground and endlessly moaning.

Well, apart from one.

He'd knocked on the door, but with no reply had started walking back to his car. He was about to get in and drive off when the door to *Bear Studios* opened and a portly, middle-aged man in a sweatshirt and jeans emerged.

'Can I help you?' he asked.

'Was passing by, thought I'd pop in and have a look,' Andy forced a smile. 'I recorded my first album here back in the eighties.'

'Oh,' the man smiled, but it was a harsh, bitter one. 'If you want to record another you'd better hurry up. We're being evicted in a month.'

Andy nodded.

'I heard,' he said. 'Something about the land being turned into a haulage company or something?'

The man spat to the mud beside him. 'More the *or something*,' he muttered. 'The studios have only been used for rehearsal space these days. No money's coming in. And unless we find half a million by the end of June, it'll be sold, closed and likely dismantled and demolished.'

'Shame,' Andy looked around the clearing he was parked in. 'I was here when it was still being built.'

'Oh, so you're one of *them*,' the man nodded, knowing exactly who Andy now represented. 'Selling your back catalogue, aren't you? How about you throw some of that cash our way?'

'That's just a rumour,' Andy shook his head. 'I'm probably as broke as you are.'

'Not driving around in that fancy Merc, you're not,' the man cricked his neck and looked back at the studios. 'And currently, nobody's as broke as me. When Keith, the old owner died, he left me a real money pit when I took this over. Best thing I could probably do is tear it down.'

'Don't say that,' Andy snapped. 'I'm sure someone will ensure this stays going for a long time.'

The man shrugged at this.

'Yeah, we'll see. I suppose you want a tour now you're here?'

'If there's one going,' Andy closed the door to his car, walking over to the man, holding his hand out. 'I'm having a bit of a nostalgia binge at the moment. I'm Andy.'

'Errol,' the man replied, shaking it. 'Come on then, not as if I've anything else to do right now.'

And as Errol entered the studios, Andy paused, staring once more at the building. He had to find a way to save the studios, as the last thing he wanted was for the place to be torn down.

There were too many *secrets* in there that could be revealed.

Shaking himself to clear his head, he followed Errol in. If he'd been more aware of the present, he would have noticed the battered, navy blue Ford Fiesta parked at the junction of Dawley Road and Botwell Common. He would have seen the man, in his late sixties, a tweed flat cap on his head bring the binoculars down from his eyes and, placing them on the passenger seat, note the time on his watch and write it down in his notebook.

But Andy Mears hadn't noticed the car, or the man inside watching him, because he had already entered the studios.

It was time to face the *ghosts* once more.

———

8

ROADKILL

BILLY ENJOYED SITTING AT HIS MONITOR DESK WHILE THE others left for the field; he'd never been a fan of the face-to-face aspect of detective work, always preferring to be in the shadows, working things out and solving cases in the cyber-space world rather than the real one.

Of course, the fact that since joining the *Last Chance Saloon* he'd had his fair share of assault rifles aimed at his face was irrelevant, but he truly felt that here, behind the keyboard, he could make a solid difference.

However, that didn't stop the real world from coming to him, and Billy was quite surprised to receive a call from the front desk telling him he had a visitor.

Billy never received visitors. He liked it that way.

Pulling his suit jacket on and walking down the stairs to the main entrance, Billy walked out of the Temple Inn Command Unit to find his visitor standing on the pavement outside, staring out at Temple Inn, puffing on an e-cigarette. Rufus Harrington was young and successful, maybe mid-thir-ties at best, and wearing one of his usual navy blue *Ted Baker* suits, his brown hair shaved at the sides and slicked back, the amount of gel in it ensuring that even the strongest of hurricanes wouldn't move a single strand. As was his habit, when he wasn't taking puffs from the e-cigarette, he nervously played with the large masonic signet ring on his left middle finger.

He hadn't noticed Billy, who took this moment to observe Rufus, trying to work out what the conversation was going to be about. The last time they'd really spoken, Billy had turned down a role in *Harrington Finance,* rejecting a rather well-paid job complete with stock options, heading the Cybersecurity department, all for the small bank of monitors in Temple Inn that he now sat in front of.

It was a career decision that he didn't regret, not even when he saw his great-uncle a few weeks back and was reminded of the opulent lifestyle he'd effectively turned down when he walked away from the Fitzwarren clan.

Rufus glanced at the door and saw Billy walking down the steps.

'William,' he smiled, but it was a nervous one. 'Time for a chat?'

'I hope it's not another job interview,' Billy smiled back. 'You know my answer.'

'God no,' Rufus shook his head vehemently. 'It's actually, well, it's work related. *Your* work, that is.'

Billy nodded at this, indicating for Rufus to follow him out of the Inns of Court entrance, situated to the right of the Command Unit.

'Come on,' he said. 'There's a place we can chat just outside.'

Nodding nervously, glancing around as if expecting to be taken down by snipers at any moment, Rufus followed

Billy out into Tudor Street and to a wine bar across the road.

From the outside it looked like a simple bar, with blacked-out windows and minimal flamboyance, but once inside, it was a different experience. Mirrors lined the walls, reflecting into the bar, with comfortable chairs and expensive looking oak tables on either side of the hardwood floor. Along the top of the walls were old drinks adverts, lit by small lamps and a selection of fairy lights, stapled up so that they were strewn across the ceiling.

Billy nodded to Rufus to take a seat.

'What do you want to drink?' he asked. Rufus shrugged.

'Sparking water if they have it?' he suggested. This surprised Billy, as in the short time he'd known the man, he'd never seen Rufus drink a non-alcoholic drink.

'Okay, now I know there's something wrong,' he said.

Rufus forced a smile back, but it was a sickly looking one.

Taking this as a cue to get on with things, Billy walked to the bar, ordering a sparkling mineral water and a small lemonade. Eventually, with both drinks in hand, he sat opposite Rufus at one of the expensive-looking side tables, passing his drink over.

'So go on then, what's the problem?' he asked.

Rufus squirmed for a moment, and Billy couldn't help but take a brief moment of glee in this discomfort.

'I heard on the grapevine that you're involved in that occurrence at Eastcheap last night,' Rufus said.

'If you mean the Manford death then yes,' Billy replied. 'Why?'

'I was there,' Rufus answered softly.

Billy leaned back in the chair.

'I've seen the guest list,' he replied carefully. 'I didn't see your name on it.'

'The list was for the potential buyers,' Rufus explained, sipping at the water and obviously sweating. 'I was there in a different capacity.'

'And that was?' Billy observed Rufus, unsure of the best way to continue this. If Rufus was about to admit to being connected to Dave Manford's murder, then someone higher up should be the one to take him in.

'I was working as a broker for the band,' Rufus explained. 'They're looking to—'

'Sell the back catalogue, we know,' Billy interrupted. 'But Dave was *persona non grata* to them, wasn't he?'

Rufus nodded. 'He still had a right to the money,' he explained. 'I was there to talk to him and his manager after the gig, convince them to accept a low-ball offer rather than wait for the larger payout. The band wanted him out of the picture, full-stop.'

'And then he died. That's convenient.'

Rufus looked at the table. 'That's the issue here. You see, I was rather public on the weekend,' he mumbled. 'Stated loudly during a polo event that if Dave was to suddenly die, the money *Alternator* would make would double. You know, with all the extra exposure and all that. And everyone knows you always make more from an artist once they're dead.'

He looked back at Billy.

'And then whoosh, a couple of days later, he's lit up like a sparkler. I'd left by then, but my assistant, Carol, she saw everything. She said he looked out, said something to someone in the audience and then... well, you know.'

Billy considered this.

'Did you do it?' he asked, his tone a little more formal now.

Rufus shook his head, his eyes widening like saucers.

'God no!' he exclaimed. 'But you have to see what it looks like!'

'Yeah, but a comment like that wouldn't go far,' Billy said. 'It'd be taken as jest.'

'Not by those who were around when I said it,' Rufus moaned. 'There were a few big names there, a couple of the Rothsteads, even Trisha Hawkins.'

Billy shrugged at the name. 'Should I know her?'

'She's been Francine Pearce's number two since Pearce was in custody,' Rufus leaned in. 'She's worse, believe me. I mean, Pearce is a sociopath, but Hawkins is a full on psycho.'

Billy nodded, finally realising.

'*Will no one rid me of this turbulent priest,*' he muttered. Anyone who studied medieval history well knew the phrase, as it was the words believed to have been uttered by King Henry the Second in 1170 and which led to the death of Thomas Becket, the then-Archbishop of Canterbury. It was accepted as a phrase uttered in rage, but several knights on hearing this had travelled to Canterbury and viciously murdered Becket, believing the King had wanted this.

Whether he did or didn't was irrelevant.

The fact of the matter was that for years after, Henry claimed this wasn't his doing, even though to some people it was, and he spent the rest of his life trying to make up for an assassination he hadn't *technically* caused.

'These days, it's called *stochastic terrorism*,' Rufus replied. 'Public speech that can be expected to incite terrorism, without a direct organisational link between the inciter and the perpetrator.'

'It's still just you mentioning something and then randomly someone doing it,' Billy shook his head. 'Whether this is thanks to the Rothsteads, or Hawkins, or not. Besides, she doesn't pull the strings at *Pearce Associates* anymore as it no longer exists, and Francine—'

He stopped, remembering his conversation earlier that day with Declan.

'They released Pearce from custody yesterday, before the murder,' he finished.

Rufus nodded.

'This is how conspiracies start,' Billy muttered. 'Francine isn't doing anything that puts her on the radar right now. This isn't on you.'

Rufus almost sighed with relief as he leaned back in his seat.

'I knew you'd have the answer,' he smiled. 'Thank you, William. And if there's anything I can do in return...' he left the offer hanging, and Billy quickly jumped at it.

'Actually, yes,' he replied. 'I saw my great-uncle a few weeks back, and he said he was going to mend some fences with my family. I wondered if you'd heard anything?'

Rufus shook his head. 'Sorry, old chap. But then I've not really seen any of your clan around recently. They've all gone to ground.'

'They have?' Billy stroked at his chin. 'Any idea why?'

Again, Rufus shook his head. 'Really wish I could help you,' he said. 'If I hear anything, you're the first person I'll tell.'

Billy nodded, looking around the bar as he sipped at his lemonade.

'You're not a suspect,' he continued, 'but at the same time, you are still a witness. Did you see anything that struck you as odd last night? Any other faces that were there but weren't on the list, like you?'

Rufus shrugged.

'I didn't know anyone there,' he replied cautiously. 'That is, I knew of some of them, I mean, they're some of the biggest hedge fund managers out there, but I wasn't there to speak to them.'

'You were there for Dave Manford and Lydia Cornwall.'

'Exactly. I'd already spoken to Cornwall, explained why I was there, and offered to make her a deal right then. Said that this was all going to be a terrible embarrassment for him, and that if they agreed to a new non-compete deal that stopped them pushing for their own agreements with financiers, they could make a tidy sum without having to do anything.'

'How much was the offer?'

'Quarter of a million.'

Billy whistled. 'That's what the small offer is?' he asked. 'How much is the back catalogue going for?'

'Close to ten mill,' Rufus replied. Lowering his voice, he leaned closer, looking around.

'The biggest problem is the *Secrets and Lies* album. Bloody well everyone seems to have to be paid off on that. And that's the album everyone wants. At least seven or eight million is purely for that bugger, as its got the bigger hits on it. And they needed it rushed through.'

'How so?' Billy asked, interested now.

Rufus shrugged.

'Look, *Harrington Finance,* well, we finance things,' he explained cryptically. 'Sometimes we end up on both sides of the fence with these deals. All I was told was that as the broker for the deal, they needed me to ensure that Dave waived away his rights to the back catalogue in the next week or two.'

'Why so soon?' Billy sipped at his lemonade as he watched.

Rufus took a sip of his own water, as if his throat was suddenly too dry.

'Look, this is only a thought,' he said. 'It might mean nothing. But I was told that *Alternator's* management, such as it is, wanted this back catalogue deal finished, and the money in the band's account by the last week of June.'

'That seems a little rushed,' Billy frowned. 'That's not giving a lot of time for negotiations.'

'Exactly,' Rufus nodded. 'We assumed this was a tax-related thing, as their deadline was right before the end of the second quarter accounts, or because they knew something that we didn't about the songs losing their lustre after summer or something. But I don't think that was it at all.'

'What do you think it was?'

Rufus steepled his fingers in front of his mouth as he spoke, as if scared to let anyone even read his lips.

'*Bear Studios*,' he whispered. 'Where they made *Secrets and Lies*. There are a lot of rumours about the place, that Nick had done something real shitty there and everything was hushed up, hence why everyone was given shares in the album as a sweetener. Nobody knew what it was, and nothing's ever come out, but there're secrets in those walls. And the land it's on? It's up for sale.'

'How do you know this?' Billy leaned closer.

Rufus shrugged.

'As I said, we finance a lot of things,' he said. 'I was told about this plot on Dawley Road, in Hayes. Close to Heathrow and London, great transport, about to link up with Crossrail, a developer's dream. Easily enough space there to build a solid housing estate for London commuters. Several of my clients want me to arrange bids for them.'

'Bids?'

Rufus nodded.

'The land where *Bear Studios* is, it's being sold at auction,' he replied. 'On the thirtieth of June.'

Billy noted the date.

'And you think *Alternator* wants this money so that they can buy the land and stop the developers?' he asked. 'Maybe they want the studio to keep going?'

'True,' Rufus smiled. 'Or, rather, they don't want anyone tearing it down, finding what's buried under the patio? Andy Mears has put offers in several times over the years, and was always rebuffed by the owner.'

'So what's different now?'

'Owner died a year back,' Rufus shrugged. 'I mean, he was close to ninety so he had a good run, but his death brought to light how deep the place was in debt.'

Billy leaned back now, considering this.

'It's a line of enquiry,' he agreed. 'I'll pass it up the chain, see what happens. If you keep me in the loop from anything your end, that is.'

'Of course.'

Billy thought for a moment.

'You mentioned the Rothsteads at the polo,' he said. 'I know a couple of them in passing, and there was a Rothstead name on the guest list. Mason Rothstead.'

'And?' Rufus sipped at his drink. 'Mason attends the opening of an envelope.'

'I've watched the CCTV footage, and he wasn't there,' Billy said. 'I didn't see you, either.'

'I left way before the show started,' Rufus smiled. 'Check about an hour earlier, you'll see me. But I was there as a messenger, not as fanboy. I left as soon as I could.'

He leaned in, as if giving a massive secret.

'And the Rothstead invites were used by others.'

'How so?'

'Eden Storm, dear boy,' Rufus finished his sparkling water, rising from his chair. 'He *is* a Rothstead from his mum's side.'

He stopped, remembering something.

'One more thing,' he said. 'Peter Suffolk, the lead singer of *Alternator* was there.'

'We know,' Billy replied. 'We're talking to him today. He's on CCTV.'

'You won't see him leave, though,' Rufus smiled. 'Because he didn't leave out the main door.'

'What do you mean?' finishing his own drink and rising, Billy stared at Rufus in confusion.

'I saw Peter there, but before the gig started he was gone,' Rufus explained. 'However, when I was outside later, I saw him down the small lane beside the bar.'

'Why were you outside?'

'I didn't hang around for the gig,' Rufus replied. 'I found a quieter place to have a drink on the same block while I waited for it to finish, so I could go back and repeat the offer once it had all ended. But when the bloody bar I was in lost power, I wandered back to see what had happened, as the whole damn street was down. I thought it might have ended the show, but not...'

He breathed heavily, as if forcing back the urge to be ill.

'...but not in that way,' he continued. 'And there was Peter, at a side door with *Metropolitan Warehouse* on it, talking to someone. Like really going at it.'

'Who?' Billy was internally cursing the fact that *Eastcheap Albums* hadn't set a CCTV camera down Lovat Lane.

Rufus tapped his nose.

'Some really old guy, in chunky glasses and a cravat,' he said. 'Neither of which should have been there, it seems as they were both arguing about *people knowing*. They saw me and instantly stopped, walking off. But it was the pair of them, I swear.'

'You know who the old man was?' Billy walked with Rufus to the bar's door.

'I think I know, but I'm not completely sure,' Rufus emerged into the London air. 'He was in the meetings when the couple who hired me to broker the deal discussed terms. Benny something, the old manager.'

Billy stopped outside the bar.

'Benny Simpson?'

'That's the one. Creepy old bastard.'

'Was he in a wheelchair?'

'You know, that confused me too,' Rufus nodded. 'When I met him, he was. Three cans short of a six-pack, too. I assumed they had him there purely because of some contract clause when he was manager. But last night? He was standing just fine.'

Billy went over Rufus's statement in his head.

'Who hired you again? This couple?'

'Oh, sorry, I didn't say,' Rufus looked mortified. 'It was Andy Mears, the guitarist, and his girlfriend.'

'And his girlfriend,' Billy continued, putting the pieces into place. 'Her name wasn't Marna, was it?'

Rufus tapped his nose again and winked.

'See, you picked the right profession after all,' he said as he waved for a taxi, heading towards Fleet Street.

'Wait,' Billy grabbed Rufus by the arm. 'You mentioned Carol heard him speak to someone in the audience before he died. None of the other witnesses heard it clearly. What did he say?'

'Oh,' Rufus thought for a moment. 'It was odd, really. Basically, said *you shouldn't be here, you're not real* and then zap! He died.'

And, with a last nod, Rufus Harrington hailed down a cab and, getting into it through the side door, left Billy alone in the street with a ton of questions running through his head.

Andy Mears was seeing Marna Manford, and Benny Simpson was at the meeting.

Benny Simpson, who retired twenty years ago, and who was supposed to be wheelchair bound and in a nursing home in Surrey, suffering from early onset dementia.

Benny Simpson, who was apparently at the gig last night.

Billy turned back towards the entrance to Temple Inn.

It was going to be a long day.

———

9

I AM THE LAW

ANJLI HAD ARRANGED TO VISIT ANDY MEARS WITH DECLAN, as they'd both finished around the same time, but rather than find him at his Archway address, she'd been informed by his PA that Andy was out completing chores today, and was currently in West London, visiting an old studio. And so Declan had met Anjli outside *Bear Studios*, on the Dawley Road shortly before two in the afternoon.

There was a black Mercedes A-Class outside the front of the studios; with the ground only packed mud for the surface and the buildings around the clearing basically one storey barns, brick buildings or pre-fabs, the car seemed incredibly out of place.

Declan's battered Audi, however, didn't.

Declan emerged from his car as Anjli pulled up. She'd had her car, a police-issued Hyundai IX35 for about a month now, and although not as sleek or cool looking as the Audi, the raised height of the car made her feel a little more superior in traffic as she looked down at the other drivers. The only issue she had was that it was white, which was a nightmare to keep clean, while the mud seemed to just merge into the charcoal grey of Declan's vehicle.

'How was the billionaire?' Declan asked as she walked over to him.

'Very... friendly,' she replied, a hint of hesitation at the start. 'I think I might need to meet with him again.'

Declan raised an eyebrow at this. 'What kind of meeting?' he asked, a slight smile playing on his lips. 'Somewhere secluded, perhaps?'

'Shut up,' Anjli was already regretting opening her mouth, looking around the clearing. 'Well, this is what I'd call bloody secluded.'

Declan nodded at the car. 'That's Andy's,' he replied. 'Number plate matches.'

As if hearing his name, Andy Mears walked out of the studio door, staring at the two officers.

'Looks like you have some clients,' he called into the door as a smaller, portly man emerged behind him.

'No,' the man replied tersely. 'We're not talking to developers or buyers or any of you bastards.'

'How do you know we don't want to hire you?' Declan asked. The man peered at him from across the muddy clearing, eventually shaking his head.

'Unless you're a manager, there's no way someone like you would be here to see us.'

'You're right there,' Anjli replied, pulling out her warrant card. 'We're here to see *him*.' She pointed at Andy, now frozen to the spot, half-walking to his car. 'I'm Detective Sergeant Kapoor, that's Detective Inspector Walsh. We're here to talk about Dave Manford.'

'Arrange a meeting with my PA,' Andy started towards his car once more, but Declan moved to block him.

'We did,' he said. 'She told us you were here, and that you had a free afternoon.'

'I need to get a better PA,' Andy muttered.

Anjli looked over to the studio.

'Our Detective Superintendent's a massive fan of yours,' she said. 'She's massively pissed off that we get to come here. *Secrets and Lies* was recorded in there, right?'

'Yeah,' the portly man said, holding a hand out. 'I'm Errol Ford. I own the place for my sins.'

He paused.

'Well, at least for the next month or so, anyway.'

Declan nodded. Billy had texted him and Anjli half an hour earlier, updating them on the conversation he'd had with Rufus Harrington. 'It's an auction, right?'

'Yeah,' Errol moaned. 'Starting bids around a quarter of a mill, and I already know there's offers in that'll push it over a million.'

Anjli looked over at Andy. 'You thinking of buying?'

'It's costly right now,' Andy admitted. 'It's a cash auction, and I have a lot of my capital tied up in property.'

'But you wouldn't if the back catalogue goes through beforehand,' Declan replied. 'You'd easily have enough.'

'True, and there's a case for nostalgia if that happened,' Andy nodded. 'We could always record the next album here.'

'Or you could do it at Peter Suffolk's house,' Declan suggested. 'He has a studio in his attic. He showed me before I left him earlier today. Small, but I'm sure you have similar in yours.'

Andy didn't speak for a moment, and Declan knew this was because he was processing the new information received.

Peter Suffolk had been talking to the police.

'And why were you talking to Peter?' he asked.

Declan shrugged.

'I'm talking to all of you,' he lied. 'Peter was closest at the time. I'll be looking for your drummer next.'

'Do you want to come in for a tea?' Errol offered.

Declan smiled.

'Oh, definitely,' he said. 'And I'd love a photo in the recording studio where they did *Secrets and Lies*, just to annoy my boss.'

'Well, enjoy—' Andy walked to his car, but Declan casually leaned against the door, barring his way, stopping Andy's words as they left his mouth.

'One cup of tea won't take you long,' he said lazily. 'And it saves you having to come into the station for a formal interview.'

Andy paled.

'Why would I need a formal one?' he asked.

'Well, with Dave Manford dead, your back catalogue just rose in price,' Anjli walked over now. 'You sent a man to buy him out the same night, but he refused. Convenient that he died right after.'

Andy sighed.

'None of that was my idea,' he muttered. 'Speak to Marna.'

'Oh, we'll be speaking to your girlfriend later,' Declan smiled. 'But first, let's have a nice cup of tea.'

Reluctantly, Andy Mears turned and walked back into the studio, past the grinning Errol.

'Oh, and could you sign something for my boss?' Declan shouted after Andy, looking at Errol as he passed.

'Something funny?' he asked the old man.

'Watching him get a dressing down?' Errol's grin was wide. 'I've just spent half an hour with him. Prick thinks he's royalty, was actually telling me how my studio should be run. Good to see him taken down a peg or two.'

INSIDE, *BEAR STUDIOS* APPEARED SMALLER THAN IT WAS ON THE outside, but Errol had explained that the walls were extra thick because of the sound dampening material.

There was a corridor that led to a main room, wide and tall, with square ceiling panels pointing down at them, cut into shallow pyramids. The entire front wall was a mixing desk, built into a walnut coloured unit, with small speakers on the top of it, a window in front the only way to see into the recording space on the other side of the wall. On either side of the windows were large, blue and black speaker units, easily three feet high by four feet wide, angled at the centre of the room, and with five small speakers visible on each.

Along the side were banks of dials and knobs, all equalisers, a MacBook Pro connected beside them, and to the right was a selection of microphones, for the moment discarded. On the wooden floor were two black leather office chairs, and at the back, beside the door into the room was a three seater sofa made of a grey tweed, which now looked far browner than its original colour.

'This is the magic room,' Errol explained proudly. 'That's a 42-input *MCI 500-series* console right there, cost a pretty penny, I'll tell you. We also have some vintage *Neve 1061* and *API 550a* modules, and some *Rosser Electronics* consoles that were rebuilt into the new desks when we upgraded in the nineties.'

Declan looked around the room, impressed.

'There's got to be a thousand different dials,' he said,

looking at the mixing desk. 'How do you know what you're doing?'

'Experience,' Andy sniffed. 'You never use them all, but a good producer will know what works, where to fade, all that.'

'We also have *Neumann U67* and *KM64* valve mics and a couple of *AKG C28s* in the rehearsal room.' Errol was still being a tour guide.

'And how many rooms are here?' Anjli asked.

'This one, the studio the other side, although that's just used for boxes these days, a large rehearsal room behind that, and there's a kitchen area and toilet across the corridor.'

'I thought this was a residential studio?' Declan asked. 'Surely they don't sleep on the sofa?'

'We've not been residential for a good few years now,' Errol admitted. 'We used to have a deal with *The Bear* pub across the road. They had rooms upstairs, and we had first dibs for when bands were in. People would stay weeks in there, having their breakfasts and dinners in the pub. But it was sold and turned to flats about ten years back. Since then we've mainly been rehearsal space and demos only.'

'And you stayed here?' Declan asked Andy, who shook his head.

'I was a session to start,' he explained. 'That is, I was a session musician, work for hire, brought in to replace Bruce when he stormed out. I'd known the original owner of this place, when he was building it, and he needed some press so, when I realised *Alternator* were having issues in the studio they were using, I suggested they come here.'

'Out of the blue?'

'No, I knew Martin, the drummer,' Andy continued. 'We'd been in a band briefly before he joined *Alternator*. We were having a pint in Camden while the album was stumbling about in Kentish Town and he was bitching about it not working. I suggested they move there.'

'That must have helped the rep of the studio,' Anjli said.

Andy shrugged.

'The band and the Manfords were unknown back then,' he replied. '*Secrets* made them massive. I guess that rubbed off on this place, but I've not been back here for thirty-odd years.'

'And yet you come here the day after Dave Manford dies,' Declan said as Errol left the room. 'Any reason?'

'Nostalgia,' Andy replied. 'I was in the area today, and I thought I'd pop by. For old times' sake.'

'Not to put an offer in then?' Declan asked.

Andy chuckled, glancing at the door, ensuring Errol couldn't hear.

'No offence to the guy out there, but if I bought this place? It'd be to buy the land, raze it to the ground and build some houses,' he whispered. 'Nobody comes here anymore. And as much as it created an amazing album, nobody involved with it has good memories.'

'Why so?' Anjli was looking at the mixing desk as she spoke. Andy cricked his neck, loosening his shoulders.

'The day they moved here, Bruce was on the verge of quitting, Nick was spaced out on Christ knows what, Dave was claiming he was keeping Nick in check while actually making him worse, Benny was complaining about every penny spent and Martin and Graham were trying to shag anything that moved. I met with them twice before Bruce trashed the place and when he went, I slipped straight in on replacing his pieces, having watched him in the rehearsals.'

'Trashed the place?' Declan looked around the room. 'Before or after all this?'

'Oh, all this is new,' Andy admitted. 'The old desk was more basic. But Bruce kicked a fight off with Nick in the rehearsal room in the first week, which pretty much destroyed Martin's drum kit, and that also caused problems. The poor sound engineer on deck that night fair shit himself. He was a teenager, thought he was getting fired for letting it happen. But the next day Nick paid for the damages, and we carried on. To be honest, we were lucky, because as the place was still half-built, the things Bruce trashed weren't yet finished.'

'Did you still see Bruce?' Declan asked. 'Before he died?'

Andy shook his head.

'No,' he replied sadly. 'And the only time I heard his name mentioned was three years back, after he got pissed up and drove his *Land Rover* off some quarry cliff.'

Declan thought for a moment.

'What do you think about the curse?' he asked.

'The album one?' Andy shook his head. 'Bollocks, all of it. There were people older than me on that job, so of course they'll die. Nick and Bruce? Pressure got to them. Dave? Bad wiring—'

'You don't think Nick's still alive?'

Andy shook his head.

'He died a long time back,' he replied. 'He couldn't let the past lie.'

'He was recording here, you know,' Errol said cheerfully as he returned with a tray of steaming mugs of tea. 'Was even here on the night he died.'

'What do you mean?' Anjli asked. 'We have him touring with *Alternator* when he disappeared.'

'Oh, yes, he did that too, but he'd booked the studio back in '98 for six months,' Errol continued, passing mugs out.

'Must have literally driven here, recorded and then driven back. There's sugar in the pot on the tray.'

'Nick had been talking about a solo album for years,' Andy argued. 'He would book studios out just in case he had the urge. But our tour had dates moved, so he probably forgot and you made a mistake in the book.'

'No,' Errol smiled. 'I think we even have master tapes of him from when he was here, somewhere. He made about six or seven songs, but then he disappeared.'

'And you just kept them?' this surprised Declan.

'His request,' Errol replied. 'I was only here a few years back then, still learning the ropes as a sparks. But I remember him stating that these were his own personal works and not connected to the band. And, as he was never declared dead, they've never been passed on.'

'You need to give those to me,' Andy demanded. 'They're not yours to keep.'

'We'll have to check into that,' Declan interrupted. 'However, we'd like those works, as they might be connected to the death of Dave Manford.'

'I'll sort out a copy for you, if I can find them,' Errol nodded. Declan could feel Andy seething next to him. This was news he hadn't expected, and it was visible.

'Is there anything else, officers?' Andy snapped. 'Or can I leave this miserable bloody place?'

'Where were you last night?'

'Charity function in Staines,' Andy replied testily. 'Marna Manford was there too, and I can give you a hundred witnesses.'

Declan noted this down.

'When was the last time you spoke to Dave?' Anjli asked.

Andy shrugged.

'Years back,' he muttered. 'Dave's request, not ours.'

'How well do you know Eden Storm?' Declan asked, and was surprised to see Andy flinch.

'I'm done here,' he snapped. 'These questions aren't valid to the case. You're looking for gossip for your boss. You want me? Bring me in for questioning, and I'll bring a solicitor.'

And with that, Andy Mears slammed his mug of tea onto the tray and stormed out of the studio. A moment later, there was the faint rev of an engine as his Mercedes sped out of the car park.

Declan looked at Errol, who was trying his best to hide a smile.

'So, can we continue that tour?' Declan asked.

It was another fifteen minutes before Declan and Anjli left *Bear Studios,* walking over to their respective cars.

'Do you think that the new songs could have been connected to the murder?' she asked.

Declan shrugged, looking out of the gate, across Botwell Common.

'Unlikely,' he replied. 'But it could explain Nick's death.'

'You think they're connected?' Anjli opened her car door, but Declan had walked past his, exiting through the main gates and walking across the road, heading towards the T-junction between Dawley Road and Botwell Common Road, and a navy blue Ford Fiesta that was parked there. Stopping at the door, he pulled out his warrant card, tapping it against the passenger window.

'Police,' he hissed to the man in the car. 'Mind winding down the window?'

The man in the car, wearing a tweed cap and with binoculars on the passenger seat pressed a button, and the window lowered.

'Couldn't help but see you when we turned up,' Declan explained. 'Looked like you were taking notes. Last time someone did that to me, a pub exploded, so I'm a little curious why you're here.'

The old man in the tweed cap nodded.

'Same as you,' he said. 'Solving a case.'

He looked up at Declan, pulling his cap off, exposing his white, shaved scalp.

'Detective Sergeant Ronald Brookfield, retired,' he said. 'And I think I can help you and your partner over there.'

'You have information on Dave Manford's death?' Declan was surprised at this, but not as surprised as Ronald was.

'Oh,' he replied. 'I thought you were here for the same reason I was.'

'And that is?' Declan asked, waving back at Anjli, telling her to wait by the cars.

Ronald shrugged.

'Cold case, from 1986,' he replied. 'The disappearance of Lorraine Warner, last seen at *Bear Studios*, in the company of the band members of *Alternator*.'

10

SPIES LIKE US

BILLY DIDN'T IMMEDIATELY RETURN TO TEMPLE INN AFTER speaking to Rufus Harrington. Instead, he sent a text message, walked across Fleet Street to a small coffee shop, ordered a flat white and then waited by the window.

Ten minutes later, a black cab pulled up outside, and a young woman emerged from it, paying the driver in cash before closing the door and walking over to the entrance.

Trix Preston, laptop bag over her shoulder, entered the coffee shop, spotting Billy and walking over, glancing down as she crossed the floor. Trix was short for *Trixibelle*, and she'd been an intern at the unit a few months back, before being forcibly removed when it was discovered she was a mole for a suspect in a murder case and had been working for *Pearce Associates* the whole time. She'd bugged the rooms in the Temple Inn Command Unit and, even after she'd left, left virtual back doors into the Unit while working for *Section D*, back doors that not only gave the Unit proof of who attacked Monroe late one night, but also assisted Declan from escaping from custody.

She'd been both enemy and ally but her heart was in the right place, and she'd assisted Billy a couple of times in the last couple of months. No older than twenty, she'd dyed her hair peroxide blonde, hidden under a baseball cap, a hoodie and a pair of jeans to make sure she was completely nondescript.

Billy had picked a spot away from the cameras, but by the time she sat down, Billy knew Trix had already worked out the location and range of every camera in the place.

Hell, she probably controlled them from the moment she left the taxi.

'Nice three-piece,' she grinned. 'Way to stand out from the crowd, pretty boy.'

'Hey, we're in the City here,' Billy replied. 'Here it's people in hoodies and caps that stand out.'

'Tourist season,' Trix shrugged. 'I can still carry it. What's up?'

'Personal favour,' Billy carried on. 'For Declan.'

'I thought we'd done giving favours?' Trix raised an eyebrow, and Billy noted it was newly pierced. 'I mean, saving him from jail, sticking his parents' killer in a bloody great big hole—'

'Yeah, that's the reason you owe him another favour,' Billy leaned closer. 'Seems your uncontactable black site is a little too contactable.'

Trix didn't reply; instead, she opened her bag, pulling out a small, slim tablet computer.

'Yeah, Tom mentioned the guards seemed chummy,' she said. 'We're looking into things, making sure there aren't any loose ends we missed. This is to do with that?'

'In a way,' Billy looked around the coffee shop, still worried. 'Can I get you a drink?'

'I'm good,' Trix replied. 'What's the favour then, posh boy?'

'Karl Schnitter, when he spoke to Declan, mentioned something about Declan's daughter,' Billy started.

Trix looked surprised at this.

'Jess?' she asked. 'If he's playing around with her, I swear I'll go throttle him myself.'

'That's what we're not sure about,' Billy admitted. 'Apparently Karl described a GCSE exam she was in, stating that Declan should have been a better father because he didn't know Jess almost walked out, but then settled down and finished the exam.'

'Could be a trolling technique,' Trix replied. 'Screwing with Declan, knowing Jess probably didn't talk in depth about her exams.'

'That's the problem,' Billy opened his phone, showing a photo. 'This is a screenshot from Declan's phone, when he asked her.'

Quick question, how did your exam go? Any problems?

I thought we already talked about the exams?

I know, but I heard you almost left or something, but stayed?

How did you know that, dad? I never told you.

'Son of a bitch,' Trix was already using a pen on the tablet, scrolling through feeds. 'He must have hacked the cameras.'

'Yeah,' Billy replied. 'And this was after you guys took him, so he's managed it while in your secure black site.'

'Black sites aren't black holes,' Trix mused as she scrolled through lines of data. 'People can still find things, addresses, people if they really want to. Do you know when the exam was?'

Billy showed a text from Declan, a copied reply from Jess that gave the required information. Nodding, Trix started working.

'Do you need the school?' Billy asked.

'Please,' Trix replied, not as a request, but more in a dismissive *you're an idiot for thinking that* kind of way. Feeling a little reprimanded, Billy looked at the tablet.

'You sure you should use public Wi-Fi—' he stopped at another withering glance from the twenty-year-old, '—of course you're not using a normal Wi-Fi. Ignore me.'

'In that suit, it's difficult,' Trix grinned, watching the code as she typed on a small, foldable keyboard. 'Did you overindulge in Sean Connery *James Bond* movies or something as a kid?'

'It's the trend,' Billy protested, expecting Trix to make another dig at him, but instead she spun the tablet to face him, swiping up.

On the screen was a CCTV camera in a hall; lines of desks were laid out, each with a student writing at each.

'This is a recording of the feed in the exam hall,' Trix said, zooming in on the bottom corner. 'That's Jess there.'

Billy stared at the girl in the bottom corner as she leaned back, obviously frustrated. Then, pushing the exam paper to the side, she placed her personal items together, as if finishing the exam. She rose to leave—but then stopped, turning this into a full body stretch as the examiner at the top glanced up.

Billy could see that Jess was torn, even from this distance.

Her body language screamed out that she just wanted to leave, to get out but, with a shake of her head to dispel whatever negative thoughts she had, she sat back down, pulling out a pen again and drawing the paper across the desk, looking down at it.

'I'd say that pretty much matches what she told Declan,' Trix commented. 'And also what Schnitter told him. Shit.'

She leaned back.

'We have a leak. So why didn't you find this yourself?'

'Police red tape,' Billy explained. 'I brought you here because the amount of hoops I would have had to jump through, as a policeman, to get this would have taken days.'

'And you knew I would have a sneakier, less legal way in?' Trix grinned, already typing on the keyboard. 'Billy. You say the nicest things.'

She stopped as a line of text appeared on the screen.

'Phoenix,' she said.

'Is that a hacker?' Billy asked. Trix shook her head.

'*Phoenix Industries*. It's effectively the amalgamation of *Pearce Associates* and *Rattlestone*,' she said. 'They'd been around for years as a subsidiary, little more than a shell company name, but now everything's going through them.'

She tapped some more.

'So about eight months ago, they gained the licence from the Government to provide security for secondary schools in England,' she read from the page. 'They installed military level security, after claims that paedophiles were gaining footage from badly guarded Wi-Fi servers.'

'Is that true?'

'Of course not,' Trix scoffed. 'They were having issues with the *National Union of Teachers* at the time, and probably hoped they could gain some staff room antics. But they weren't allowed to peek until they owned the company that did it legally.'

'So the only people who could have gotten in here without the dodgy stuff you use is *Phoenix*,' Billy mused. 'Would they have left a footprint?'

'Dude, the dodgy stuff *I* use is government and military grade,' Trix tapped on the tablet, closing the screen down. 'It's the same thing they have.'

After a few more moments of typing, she read the screen before looking back at Billy.

'Security servers were down at Jess's school at the time of the exam,' she said. 'Routine maintenance. That way, there's no proof anyone was in the system. Convenient.'

'Thanks,' Billy nodded. 'I think that's enough proof that someone was watching Jess, and that somehow they got into your black site.'

'That's easy enough, to be honest, knowing this,' Trix replied. '*Rattlestone* and *Pearce Associates*, the Government heavily funded them, as you know. Chances are, when *Phoenix* picked up the pieces, some of those assets moved across.'

'Great,' Billy rose from the table. 'So it's a supervillain team up.'

He stopped.

'*Phoenix* isn't run by Trisha Hawkins, is it?'

'How did you know?' Trix zipped up her messenger bag as she followed him. 'She's not the face, but she's pulling the strings.'

'Second time I've heard her name today,' Billy sighed. 'And that never bodes well. Can I get you a to-go at least, for what you did here?'

'You don't owe me, Declan does,' Trix grinned. 'And I'll be calling in that favour soon. Expect a package in the post.'

'I heard,' Billy said as they walked into the street. 'A USB drive?'

'An image on one, but yeah,' Trix stopped by the curb and the same taxi, complete with the same driver, pulled up. 'I'll send it.'

'Oh, *that's* a good trick,' Billy said, impressed as with a wave, she closed the door behind her, the taxi already driving off. 'That's a good trick indeed.'

Alone in the street and realising that he was now talking to himself, Billy started back for Temple Inn.

———

EDEN STORM WAS NOT A MAN WHO LIKED TO BE KEPT WAITING. However, unlike many of the people who embraced this term to the point of dickishness, Eden understood that not everyone could travel unmolested, either by helicopter, private plane or SUV, and so he'd learnt over the years to take meetings in a more fluid, less linear format.

The problem was when there were set-in-stone times—for example a flight to Manchester—that were being delayed, and when it was pretty much only because he'd met with someone who was now running late, this annoyed him.

The SUV in which Eden sat was parked on Sloane Square and Eden had kept the windows tinted; partly so people couldn't look in and see him, but also because he didn't want to see them. Sloane Square and the 'Sloanies' of the eighties and nineties was where his mother had cut her teeth. It was even a local nightclub down the Kings Road where his mother had first met Nick Manford.

I wonder what would have happened if they'd never met, he thought to himself. He knew the obvious answer was that he would never be born, but at the same time there was a thought, a soft, unspoken one that said that if Tamara hadn't met Nick that night in a Chelsea club, they might both still be alive.

He didn't get to think on this any further because Wardler, his shaved bear of a bodyguard, exited out of the front passenger door, speaking to someone outside. A moment later Wardler opened the back passenger door and a man in his late twenties, with a haircut that seemed to involve having everything beneath the tips of the ears shaved clambered in, his black shirt and trousers blending into the black seats so that in the tinted-window gloom, Dan Wooten, the *Eastcheap Albums* bar manager looked like a floating head with a silly haircut.

Dan nodded to Eden.

'I got what you asked for,' he said. 'Sorry it's taken so long to get back to you, but the police were very diligent, and I couldn't get a copy of the CCTV footage until they'd gone. It's all on here, though, every camera.'

He passed over a USB drive, and then added an A5 envelope to it.

'What's this?' Eden asked, reluctant to open it.

Dan smiled.

'A little extra,' he said. 'After the police went, one of our bar staff came in. She'd been near the front of the stage before Dave started, and she took photos of the audience. We were going to use it for promotional purposes, but I printed them out for you. An addition to what you asked for, as it pretty much shows the entire audience.'

'Including me?'

'Yeah, sorry, you're tagged on the CCTV too,' Dan apologised, but Eden shrugged, opening the envelope.

'I already know,' he said. 'The police came to see me.'

'Look,' Dan seemed jumpy now. 'I don't want to seem rude, but I just risked my job to get you that.'

Eden nodded. 'Understood,' he said. 'Give your bank details to my bodyguard as you leave, and he'll wire the ten grand today.'

'Any chance of cash?' Dan nervously replied. 'That way, there's no paper trail. Me getting ten grand from you the day after a man dies in my club...'

Eden smiled.

'Yeah, that probably looks bad. We'll sort it,' he said, returning to the images. 'And seriously, man, thanks for this. Maybe—'

He stopped as he stared down at one image.

'Did you see this man in the bar?' he asked, turning the sheet around to show Dan. 'This one here?'

Dan peered at the image; it was a man, also in a hoodie and jeans, but his hood was up, half covering his face, however the flash of the camera had lit the visible part up, giving a bleached face that had a dark strip of beard under the lip, and a pair of John Lennon style sunglasses on. He had a phone in his hand and was watching it, as Dave Manford, on stage, was tossing his bottle of water to the side.

'No,' he shook his head. 'I would have remembered him if he appeared at the bar. Why?'

'It's fine, don't worry,' Eden smiled, but it was a forced, fake one. 'See Wardler, and he'll arrange some cash. Fifties okay for you?'

Gratefully, Dan the bar manager left the SUV, the door shutting behind him as he now stood outside and chatted to the giant bodyguard. Eden, however, had forgotten that Dan even existed, as his attention was once more locked onto the man in the image.

A man who bore a striking resemblance to Nick Manford, Eden's father.

A man who, if it was Nick, had been missing for over twenty years, and was currently in the process of being declared *dead*.

Eden swore as he leaned back in his chair.

'Wardler,' he said as the bodyguard clambered back into the front passenger seat. 'Do me a favour and call Manchester, I'm going to have to delay my trip.'

'Problem?' Wardler looked back at Eden. He'd been his right-hand man and bodyguard for over five years now and could tell from even the slightest of micro expressions the mood of his client.

Eden Storm didn't have micro expressions on his face as he passed the photo across. His face was maximising everything as his brain tried to comprehend this.

'We need to find this man,' he said. 'We need to see if it's my *father*.'

―――――――――

11

UNDER YOUR THUMB

'I WAS NEW TO THE PLAIN CLOTHES DEPARTMENT BACK THEN,' Ronald said as he sipped at his pint of bitter. 'I was wet behind the ears and only just out of my uniform.'

Declan nodded as he glanced around the pub, apparently named *The Carpenter's Arms* and (as Ronald had reliably informed him as they arrived in the car park) one of the last pubs left in Hayes.

The Carpenter's Arms was a large, roadside pub off the Uxbridge Road, better known as the A4020, a dual carriageway that travelled east from Uxbridge (currently a couple of miles to the west) through Southall, Ealing and Shepherd's Bush, where it merged with the A402 and carried on past Bayswater and Hyde Park, eventually turning into Oxford Street once it hit Central London. This far out, however, there was nothing city-like about the area, and the only reason that Declan could assume that they'd been brought the ten minutes north of *Bear Studios* was because this pub was in spitting distance of the local police station;

Hayes Command Unit was only a couple of minutes' walk across the dual carriageway from there.

'One of the last left,' Ronald added, noting Declan's glance. '*Bear Studios* used to be named after *The Bear* pub, but that closed in 2008. *Blue Anchor* and the *Golden Cross,* both around the same time. *Royal Oak* mysteriously burned down one night and was turned into houses, *Heath Tavern, Hambro Arms*, all the same way. Even this place was sold off a couple of years back. Luckily someone took it over so we didn't have houses put up here.'

'Sounds terrible,' Anjli said, sipping at her own drink, a lemonade with ice, and although Declan could tell that she was mocking slightly, Ronald took that as affirmation.

'Indeed,' he said. 'Indeed.'

'So, you were going to explain why you were watching the studio?' Declan asked. At this, Ronald nodded, his demeanour becoming more professional as he leaned closer.

'Look, I'm not a conspiracy nut or a looney,' he breathed. 'And I know how it's going to sound. But nobody looked out for her, and it was my first case.'

'Lorraine Warner,' Declan added. Ronald's eyes darkened slightly, although it could have been because of the shadows in the bar.

'Aye,' he muttered. 'My first case, that was. Sweet girl, no older than nineteen. She'd been the barmaid at *The Bear* for about a year, although she'd been hanging out there with her friends before she was legal. I knew her because my parents lived in Princes Park, and it was a five-minute walk on a Sunday, when I visited them.'

'Were you sweet on her?' Anjli asked. 'I'm just asking because it sounds like you were a little.'

'Only because she was a wonderful person,' Ronald

snapped. 'I was thirty-three, love. Back then you were called a *cradle-snatcher* if you went for someone that much younger.'

'So no flings?' Declan continued. Ronald blushed.

'One Christmas kiss, nothing more,' he admitted. 'And I never would have. Her family would have kneecapped me. And besides, she had her pick of the locals, although she never dated any of them. They all loved her, especially the ones too young to know better.'

Declan nodded. 'And then she disappeared?'

'Thursday July 24th, 1986,' Ronald stated the date as if something etched it into his soul. 'That was the last time anyone saw her alive.'

'And *Alternator* were around then?' Anjli asked.

'They turned up a couple of weeks earlier,' Ronald replied. 'Reckoned they'd spent months in some fancy London studio getting nowhere and wanted a bit of the rough. Northerners, mainly.'

'Did you have any run-ins with them?' Declan asked. 'before the disappearance?'

Ronald nodded.

'A few, yeah. The younger Manford? Nick? He was a coke-head. Constantly on the scrounge for drugs. First name basis with most of the scum in the area, and believe me, there was a lot of scum to know back then. Got in with a local traveller clan called the Randalls, pretty much bankrolled them while he was here. We picked him up a couple of times, but he always had fancy lawyers to get him out. Prick.'

'And did he know Lorraine?'

'Yeah, she introduced him to the Randalls in the pub one night, but I don't think she realised how much of a druggie Nick was then,' Ronald sipped at the bitter. 'But the band all knew her, as they were in there every night. Apart from the new guy, Andy. The one you were with today. He was local back then, commuted in and out. The rest of them did the usual.'

'And the usual was?' Anjli asked. 'Pretend we're not local.'

'Sorry,' Ronald nodded. 'I don't often talk to people who aren't local. *The Bear* had a selection of rooms above the bar. The studios had first booking rights on them, and the pub was happy to have long-term rentals. *Alternator* moved in at the end of July. They got their breakfasts and their evening meals in the pub, but to be honest, they weren't there for the latter much and were usually staggering to bed when breakfast was being served.'

'Just the band?' Anjli asked.

'Dave had a girlfriend who was with him all the time, so she'd be staggering in with them too.'

'Did you get a name?'

'Lydia something. Sounded foreign.'

'So they worked long hours?' Declan asked, but was rewarded with a bark of a laugh.

'Bugger that,' the retired police officer laughed. 'They'd sleep until noon, bugger about in the studio until seven or eight, come back to *The Bear*, drink until closing and often past that—'

'Lock-ins were common?'

'Lock-ins were consistent,' Ronald nodded. 'And then about one in the morning they'd all piss off back to the studio and drunkenly jam until people were going to work. There wasn't anyone living around them at night, and there was a golf course being created to the back. They could scream their heads off and nobody would hear them.'

His eyes narrowed as he stared into his beer.

'Nobody would hear the screaming,' he whispered.

'You said a few run-ins,' Declan attempted to bring Ronald back on course. 'Was it just Nick?'

'No,' Ronald's face darkened. 'Two of the band, Hagen and Reilly, were on our shit list too.'

'Why?' Anjli asked.

Ronald pulled his jacket off, placing it on the back of his chair.

'Weekend before Lorraine disappeared, two girls claimed that Hagen and Reilly had appeared at a party in West Drayton, a few miles west. They'd played the 'rock star' act, pulled the two girls, but they reckoned they'd been slipped something in their drinks and that Hagen and Reilly had, well, the term these days is *date rape*.'

'That's a pretty big statement to make to the police,' Declan commented.

'That's the problem,' Ronald shook his head. 'They never told the police. They mentioned it to a couple of people but then Dave's girlfriend 'had a word' with them, pointed out that *Alternator* were backed by EMI, and would have fancy lawyers, so it was a word against word deal. And the girls had been seen at the party completely out of it, so there was a very strong chance that Hagen and Reilly hadn't given them anything and they were looking for an excuse for why they acted as they did. Basically, she put the fear of God into them.'

Anjli was furious.

'So Lydia forced them to keep quiet?'

'Pretty much. Said that if they shut up, they could have a comfortable life. I believe they were given a grand each as hush money, but when this got out, it labeled them among the locals as whores, and Lydia was nicknamed *the pimp*.'

'And you did nothing?'

'What could I do?' Ronald muttered. 'Until the girls made a statement, our hands were tied. So we watched Hagen and Reilly like hawks, and the local lads gave the two of them a belting a couple of days later. Told them to finish the recording fast and get the hell out.'

'And that was it?'

'Until Lorraine arrived,' Ronald carried on staring at his drink. 'She found out about everything when she broke up the fight. When she heard what happened, she told the lads to leave it to her. She was good friends with the two girls. She took it personally.'

'What did she do?' Anjli leaned in.

'Nothing that we ever knew of,' Ronald explained. 'It was a Thursday. I remember because it wasn't until the weekend that she was reported missing, and the Commonwealth Games had just started. She was on the Thursday shift but finished at closing. She never usually joined the band for a drink, but this time she did.'

'Are you sure this wasn't because she was attracted to one of them?' Anjli asked.

Ronald shook his head.

'Sure, they were shiny and new,' he explained. 'They'd had small chart success, and they were the most famous people in the pub. And, they weren't bad looking chaps, especially if you got past the bad habits and severely questionable behaviour.'

He sniffed.

'I suppose you didn't really have unattractive guys in bands in the eighties,' he said. 'Apart from that guy in the—'

'So the Thursday, she disappeared?' Declan once more steered Ronald back on track.

'Yeah,' Ronald replied. 'They went back to the studios,

and a couple of local girls, not the ones that had been at the party, went with them. Lorraine went along too.'

'You think she went along as a chaperone?' Anjli asked. Ronald nodded.

'Teetotal all her life,' he admitted. 'Never touched drugs. Her family would have battered her if she did. She even gave Hagen and Reilly a bottle of champagne each during the evening, apologising for the attack the previous day.'

'So when did people know she was missing?' Declan was writing in his notebook. Ronald shrugged.

'She wasn't scheduled to work on the Friday, so the pub thought nothing was wrong, and she'd often end up crashing the night upstairs when there was a room free and she was on an early shift the next day, so her family were used to her being away for a couple of days. So it was Saturday when they came in looking for her.'

'The twenty-sixth?'

Ronald nodded.

'The pub was in the dark as much as her family were, so they went to speak to the band. They claimed the girls had left around two in the morning, Lorraine with them. They were clueless about anything else.'

'The girls?'

'Too drunk to remember,' Ronald replied. 'Pretty much blanked out the night. They believed she left with them, but couldn't confirm it. Nobody could remember where she was at any time.'

'So she was a missing person.'

'Yeah,' Ronald agreed. 'And to be honest, there wasn't that much of an impetus to find her at the start. She was a sweet girl, but she liked her own company more than groups. Nowadays, she'd likely have been called bipolar, but we didn't have those sorts of clever diagnosis back in the eighties. People thought she'd had one of her moments, her spells, and had just taken off for a while. And as I said, she had family that travelled a lot so people assumed she'd pissed off until *Alternator* did the same.'

'And nobody followed up?'

Ronald shook his head. 'There were bigger problems around then,' he explained. 'The Monday after Lorraine Warner went missing, Kenneth Erskine was arrested in London. He was known as—'

'The *Stockwell Strangler*,' Anjli interrupted. 'We learnt about him in Hendon. But he wasn't around here, and he only went for older people.'

'True, but the moment he was picked up and his name was announced, someone called in, said that he'd been seen in the area the day after his last killing on the twenty-third, in Fulham,' Ronald explained. 'It's not that far from Hayes, and would have placed him in the area on the day Lorraine disappeared. Because of the timings, any missing person cases at the same time and location got moved to Scotland Yard and, when it was realised Lorraine didn't fit his bill and it was dumped back down to us, the case had moved on and the band were finished and gone.'

He sighed.

'And now she was gone, the rumour mill went ballistic. There was suddenly talk of her having suicidal tendencies, or that she might have had a secret boyfriend and gone off to elope. Remember, we didn't have Facebook status updates back then, and everyone with an opinion was giving it. We were inundated with sightings, or comments from friends of friends, all that malarky.'

'But you didn't believe this?' Declan asked.

'Bollocks, all of it,' Ronald spat. 'The only people who knew what really happened to her were in that studio, and they were all keeping quiet. The story was that she left early and everyone stuck to it.'

'Maybe it was the truth?' Declan suggested.

'The story was too complete, too word for word and nobody deviated from it,' Ronald explained. 'I might have been new to CID, but I'd been a copper on the streets for over a decade. I knew when something was being covered up, or when people had been coached to say the same thing. They were word for word identical.'

He leaned back in his chair, looking up at the ceiling.

'And around this point, they suddenly do this deal. You must have heard of it. Everyone involved in *Secrets and Lies* gets an equal share of the album sales, no matter how small their role was. But it wasn't *everyone*, just the people there that night.'

'We heard it was because they didn't have the money for the studio move,' Anjli replied. 'That this was the only way people would work for them.'

'Bullshit,' Ronald shook his head. '*Bear Studios* would have taken them for free for the press it'd give them alone. *The studio that succeeded where EMI failed?* Come on. It was an open goal. And the recording crew were mostly kids, anyway. Peanut was only just out of his 'A' Levels.'

'Peanut?'

Ronald smiled. 'The sound engineer. Never knew his real name, scrawny runt, working the summer holidays before going off to wherever. But he idolised Nick when he wasn't mooning over Lorraine in the pub. Followed him everywhere. He didn't need no special deal. He would have *paid Alternator* to let him help with the album.'

'But you think this deal was to keep people quiet?' Anjli continued.

'Seems convenient that they had a deal with NDAs up to the roof, saying that *nothing about the time spent in the studio could be talked about,* and if you did you *not only lost your share, but had to pay back what you'd already been given,*' Ronald replied. 'People thought it was because of Nick's drug habit, keeping it from the press, but I think it was because of what happened that night.'

'And what do you think happened that night?' Declan asked.

'I think Lorraine Warner died,' Ronald said flatly. 'Overdose, murder, accident, whatever. They then got some record company fixer in to remove the body and the lawyers made a deal with everyone there.'

'And you're still trying to solve the case?' Declan asked.

Ronald straightened as he spoke.

'I keep an eye on the place, and have people that tip me off when anyone visits. If it's the last thing I do, I'll put her soul to rest.'

Declan thought for a moment.

'What do you think about the curse?' he asked.

Ronald laughed at this.

'Oh, I think it's karma, coming back on them tenfold,' he replied. 'Those buggers deserve everything they get. Well, maybe not the new guy, he's only been there a handful of years and the bassist arrived after the fact as well, but the Manfords, Andy Mears, Martin Reilly, Graham Hagen, Bernard Simpson, Bruce Baker, even the *Bear* crew. Anyone making money from that album, and who knows anything about that night, deserves to face justice for what they did.'

Declan was writing the names.

'Can you confirm where you were last night?' he asked.

'Oh, as much as I want them to pay, I don't want them dead before they get taken down,' Ronald responded. 'I want them in court. Not in coffins.'

Declan nodded as he placed away his notebook.

'The studio said that Nick returned in 1998,' he said. 'That he was recording something new there. If you've been researching this case since the eighties, can you confirm this?'

'Oh yes,' Ronald nodded. 'He was there from October 1998 until he disappeared. Came in whenever he had a gap in touring. But he was a different man then. I spoke to him in the bar a couple of times, trying to find out information.'

'How so different?' Anjli leaned closer. Ronald shrugged.

'I mean, he seemed to be clean by then, but was haunted,' he said. 'He was unhappy, too. Whether it was the band or his wife, I don't know. He never knew I was police, I was just some bloke he drank with at the bar. But it wasn't a surprise that he killed himself.'

'You think he committed suicide?' Declan asked.

Ronald finished his pint before replying.

'I think that was PR bollocks too,' he stated. 'Because the day they reckon he was walking into the sea after that gig in Brighton? He was in *Bear Studios* by midnight, because he came into the pub to get the key.'

'You're absolutely sure of this?' Declan looked at Anjli, who was also writing this down. This matched what Errol had mentioned only an hour earlier.

'I couldn't swear on a bible, but I'm sure of it,' Ronald admitted, passing Declan a card with a mobile number on it. 'But if you hear anything, please let me know.'

'I will, Detective Sergeant,' Declan passed his own card

over. 'And the same goes here. If you see anything else odd, contact me immediately.'

'It's just Mister now,' Ronald said sadly. 'One piece of advice from an old man? Don't take early retirement. It's boring as hell.'

With these words as his last message, Ronald nodded to them both, pulled his jacket from the chair and put it on, placed his flat cap back on his head and walked out of *The Carpenter's Arms.*

Declan looked back to Anjli, now placing her notebook away.

'You know, just once I'd love to have a simple case,' she said. 'You know, blood covered man walks in, says 'I did it' and job done.'

'You'd be bored,' Declan rose from the table, pulling his own jacket on. 'Come on, it's going to take close to an hour to get back to the office from here.'

'Race you,' Anjli grinned as they made for the door.

Declan walked to his car, considering what they had learnt so far. A single death in an East London bar was rapidly becoming a multiple murder enquiry.

Declan just hoped they worked it out before anyone else died.

————

12

LIVE TO TELL

'Right then, my little detective darlings, get in the briefing room,' Monroe called out of his office, disappearing a moment later. Declan looked over at Anjli.

'You know, I liked him better when he was miserable all the time,' he said as, notebook in hand, he rose from his desk and started towards the glass-walled briefing room.

'I know what you mean,' Anjli replied, following. 'I think Doctor Marcos is becoming a good influence on him.'

'On who?' Doctor Marcos, already sitting in the briefing room and, luckily for Anjli, only hearing the last part of the statement as they entered, looked up from her iPad.

'De'Geer,' Declan lied quickly. 'I think that his continued work with forensics is making a better officer of him.'

'When he's not making gooey-eyes at Joanne,' Doctor Marcos smiled. 'Where is he, anyway?'

'He's gone to pick up Lydia Cornwall for questioning,' Anjli sat down in her seat.

'Right then. Settle down,' Monroe said as he entered, Billy and Bullman walking in behind. Billy walked over to his usual spot, connecting his laptop to the plasma screen, while Bullman continued to hover around the door.

'So, what do we have?' Monroe asked. 'Seems to me you're collecting cold cases instead of playing with the toys I've given you.'

'Not sure if they're connected, Guv,' Declan smiled. 'Best to check on them though.'

Monroe nodded and, on the screen, the photo of Dave Manford, dead on the stage of *Eastcheap Albums* appeared on the plasma screen.

'Any more on Mister Manford?' he asked Doctor Marcos, who stood up, making her way over to the plasma screen.

'Actually, yes,' she said. 'Earlier we talked about how he'd been electrocuted by what seemed to be a faulty amp connection, something that often happened to guitarists when their metal strings touched the stands when they weren't grounded.'

'Did we? I think I fell asleep during that part,' Bullman smiled. 'You're telling me you were wrong?'

Doctor Marcos stared for a moment at Bullman before replying, and Declan recalled how the first time they properly met in Birmingham, Doctor Marcos had held a scalpel to Bullman's throat.

'No, but we've worked out the cause,' she replied calmly. 'We believed the device retrieved from the murder scene had artificially created a difference in potential, and thus electrocuted Manford, but on examination we learnt it was purely the on-off switch.'

'So how did he get electrocuted, then?' Declan asked.

Doctor Marcos tapped on the plasma screen and another picture appeared, that of the late Dave Manford's right hand.

On it, on the ring finger was a silver band, the hand charred with black soot around it.

'This,' she said. 'The ring connected with the microphone and carried the charge. It's a silver ring, and that's incredibly conductive to electrical current.'

'Ah, the *Vena amoris*,' Monroe mused. 'The vein of love, running from the ring finger directly to the heart.'

'If you ask a Roman or an Egyptian, yes,' Doctor Marcos replied. 'But these days we have *science*, and that's just a myth. All fingers connect to the heart, eventually. They start off small and then keep joining other veins, becoming bigger the closer to the heart they get.'

She tapped the screen, and the image changed to a closeup of the ring, on a metal table, sawn in half.

'We had to saw the ring off, as it'd pretty much melted to the skin,' Doctor Marcos explained. 'And when we did, we noticed that through the middle was a sheet of copper, sandwiched in between the layers, and with three small visible prongs attached to the inside, made to mimic a smart-tech ring.'

'But it wasn't.'

'No, there's no circuitry in it, and to be honest most of the rings on the market are ceramic,' Doctor Marcos shook her head. 'This was simply a silver and copper ring, made to look like one. Which isn't common, because a copper and silver ring can self destruct.'

'Like actually explode?' Anjli was surprised at this. Doctor Marcos waggled her hand in a *maybe* gesture.

'Galvanic corrosion,' she explained. 'A galvanic cell is what's created when you connect two different metals in the presence of an electrolyte. It makes an electrochemical cell, and electrical current is produced.'

'The ring becomes a battery?' Declan asked.

Doctor Marcos nodded.

'It's formed by the copper and silver when the ring gets wet,' she added. 'Things like salts on the skin, lotions and soaps or other substances in the water create an electrolyte. This current will flow from the more negative metal to the more positive one. When this happens, galvanic corrosion causes the more positive metal to dissolve, or corrode into the electrolyte and the more negative metal is inhibited from corroding. But, yeah, a battery gets made. So if you have it on and you're nervous, the sweat hits the ring. And then when you touch the microphone and complete the circuit...'

She left the statement hanging.

'Ouch,' Bullman muttered. 'I'm guessing this isn't a normal thing for a ring to have?'

'No,' Doctor Marcos looked at Billy, who tapped on his keyboard. On the screen, images of Dave Manford, all taken in the last couple of years appeared.

'In these, Manford doesn't wear a ring,' Doctor Marcos explained. 'But last night he willingly put on the ring that killed him, one that looked like a heart rate monitor device, but was designed purely to help electrocute him.'

'Let's hope Lydia Cornwall has something for us on that when she arrives,' Monroe nodded. 'Okay, what else do we have?'

'Peter Suffolk was there because he was secretly strengthening Dave Manford's voice through video exercises,' Declan continued, reading from his notes. 'He left before the performance out of the back door, angry that Lydia had arranged for some paparazzi to be hanging around. He was concerned that *Alternator* might fire him if they saw him with Dave, and she seemed to have deliberately set him up.'

'Was he caught?' Monroe asked.

'No,' Billy replied. 'But Rufus Harrington said that after the power went, he was standing outside the venue and saw Peter Suffolk and Benny Simpson, the band's old manager, having a row down a side lane.'

'Benny who's apparently in a wheelchair and has dementia?' Monroe asked. 'The obvious aside, would he even know Suffolk?'

Billy tapped on a screen and a driving licence appeared for ANDREW PETER KNYTTE, with Peter Suffolk's photo on the side.

'Peter Suffolk,' Billy said. 'Fifty-three years old, born in West Drayton. Changed to his stage name after graduating from the Central School for Drama in 1991.'

'Understandable,' Monroe commented.

Declan took over now.

'Peter joined *Alternator* in 2011 after Jesse Morrison, their old singer was effectively fired after breaking his leg, and he reckoned he'd known them a few years before that, but nothing more. And Benny Simpson retired from management in 2002, so I can't see them knowing each other from his time as manager.'

'So why would they be arguing?' Monroe looked at Bullman, who shrugged.

'Maybe Benny wants a slice of the *Alternator* back catalogue money, and Peter was the first person he saw?'

'Maybe,' Monroe nodded. 'But if Benny was there, and he wasn't a wheelchair-bound man with dementia, then we have another murder suspect, if he entered through the back.'

He sighed audibly.

'Okay. What else?'

'Andy Mears was at *Bear Studios* today,' Declan added, glancing at Bullman. 'We took some photos for you, boss.'

'Good boy,' she said. 'Anything come from it?'

'Nothing from Andy, although he gave us an alibi for last night. And Errol, the owner was convinced that Nick Manford was creating a solo album there the month he disappeared,' Anjli said. 'Usually that's the first step for a solo career, right?'

Bullman nodded.

'He wasn't happy back then, that's for sure.'

'And as we all know now, DS Kapoor and I also met a retired detective sergeant who's now trying to solve a missing persons cold case on a *Bear* barmaid named Lorraine Warner, that he's convinced comes from a late night recording session of *Secrets and Lies*,' Declan continued. 'He believes that something brutal happened to her on a particular night, and the whole 'equal share' plan of that album was pretty much hush money for all involved.'

'Also, he said that a few days before the incident, Martin Reilly and Graham Hagen were reported to have spiked the drinks of two teenage girls who were then forced to have sex with them at a party, although charges were never brought up,' Anjli added.

'Oh, did they?' Monroe's face darkened with anger. 'Let's get those wee little shites in.'

'We don't know if it was true or not as nobody came forward, but it was suggested that Lydia Cornwall, then apparently Dave Manford's girlfriend threatened them, scaring them into silence. Then, three days later they were attacked outside the pub, Lorraine Warner stops the beating and then the next day buys them champagne as an apology from the pub, agreeing to visit the studios after a lock-in for the first time.'

'If it was me, I'd have spiked the champagne,' Anjli muttered. 'Give them the same as they gave the girls, with maybe some hallucinogens and a couple of laxatives thrown in.'

She stopped.

'Christ, what if she actually did that? What if that's why she was killed?'

'Seems far-fetched,' Doctor Marcos said from the back of the room. 'But then again, it's actually quite restrained for us. Usually we have more out of left field bombshells hitting.'

'Oh, I've got one of those for you,' Anjli grinned. 'Eden Storm.'

'Oh yes?' Monroe leaned closer now. 'Tell us about this billionaire. I hope you gathered some funds for the office Christmas party. I'd like it to be in Barbados this year.'

Anjli nodded to Billy, and an image of Eden Storm appeared on the screen.

'Eden Storm, age thirty-four,' she said. 'Born in LA in January 1987 to Tamara Rothstead-Page, the daughter of Harvey Rothstead, owner of *Klaude-Rothstead Pharmaceuticals.*'

Doctor Marcos whistled. 'Born with more than a silver spoon in her mouth then,' she said.

Anjli nodded to Billy, and another photo appeared, an image of a young girl, obviously drunk, in a skimpy dress and on a table in a nightclub. It was a photo obviously taken from a newspaper front page.

'Tamara was quite the 'It Girl' in the eighties, carving up a scene in London well before the more known 'wild child' socialites like Tara Palmer-Tomkinson or Amanda de Cadenet hit the town,' Anjli explained. 'Sometime around here, in early 1986, she met Nick Manford in a Chelsea club, and after a short fling, she returned to LA and gave birth to Eden. Nick couldn't publicly accept the baby as his, because she was engaged to Los Angeles property magnate Ethan Page, and wasn't intending to drop that golden goose for a penniless rock star any time soon, but apparently over the years Tamara's attitude softened.'

Declan was counting on his fingers.

'So they conceived Eden in April or May 1986,' he said. 'Right before the band moved to Hayes.'

'This might have been why Nick couldn't concentrate in the first studio,' Monroe chuckled. 'Pretty girl on your arm and all the cocaine you can eat. And why was Eden Storm at the gig last night, then?'

'Invited personally by Dave,' Anjli read through her notes. 'He seemed a little secretive about some things though, and I got the impression that Dave had gained a loan from him in the past, but one thing he *said* was that he was Nick Manford's biological son, so I'll look to meet with him again before he returns to America.'

'Anjli and Eden hit it off,' Declan winked, and ducked as a pen was thrown at him.

'Right then, billionaire illegitimate child, that's more down our street,' Monroe nodded. 'Anything else?'

Billy put up his hand.

'For Christ's sake, laddie, we don't do that here!' Monroe exclaimed.

Billy grinned.

'Couldn't help it,' he said. 'Rufus Harrington. Turns out his company is handling the brokerage of the *Alternator* back catalogue, at the request of Andy Mears and Marna Manford. Who, apparently, are an item.'

He tapped on a key, and on the screen an image of *Bear Studios* appeared.

'However, this sale might have more going for it than just money. Apparently Rufus has been told to get things sped up and sorted out by the end of June.'

'Which is when *Bear Studios,* or at least the land it's on, goes up for auction,' Declan added. 'So, if Andy wanted to buy it, having the money by then would be favourable. Especially as he's made several offers in the past, but currently doesn't have enough liquid assets to buy outright.'

Anjli looked at Billy.

'Can you do me a favour?' she asked. 'Find out from your friend what happens when land is sold?'

'Thinking of putting a bid in?' Declan asked.

Anjli shook her head.

'I'm thinking more about the master tapes that Errol, the guy at *Bear Studios* told us about,' she said. 'Nick disappeared before finishing, and the bill was never paid. And they're not *Alternator* songs, and weren't even known about by Andy until he heard the same time as we did, so they're not part of the back catalogue.'

She scratched at her nose.

'Now I'm no lawyer, but surely whoever buys the land, buys the studios and all that's in it?'

'Including these never-heard-before songs,' Declan nodded. 'Yeah, that's possible. Although surely someone would have leaked these out by now. Even the fact that Nick was in the studio that night.'

'Unless only the sound recordist knew on that particular evening that Nick was in town,' Billy suggested. 'Oh, and

Rufus said that his assistant heard Dave say something to one of the audience.'

'We've had a few people confirm that,' Anjli added. 'But it was mumbled and the microphone fed back over it.'

'His assistant was front and centre though, and heard it clearly from the source,' Billy looked at his notepad. '*You shouldn't be here, you're not real.*'

'Dave knew his killer, then, or at least hallucinated them,' Declan looked at Monroe. 'Oh, one more thing. Marna and Lydia are half-sisters.'

'Of course they are,' Monroe sighed. 'Because what we really needed in this was bloody sisters.'

He looked at his watch.

'It's nearing rush hour, so travelling anywhere is going to be a bitch,' he said. 'De'Geer should pick Lydia Cornwall up any time now, so we can ask her about all this when they get back.'

He looked back at the plasma screen as he composed his orders.

'In the meantime, try to get hold of the other members of the band, as well as this Marna woman, and book times to talk to them tomorrow. Declan, have another chat with Mister Suffolk about his conversation with the ex-manager when you can, and after we've spoken to Miss Cornwall tonight, I'll go have a chat with Mister Simpson in the morning, see just how decrepit he really is, before visiting those two wee shites to discuss their party antics in the eighties.'

As if by magic, the phone in the briefing room buzzed, and Billy, being closest to it, leaned over and took the call. After a moment, he placed the handset down without saying a word on the line, looking back to the others in the room.

'That was the front desk,' he said. 'They had a call from

De'Geer in Hackney. Seems he went to Lydia Cornwall's flat, but there's been a, well, a development.'

'And what sort of development is that, laddie?' Monroe asked. 'Because from your tone and manner, I'm thinking it's a fatal one.'

Billy nodded.

'There was no response when he knocked, so he checked through the letterbox and saw a body on the floor. He broke the door down, went in with PC Cooper and they found Lydia Cornwall on the floor, dead.'

'Cause?' Doctor Marcos was already rising, gathering her things and preparing to attend the scene.

Billy swallowed.

'They don't know,' he said. 'De'Geer said it looked like a screwdriver or something like that had been rammed into the side of her throat, and she'd bled out on the floor, but it didn't seem right somehow.'

Doctor Marcos nodded.

'He's got a good eye, so I'll trust that concern. I'll get Davey from downstairs and we'll go check it out.'

She turned to Monroe.

'Do you need us to take anyone with us?'

Monroe shook his head.

'It's late, and you won't have anything clear until tomorrow, I'm guessing,' he said. 'Find out what you can and keep us informed.'

Doctor Marcos nodded and left the briefing room. Declan looked back at Monroe, who was only just holding back his anger.

'Two murders on two successive days,' he muttered. 'And all we have is some bollocks about an album over thirty years ago. I want more.'

He turned and stormed out of the briefing room.

'*I want more!*' he yelled before the sound of his door slamming echoed around the office.

As the echo stopped, Anjli looked at Declan with a faint smile.

'Well,' she said. 'I don't think you need to worry about his good mood anymore.'

———

13

OUR HOUSE

PC Morten De'Geer stood at the door to Lydia Cornwall's Hackney flat and considered that he'd seen more dead bodies while working at the *Last Chance Saloon* in the last few months, than in all of his time at Maidenhead.

The cases seemed to *collect* them.

Today was supposed to have been a simple one; Lydia had agreed by phone to come into the station to answer questions, but following the previous night's events, Monroe felt it best to send someone to pick her up. And so De'Geer and PC Cooper, a new recruit to the uniformed aspect of the Temple Inn Command Unit and newer to the force than even De'Geer was had borrowed one of the Unit's two squad cars and had driven to Hackney to pick her up.

However, when they arrived at her gated apartment and gained entry there was no answer. He'd asked the main desk at the Unit to try calling her by phone, and although he could hear it ringing in the building, there was no answer. De'Geer had wondered whether Lydia had either wandered out, maybe to the shops, or whether she'd misunderstood Monroe and was making her own way to Temple Inn.

After about ten minutes of waiting around, ten minutes of Cooper asking De'Geer about previous cases that the unit had worked on, but annoyingly none of which De'Geer had actually been involved in, De'Geer had eventually tired of this and leaned against the door, trying to peer into the building through the frosted glass pane in the middle of it.

The building itself was more towards Dalston than Hackney Central, and was on a recently built estate named *Stannard Mews*, a series of small yet pretty pale blue-doored buildings, of which Lydia owned a two bedroom, first-floor apartment. The door that De'Geer stared through led to a set of stairs, of which, at the top and to the right, was another door that led into the first-floor apartment. If anyone was in there, De'Geer would not have been able to tell without taking a ladder to the wall and climbing up to look, something he was getting very close to doing, but through the frosted glass he could see there was something at the top of the stairs, a mound on the landing floor, half through the open door.

Kneeling, De'Geer opened the letterbox, trying to peer up the stairs through the narrow slit, but again all he could see was what looked to be a prone body at the top. Rising, he looked at Cooper.

'You got a lock pick set yet?' he asked as he rummaged around his fluorescent jacket. Cooper, confused at this, shook her head as De'Geer pulled out a small leather pouch, opening it to show several metal tines.

'You should get one,' De'Geer replied, already placing in one of the metal tension rods, pushing it to the side as he started picking the door lock with another pin. 'DI Walsh gave me this one. Explained that it's far better to pick the lock than smash the door open.'

'Why would we smash the door open?' Cooper was even more confused now as with a click, De'Geer stood back up, putting away his lock picks.

'Because I think there's a body at the top of the stairs, and if I'm right, we might need to call an ambulance,' he replied calmly, pushing the door open.

'And, as it's not been forced, we can say it was open, and that's why we could enter,' Cooper nodded as she entered behind him. De'Geer knew this was a grey area, to be honest; technically neither of them should have entered unless there was an actual threat to life going on in there, but the body that De'Geer saw, even if it was just forgotten laundry, was enough to give cause for concern.

As it was, as he'd climbed the stairs, he'd seen that it was indeed a body, that of a woman in her sixties, her neck awash with blood. He'd called it in immediately, knowing that the sooner forensics got here the better, while Cooper left the building rapidly to be sick in a recycling bin.

And now, half an hour later, a still-pale Cooper was controlling crowds at the main gated entrance of the Mews, while De'Geer was acting Scene of Crime officer. There was a blue tent now in front of the stairs, the neighbours had been removed temporarily, and DC Davey and Doctor Marcos, both in their PPE suits were now examining the body before moving it.

'You were right,' Doctor Marcos eventually said as she walked down the stairs, pulling down her face mask as she did so, leaving it on her chin. 'It looks like she was stabbed with a screwdriver, maybe a very thin tube, and it's definitely not feeling right.'

She looked around the courtyard.

'Gated community,' she continued, peering at the entrance. 'Surely there must be CCTV around here.'

'DC Fitzwarren is already on it, I've been told,' De'Geer replied as formally as he could. He wanted to transfer to forensics down the line and he wanted to stay in the Unit, which meant that he needed to stay on Doctor Marcos' good side. She nodded absently, only half listening, already looking at the door.

'No forced entry?' she asked. De'Geer shook his head.

'Not that I saw,' he replied. 'Although I gained entry myself.'

'From the position of the body, I'd say she was leaving the apartment, not entering,' Doctor Marcos mused. 'That to me says she was backing away from her killer who was inside, not from this door. Which means—'

'She knew them,' De'Geer finished the sentence, but then stopped. 'Sorry, Doctor. You probably wanted to say that.'

'It's fine,' Doctor Marcos was already pulling the mask back on. 'I'd rather you got it than I had to explain it to you.'

She looked to the gate, where Monroe was passing through the small group of photographers that had gathered there.

'Mask, gloves and boots,' she said as he approached. Monroe was already pulling on his gloves as he grimaced.

'Bloody hell, woman, I'm not a wee lamb that needs to be told how to walk,' he muttered. 'I know the drill.'

Pulling on his plastic booties at the doorway, he looked at De'Geer.

'You okay, laddie?' he asked with genuine concern. 'Cooper looked like she'd jettisoned her lunch.'

'She's not used to it,' De'Geer put on a brave face, but Monroe shook his head.

'You should never get used to it,' he replied with a nod. 'Get someone to take over for her. And you. There's a couple of sergeants came with me, they can do it.'

'I'd rather help, sir,' De'Geer stiffened, but Monroe just smiled.

'I know, laddie,' he said. 'That's why you're putting on one of these bloody silly Smurf suits and helping Davey and Rosanna. God knows you've probably been champing at the bit to do so.'

As De'Geer gratefully passed his responsibilities over to one of the freshly arrived officers and ran off to find a spare PPE suit in his size, Monroe fixed the mask to his face and entered the building, walking up the narrow staircase to the first floor, and the body of Lydia Cornwall.

'What do we know?' he asked.

Doctor Marcos, kneeling beside the body, motioned for Monroe to move around the corpse and stand beside the door where, at this better angle, he could see the black crusty blood from the neck wound.

'Sharp force injury because of a traumatic separation of tissues,' she said. 'Basically something less than a centimetre wide but at least four inches long slammed into the side of her neck here,' she showed the wound, 'and punctured the skin right here, causing the victim to collapse, bleeding out.'

'Do we know the exact force used?' Monroe wanted to move closer, but this wasn't his expertise. Doctor Marcos shook her head.

'The variables we need, such as sharpness of weapon, angle of attack and relative movements of the people involved, until we know these, I can't work these out,' she replied. 'I can say there was a considerable force, and a strange wound left.'

Monroe nodded. 'More than one stabbing motion?' he asked. Doctor Marcos shook her head.

'It's a weird one,' she leaned back. 'The wound looks different than usual. I'll have to do a full autopsy here. It almost looks like they stabbed her with a shard of metal rather than a solid lump of it.'

Monroe looked into the apartment.

'Keep me updated,' he said, entering the corridor that led into it.

The first-floor flat was entered through another front door, the *Chubb* lock high and to the right of what looked like a standard interior door handle. Through this was a small corridor, white-painted and with no pictures or mirrors on it, which led to two doors on the left, the first leading to a small kitchen, the second to a small airing cupboard while a door on the right led to a sandy tile-walled bathroom, complete with toilet and spacious white bath, and one final visible door straight ahead that led into a small living room. Before that, though, the corridor turned to the right, leading to the two bedrooms of the property; a door to the left led Monroe to a narrow room with a double bed and wardrobe, while the one directly ahead was an office with a desk in the middle, and posters and album covers in frames on the wall.

All the posters and albums were from *Alternator*.

Walking back into the living room, Monroe found DC Davey, in her blue PPE suit, examining a coffee table in front of a black leather sofa. On it were two cups of tea, barely touched.

'Anything?' Monroe asked. Davey nodded.

'The victim knew her killer,' she said, pointing at the mugs. 'Well enough to make them a cuppa.'

'Milk and sugar?'

'Milk, but sugar's on the table so we don't know if they used it or not yet,' Davey leaned closer to the mugs, which had a dark dusting of powder on them. 'Only one set of prints on them both, too, so the killer was offered a drink, but didn't take it.'

'Probably knew they'd leave DNA,' Monroe nodded. 'Which could mean this wasn't an accident, and they came here deliberately to kill her.'

'The victim fell in the doorway, as if trying to run from the apartment,' Davey pointed down the corridor towards the entrance door, where Doctor Marcos was still working on the body. 'I think she invited the killer in, they talked, something happened and the killer attacked her. She ran, but was caught at the door.'

'Why do you think they attacked her here?'

Davey pointed at the door, where to the side a small pile of books had tumbled.

'The entire apartment is spotless, except for that pile by the door. Which, if you turned from the table and the mugs, is a direct line for the way out. Also, we found this there.'

She turned to a box on the floor, a holdall for forensics, and pulled out a clear baggie. In it was a gold necklace, with what looked like a small red phial within the clasp.

'It's a necklace, snapped at the back,' she explained. 'As if grabbed and pulled.'

'So the killer wore a necklace, Lydia grabbed it and it snapped off,' Monroe nodded.

'Or it's the other way around,' Davey suggested. 'The

necklace seems to be a phial of liquid, so we'll have a look, see if we can get any DNA off it.'

Monroe walked around the room, noticing additional photo frames on the wall. Looking closer, he saw that they were images of Lydia, taken over several decades, and apart from a few wedding shots of a younger Lydia and Ray Cornwall, the rest were with members of *Alternator*. The most recent ones were with Dave Manford, but there were a couple of a younger, smiling Lydia next to a man with shaggy brown hair and rounded Lennon spectacles, a slim sliver of beard under his lip as she kissed his cheek.

Nick Manford also knew Lydia well, it seemed, and Monroe wondered whether this was before or after Marna snagged him for a husband.

'Anything else?' he asked, but Davey shook her head.

'Nothing so far, but we've only just started,' she replied as De'Geer, now in full PPE, entered to join her. 'We'll likely be here all night, and that's before we start on what the hell actually killed her.'

'Thoughts on that?' Monroe asked. Davey shook her head.

'Something like a tube, maybe the hollow end of a screwdriver?' she suggested. 'You know, the ones with the interchangeable heads, where they slot into an inch-deep holder? Something like that perhaps.'

'Keep on at it,' Monroe looked around the room one last time. 'De'Geer, if you're making yourself useful, see if there's anything in her office that can help us.'

Now feeling like he was simply in the way, Monroe exited the apartment, standing once more beside Doctor Marcos.

'What, you want a goodbye kiss?' she said, still kneeling close to the body. Monroe almost grinned, but staring down at the body of the dead woman, he felt all the humour drain from him, replaced by the same anger he'd felt earlier that day.

'Keep us updated, yeah?' he asked.

Doctor Marcos looked up, fixing him with a withering gaze.

'Oh, really?' she replied. 'I was thinking about keeping it to myself. Me, Morten and Joanne. We were going to sit in the back of the briefing room and act all holier than thou because we knew stuff that you didn't. Will you just bugger off out of my crime scene, please?'

Monroe made his way gingerly down the stairs, waving without looking as he left. Now outside, he looked around the courtyard. It was well maintained, with greenery interspersed between the parking spaces.

'The gate,' he asked PC Cooper who, although she was still pale, was now standing guard on the door. 'How did you get through it when you came here?'

'PC De'Geer buzzed for entry, Guv,' PC Cooper replied queasily. 'There was no answer, but a car was leaving and the gate opened, so we just drove in. We checked the reg, it was a neighbour.'

Monroe nodded, staring at the gate. A gated community was only as good as the people entering and exiting out of the entranceway. If someone could slip in, it negated the whole point. Walking out of the gates and past the reporters, giving a polite 'no comment' to any who asked him for news, Monroe now stood on the pavement, looking left and right up Stannard Road. The area really was a mixture of old and new, but to the south was a T-junction with Graham Road, a black, wrought-iron gate barring the way in or out, a blue sign on it stating EMERGENCY ACCESS - DO NOT OBSTRUCT.

Which meant that if someone came here by car, they had to come from the north. And, as he walked to the T-junction with Ritson Road, only fifty yards northwards, he saw, on the streetlight facing him and attached about twenty feet in the air, a white box with an image of a cat, and the word STRYKER underneath.

Monroe smiled.

'Got you, you little bastard,' he said.

Because if the killer came from the north, he or she would have had to have passed the detecting view of the *Stryker Polecat* surveillance device that this street had guarding it, set in almost the perfect location to see them.

Of course, if the killer went south, Monroe had nothing.

Best not to think of that, he thought as he walked back to his car. *Best not to think about that at all.*

Unfortunately for him, he also didn't look to the south, and more importantly across the road where, standing in the shadows of a bus stop, a bald man watched him carefully, smiling as Monroe walked off.

Derek Sutton wanted nothing more than to shout out, call across the street to his onetime friend, but he couldn't let Monroe know he was in London.

Because Derek Sutton had a *job* to do.

14

MEAT IS MURDER

Declan had left the office at 6pm, calling it a night. Usually he would have spent more time there, often working late into the evening, or more often would take his work back home to Hurley, where he'd end up discussing the casework files into the early hours with Anjli, which probably wasn't good for either of them. But tonight was a different matter, because he was meeting up with Jess.

She'd turned sixteen a few weeks earlier, and this was sitting heavily on Declan. *How was his little girl sixteen?* In his mind, she was still seven, playing with dolls and cutting her hair short with kitchen scissors.

Though, being honest, Declan couldn't actually remember her playing with dolls.

And now, with her GCSEs done and with a break before she started her 'A' Levels, still intending to join the police force, Declan had finally arranged a slot in both of their schedules where he could take her out for dinner.

Of course, to a sixteen-year-old, the idea of 'dinner' was completely different to a man in his early forties, so while

Declan had been considering some of the more expensive restaurants in the City, Jess had found a couple of vegan friendly places off Neal's Yard, north of Covent Garden.

'I don't know what I'll be able to eat,' Declan moaned to Anjli, who'd been dragged along as moral support. 'No meat. What else do I need to know?'

'I'd not so much think about the things you'll lose, and consider it as an exciting chance to try a plant-based diet,' Anjli smiled. 'And, as much as watching you eat a tofu burger delights me, why exactly am I coming with you?'

'Jess asked for it,' Declan replied. 'Liz is still twitchy after Hurley. It's been hard to get her to let me see Jess without a chaperone, and for some reason Jess thinks you're a good influence on me.'

'It's because I've bought us a cool coffee machine,' Anjli replied knowledgeably. They were walking along Long Acre now, having turned off Kingsway and heading towards Covent Garden. 'And Liz needs to lighten up. Hurley was months ago, and Jess hasn't been in danger of dying for ages now.'

She smiled.

'Maybe your criminal girlfriend could talk to Liz?' she offered. 'Liz seems to listen to her.'

'First off, Tessa isn't my girlfriend.'

'But she's still a criminal?'

'Of course,' Declan replied. 'She's in court next month on charges of murder, so I think she's pretty much crossed that divide.'

'But you still fancy her.' Anjli was grinning now. Declan sighed.

'So, this Eden bloke,' he said, changing the subject. 'You called him yet?'

'I've made another appointment to speak to him about the case, yes,' Anjli replied cautiously.

'Was it by email?' Declan asked.

'Yes,' Anjli replied slowly, unsure where this was going.

'Did you end it with kisses?' Declan ducked as Anjli threw a punch at him. 'Always let them know when you fancy them.'

'You're a dick,' Anjli said, but she was smiling. 'You act like this with your jailbird girlfriend and she'll shank you in the showers.'

Turning into Neal Street, a pedestrian road with clothes shops on either side, Declan decided not to continue this conversation. For a start, he found he had a strange feeling of jealousy over Anjli's interest in Eden, but this was most likely because for the last month they'd become close as housemates, and a new man, especially a billionaire coming into the mix could upset that.

And besides, Tessa Martinez was his childhood crush, not his adult one.

Do you even have an adult crush?

Declan was about to tell his inner voice to *go do one* when Anjli pointed at a side alley.

'Neal's Yard,' she said. 'Where carnivores go to die.'

'You can't mock me,' Declan replied testily. 'You eat meat.'

'Yes, but I'm open to new experiences,' Anjli grinned.

Declan looked over to the entrance to the alley and saw a young woman, sixteen years old, her hair dyed black and cut into a wedge, matching her leather biker jacket and black Levi jeans. In fact, if it wasn't for the pillar-box red Doctor Martens she wore, she'd be completely monochrome.

'Interesting look,' Declan said as he hugged his daughter. 'You sure wearing leather to a vegan café is a good idea?'

'Faux leather,' Jess replied with a smile. 'Likewise, the boots.'

She looked at Anjli and before she could say anything, Anjli found herself also on the receiving end of a hug.

'Um, thanks,' she said, confused.

'You saved my life, Anj,' Jess stated. 'That makes you family.'

Anjli looked a little taken aback by this, and now it was Declan's turn to smile. Anjli had indeed saved Jess when she was captured by Ilse Müller in Hurley a few months earlier, but as far as Anjli had been concerned, it was part of the job.

'Come on,' Jess said eagerly, pulling Declan towards a café in the yard. 'I got us a table for four.'

'We expecting another?' Declan asked. Jess shook her head.

'Even numbers,' she said. 'No tables for three.'

The café that Jess had picked was a small, cosy one, with wooden benches lined in rows against the wall, split into sections of four. It was colourful and quite welcoming. Declan could think of more than a few places where he'd felt actively oppressed while eating. Obviously used to the café, Jess was already greeting the server like an old friend as she waved Declan and Anjli to the bench beside a window. After a few moments, she sat down beside them once more.

'Just ordered some kombucha teas,' she said. Anjli nodded at this, as if it was the most obvious statement that could be made, but Declan wasn't sure if he heard correctly.

'And what's that again?' he asked. Jess grinned.

'It's tea, dad,' she replied. 'Just created slightly differently to how we do it.'

'It's not in a tea-bag, for a start,' Anjli smiled. 'Kombucha teas help with digestion and diabetes, strengthening the immune system, reducing blood pressure and detoxifying all that crap you've built up over the years.'

'I might like all that crap I've built up,' Declan muttered.

'Kombucha also helps against rheumatism, gout, haemorrhoids and even fights cancer,' Jess added. 'So sue me if I want you to try something that might actually extend your life.'

'Hey hey,' Declan held up his hands in defence. 'I didn't say that I didn't want it!'

'Good,' Jess passed him a menu, printed on double sides of a piece of paper. 'You have a choice of wrap, salad or soup.'

Declan stared mournfully at the menu, realising that even aside from the lack of meat, his meal options were now ranging from healthy to *incredibly* healthy.

'Can I just move on to the desserts?' he asked.

'A salad won't kill you for once,' Anjli laughed, looking up at the server who'd walked over to the table. 'I'll have the jackfruit and potato wrap, please.'

Jess ordered something involving hemp cheese and *biodynamic pulled mushrooms*, and Declan ordered a falafel style chickpea wrap, mainly as falafel was one of the few words that he knew there. And with some sides of sliced avocados and marinated olives on the way, Declan looked back to his daughter, noting that she was already distracted, staring across the café at a girl wearing a denim hoodie, a pair of *Bosé* headphones on as she read a book while eating.

'She looks familiar,' Declan said. Jess nodded.

'That's Prisha,' she replied. 'She's a year above me, about to start her second year of 'A' Levels at Henley College.'

'One of Nathanial Wing's friends,' Anjli continued, recognising her. 'Strange she's in London though.'

'She's spending the summer in a scheme made by the

London School of Economics,' Jess replied with the knowledge of someone who was very clued in about the movements of an effective stranger she met twice. Declan raised an eyebrow.

'Is *she* the fourth person?' he asked with a smile and was surprised to see Jess blush a little.

'I'm just going to go say hi,' she said, rising from the chair and walking over to Prisha, who looked up, smiling as she approached.

'I'm guessing you didn't know they kept in touch?' Anjli asked.

Declan looked back at her, conflicted.

'I thought she fancied Morten?' he asked. 'Now she's after some older girl?'

'Morten is a man in his early twenties,' Anjli replied, her tone colder. 'Are you saying that you'd rather she was still after him than a girl only a year older than she is?'

Declan shook his head, already aware of the hole he was digging for himself.

'I just didn't know,' he said.

'Well, now you do, so now you can be supportive,' Anjli replied. 'Christ, Dec, she might just be experimenting, finding out what she's into. Didn't you experiment in your teens?'

'By her age, I'd already met Kendis,' Declan replied, stopping as he looked back at Anjli. 'Wait, are you saying *you* experimented?'

Anjli sighed despairingly at Declan as now smiling widely, Jess walked back over.

'I spoke with Billy today,' she said matter-of-factly. 'He's helping me with some computer summer work. What's this about a billionaire boyfriend?'

Anjli groaned. 'I met Eden Storm today, and he was... well, he was nice,' she replied.

'Eden Storm?' Jess whistled. 'He's massive! You should totally get in there.'

'I don't know,' Anjli was squirming a little now. 'I don't think he's my type.'

Declan went to laugh, but a glare from Anjli stopped him.

'And don't you dare mock me, with your jailbird girlfriend.'

'Tessa isn't anything like that,' Declan replied. 'She just needs a friend right now.'

Jess watched her dad, looked at Anjli, and then smiled.

'You'd make such a cute couple,' she said.

'Me and Tessa?' Declan was confused.

'No, you dick. She's talking about us,' Anjli said as she looked back at Jess, now giving the full power of her glare to the smiling sixteen-year-old. 'Which is just proof positive that you've failed as a father and she's on some serious mind-altering drugs.'

Jess simply shrugged, the smile still plastered on her face.

'Hey, why were you asking about my exams, anyway?' she asked. 'You never explained how you knew?'

Anjli glanced at Declan as he smiled. He'd expected the question, and he'd already prepared for the lie.

'Billy was testing CCTV log ins, and he got into your school,' he replied. 'By random chance he caught the saved feed of your exam.'

'Wow,' Jess looked at Anjli. 'That was a terrible lie. You want to have a go?'

'She's sixteen, Dec,' Anjli said, looking at Declan. 'I'd want to know if I was that age. She needs to be informed, so she can be prepared.'

'Prepared for what?' Jess asked, now concerned.

Declan signed.

'Karl Schnitter had someone watch you,' he said. 'Hack into the CCTV just to wind me up.'

'Karl Schnitter's in a hole somewhere,' Jess said, paling. 'You said he'd never bother me again.'

'And he won't,' Anjli leaned in, placing a hand on Jess's own. 'He did this to prove a point, that he has powerful friends. He wanted leverage for a message being passed to his own daughter.'

'If he wanted to do anything, he would have by now,' Declan added.

Jess groaned.

'Way to sugarcoat it, dad.'

'You're safe,' Anjli leaned in. 'Me and your dad? We'll kill anyone who comes near you. Morten too. You're part of the Unit, and we look after our own.'

'But please, don't tell your mum,' Declan pleaded. 'I only just calmed her down.'

Jess nodded. 'The exams were weeks ago,' she said, as if convincing herself. 'Okay. It's fine. It's all fine—'

'It is,' Declan interrupted, placing a hand on his daughter's own. 'I'll make sure of it.'

'Just promise me you'll ensure nothing happens.'

'Pinkie promise.'

Jess smiled once more, seemingly placated by this gesture.

'So, what's the case?' she asked, changing the subject. Looking back at Prisha and deciding that he wouldn't enquire about her personal life until Jess was ready to tell him, and hoping that she'd do the same in return, Declan shrugged, grateful for the scene change.

'Old pop singer died, now his manager is dead too,' he said. 'Band's about to make millions—'

He stopped as three mason jars, filled with tea and with ice in were placed on the table.

'So kombucha is iced tea?' he asked.

'It's more than that,' Jess smiled as she passed two paper straws to Declan and Anjli.

'You don't use a straw?' Declan asked as he tore the paper wrapping off his. Jess was already rummaging in her bag.

'I do, but I bring my own,' she said, pulling out what looked to be a neon-coloured plastic straw. 'Disposable straws are—'

'Destroying our planet,' Declan replied before Jess could continue. 'You're the second person who's mentioned that to me today.'

He thought back to Peter Suffolk's words in Highgate.

I even have a stainless steel one I take everywhere with me!'

'A stainless steel straw,' he blurted. 'They'd be the same width as this, right?'

He was looking at his own straw as he spoke, already working out that it was around half a centimetre in width.

Anjli watched him, realising a second after him what he was thinking.

'Peter Suffolk had a straw like that?'

'That's what he told me,' Declan was already rising from the chair, pulling his phone out, looking at the screen as he did so. 'I need to call Monroe, but there's no signal in here.'

Walking quickly out of the café, Declan exited Neal's Yard as he dialled Monroe, stopping at the junction of Short's Gardens and Neal Street.

'I thought you were off tonight?' Monroe asked as a form of answer.

'I am, but I think I might have something,' Declan said. 'Actually, it was more something Jess did, so credit where it's due. Are you still with Doctor Marcos?'

'*I'm outside the house and about to drive back to the Unit,*' Monroe replied. '*But I can get back if you want.*'

'Yeah, if you're able,' Declan was looking around the street as he spoke. 'Ask her if the wound in Lydia Cornwall's neck could have been made with a stainless steel straw.'

'*Christ, that's specific,*' Monroe said, and Declan could hear that he was walking now, most likely back to the crime scene. '*But having seen the wound, I can see how that could be it. Now go see your daughter and we'll discuss this in the morning.*'

'If she agrees, it might be worth pulling in Peter Suffolk,' Declan continued. 'He's the one who was talking about straws earlier today.'

'*Leave it with us,*' Monroe finished the call, disconnecting as Declan stared across the street.

Just past the crossing, there was a dark blue BMW parked half on the pavement.

It was most likely a driver waiting for their client, but there was something that felt wrong here, and as Declan walked towards it, he saw the driver start the engine; the lights turning on.

'Stay right there,' Declan stated as he placed himself in the road now, stopping it from driving as he showed his warrant card. 'You move, you're nicked.'

'Are you saying that a car can't be parked now?' the woman who spoke had emerged from the back of it now, facing Declan as he stopped. Her black bob was familiar enough, but the voice would have given it away even with his eyes closed.

Francine Pearce.

'Am I supposed to believe this is a coincidence?' he asked. 'That you happen to be here at the exact moment I am?'

'Oh, we're not following you,' Francine smiled, staying beside the car. 'We're watching someone else.'

Declan went to reply, but then felt a sliver of ice slide down his spine.

'You're following *Jess*,' he hissed.

Francine didn't reply at first, letting the moment stretch out.

'Such a brave little girl,' she said. 'And with her whole life ahead of her. I hope she never has her whole world ripped from her, like I did.'

'Are you seriously playing the victim here?' Declan was stunned. 'You shot at me. You set me up for the police when I needed your help.'

'I knew the gun had blanks, I was playing the part for Susan,' Francine replied calmly. 'And when you broke into my house, you were a suspected terrorist. Of course I'd call for help.'

Declan moved closer.

'I get you have a problem with me,' he said. 'But Jess is off limits. Stop following her. You want to continue whatever we have, I'm right here, right now. Get whatever issues you have off your chest. I'll even go completely off the record if it helps.'

'I'm sure I don't know what you mean,' Francine's perpetual smile was irritating Declan now, and he wanted more than anything to arrest her. But he knew she probably had an army of solicitors in the back seat of the car, just waiting for the opportunity to leap out.

So instead, he leaned in.

'You go near my daughter, you talk to my daughter, you

even look at my daughter and I will *kill* you,' he hissed. 'I've been a copper for a long time. I know how to make you disappear. And my army training will ensure you *know* you're dying.'

'Is that a threat?' Francine put on a brave face, but she was shivering as she spoke.

'It's a prophecy,' Declan hissed before turning and walking off. 'I don't want to see you near my daughter again. And move your car before I have it clamped.'

Francine Pearce took a long moment before doing anything.

And then she turned to the woman in the back seat of the car, out of sight for the conversation.

'Did you get all that?' she asked. 'Tell me you got all that.'

'I did,' Trisha Hawkins said, turning off the dictaphone and placing it into her jacket pocket.

'I got every word of his death threat, nice and clear.'

15

EVERY BREATH YOU TAKE

AFTER RETURNING TO THE CAFÉ, DECLAN CONTINUED HIS plant-based dinner with Jess, finding it surprisingly easy in the process, although he'd have much preferred a normal mug of builder's tea than the mason jar with a straw in. Jess asked more about the case and Declan provided her with as many facts as they had, allowing Jess to consider the options. He knew Liz didn't want Jess in any investigations, and after Hurley he totally understood that, but he knew Jess still wanted to be a police detective like her father and grandfather, and nothing was going to stop that, so it was better to lean into it.

As it was, Jess didn't have any new aspects to the case, pointing out that the last studio album that *Alternator* had brought out was *before I was born, dad,* so after dinner Declan hugged his daughter goodbye and offered to take her home. Jess pointed out that as she was sixteen, she was fine to catch a tube train and there was an awkward moment when neither left the café, until Anjli said her farewells, dragging Declan out by the arm and, only when they were walking back towards Covent Garden, with Declan calming once he saw that the BMW was now gone, Anjli finally explained to him *Jess wasn't going home yet, was likely to start her second catchup of the evening with Prisha, and the last thing she wanted was her dad there.*

As they were going back to the same house, Declan and Anjli car-shared to Hurley, leaving Anjli's car at Temple Inn and, the following morning car shared back into the station, using the time to discuss the case. In fact, Declan already realised that Anjli was discussing every part of the case except for Eden Storm, but decided not to press her on the subject. In a strange way, he was quite happy for the billionaire to be forgotten.

It was around fifteen minutes to nine when they entered the Command Unit, being buzzed through by the Desk Sergeant and making their way upstairs, nodding to Doctor Marcos as she looked up from her desk in forensics as they passed her office.

Billy was already at his station as they arrived.

'What's new?' Declan asked. Billy pointed his thumb at Monroe's office.

'He's been waiting for you,' he said. 'Peter Suffolk was brought in this morning, about half hour back. Monroe wants you to take lead.'

'I thought Bullman would want this one?' Anjli commented, but Billy simply shook his head.

'She's seen this guy sing with her favourite band every two years when they've toured, for around a decade,' he explained. 'She doesn't want to interview him for murder.'

'It does kill the magic slightly,' Declan admitted. 'Anything from the *Stryker* CCTV people?'

'Waiting for footage to be sent over now,' Billy replied.

'Currently I'm just going through old album credits, trying to work out who was involved in the *Secrets and Lies* recording and who's died, but there seem to be discrepancies in the linings of both the album and the CD.'

'Speak to Bullman, she probably has both in pristine condition,' Anjli grinned as, across the office, Monroe's head popped out of his doorway.

'You ready for some work?' he asked. 'Or do you need your morning *wakey wake* first?'

'I was going to make a coffee, yes,' Declan smiled. 'Sounds like you've already had yours, sir.'

Monroe exited his office, walking over.

'Good catch with the straw,' he said. 'When we picked him up, he had one in his inside jacket pocket. It matches identically to the wound.'

'Is it the murder weapon?' Anjli asked.

'It's likely to be the same as it, but these things are ten-a-penny,' Monroe said. 'It's not exactly a *ruthenium letter opener*.'

Declan nodded at this. Monroe was referencing a particular type of letter opener used as a murder weapon that had been so specific, it had led them straight to its owner a few months earlier. But a stainless steel straw that could be bought in packs of five online wasn't so exclusive.

'Still, it gives us a starting line,' Monroe smiled. 'Grab your coffee, laddie. We start in five minutes.'

Declan nodded, looking back at Billy.

'Anything else we need to know?' he asked. Billy shook his head.

'Moment I get anything, I'll let you know,' he said, returning to the screens. Declan nodded and headed to the canteen.

He had a feeling he'd be needing a lot of coffee today.

PETER SUFFOLK WAS IN THE INTERVIEW ROOM WHEN DECLAN and Monroe entered, a stern-looking woman in her late forties or early fifties, her blonde hair pulled back over her black suit, her burgundy-framed glasses looking as stern and imposing as she was, sitting beside him.

'I'm Carrie Woodstock,' she said without offering a hand or rising. 'I'm Mister Suffolk's legal representative.'

'Pleasure,' Monroe replied as he sat at the desk opposite, although there was no sign of this on his face.

The room was small and empty of all furniture except for a table with a recording device on, and four chairs, two on either side, with Peter and his solicitor on one side, and Declan and Monroe on the other. Once everyone was settled, Monroe turned the recorder on.

'The time is nine oh-five,' Monroe stated into the microphone. 'Interview of Peter Suffolk, aka Andrew Knytte, his solicitor Carrie Woodstock in attendance, by DCI Monroe and DI Walsh.'

He leaned back in his chair, watching Peter silently. He was in jeans and a sweatshirt, his hair ruffled, as if he'd been woken up and brought here without a chance to shower. Which, in a way, was true.

'Where were you yesterday—'

'Look, what's going on?' Peter suddenly exploded. 'I'm woken up at stupid o'clock in the morning, dragged here and dumped in a holding cell and now I'm being treated like a killer!'

He looked at the solicitor.

'Even she hasn't been bloody told! I spoke to your man

there—' he indicated Declan '—yesterday, and I answered every question honestly!'

'But you didn't,' Declan leaned forward now. 'You stated that on the night of Dave Manford's death, you exited through the back door and dealt with a paparazzi. To quote —' he pulled out his notebook, flicking through it until he found the phrasing he needed '—*There was one pap there, taking shots, but I paid him twenty quid and deleted the images from his camera. Far cheaper than trying to do that to all of them.*'

'So?' Peter muttered sullenly. 'What's one pap got to do with this?'

'We have a witness that states that he saw you in Lovat Lane, after the murder happened, arguing with Benny Simpson, the onetime manager of *Alternator*.'

Peter stared at Declan now, his mouth half open.

'For the recording, the suspect is silent,' Declan said.

'The old guy was Benny?' Peter shook his head. 'No way. Benny lives in a nursing home and is spoon fed baby food. No way this was him.'

'But you spoke to this man?' Monroe asked.

'Sure!' Peter replied. 'He was the pap I talked about! Took a photo as I walked out, I paid him off and deleted it. I assumed he was an amateur who lucked out. Lots of pensioners do this to gain a little extra money.'

He looked at his solicitor.

'I don't even know him,' he said. 'He quit as manager like eight years before I even turned up. Sure, I heard the name and that, usually when the band were pissed and complaining about the old days, but that was it!'

'If that's all you have on my client—' Carrie started, but Monroe held up a hand to stop her.

'We're not here for that,' he said. 'We've brought in your man here because of the murder of Lydia Cornwall.'

At this, Peter almost fell off his chair in shock.

'Lydia's dead?' he asked softly. 'How?'

'We believe that someone rammed a stainless steel straw into the side of her neck, severing the artery and causing her to bleed out,' Declan replied. 'And considering that not only did you have one in your possession when we arrested you, and that you also mentioned it to me yesterday, we also have you on CCTV as one of the last people to see her alive, and you ended that conversation with a pretty heated argument.'

'I didn't want her dead,' Peter shook his head. 'She winds me up—*wound* me up, but she was pretty decent.'

He looked back at Carrie.

'I have a dozen of those straws,' he said. 'I use them everywhere.'

He looked back at Declan.

'And so does the band,' he said. 'Especially Andy, they all have them. I got them into it after the second tour we did. They all lost their voices, but I was clear as a bell. I bought them all straws.'

Declan looked at Monroe. If this was true, then Peter might not have been the prime suspect after all.

Declan slid a photo across the table, a forensic picture of the gold necklace.

'Recognise this?' he asked.

Peter looked at it for a long moment before shaking his head.

'Sorry, no,' he replied. 'Should I?'

'Where were you around four pm yesterday?' Monroe asked.

'Was that when she died?' Peter replied. 'I was at home. In my house.'

'Can anyone vouch for this?' Declan asked.

Peter shook his head.

'No, I was alone—'

He stopped, his eyes widening.

'No, wait!' he exclaimed. 'Yeah, I have about a hundred people who can vouch for me!'

'You're going to have to explain that one,' Monroe said, leaning back. Peter nodded urgently, as if aware that this was his only opportunity to clear himself.

'Three pm yesterday was ten in the morning in New York,' he said. 'I was at the memorial for Randy Watts.'

'Randy who?' Declan asked. Peter looked at him.

'Randy Watts!' he repeated. 'Big time jazz musician. He'd been on a couple of the cruises I'd been on, and he died a month back, heart attack. They organised a big online memorial for him, as the family only wanted a small, close-knit funeral. So yesterday we did an online one, about a hundred and twenty of us. There were some memories spoken, a gospel choir did some songs... I added nothing because they already planned it out before I was told, but I was there.'

'And we can prove this how?'

'It was on that chat software, *Zoom*,' Peter replied. 'The video conference thing. We were muted so as not to affect the readings, but I had the camera on. We all did. You can see all of us on it, and they put it on *YouTube* afterwards so it'll be there. It was about two and a half hours in total, ended around five fifteen. After that, I went around Andy's gaff. He lives up the road from me. I checked in, let him know I was keeping the party line and all that, and got back home about seven.'

'Andy Mears?'

'Yeah.'

Declan looked at Monroe. It was looking more and more like Peter had a solid alibi for the murder, and an explanation for the murder weapon.

'Look,' Peter added. 'I get that I'm a suspect because of the video and the straw. I do, but I never knew Dave. I wasn't in the band when he was, or Benny was, or even Nick. I was in drama school when they made *Secrets and Lies,* and I get nothing, not a single bloody penny when they sell the back catalogue. In fact, I lose out because they probably won't be able to re-record any *best of* albums with me if they sell, because they'll have to licence the songs back. Of everyone involved in the whole thing, me and Chris Joseph, the current bassist? We're literally the guys who have nothing to gain here.'

'How can we find this video of you unedited?' Monroe asked. Peter looked at Declan.

'Look, the guy who set it all up, he'll have all the original feeds. You'll see me. If I can get my phone, I can forward you the details, and you can watch it yourself. I'm literally sitting at my kitchen table, staring at the screen for around two hours or so.'

Declan nodded, rising. 'Pausing interview until the video has been watched,' he said, leaning across Monroe and turning the recording off. 'We'll pass you the phone and we'll check this out, but you'll have to stay here until we sort it. Okay?'

Peter nodded.

'Honestly? If someone's out there offing people connected to the band, I'd much rather be here.'

'And how much longer do you think the band will exist?' Monroe muttered, walking to the door. 'If this money goes through, they'll never need to tour again. And where will that leave you?'

Following Monroe, Declan left the room, fuming.

If Peter's alibi checked out, they were back at square one.

'PETER'S ALIBI CHECKS OUT,' BILLY SAID, POINTING AT THE screen. 'The memorial's already had over a hundred thousand views on YouTube. It's about two hours long, and everyone involved with him is seen, edited 'live' into the video at some point. I emailed the guy who did it, Kaz something, and he came back immediately.'

Billy tapped on the keyboard and a video popped up, a full-screen image of an empty kitchen.

'This is Peter's feed,' he said. 'All of them were recorded individually through the app by Kaz and combined at the other end.'

On the screen, Peter walked into shot, sitting down and smiling at the screen. All that was visible on the table was a mug and a water bottle.

'This is before the memorial started,' Billy explained.

'Hi everyone,' the video of Peter said. 'Let me sort my video out—yeah, hey Ali, it's good to see you too. Just give me a moment and I'll mute everything.' He fiddled with the video camera, and Declan assumed he had a web camera attached on top of the screen. The image went dark for a second and then returned as Peter kept fiddling. He eventually sat back down.

'*That better?*' he asked, now fiddling with a pair of ear buds now placed in his ears. '*Good, I can hear you. I'll mute now. Good luck, guys. All my love.*'

He pressed a button on the keyboard and then... did nothing.

'This is roughly when the memorial started,' Billy explained. 'For two hours, we literally have him as an audience member.'

Slowly, Billy skimmed through the video. On it, now at four or even five times the speed, Peter fidgeted at speed, laughed, nodded, left for a moment and returned—

'Stop,' Declan said. 'What happened there?'

Billy looked at the timestamp. 'He leaves for about forty seconds,' he said. 'Probably a loo break.'

Speeding through again, they watched Peter drink from the water bottle, leave again and return a minute later with a fresh mug, which he drank as he watched the last part. And then it froze.

'What happened here?' Declan pointed.

'It's five-fifteen, and the feed ended,' Billy replied. 'They ended the call, so the video would have stopped recording.'

Monroe stared at the image, frozen on the screen, of Peter Suffolk, a bottle of water and a mug of some hot beverage on his desk.

'Shite and dammit,' he muttered. 'He couldn't have gotten to the house before six, and by then De'Geer was there.'

Declan looked at the apologetic Billy.

'Is there anything we can use here?'

'To convict him? No,' Billy replied. 'This is pretty set in stone. And I have something else, anyway.'

He started clicking on his mouse and on the second monitor a full colour CCTV image appeared.

'This was taken by the *Stryker* security camera the Guv saw,' Billy explained. 'It was taken around four-ten in the afternoon, which matches time of death pretty well.'

On the image was a man in a black hoodie, walking towards the T-junction with Ritson Road. Billy zoomed in on the face.

'It's not great, but it's enough quality to make out a couple of things. In particular, the black soul patch beard under the lip, and the rounded Lennon specs that the subject is wearing.'

Declan peered at the image as Billy pulled up another photo, that of Nick Manford, taken six months before he died. In it, he was also sporting his trademark Lennon shades, and wore a black strip of beard under his lip.

'Rufus told me that before he died, Dave said *you shouldn't be here* to someone in the audience,' he said. 'What if he was saying this to someone who should have been dead? What if he was saying it to Nick Manford himself?'

Declan stared at the image of a man who could have been Nick Manford.

A man who was never declared legally dead, and whose body had never been found.

'Bloody marvellous,' he muttered.

16

NO EXPLANATION

'So what do we know?' Monroe asked, sitting on one of the empty desks. 'Give me something, Anything. Because I just watched our best opportunity walk out of the Unit ten minutes ago.'

Declan leaned back in his own chair and stared up at the ceiling. After the video had proven that Peter Suffolk had been involved with the online memorial and was in his kitchen, on live video while Lydia Cornwall was murdered, they'd been forced to let him go, even though he'd had the murder weapon in his pocket.

No, that's not right, Declan thought to himself. *It wasn't the weapon; it was the type of weapon. Completely different.*

In his defence, Peter had been very understanding about this when he could have been an utter diva; woken up, dragged out of his house and accused of murder only to be cleared a couple of hours later wasn't an easy thing to put aside, but Peter had shrugged his shoulders, thanked his solicitor and then shaken everyone's hands before leaving, promising that he'd help in finding the killer of Dave and

Lydia, even suggesting they hunt down Martin Reilly and Graham Hagen, who apparently would have gone to ground together, as well as implying they speak to the only other person in the band who used the straws.

Andy Mears.

Unfortunately, Andy Mears also had an alibi for the afternoon; after leaving *Bear Studios,* he'd been in *Harrington Finance* with Marna Manford, in crisis meetings with their broker, Rufus Harrington. Who, five minutes after Peter had left, had texted Billy to inform him of this. Not because he wanted to provide an alibi; Rufus had texted because Andy had pushed forward on selling the back catalogue quicker than previously agreed, claiming that the official death certificate of Nick Manford, which would provide Marna with all rights as his widow, was due any day now.

'Would have been nice if he'd texted you about this last night,' Monroe muttered.

'In fairness, we would still have brought Peter in,' Declan suggested.

Monroe sighed, almost theatrically, but Declan knew it was a sign borne from frustration.

'So come on then you *bampots*, what do we know?' he snapped again, and the strong Glaswegian inflection to his voice was even more proof that he was stressed.

'There's two possible options to Dave Manford's death,' Anjli suggested. 'Either it's to do with the money being offered for the back catalogue, or it's something that happened back in 1986.'

'Agreed,' Monroe nodded. 'I think it's the former that's actively pressing the latter. The catalogue being offered for sale is bringing things into the light, things that the band hoped would be hidden when *Secrets and Lies* was produced.'

'Maybe not the band,' Billy continued. 'Maybe only Nick and Dave Manford.'

'I dunno,' Anjli shook her head. 'Andy Mears seemed pretty put out when he was talking to the guy at *Bear Studios*.'

'That might have been because he didn't know about the new songs by Nick,' Declan mused. 'That or he knew and didn't want anyone else to know what they had.'

'Either way, the only way *Bear Studios* makes serious money off the auction in June is if someone knows about this,' Monroe said, straightening up as Doctor Marcos entered the office through the main doors. 'You look like a woman with news.'

'I have something, but I'm not sure,' Doctor Marcos nodded. 'I needed to speak to Buttercup here.'

She pointed at Billy, and he smiled.

'So I'm Buttercup now?' he asked. 'I've had worse. What's up?'

'I uploaded a file, have a look,' Doctor Marcos sat on the table next to Monroe, a little closer than someone would usually sit, but then everyone knew about their still-believed-secret relationship.

Billy opened a file on the screen, and a couple of small schematic images appeared. They appeared to be flowcharts, or some kind of electrical follow through designs.

'What are we looking at?' Monroe asked.

'NFC technology,' Billy was zooming in on the image. 'Known as *Near Field Communications*.'

'To who?' Monroe asked. 'Because I've never heard of it.'

'That's because you have a police issue car,' Doctor Marcos smiled. 'The new cars out there, however, use this, mainly so someone can walk up to their car and get in with no key. Their phone does the work.'

'So it's like bluetooth?' Declan asked.

'Similar,' Billy nodded. 'Car companies are using several types right now. *Ultra Wide Broadband* is a form of radio transmission, where the sensor in the car can tell the direction of the signal, so a bit like a tiny radar. When you ping, the door opens. But NFC is different.'

He picked up his iPhone from the desk, showing it to the others.

'It's an industry-standard, contactless technology that's designed to work only across short distances,' he explained. 'You ever used *Apple Pay*? Your phone uses NFC to make that work. I mean, it's more complicated, but you get the gist of the idea there. And in the same wallet where you store your virtual card, there's a thing called *Car Keys* on Apple phones, a digital protocol that lets an iPhone or Apple Watch with NFC capabilities unlock, lock, start, and otherwise control an NFC-capable vehicle. All you do is place it near a specific location.'

'So it's a magic door opener,' Anjli nodded. 'How does this relate to us?'

'From what I know, unlocking a car with this involves holding an Apple Watch or iPhone near an NFC reader located inside the car, is that right?' Doctor Marcos asked.

Billy nodded.

'When the NFC reader detects the digital key stored in the iPhone or watch, the locking mechanism in the car activates.' He was scrolling along the line now. '*Hyundai, Tesla* and *Ford* are all looking at combining Bluetooth and NFC, while *Volkswagen* is talking about UWB.'

He leaned closer as he examined the image.

'This isn't from any of those, though,' he said. 'There's a logo on it. *Edisun.*'

Anjli sat up at this.

'Edisun?' she repeated. 'With a 'u'?'

'You know it?' Monroe asked. Anjli nodded.

'It's the *Tesla* car rival that Eden Storm is building.'

'Then that's very interesting,' Doctor Marcos stood up. 'Because that's from the device we found in the amp, the same device that was turned on remotely.'

'Of course,' Billy nodded. 'Use NFC technology to open the circuit.'

He looked back at the group.

'That means that the killer had to be in the room, as you can't be over ten, maybe twenty feet away from the device. More importantly, this is a device that's been bastardised from what looks to be Eden Storm tech, and that tech doesn't exist yet,' Billy rubbed at his chin in thought. 'If it was out, I'd know.'

'And the only reason I know is because Storm told me,' Anjli admitted.

'Well, if Storm's own tech lit up Dave Manford, then it's even more suspicious why he was there that night,' Declan suggested. 'I think we need to have another chat with him.'

'He's a billionaire,' Anjli protested. 'What reason would he have for killing Dave Manford or Lydia Cornwall?'

She stopped.

'They were always trying to gain money from him,' she said, remembering another line Eden Storm had said to her. 'He mentioned Dave had already had a loan from him. Maybe he had enough.'

'Why would he give a loan to Dave Manford, though?' Declan asked. 'I mean, it's not like Nick and Dave were close at the end, from what we're hearing.'

'What if it was guilt money, or *shut up* money?' Anjli considered.

'Okay,' Monroe was pacing around the office now. 'You're Eden Storm, billionaire. You're the son of Nick Manford, although he doesn't seem to acknowledge you, and Anjli fancies you.'

'I don't think that last part matters, Guv,' Anjli replied.

'My hypothesis, my rules,' Monroe smiled. 'Why would you, with all this, kill Dave or Lydia? And why personally? You could literally pay an army to do it for you.'

'Maybe he did,' Declan mused. 'Maybe he was just there to watch. He leaves before Dave starts the set, remember?'

Billy tapped on the screen, pulling up the CCTV of Eden Storm before leaving the bar. In the background Dave Manford was speaking into the crowd as, in the foreground, Eden's face was just visible on the screen.

'If he leaves the building, the brickwork alone would ensure there's no way he could connect to the device.' Billy explained. 'And Dave is electrocuted two seconds later after Eden walks out into the street.'

'So Eden didn't do it.' Declan could almost hear a hint of relief in Anjli's voice.

'Do we have anything else CCTV wise?' Monroe asked Billy, who nodded.

'I'm still working on the images, but I do have a couple of things from the bar camera's feed,' he replied, pulling up a video onto the screen. It was footage of Lydia standing with Dave, shortly before the show started. 'This is from about five minutes after Peter Suffolk left, and if you watch...'

On the screen, Lydia passed an item across to Dave who, after staring at it for a moment placed it onto his right hand.

'Lydia gave Dave the ring that killed him,' Monroe

muttered. 'Jesus, was she the murderer? Eden's accomplice perhaps? Did Eden kill her to stop her speaking out?'

'Maybe Eden Storm isn't involved at all,' Billy paused the video and zoomed in on the top left corner of it, focusing on the wall in the background. It was blurry and over pixellated, but everyone in the room could see the shadowed figure crouched down.

'This is the only point someone goes near the amp,' Billy explained, scrolling through another feed, stopping at a view of the audience as the show was about to start, a black hoodie wearing figure standing in the midst of it. 'This man, in fact.'

'Our mysterious lookalike. Good work, laddie,' Monroe nodded as PC De'Geer entered the office through the main entrance, walking over to them. 'Anything new?'

'We located Chris Joseph, the bassist for *Alternator*, but he's been in Los Angeles for the last three weeks, working on an album with his other band,' De'Geer shook his head. 'I was hoping you might have something.'

'We might have *zombies*, laddie,' Monroe raised his eyebrows as, on the screen, the image of the Lennon-glasses-wearing man in the hoodie leaving the street where Lydia Cornwall had been murdered popped up, next to the blurred, zoomed image of a hoodie wearing man in *Eastcheap Albums*.

'Nick Manford sported the same soul patch and shades, so this is definitely someone trying to look like him,' Declan stated. 'Or, it is him, and he faked his death twenty years ago.'

There was a *ding* on Billy's phone and, looking at it, Billy looked at the others in a mixture of triumph and shock.

'I might have something else,' he said, spinning back to his computer, tapping on the keys, pulling up an image attachment on the email he'd just read. 'About a hundred feet down Lovat Lane, beside *Eastcheap Albums,* it curves to the right and there's a side road, well more a passageway east, called Botolph Alley, opposite St Mary-At-Hill Church.'

'I'm hoping this is going somewhere,' Monroe muttered.

'On that building, when I looked at it on Google Maps, I saw it had two CCTV cameras, one aimed north up Lovat Lane, and the other up Boltolph. It's not on the same block so wasn't affected by the power outage, and doesn't have a line of sight of *Eastcheap Albums*. Checking into it, I found it was a residential property, a four bedroom, semi-detached house that's currently empty and up for auction.'

'Let me guess, the cameras are there because it's empty?' Declan asked.

Billy nodded.

'I spoke to the management company, explaining the situation. They promised to send me any images from the CCTV footage in the five minutes before and after the electrical outage, in case anyone walked past. They just sent me this picture.'

On the screen now was an image of a man, walking south down Lovat Lane, his head down and half hidden by his hoodie, a half-hidden logo on the chest clearly visible.

But his Lennon style glasses were a giveaway.

'They said in the email that this was the only person who walked away from the bar the entire time, and the timestamp in the corner has it as literally forty seconds after the power went out.'

'Easily enough time to walk out and head south,' Declan leaned closer once more. 'Do we know if there are any other cameras?'

'Only at the other end, where the lane hits Lower Thames Street,' Billy said. 'There's a pub named *The Walrus and The Carpenter*. They have one, but it's aimed at the front of their pub, not onto the surrounding area. And once there, he could have disappeared anywhere.'

'So the same person who was caught walking from Lydia's house, and who's playing with the amp is seen leaving *Eastcheap Albums* right after the murder,' Monroe shook his head. 'This isn't a coincidence. This is the guy. We need to know though whether he worked alone or with help, billionaire or not. What's the logo on the hoodie?'

'I'm trying to work it out,' Billy said.

'It rings a bell,' Bullman, who'd appeared out of nowhere, was peering at it. 'I might have an idea about that.'

'Christ, woman, don't sneak up on me,' Monroe snapped.

'You mean Christ, *Ma'am*,' Bullman smiled sweetly.

'I'll go through the CCTV again,' Billy offered.

Monroe nodded.

'Do that. And find out anything you can about this curse. I'm still wondering how many people were supposed to make something from that album, and how many have died.'

'You still think something happened during *Secrets and Lies?*' Declan asked.

Monroe shrugged.

'Your retired copper did, and we owe it to him to at least look,' he said. 'Professional courtesy and all that.'

He looked over at De'Geer.

'Find the other band members, Martin Whatshisname and Graham Doodah,' he commanded.

'Martin Reilly and Graham Hagen.'

'That's the ones. Find them, bring them in. I'm sick of buggering around here. Anything on that necklace yet?'

Doctor Marcos nodded.

'It's a blood pendent,' she said. 'They were big in the late nineties and became famous when Billy Bob Thornton and

Angelina Jolie wore them. You take a drop of blood and seal it in the necklace. Machine Gun Kelly has one with Megan Fox's blood in it.'

'And Machine Gun Kelly is a singer, not a forties gang-ster?' Monroe asked.

'Singer, rapper, actor, lots of things,' De'Geer added. 'I'm a bit of a fan.'

'And this phial had blood in it?' Monroe looked at Doctor Marcos again. 'Whose blood?'

'We're still checking into it,' Doctor Marcos said. 'But, with the way these work, whoever it is was likely to be the love of the wearer's life, or both sides of the relationship.'

'Keep at it.'

Bullman ran a hand through her hair.

'If I'm right, Nick Manford had something like this on the cover of the fifth album, in 1996.'

Billy was typing now, and an album cover appeared. On it was the 1996 line up of *Alternator*; Nick, Dave, Graham, Martin and Andy. It was called *Royal Blew* and had the band lined up in a photo. On it, though, Nick Manford was further forward than the others, with a necklace over his hoodie.

'Christ,' Monroe said. 'It's the same necklace, and the same bloody hoodie.'

The image showed that Nick's hoodie had a logo on the chest; the logo of his *alma mater,* Hull University.

'I knew I recognised it,' Bullman nodded.

'So a man that looks like Nick and wears his hoodie was seen leaving Lydia's house, where a necklace that belongs to him was torn off?' Declan shook his head. 'Are we sure it's *not* him?'

Monroe looked at Declan now.

'Take DS Kapoor and go hammer on Marna Manford's

bloody windows too,' he ordered. 'There's more going on with that grieving widow than we thought.'

'I was going to speak to Eden Storm—' Anjli protested.

'I'll be seeing Mister Storm,' Monroe interrupted. 'No offence, but I think we need *bad cop* time. If it comes out he's been playing us, I want us ahead of him for once. Is there anything else I'm missing?'

'What killed Lydia Cornwall?' Doctor Marcos suggested. 'I mean, we know it's a stainless steel straw. Good catch there from ol' Deckers.'

Declan glanced at Anjli, who shrugged. 'Not a fan of this nickname thing you've got going, Doc,' he said.

'Don't care,' Doctor Marcos grinned. 'I'm adorable, so you'll let it waive. But here's my hypothetical comment on the situation. Lydia is Marna's what, half-sister? They don't talk much, but they talk. Lydia's also managing Dave and they seem to be incredibly close, have been since she was some kind of groupie in the eighties, even though she married Ray Cornwall in the late nineties.'

'Okay,' Anjli replied. 'I get that.'

'So Lydia opens the door and surprise! Someone's there. She invites them in. She makes them tea. And then she runs, but is killed by a straw in the throat, half falling out of the door.'

Doctor Marcos shrugged.

'It's a common scene, we've seen it ourselves many times. But here's where things go off track.'

She pointed at the image of possible-Nick walking from Lydia Cornwall's house.

'You don't invite a man who you've believed to have been dead for twenty-three years in for a cuppa,' she said. 'You stand in the doorway and faint, especially if you're suffering from PTSD following a brutal death the night before. And even then, having Nick appear the day after Dave dies? Or someone else dressed as him? On your doorstep? Surely I'm not the only one who'd have warning bells?'

Declan nodded as he stared at the screen.

'If it's Nick, then Lydia must have known he was alive,' he said. 'And if it wasn't, and it *was* someone dressed as Nick, she must have known who they were, and more importantly why they were dressed that way, to invite them up the stairs and into her apartment. And now we know she gave Dave Manford the fake ring that killed him, we have to wonder how involved she was at that point.'

Declan stared at the three images on the screen, three different CCTV pictures of what looked like Nick Manford, taken less than twenty-four hours apart.

Someone was playing a clever bloody game, and it was time to end it.

17

LIFESTYLES OF THE RICH & FAMOUS

MARNA MANFORD LIVED IN A LARGE FIVE-BEDROOM HOUSE ON The Bishops Ave, in North London. It was a wide, very opulent street just north of Hampstead Park, and in the thirties was known as *Millionaire's* Row.

Now, it was known as *Billionaire's* Row.

Declan climbed out of Anjli's Hyundai IX35, staring down the avenue at the magnificent mansions on either side. Or, rather, staring at the top parts of these buildings, as the enormous brick walls that most of these estates had kept the public from truly seeing in.

'How the hell does someone like Marna live here?' Declan asked Anjli as they walked down the road. 'These houses are twenty, thirty million at worst.'

'You'd be surprised,' Anjli, with her usual estate agent level of knowledge, smiled. 'A few years back, sure, all these houses were owned by oligarchs and Saudi families, but that's changed now.'

'How so?' Declan stopped at one wall. It was a hoarding, and on the side of it was written FANTASTIC FREEHOLD

OPPORTUNITY while behind, seen in the gaps in the chain-link fence, was a building that didn't look like it'd been lived in for years.

'A lot of the street is like that now,' Anjli said as she looked through the fencing with Declan. 'At one point someone worked out that all the mansions on this street, of which there's about sixty, was worth five hundred million combined. Members of the Iranian royal family, fleeing the fall of the Shah, lived here. The Sultan of Brunei owned a house down there on the right. Saudi Arabian princes followed, and even Elton John sang about the place, although to be honest he might have been on about Holland Park, which is also called Millionaire's Row.'

She carried on walking.

'Of course, half of these houses are filled with squatters, as nobody lives there.'

'What?' Declan couldn't believe this.

'Shell Corporations buy the houses, mainly for the land,' Anjli explained. 'It's mainly the real estate that's worth the money. But a couple of years ago the Government clamped down on taxes being paid. You own a ten million pound mansion, you shell out a million in stamp duty. But because of this, the prices fluctuate. The house Marna lives in? I looked it up. They sold it to Nick in 1996 for just over a million. It's probably worth five now.'

'Sounds like she doesn't need the money then,' Declan said.

Anjli shrugged.

'Depends what the upkeep of the house is,' she said. 'And it depends on what's being offered.'

Marna's house was a red brick building on the corner of a side road, with a low, similarly red-bricked wall topped with black-painted metal tines. It was easily three times the size of Declan's house in Hurley; the front garden and driveway alone held the same footprint as his own house, and beside the wrought iron double gates was an intercom and buzzer. Pressing it, Declan waited patiently. Instead of an answer, however, the gates simply swung inwards, allowing them entry. Walking up to the large, wooden door that barred the way into the house, they saw that this, too, was now ajar.

Pushing it open, Declan nodded for Anjli to enter.

'Why am I the one to go first?' she hissed.

'Because you know this street,' Declan smiled.

In front of them was a marble floored hallway that led towards an ornate double staircase leading to the higher levels. To the left was an open door through which Declan could see a corridor heading towards a library, while to the right was a closed door. As he looked at Anjli, unsure what direction to go, the closed door opened, and a blonde woman in her early fifties stood waiting for them.

'You are the detectives?' she asked.

Declan nodded.

'DI Walsh and DS Kapoor,' he said, pulling out his warrant card to show her. The woman opened the door wider, and Declan could now see that she was painfully slim, and dressed head to toe in black lace. She looked like one of ABBA, but created by Tim Burton.

'Go into the study,' she breathed, her voice holding the slightest of accents to it as she pointed across the hallway, through the open doorway before walking out of view, back into the room.

Anjli smiled. 'Impressive house, right?'

'I've seen better,' Declan whispered back. 'Devonshire House for a start.'

'Someone tried to kill you on the roof of Devonshire House,' Anjli reminded him.

Declan grinned.

'People tried to kill me on more than just the *roof*,' he replied as he led Anjli across the hall and through the door, into what turned out to be a corridor that ended at a small and well-defined library.

There was a low table in the middle of the room, a small pile of books on it; many of them were what Declan would have called *coffee table* books, that was to say that they were impressive looking *cool* books about style and photography. On either side were leather Chesterfield armchairs, four of which were spaced equally around the table. Declan sat in one, and Anjli followed suit, slumping into the one to his right with a sigh.

'We need one of these,' she muttered, half to herself.

Declan wiped a finger along the top of one of the books.

'It's dusty,' he said. 'The house looks spotless, but this room hasn't been cleaned recently.'

After a couple of moments, Marna Manford entered the library, a drink in her hand. It was clear and had ice in, and Declan assumed it was either vodka or gin. She'd also freshened up, as the makeup on her face was now freshly applied.

'I hate this room,' she muttered. 'I try not to come in here. It was Nick's, you see. I have my own library.'

Of course you have your own library, Declan thought to himself. *I bet you never had a secret room with a crime board on it, though.*

'We're happy to go elsewhere if this makes you feel uncomfortable?' he asked. Marna shook her head.

'I don't want you clumping mud all over the floors,' she

said, sitting opposite. 'I hope you understand the reasons for the drinking. I'm grieving.'

Declan nodded. Lydia had been Marna's half-sister after all.

'Did you keep in touch?' he asked.

Marna looked confused.

'With the dog?' she replied. 'How would I do that?'

Declan shifted in the chair.

'I assumed we were talking about something else,' he said politely. 'What are you exactly grieving for?'

'My prize greyhound was taken from us two days ago,' Marna replied sadly. 'She was only seven. Poor girl.'

Anjli closed her notebook.

'As sad as that is, and you have my condolences, but we're not here about your greyhound.'

Marna blinked a couple of times.

'You're not here to find the person who took her?'

'No, Ma'am,' Declan spoke now. 'We're here in connection with the murders of Dave Manford and Lydia Cornwall.'

Marna's whole body language altered. Now it was more confrontational.

'If I'd known that, I wouldn't have let you in,' she muttered. Declan was tiring of this.

'Yes, you would,' he replied flatly. 'Or we'd have simply brought you in as a murder suspect.'

Marna stopped drinking, the glass held at the mouth.

'You think *I* did this?' she asked.

'Well, Ma'am, your brother-in-law and half-sister have both been murdered and you don't seem to be shedding as many tears for them as you are your dog,' Declan replied.

Marna shrugged.

'I loved that dog,' she said. 'I couldn't give a shit about those two freeloaders.'

Declan looked at Anjli as she wrote this down.

'When was the last time you saw either of them?' he asked.

'In person? Years ago,' Marna placed the drink on the table. 'Through intermediaries, last week. They've been trying to squeeze money from us over a potential deal.'

'The back catalogue,' Declan replied.

Marna nodded.

'Nick had the rights, not Dave. Nick and Andy wrote the songs.'

'And before Andy Mears arrived?' Anjli asked.

Marna fixed her with a glare.

'Well, I suppose Dave has a say on those. The shit ones on the first album. But his demands were insane.'

'Insane enough to kill?'

'Insane enough to get a solicitor to tell him to piss off,' Marna laughed. 'Why kill a man who's been pretty much dead for years? We'd all forgotten about him before he popped back up.'

'You're the manager of *Alternator*, yes?' Anjli was writing in her notebook again. Marna waggled her hand.

'We are all our managers,' she said. 'Well, Andy and I, anyway. The others, they don't care as much. They just play the music or they get replaced by more willing musicians.'

'Like Peter Suffolk and Chris Joseph.'

'Exactly.'

Declan leaned back. 'How long have you known the band?' he asked. 'Did you meet them at the same time as Lydia? Or was it after—'

'Why don't you ask what you really want to know?' Marna snapped, interrupting him. 'What they *always* want to know?'

'And that is?'

'How many of the band did I *screw* before I snagged myself the lead singer,' Marna replied, and Declan could feel the resentment dripping off her voice. 'That's what they all think. That I was a slut like Lydia, screwing my way through the ranks.'

She looked away, staring at a bookshelf.

'That was her,' she muttered. 'Not me.'

Declan thought back to the conversation he'd had with Peter Suffolk; he'd mentioned Lydia's antics as well.

'Lydia? She just wanted to sleep her way through the band.'

'So you only had eyes for Nick?'

'God no,' Marna half laughed. 'When I met him, I was an innocent girl, only nineteen or so. It was early 1989, and he was, well, not that impressive. I was more interested in Andy Mears. But he was married.'

'So nothing happened?'

'Not with Nick,' Marna had a sly smile on her lips. 'Andy however...'

'You had an affair?' Anjli looked up.

'No, not as such,' Marna replied. 'To state *affair* implies a continual secretive liaison, whereas all he did was roughly take my virginity in a back room of the Brixton Academy before going on stage. Not that impressive to be honest, so later that year I taught him how to truly please a woman in a three-man tent at the 1990 Glastonbury Festival, while Sinead O'Connor sang bloody awful sad songs at people.'

'And he was still married then?'

'He was still married until early ninety-eight,' Marna replied. 'And I wasn't the one who caused *that* implosion. By then I was with Nick. Me being with Andy? It made me forbidden fruit. And Nick upped his game and paid me some major attention. We married in ninety-four.'

'How did Andy feel about this?'

'Relief I'd moved on, I think,' Marna didn't hide the smile. 'The rumours were already circling. Tents aren't soundproofed, and I'm very loud.'

Declan nodded at this, stopping when he realised he was effectively agreeing with her about her vocalness.

'So you arrived on the scene after *Secrets and Lies?*' Anjli asked, changing the subject to Declan's relief.

Marna nodded.

'Lydia knew them before, but I wasn't interested until I finished school.'

'And how did Lydia meet them?'

Marna shrugged.

'I'd tell you to ask her, but obviously you can't now. We weren't close, never needed to be. We shared a father, nothing more, and she resented my mother turning up after hers died. Only thing we had in common was the surname, well, that and a terrible taste in music.'

'You don't seem to have done too bad out of it,' Declan stated.

Ignoring the comment, Marna rose, walking over to the window, staring out.

'Look, I don't want to be a party pooper, but what's all this got to do with their deaths?' she asked. 'All of this is ancient history.'

'Where were you the night Nick Manford died?'

Marna looked back across the room.

'I still don't believe he's dead,' she said.

Declan nodded. 'Went missing, then?'

'Seventeenth of December, worst day of my life,' Marna replied. 'I wasn't there. It was the last of their gigs before the Christmas break, Nick was planning to drive back here after the Brighton concert. Instead, they found his car at six am the following day at a nearby beach. He drove there directly afterwards.'

'What if I told you he didn't?' Declan asked.

'I'd say you're as insane as all the other conspiracy theorists out there,' Marna retorted.

'We have a witness that states that Nick Manford was recording in West London directly after the gig,' Declan continued. 'He left there around three in the morning, and the car was found three hours later, on the south coast.'

Marna, for the first time, was silent.

'I'm guessing you didn't know,' Declan finished.

Anjli leaned in.

'We've heard that you and Andy are a couple now,' she said. 'When did this begin?'

'We'd—we'd always been close,' Marna replied, but gone was the calm demeanour. Now she was thrown off kilter. 'About five or six months after the disappearance, the constant press intrusion was too much for me, and Andy stepped in, my knight in shining armour.'

'And you've been together since?'

Marna nodded.

'Why have you never claimed that Nick was deceased?' Declan asked. 'Never pushed to have him made legally dead?'

'Because at the start we thought he was just being a dick,' Marna admitted. 'You know, taking a sabbatical, pissing off to Tibet and buggering around with the monks. But then after the years passed, he didn't appear.'

She slumped back into a Chesterfield.

'But I know he's still out there,' she said. 'He still takes his yearly fee.'

Anjli looked at Declan.

'What fee?'

'His bug-out bag,' Marna explained. 'He always talked about escaping, to find a way to just get away from it all. He set up an account in the Cayman Islands about five months before he disappeared, with fifty grand a year to be put in. He reckoned we could live easily in the Caymans on that, like some hippy beachcombers or something. But I wasn't interested in leaving and told him it was idiotic. Still, every year, that goes in.'

'You never stopped it?'

'Why would I? It was his money,' Marna leaned closer. 'And besides, I get a statement report every year. A week after it goes in, it's always removed.'

She sat back in her chair.

'Only Nick could remove it. This for me is proof positive that he's alive.'

'Yet you're moving ahead to have him claimed as deceased?' Anjli asked.

A shadow fell across Marna's face.

'Not by choice,' she replied. 'He's had over twenty years to sort his shit out. And now it's affecting *my* shit.'

'The back catalogue.'

'Yes,' Marna nodded. 'Over twenty million dollars on the table now. And I can't do anything until I have the rights.'

'And who gains that money?' Anjli continued. 'Hypothetically, when the papers are signed?'

'Well, a chunk is tied up in that bloody stupid *Secrets and Lies* deal, a good eight or nine million, but the rest goes to the band. Well, mainly Andy and Nick, as they wrote the songs, but Martin and Graham do well overall.'

'Would the money go to you on his death?' Declan asked. 'Or would they go to his heir?'

'Nick doesn't have any children,' Marna seemed convinced about this.

'What about Eden Storm?' Anjli added.

Marna laughed, as if expecting this.

'Tamara Rothstead was a crazy bitch, and it's never been proven,' she snapped.

Declan nodded at this.

So Eden's believed parentage was known.

Marna, however, just stared at Declan.

'It didn't surprise you when I said he might be alive,' she said.

Declan nodded, pulling out his phone, scrolling through the images.

'It's a line of enquiry,' he said, stopping at a particular one. 'And we'll need to know where you were both times of the murders. And if you recognise this man.'

He showed the image on the phone, the hooded man that left Lydia's house.

'We believe this was the killer of Lydia Cornwall.'

Swipe. Now he showed the image of the hooded man leaving *Eastcheap Albums.*

'And this is him leaving the murder scene of Dave Manford.'

Marna looked up in surprise.

'That's Nick,' she said. 'Or at least someone who looks bloody like him.'

Declan nodded. 'You sure you've had no contact?'

'None.'

'What about Benny Simpson?'

'That prick? We've not seen him since he retired.' She snorted. 'Rather jumped off the cliff before he was pushed, that is.'

Declan now showed the picture of the blood pendant.

'Do you recognise this?'

Marna paled.

'That's Nick's,' she said. 'It's our blood, in two halves, in a tube. I have one too, we did it in 1997.'

'Do you still have yours?' Anjli asked.

Marna nodded, pulling a necklace out from around her neck.

'I still wear it,' she said. 'Well, when I'm not with Andy. He's a little jealous.'

'Can we borrow it?' Declan enquired. 'We don't have any DNA of Nick and it could help with the enquiry.'

Marna unclasped the necklace, passing it over. Declan placed it into a clear plastic bag as Anjli listened for a moment.

'Can you hear that?' she interrupted. 'It's like a whine.'

Declan rose, hearing the incredibly faint, distant sound as well. Triangulating the sound, he walked to a side door in the library.

'That goes to the basement,' Marna replied. 'It's never opened, as nobody ever comes in here. All that's down there is Nick's forgotten old junk, in case he ever came back wanting it.'

Declan opened the door and stepped back in shock as an anxious and yelping greyhound came bursting through it. Marna raised up her hands in joy.

'You found my baby!' she cried as the dog jumped onto

her, frantically wagging its tail. 'Oh, you silly button, how did you get trapped down there?'

Declan looked at Anjli—Marna was no good to them anymore, and to be honest, he didn't think he was going to be getting anything else from her that day.

'We'll leave you together,' he said as Anjli joined him at the door. Marna didn't reply, snuggling with her dog.

'How do you misplace a dog in a cellar for two days?' Anjli asked as they walked out of the house, towards the street.

'Same way you misplace your husband for twenty years, I suppose,' Declan looked back at the house as they walked out of the gates. 'Am I the only one that finds it suspicious that she gets together with Andy, but can't stay with him because he's married, then six months after he's available Nick disappears, and six months after that they're together?'

'We're not here investigating Nick's death, though,' Anjli muttered. 'But yeah. She's guilty as hell of something.'

'I might be able to help you with that,' a voice spoke and, as they looked to the corner of the street, they saw Peter Suffolk standing there.

'I saw your car,' he said to Declan. 'I assumed you'd be coming here. So, I waited.'

'Not stalkerish at all,' Anjli replied.

Peter shrugged.

'Look, can we go somewhere else?' he requested. 'I don't want her looking out her window and seeing me talk to you.'

'Are we talking then?' Declan asked.

Peter smiled.

'Oh, I think we'll be doing a lot of talking,' he said.

18

NOTES IN THE MARGIN

BILLY CLOSED HIS EYES AND LEANED BACK, STRETCHING. ONE issue he had sitting in the office most of the day was that it played havoc with his posture.

One of the other problems he had was the boredom. Sure, he could control three or four things at once, and sometimes he had the power of God when he was connected to the ethernet, but the power that he wielded relied on other people.

People who weren't as productive as he was, and took longer to come back to him with his requests.

Today was one of those days; he was waiting for several requests to come back while also holding off filling out a requisition form before DC Davey sent him information on the device they were still investigating, and this meant he currently had half an hour of *nothing* time. It was too short to go out and grab some lunch, while at the same time it was thirty slow, boring minutes of dullness.

Looking at his desk, he stopped, however, as he found something he'd forgotten in yesterday's rush after Lydia

Cornwall's murder. A manilla envelope from Whitehall, with a USB drive in it. The copy he'd been promised of Karl Schnitter's message to his daughter.

Tearing it open, he let the drive slip to the tabletop as he rummaged through the drawers of his desk. They were under-desk filing cabinets, used purely for the space that each one gave, allowing him to keep various oversized items within them. And, pulling out a leather case, he opened it up, releasing the hidden away laptop to the office.

This was Billy's pride and joy, never turned on when a Wi-Fi connection was present, and set up in a literal Faraday cage, or in this case a cottage while on holiday in Scotland with no Wi-Fi, phone signal or even working consistent electricity, where he opened it up with his tools and physically removed anything that could compromise him. This laptop could not and *would* not be able to connect to the internet. Ever.

And that's what he wanted.

The term *air gapping* referred to a well-discussed hypothesis that there's a gap of air between the computer and other networks. If it isn't connected to them, it can't be attacked over the network, or through other, online means. An attacker would have to find a way across this *air gap* and physically sit down in front of the computer to compromise it.

Of course, there were ways to do this; Billy had seen Russian hackers show how they could gain information from hacking into the laptop's speakers, even the fan, making it change speed, using the audio from this, recorded nearby to turn into data. Often, a simple USB drive was all that was needed to corrupt it.

Billy stared at the USB drive on the desk as he booted the laptop up. He assumed that, of all the people who *wouldn't* be screwing around here with Malware, Whitehall's security service probably wasn't high on that list. That said, Trix, who had sent the USB, had a dozen other ways to get through the Unit's security if she wanted; Billy was still finding back doors she'd left to the network even all these months later.

He was seriously impressed.

And because of this, he didn't think there would be any issues placing the USB into the drive, as he closed his eyes, crossed his fingers and did so.

There was one file on the drive.

Liebchen.jpg

Liebchen. The German word for sweetheart, a term of endearment for a loved one. Which made sense, considering this was supposed to be a message to his daughter. Opening it up, Billy saw it was a letter, written by hand by Karl Schnitter, and directed to his daughter, Ilse Müller, currently held in a separate Women's Maximum Security Prison.

Once finished, the letter had been placed onto a table and this photo of it had been taken by someone, most likely a guard, ensuring that all four corners of the page had been included in the frame. The text was sprawling and half of it was unreadable. Even if he could have made it out, Billy wouldn't have been able to work out what was said, as he couldn't speak much German.

That said, he knew the text of the letter would have been sent to a dozen linguistics experts, and an equally sizeable amount of cypher gurus by now. *Was Karl leaving a note in the text? Was there a code there, instructions that nobody else could find?*

Billy leaned back as he stared at the image. The problem

was that Karl would only have been able to write the note while being watched, and he would have known that it would have been looked over by experts.

But, at the same time, he didn't send the note.

He sent a *photo* of the note.

And Billy knew what could be done with a photo. It was easy, and barely anyone ever looked.

Closing the photo, Billy opened a notes application on the laptop, clicking and pulling the image into it. No longer able to show the image while in a text-based application, instead, the photo was broken up by the program into a mixture of text and ascii characters scrolling down his screen.

Moving through it, his eyes followed down the random symbols and glyphs.

What he was looking for was a skill called *steganography*, the art of encoding messages and hiding them in plain view; in this case, the basic building blocks of the image, unseen by anyone unless they hacked into the actual source code.

The lines were filled with garbage for most of it, but the last line caught his eye.

135165ÿ·,BExifΔ¿Δ¿AVengEΔ¿me¿
51.577665492248464,ÿ0.024399135165608734

Billy copied the final part of the line, placing it into another open page on the text app, this time adding spaces and removing some random symbols, clearing the message up.

AVENGE ME 51.577665492248464,
0.024399135165608734

Latitude and longitude directions for a location and a command.

And, when Billy placed the coordinates in, he found it aimed at a nondescript business park in the middle of nowhere, an hour or so out of London.

The kind of place that a black ops site could be.

Quickly, he picked up his phone, sending a text.

You need to check the steganography of the image

A moment later, a message from Trix.

I know, we saw it. Moving package this week.

And then, a rather reluctant

Nice catch

Billy grinned as he closed the laptop, removing the USB drive. He'd not only cracked a code, but he'd also learnt the location of a top-secret site, although the chances were that this was already being dismantled, especially if Karl knew where it was.

Bullman emerged from her office and, seeing him at his station, walked over, a gatefold vinyl album copy of *Secrets and Lies* in her hand.

'Look at this,' she said, opening the album. In the inside Billy saw the lyrics of the songs printed out, as well as a column of text that included all the small-print of the back matter; locations, printers, instruments used, all of that. And, on the bottom right was a small box, with text in it.

Shareholders
BB / GH / AK / DM / NM
AM / CN / MR / BS / LV / SW

'See this?' Bullman pointed at the box. 'This isn't on any other copies I've seen. This album is a first pressing. I bought it the day it came out. When the CD was released, it was missing.'

'It looks like the initials of everyone involved in the making of the album, in alphabetical order,' Billy nodded, already typing up the names. 'BB is Bruce Baker, the guitarist that Mears replaced during the recording. Then we have Graham Hagen, Dave Manford, Nick Manford, Andy Mears, CN must be Clive Newton the producer, Martin Reilly and Benny Simpson are next, LV I'm guessing is Lydia Valkenburg—'

He looked up, confused.

'I'm not getting who AK and SW are, though?'

Bullman shrugged.

'Probably the studio techs. Although it'd have been a whole lot better if we had their actual names...'

'But why add Lydia to this?' he asked. 'According to Peter Suffolk, she was nothing more than a groupie back then, and we have her as Dave's girlfriend, gaslighting teenagers during the recording.'

'Maybe threatening the girls was enough to get her on the list,' Bullman shrugged. 'Or she sang backing vocals? But it explains how she could keep the apartment, I reckon there's been a sizeable album royalty over the years. But that's not all I was going to show you.'

Bullman had already brought out a CD of the album,

placing it on the desk. Billy opened it up, looking for the same piece of the backwater that the list was on.

'That's interesting,' he said. 'It's not there. Instead, there's a credits list. And look here—' he held up the case, showing it to Bullman. '*Brass section by Miles Walters. Backup vocals on No Cares To Give, Michelle Wylde.* Why aren't either of these on the list?'

'Maybe they weren't there when the decision was made to give shares?' Bullman suggested. 'Although if that was the case, it means we're now looking at a particular moment, possibly during the recording when there was a decision made to do this, whereas the legend of the album always stated that Nick offered the shares before they started.'

Billy leaned back.

'Something happened at a particular point, and Nick gave everyone there a share in the album,' he muttered. 'Does that mean he was buying their silence?'

'If you believe Ronald Brookfield, it's probably connected to the disappearance of Lorraine Warner,' Bullman suggested. 'So, who's left alive on that list?'

Billy looked at the list once more.

'Lydia Valkenburg is Lydia Cornwall now, so she's dead,' he said. 'Bruce Baker died in a car accident, Dave Manford was electrocuted, Nick Manford is missing, believed to have committed suicide—'

'Or he's the killer,' Bullman mused. 'Christ, I hope he's not the killer, that would really piss me off.'

'Clive Newton, the producer, died of cancer years ago,' Billy was pulling up a forum screen. 'And on this group page, someone claimed that Shaun Williams was the electrician for the studio at the time, So he has to be the SW mentioned here. He died of a severe electric shock when he shorted a whole power grid back in 1989.'

'Like Dave Manford?'

'No, this was definitely an accident,' Billy read from the notes. 'He was wiring up a school Christmas lights spectacular, and, well, blew himself up in the process.'

'So not that great an electrician then?' Bullman muttered. 'Way to go out like your nickname, though.'

'He was super unlucky, too,' Billy added. 'The money from the album deal was only just starting to appear then, too. A year later, he wouldn't have been doing this.'

He looked up at Bullman.

'That's six. And that also leaves Benny Simpson, who seems to be drooling in an old people's home or sprightly and taking photos depending on who you talk to. Then there's Andy Mears, Graham Hagen and Martin Reilly, all current band members and someone called Peanut, who's not on any lists I've found so far. And *Bear Studios* was completely analogue in '86, so if Peanut was named, it'll be in a book, somewhere deep in a box rather than online.'

'Surely Peanut must have given their name at some point, though,' Bullman said, running a hand through her white hair. 'I can't see solicitors sending royalty cheques to someone's initials only.'

'We can't get the details,' Billy replied. 'Unless there's due cause and that'll take weeks.'

He brought up a document on the screen.

'I've been talking to the solicitors that covered the deal and they claim it's covered by solicitor-client privilege up to the sky, so won't give us anything.'

'Who are the solicitors?' Bullman asked. 'We're in the

Inns of Court. Maybe one of the barristers we know here can help?'

Billy nodded, typing on the screen.

'*Sutherland and Abnett,*' he said. 'They're—'

'I know them,' Bullman leaned over Billy, typing on the screen. An image of Carrie Woodstock, the blonde, bespectacled solicitor for Peter Suffolk, appeared.

'Miss Woodstock here is one of their partners,' she said. 'I'm assuming they've been *Alternator's* legal team since the EMI days.'

Billy was typing again, searching the *Sutherland and Abnett* website.

'EMI aren't clients anymore if so,' he said, pointing at a logo. 'But we recognise this one.'

The logo of *Klaude-Rothstead Pharmaceuticals* appeared on the screen, with text explaining that *Sutherland and Abnett* had been the go-to solicitor for them for over forty years.

'They would have been the family solicitors when Tamara Rothstead was a wild child,' Billy scratched at the back of his neck nervously.

'Which means that Tamara most likely provided the legal team for the contract, if they're the name on it,' Bullman leaned back against the table. 'That's too convenient. We need to know what happened that night.'

'And that's where we hit the wall, because no one is talking,' Billy complained. 'I'd probably have more chance going through the antiquated system at *Bear Studios*—'

His face brightened.

'I *could* go through the antiquated system at *Bear Studios!*' he exclaimed. 'I bet they're locked away in a computer somewhere.'

Bullman smiled. She knew Billy had an almost pathological love of retro computers, so the thought of hunting through floppy disks, while her idea of hell, was pretty much a holiday for him. 'I'd have to—'

'I could get a copy of Nick Manford's unreleased album for you, Ma'am,' Billy added, sweetening the pot.

'Go on, piss off,' Bullman said. 'But if we need you, you're back immediately. Have you finished with that video?'

Billy stopped, already rising.

'I hadn't started it yet,' he admitted. He'd intended to work through the video of Peter Suffolk watching the funeral, but it'd fallen off his list.

'Can anyone else do it?' Bullman asked.

Billy nodded.

'Then I'll get De'Geer to go through it when he returns,' she continued. 'Go on with you, we'll call when you're required back at base.'

'I don't think you'll need me,' Billy grinned.

'I don't know,' Bullman was already walking back to her office, vinyl album in hand. 'Monroe doesn't even know how to save an email attachment, so I reckon you'll be back by six.'

19

HAMPSTEAD INCIDENT

DECLAN STARED AROUND THE OUTSIDE TABLES OF THE *Spaniard's Inn* with a mild sense of foreboding.

'You know, when Monroe sees our expense accounts for this case, all he's going to see is pub lunches,' he bemoaned, looking back at Peter Suffolk, now drinking a pint of lime and soda with ice. 'So what were you doing outside Marna's house?'

'I live in the area,' Peter replied. 'But you know that because you've seen my house.'

'It's not exactly next door, though, is it?' Anjli added.

Peter shrugged.

'Look, I knew you'd be here to see her next,' he admitted. 'I wanted to catch you before you left.'

'Why?' Declan leaned back, observing Peter.

'Because your boss made a valid point earlier,' Peter replied. 'I'm just a touring singer for them. Me and Chris? We're not part of the club. If the back catalogue sale goes through, and it's likely to, they'll all make millions while I won't make a thing.'

He sipped at his drink.

'In addition, what your boss said made me call my touring manager. He's not connected to the band, just my cruise liner stuff. And he said that sometimes, when a back catalogue is sold, the band then needs to licence their own songs back for tours, which costs a ton of money. Which means touring becomes a lot more expensive, for a group of people who now don't need it. And the 'best of' album with me on vocals we were discussing, well that's likely off the table.'

'So it's losing money that brings you here.'

'No, it's more than that,' Peter continued. 'Look, this morning I was pulled out of bed and effectively charged with murder. I was innocent, but I knew the moment I was dumped in that upstairs cell that if this came out, innocent or not, they'd cut ties with me immediately. I'm expendable. And more importantly, if they're all *Hunger Games*-ing each other, I'm not going to prison for something they're doing.'

'Sounds like your loyalty's wavering,' Anjli suggested.

'It's not,' Peter argued. 'I'm still loyal. It's just that some really odd shit is going down, and with Lydia and Dave now dead, this is a little more real, and I don't want to be in the middle of it.'

He leaned closer.

'Look, I joined the group fifteen years after *Secrets and Lies* came out. Ten years after Benny Simpson left and over twenty since Nick disappeared. The *Alternator* I've worked for isn't the one from back then. Now it's run by Andy and Marna as a money-making machine, and it's purely a tribute act, touring theatres and smaller gig venues, milking the nostalgia vibe. Martin and Graham have their own little clique, they were around at the start and they resent Andy becoming de facto boss, so they only get involved in things when it affects them financially. I was brought in effectively as an employee, and I'm the same as Chris, who was brought in as bass player when they kicked out Dave. We turn up, earn our money and piss off.'

Realising he'd been ranting a little, Peter shrugged.

'I've no skin in the game, and everything to lose,' he said. 'So let me be your inside man. Let me root about and find what you need to solve this case. Because the quicker it gets sorted, the quicker we can all move on. And I'll have a better idea of whether I need to find a new band to front soon.'

'You said that really odd shit is going down,' Anjli asked. 'What did you mean by that?'

Peter shrugged. 'You tell me,' he said. 'That pap outside, the one I gave fifty pounds to, him turning out to be the old manager? Andy going on nostalgic visits to his old recording studio? Marna getting more drunk than usual?'

'How did you know she was drunk?'

'She called me an hour ago, after hearing I'd been taken by the police,' Peter muttered. 'Not to check if I was okay, but to tell them she needed some uniforms to come and find her missing dog. And I could only work out half the words, as she was slurring.'

Peter looked at the grass.

'I hoped that bloody dog was gone for good.'

'Not a fan of the greyhound?'

Peter shook his head. 'It hates me,' he said. 'Whenever I visit, it keeps barking mentally and going for me. Probably smells my cats. Look, if you need me? I'm around.'

'If you can get us a conversation with Martin and Graham, that'd be appreciated,' Declan replied. 'We can't seem to find them.'

'They went into hiding together the moment Dave died,' Peter nodded. 'They knew it'd be a press feeding frenzy. I'll see what I can do. I think one of them has a caravan somewhere. Near Chertsey, I believe.'

He started going through his phone, eventually finding a contact.

'Here, take this,' he said, showing it to Declan. 'This is Martin's number. Maybe you can do your cyber thing and work out where he is from the signal?'

Declan nodded, sending the phone number to Billy's phone.

'That might be enough,' he smiled. 'Thank you.'

'Anything that stops me from being arrested again,' Peter grinned.

'Do you think Nick's alive?' Anjli asked, as Declan had a beep on his phone. As he read the text, Peter rose from his chair.

'Honestly? I don't care,' he said. 'As long as he doesn't want his job back, I'm cool. And I'm sorry, but I have to run. I have a voiceover gig I need to get to.'

Declan looked up from his phone.

'Let us know if you find anything,' he said. 'About where Martin and Graham are.'

'Will do,' Peter gave a mock salute. 'I'll keep you in the loop.'

And with that, finishing his drink, Peter Suffolk nodded to the two detectives and left.

'You think he's on the level?' Anjli wondered as she watched him leave.

'Christ, no,' Declan replied, leaning back in his seat. 'He's as dodgy as the rest of them. He's got a secret he's hiding and we need to work out what it is. Also, what his connection to Benny is.'

'I thought he stated he mistook Benny for a photographer?'

Declan nodded. 'Yeah, he's stuck to that story, but it changed today.'

He flicked through his notebook.

'Today, he said he gave the photographer fifty quid to lose the photos. When he spoke to me before, it was twenty.'

'So he got confused?'

Declan looked at Anjli.

'If you lent me fifty pounds, right now, are you saying that two days from now you'd get that confused?'

Anjli shook her head. 'I suppose not. So what, he was lying?'

'It's easier to get the numbers wrong when they don't really exist,' Declan mused. 'One thing's for sure. Peter Suffolk was telling the truth about his financial future, as none of this incoming money will go to him.'

He closed his notebook, rising from the chair.

'But Peter has his own agenda here, and the sooner we work it out the better.'

'What was the message?' Anjli asked.

'Davey, doing follow-ups in Lydia's apartment,' Declan replied. 'Apparently they found traces of SD Alcohol 35-A and latex in the bathroom sink.'

'I don't know what *SD whatever* is.'

'Neither does she, yet,' Declan shrugged. 'But by the time we get back, I'm sure she will.'

He stopped as his phone beeped again. As he looked at it, Anjli smiled.

'She worked it out already?'

'No,' Declan still held the phone but wasn't looking at it now as he walked out into the pub car park.

'Take the car back to the station,' he said, glad that they'd taken Anjli's car to the interview. 'I'll catch the tube back. I have something to do.'

'Anything I can help with?'

'No, it's all good,' Declan smiled, hoping Anjli wouldn't see it was fake. 'Karl stuff.'

'Ah, Whitehall,' Anjli nodded, walking off towards her car. 'Good luck with that one. I'll see you back at base.'

Now left alone, Declan stared at the message. It was from an unknown number, but the message itself gave away everything he needed to work it out.

We need to meet. Now. End this once and for all. Alone, no cops, no subordinates. Say yes and I'll send a public location. FP

Francine Pearce wanted to meet.

Declan replied to the message with a *yes* and waited. A moment later, the phone beeped again and another message, obviously primed and ready, appeared with an address in East London.

It'd take about half an hour to get there, but Declan was okay with that.

Finally, he could put the past to rest.

Permanently.

'WELCOME BACK TO *PETER MORRIS IN THE PM*,' THE TITULAR Peter Morris of the show leaned back onto his armchair, his notes held in his hand as he smiled into the camera, casual in a pastel shirt and black trousers, the sleeves down and secured at the end with gold cufflinks, his hair a greying black and combed into a stylish side parting. 'We're here today to discuss the untimely death of ex-*Alternator* founder Dave Manford, with guitarist Andy Mears.'

Andy, sitting on the couch facing Peter Morris kept his face as sombre as he could, while silently loathing the fact that publicly he was still classed as the *guitarist*.

Alternator would have been bloody well dead without me.

'A terrible time,' Andy said, realising that everyone had been waiting for him to speak. 'I mean, we hadn't really spoken for years, but he was and always will be part of the *Alternator* family.'

'A family that still has a missing person in the form of Nick Manford,' Morris continued. 'Do you think he still lives?'

'Well, I hope he does,' Andy replied carefully. 'But with that, he's had years to contact us. I hope that wherever he is, alive or dead, he's at peace.'

It was a line he'd used many times in the past, an autopilot of an answer, and quietly, Andy kicked himself. He knew that Peter Morris would pick up on that.

'If that's the case, why push to declare him dead?'

Andy forced a smile.

'I'm not doing anything of the sort,' he replied. 'However Marna, his wife also needs to move on, and I believe this has been part of the healing process.'

'And the back catalogue you'll be able to sell for tens of millions will also be part of the healing process?' Peter Morris smiled back, and his was as fake as Andy's.

'You'd have to ask Mrs Manford,' Andy said, while his eyes screamed *you utter prick Morris.*

Peter nodded, looking back at the camera.

'On a happier note I understand that you are to tour again?'

'It's being planned at the moment,' Andy lied. If the back catalogue deal came through, he'd make sure he never had to see Martin or Graham ever again. But, if it didn't, they had to do something. 'And we're all just itching to get back out there, see our fans again.'

'Something I've always wondered,' Peter Morris looked back at Andy. 'How do you keep healthy while on tour? I mean, I only talk here, but I can often lose my voice. How do you ensure you keep yours?'

'Well, it's more my fingers I need to worry about,' Andy corrected. 'As you said, I'm the guitarist.'

'Yes, but you sing too, right?' Morris was pressing on something, and Andy couldn't work out what it was. 'A little birdy told us you use a straw?'

'Oh, yes, you mean the *straw technique*,' Andy smiled, a genuine one now, relieved that the interview was heading towards the more insipid type of television fare that he was used to. 'You force air back into your throat and reboot it, effectively.'

'That sounds confusing,' Peter smiled at the audience, who tittered at this. 'We have a straw here, could you—'

Andy looked at the offered straw; it was tiny, one of those juice box straws. There was no way he could do anything with that.

'Actually, I have one of my own,' he said, reaching into his pocket.

'You carry your own straw?' again, bloody Peter Morris gurned for the cheap seats. Andy was getting irritated.

'Of course,' he snapped, pulling out a black velvet pouch.

'I use it everywhere. Germs, you see.'

'Of course,' Peter nodded and was about to reply, but stopped as there was an audible gasp from the audience. Andy stared at the stainless steel straw in his hand, now pulled out of the velvet pouch—

And with the end covered in blood.

'I—' Andy looked around the studio. The Floor Manager was talking into a headset, the audience was muttering amongst themselves, and Peter Morris was staring at Andy as if he was a killer.

'I think this might be bean juice or something,' Andy joked.

'Sure,' Peter Morris said quietly. '*Human bean* juice.' He looked back at the camera.

'We'll be back after this break,' he said and, as the cameraman counted them out, he stood up, backing out of his armchair.

'Call the police,' he said. Andy rose, irritated.

'You shit!' he exclaimed. 'Someone set me up! You were told to ask that question, knowing I had this—'

A burly hand appeared on his shoulder and one of the security guards stood over him.

'You can stay with us in the green room,' the guard said. 'We'll wait for the police together.'

Confused, scared and with a bloodstained metal straw in his hand, Andy followed the security guards, of which there were many now, out of the studio while in the seats, the audience took photos, uploading them to social media.

Andy Mears was no longer just 'the guitarist' of *Alternator*. Now he was *news*.

20

MY GENERATION

THE STEADFAST NURSING HOME IN SURREY WAS SEVEN MILES south of Guildford, and although it looked close, Monroe and De'Geer had learnt after two hours of driving in one of the Temple Inn squad cars, on a journey which included the M4, the M25 and the A3, that distances were deceptive. Monroe had wanted on several occasions to get De'Geer to turn on the blues and twos and burst through the standing traffic, but his better side stopped him.

The home itself was a large red-bricked mansion a small distance off a minor A-road, a wrought-iron fence barring any passing visitors without an appointment. There was a house to the side, and an elderly man in a Barbour coat had emerged, opening the gate and waving them through the moment he saw the squad car. He didn't even ask to see identification, and Monroe wondered how often police cars, or rather ambulances, arrived unannounced at the gates.

'Records of the Steadfast estate go back to Norman times, but this was built in the late nineteenth century,' De'Geer explained as they drove along the long driveway towards the nursing home. 'There's just under fifty acres, and it's been a care home since just after the war.'

'How have you learnt all this while driving the car?' Monroe asked, genuinely impressed. De'Geer shrugged.

'Wikipedia, before we left,' he replied. 'I didn't think it was worth mentioning until now.' He pulled up outside the main entrance of the building. It was three storeys high, with the top floor built into the roof, with ivy climbing up the right-hand side of the front-facing wall. To the right of the building were newer houses, a terraced row of such.

'There's space for fifty residents here,' De'Geer continued.

'And somewhere inside is Benny Simpson,' Monroe replied as he clambered out of the squad car. A woman in a tweed jacket anxiously emerged from a set of double doors, wringing her hands together as she approached. She was well built, and Monroe thought from her looks, she'd be awesome on a women's rugby team.

'We didn't call for the police,' she said anxiously, looking around. 'Is there something we should know?'

'Not at all,' Monroe smiled, showing his warrant card. 'I'm DCI Monroe, this is PC De'Geer. We're here to speak to Bernard Simpson, one of your inmates.'

At this, the woman's face darkened.

'They're not inmates,' she said coldly.

Monroe raised an apologetic hand.

'Sorry,' he smiled. 'Residents.'

'He's in the back garden,' the woman started leading the two visitors through the main reception, a white-painted stately home entrance, which gave Monroe powerful memories of the school he went to while in Glasgow. It, too, had been built in what was once a stately home.

'How much does it cost to live here?' De'Geer asked politely, making conversation.

The woman looked at him with the gaze of a person very much aware that this was a question where the answer was way out of the asker's league.

'A 'licence to occupy' for one of our apartments costs just over four hundred thousand pounds,' she sniffed. 'That might sound a lot, but it is below the average cost of a two-bedroom apartment in the local area. And the amount is refundable to the licence holder, or their estate, once they sell it on to the next occupant.'

'Why would it be sold—' De'Geer stopped himself. '—Oh.'

'So you buy a place here,' Monroe joined in now as they emerged onto a back patio. 'That doesn't include dinners and all that, right?'

'No,' the woman replied. 'We also charge a support package each month of three thousand. This covers laundry, ironing, lunch and dinner, pretty much everything except for council tax.'

She looked at De'Geer.

'In total, that would be just shy of forty thousand a year, after purchase of the apartment,' she said. 'Should we put you on the waiting list?'

De'Geer shook his head.

'Although I might afford that when I'm old enough, if I start saving right now.'

'Is there a particular reason for your visit?' she asked. 'Is Bernard in trouble?'

'Just need to ask some questions,' Monroe avoided answering fully.

'There,' the woman, realising that she wasn't getting

anything else from this conversation, pointed at a man in a wheelchair to the left of the gardens. 'That's Mister Simpson.'

And before Monroe could ask anything else, the woman and her tweed jacket were gone.

Walking across the well-manicured lawn, Monroe approached the man in the wheelchair. He was old, in his seventies, but slim with it. His hair was almost gone, and the remnants were white, cut short with what looked like a razor. He was clean shaven and wore chunky black glasses on his face, wearing a blazer, shirt, and jeans, and his eyes were shut as he took in the sun.

'Mister Simpson?' Monroe asked gently, placing a hand on the elderly man's arm to wake him. 'Are you awake?'

Benny Simpson opened his eyes slowly, peering at Monroe with distrust.

'Are you taking me to dinner?' he asked, looking over at PC De'Geer. 'Are you?'

'No, Mister Simpson, I'm DCI Alex Monroe,' Monroe continued patiently. 'And this is—'

'I like the lunch menu more than the dinner one,' Benny said to De'Geer. 'See if you can get me that.'

Monroe watched Benny for a moment.

'Mister Simpson,' he said softly, his voice emotionless. 'I have met many people with various levels of dementia over my life in the police force. And even they, when seeing a seven foot bloody Viking in full, fluorescent police uniform don't confuse him for a bloody orderly.'

He leaned in.

'We have a witness who states he saw you in an alley in the City two nights ago, and we have CCTV that paints a pretty damning picture of you, standing up and talking quite coherently to Peter Suffolk. So how about you cut the shit, and we have a wee chat?'

Benny Simpson's eyes narrowed.

'Wheel me behind that hedge,' he muttered. 'We can chat there.'

'There we go,' Monroe smiled. 'Look at you. Talking coherently. It's a bloody miracle.'

With a smile, De'Geer took the handles of Benny Simpson's wheelchair and moved it out of view.

'Prick,' Benny muttered as he did so. 'I was so convinced I'd avoided the cameras, too.'

'You did,' Monroe smiled. 'I lied.'

'I could report you for that,' Benny muttered. Monroe shrugged.

'Who'd believe you?' he asked. 'You have dementia.'

Benny accepted this and, once the large bush blocked anyone's view, he reached into his pocket and pulled out a thin cigar, clipping off the end and lighting it.

'We're not supposed to smoke,' he said. 'But we all do.'

'Why the act?' Monroe asked. 'Surely there are better ways to be a recluse?'

'Staying alive,' Benny replied, sighing with delight as he took in a lungful of cigar smoke. 'Nicaraguan. Much better than that Cuban shite. Only became popular because Kennedy shit the bed and banned them.'

'Is someone trying to kill you?' De'Geer asked.

'Probably,' Benny grinned. 'But while I'm *dear demented daddy,* they leave me the hell alone.'

Now, finally able to be himself, he squeezed De'Geer's arm.

'Oh, I thought it was padding,' he said, leaning back and impressed. 'Very nice.'

De'Geer glanced at Monroe for help, and the DCI leaned back in, regaining Benny's attention.

'You were backstage at a crime scene two days ago,' he said. 'Why?'

'I wasn't backstage, I was at the back door,' Benny responded indignantly. 'I was waiting for the end of the show, so I could speak to Dave. I didn't know he was dead until I spoke to Peter.'

'Peter Suffolk told you he was dead?' Monroe frowned. 'He said he left before it happened.'

'Oh, most likely, but this was later, after the police arrived,' Benny waved the cigar around. 'We all had to stay where we were and Peter appeared like the bloody Christmas fairy.'

'We understand you took a photo of him,' De'Geer stated, but Benny just frowned.

'Why the hell would I want a photo of that soapy tit?' he asked. 'I was there for Lydia and Dave. Not the replacements.'

'Can I ask why you wanted to speak to them?'

Benny nodded.

'You can, but I'm not saying.'

'Was it by chance about the upcoming back catalogue deal and the *Secrets and Lies* sub clause?' Monroe smiled. 'I'm guessing those royalties have kept you happy here for seven years or so. You don't have to do the act all the time, do you?'

'God no, just when there are visitors,' Benny smiled. 'I pay a little extra for the alerts. I'd been waiting for a visit, either from you or others since Dave died, so I've been in the chair just in case.'

'Others?'

'The people Andy or Marna might send,' Benny's tone

grew colder. 'Checking in on granddad, making sure he's still too loopy to talk.'

'Talk about what?' Monroe asked.

Benny stayed quiet.

'Look, Mister Simpson, if you're here because you're in fear for your life, we can help,' Monroe said.

Benny just laughed; a short, barking sound.

'You can defend me against the dead?' he asked. 'Good luck.'

Monroe stopped at this, standing straight.

'You mean Nick.'

'He walked past me,' Benny whispered. 'The night of the gig. Hood up, but I saw the glasses, saw the beard, recognised his battered old hoodie. Bugger wore it all the time.'

'Hoodies can be bought.'

'Not this one,' Benny shook his head. 'Bloody thing was moth eaten, with a cigarette burn on the left elbow. I was there when he did that, back in 1993. This hoodie was his, believe me.'

'Was he wearing it when he died?' De'Geer enquired. Benny shook his head.

'No, and that's the odd thing,' he replied. 'He didn't take it on tour that year. So he had to either have it elsewhere, or he picked it up when he disappeared.'

'You don't think he was dead.'

Benny shivered. 'I did until that night,' he said. 'He didn't look at me, or maybe I'd be joining Dave.'

'Why would Nick kill his brother?' De'Geer now asked.

'It's not as if they were close,' Benny replied. 'And they hadn't been on friendly terms for years.'

'Since *Bear Studios?*' Monroe was fishing now.

Benny leaned back in his wheelchair, staring at the sky.

'Tell me what you know,' he said. 'That way I don't incriminate myself even more.'

'We know that something happened at *Bear Studios* in July 1986, while you were recording *Secrets and Lies*,' Monroe started. 'Something that ended with a list of people gaining shares in all profits of the album, and something that we believe is tied to the disappearance of Lorraine Warner, a barmaid at *The Bear* pub.'

'We also know that around this time Nick Manford had a sexual relationship with Tamara Rothstead, and that the alleged son, now known as Eden Storm, claims to be Nick's,' De'Geer added.

'And we know that on the night that Nick Manford supposedly drove from his Brighton concert with *Alternator* in December 1998, instead of driving straight to some beach and drowning himself, he instead drove straight back to *Bear Studios,* where he'd been working on new solo material, leaving at three that morning and then returning to Birling Gap, where his car was found several hours later. But unlike the others, you knew that piece already, didn't you?'

Benny looked at the grass.

'I knew he was recording the album, because we'd talked about it,' he said. 'Nick was unhappy for a while, he knew Marna and Andy were shagging behind his back, he'd been sent photos of eleven-year-old Eden, Tamara had died and it weighed heavy. The Randalls had put a hit on him and he was seeing killers at every corner.'

'The Randalls?'

'Pikey pricks he used to have dealings with a decade earlier. It turned sour,' Benny explained. 'He was out of rehab but everyone else was still using, he was having a guilt trip about *Secrets and Lies,* probably connected to the Randalls as he was buying from them at the time, he'd somehow picked up a gun, although Dave probably sourced that like everything else, and he wanted out.'

'You mentioned a guilt trip,' Monroe said. 'What happened that night?'

'What makes you think any—'

'*Lorraine Warner died!*' Monroe slammed his palm onto the handrail of the wheelchair. 'She died over thirty years ago and nobody's come forward. And I think it happened in *Bear Studios*, during the recording, and you paid off everyone there!'

Regaining his composure, Monroe walked away from the suddenly terrified ex-manager in the wheelchair.

'Tell us here or tell us in the interview room,' he said. 'But only one of these options keeps your secret, because believe me, if we take you in? We're doing it publicly. And if you've seen our previous cases in the news, you'll know that the Temple Inn Command Unit is *shite* at keeping secrets when they're on our doorstep.'

Benny visibly slumped.

'I wasn't there,' he mumbled. 'I turned up the following morning. It was Friday, and I was checking in. The atmosphere was off, and I knew something was wrong.'

'And?' Monroe pulled out his notebook.

Benny nodded, as if deciding.

'You want the full story? Fine. I'll tell you what I know,' he muttered. 'But you might want to sit down, because it's long and not for the fainthearted.'

And with that, the onetime manager of *Alternator* talked about a night in West London thirty-five years earlier.

21

GUNS DON'T KILL PEOPLE, RAPPERS DO

'THEY WERE SPIRALLING OUT OF CONTROL,' BENNY SAID, sitting back in his wheelchair and looking at Monroe and De'Geer as if he was a storyteller and they were his willing audience. 'EMI were talking about paying a kill fee and ending the contract with *Alternator* altogether.'

He looked around the gardens.

'I was the manager, but I wasn't able to manage,' Benny explained. 'Nick was the leader and because of his drug habit, he wasn't able to lead. And so we took whatever we could get.'

'Andy's offer of *Bear Studios*.'

Benny nodded.

'He knew the band from the rock scene, and the studios were new and needed custom,' he said. 'It seemed like the stars were aligning.'

'And the studios were happy with the shared profits rather than a fee?' De'Geer asked. However, at this Benny just laughed.

'That's the press talking,' he said. 'The story the civilians were given. We paid *Bear Studios* a fair price for what we had. There was no deal even on the table at that point.'

'EMI paid?'

'EMI were happy that there was a possibility of an album turning up,' Benny replied. 'They gave us a blank cheque. And that was the problem, because Nick had a lot of ways to spend a blank cheque. But at the same time, he was creating. They'd spend all night getting pissed up in that local pub, stagger across the road to the studios, record whatever the hell they'd worked out and then pass out. Every Friday I'd turn up, pay the bills and then leave them for another week.'

'So what happened *this* particular week?' Monroe asked.

Benny shook his head.

'Everything bad you can think of,' he said, and his body language was shifting into that of a man who really didn't want to be talking. 'Look, remember all I'm saying here is based on second-hand information. I arrived on the Friday, finding the studios in disarray. I mean, I'd seen this a couple of weeks earlier when Bruce Baker had stormed out of the band right after they first arrived there. They'd had a fight, there was some property damage, but we'd sorted that out with some petty cash. But after that, they were still fired up, bitching at each other, hot-headed... This time, they were sullen. Lost. Nobody was talking, but over the weekend I could piece together what happened.'

He stopped.

'Go on,' Monroe urged, but Benny shook his head.

'There were NDAs,' he said. 'If it comes out that I told you any of this, I lose the lot.'

He looked around the gardens.

'I have to pay back everything.'

Monroe considered this.

'I get that,' he said. 'Let's see if we can guess a little of it. That way, if it's what you *can't* say, you haven't told us.'

Monroe rose, walking around the wheelchair as he spoke.

'Nick and the band are drinking in *The Bear*,' he started. 'Maybe the engineers, maybe the producer, but there's a good session going on. At some point, in the early hours of the morning, they all go back to the studio. However, they bring with them the barmaid, Lorraine Warner, now off shift.'

'Go on,' Benny replied.

'They carry on partying, but something happens. Maybe Lorraine overdoses. Maybe there's an accident. Either way, she dies. Everyone there is shocked, and also incredibly wasted. Someone decides that they need to do something about it. The body is removed. The next day, everyone pretends that life goes on. However, it doesn't, as now there's half a dozen people who are all accessories to something terrible. Accidental death. Maybe manslaughter. Murder, who knows. And then you turn up. You learn of this. And, as a manager, you manage. You come up with a plan that the album will be equally shared amongst everyone involved there that night, on the condition that if anyone talks, they'll lose everything. You literally buy their silence with a piece of the album sales. Which, to be honest, I can't explain how that would ever work, because in the best possible way, you were nobodies back then.'

'Nick made a guarantee that if the album didn't go platinum, he'd pay them all a substantial fee out of his own money.'

'And how was he going to find that?'

'Tamara Rothstead. But then the album went multi-platinum, so he never needed to,' Benny replied softly. 'It made millions upon millions. And everyone gained their percentages. And sure, you might feel bad, but then *poof!* Another big cheque in the mail. And then another. And then you realise you've spent over a million quid. And you realise that if you ever told people about what happened, then the lawyers would not only discredit your word in court, but you'd also be forced to pay back everything you made. And you don't have it anymore.'

'So now, you have a group of people who want to talk about it but can't, and who get bonuses for their silences,' De'Geer continued. 'It's ingenious, to be honest. You could have kept this up forever. But why was Tamara Rothstead involved?'

Benny didn't answer, looking away.

'So what happened to Lorraine's body?' Monroe asked.

'And who killed her?' De'Geer added.

Benny shook his head.

'I don't know,' he replied.

Monroe spun to face him, furious.

'What do you mean, you *don't know?*' he snapped. 'How do you lose a bloody dead woman?'

'I told you, I wasn't there!' Benny angrily stood up now, past caring if anyone saw him. 'I came in the next day! All I had was second-hand comments! Half the people there thought it was a mass hallucination, that she was playing a trick on them after Martin and Graham hurt her friends earlier that week!'

'Hurt her friends?' Monroe interrupted, his expression cold. 'Don't you mean *raped?*'

'It was never proven, the girls never came forward, and it was classed as sorted when the local lads beat the shit out of Reilly and Hagen two nights later,' Benny protested. 'All I know is that within a few hours there was no corpse to be found, and nobody remembered if it had even been there! People assumed she hadn't died and had just walked off! The whole album profit deal was purely a band aid to keep them quiet until she turned up!'

'So she wasn't dead?' De'Geer asked.

Benny slumped back into the wheelchair.

'Only Nick knew the truth,' he said. 'He was the most coherent at the time, probably because he had such a resistance to drugs. He told me, years later he believed Lorraine was taken by Tamara.'

'Tamara Rothstead was there that night?' this surprised Monroe. 'Is this why he thought she'd cover any debts? Who else was there?'

'Bruce,' Benny admitted. 'He'd returned with Tamara. Seems that this was part of the reason they all fell out earlier, as Bruce had known Tamara's family for years and felt that Nick had been screwing her around. Which, in fairness, he had.'

'Christ,' Monroe muttered. 'So Tamara turns up, pregnant with Nick's child, there to probably announce this, and she finds him with a barmaid.'

He shook his head.

'It gets worse every lead we gain.'

'What if Tamara killed Lorraine?' De'Geer suggested.

'Speculation, and one that'd have the whole Rothstead-Page estate solicitors hammering down on us,' Monroe mused. 'Though if this was a secret Tamara wanted kept, this could explain why her son was helping kill Dave, or even why her family solicitors are working with *Alternator*. I'm assuming they did the legal stuff on the contract.'

'Hold on,' Benny looked at both De'Geer and Monroe. 'How's Eden connected to this?'

'He was at the concert,' Monroe replied. 'And we believe tech designed by Storm's company was used to murder Dave Manford as he started his set. I assumed you knew this, as you were seen there?'

Benny took his glasses off, pinching the bridge of his nose.

'I didn't go in,' he said. 'It was too risky.'

'Let's talk about this risk,' Monroe nodded. 'Why exactly are you in a nursing home pretending to be senile, when you can apparently come and go at your leisure?'

Benny sighed.

'Look,' he said. 'I told you about the deal and why it was created. But you were right when you said that people would still want to talk. The threat of bankruptcy, to have your name destroyed, it sometimes doesn't do enough to stop people from wanting to talk, you know?'

'Go on.'

'Nick was unhappy,' Benny replied. 'I've already said that. He was going solo, and he was cleaning up his act. *Had* cleaned up his act. He wasn't the partying animal anymore, which was probably why Marna was shagging Andy again.'

He spat out a piece of cigar onto the grass.

'Then the police catch Nick in a club in Acton, after *Alternator* did a gig in Hammersmith, where witnesses say there was an altercation between Nick and some Randall associates which ended with Nick pulling a pistol. The police didn't find it on him, but they wanted him to come in to give a statement within the next seven days. Nick had nothing to lose, his conscience was eating him up and he told me he was going to come clean, give a full statement and tell the police what he could remember about Lorraine's death. To hell with the consequences and all that. This was three days before Brighton.'

'And then he disappeared.'

Benny nodded. 'Bloody convenient, right? Anyway, I assume he's reconsidered, and he's gone to sort himself out, or he knew coming clean would definitely give him jail time and the Randalls had people inside, so he ran. But there're rumours floating about, that he'd told others of his plans and they'd tried to talk him out of it.'

'You think someone killed him to keep his silence?'

'I did and I didn't,' Benny replied. 'I knew he had this backup account which had fifty grand in, and for the next couple of years I saw money go in and out. It had to be him withdrawing it, but at the same time I couldn't confirm it wasn't Marna, that sly bitch, being clever and faking it. By then, she and Andy were effectively public, so having a 'look he's still alive' story with proof stopped the rumours that claimed they killed him so they could be together. And over the years, the sightings of Nick, the ones in Tibet or in Bali, all those, half of them were paid for by Andy and Marna.'

'Keeping the legend alive,' De'Geer commented.

'Anyway, after Nick disappeared, Marna and Andy pushed for control,' Benny continued. 'Dave pushed back, claiming he was the co-founder of the band so it was his now, but Martin and Graham were convinced it was Dave that offed Nick.'

'Why?' Monroe asked.

'Because they hated each other at the end,' Benny took a long drag of his cigar, realising it'd gone out. Relighting it, he took another drag before continuing.

'They blamed each other for the lack of success *Alternator* had in the nineties,' he explained. 'Dave claimed he'd been nothing more than a drug mule gopher for Nick in the early days, while Nick in turn blamed Dave for his increasing addictions, saying that Dave had deliberately done it to split him and Marna, before Nick had cleaned up his act. And, when Nick was gone, Andy convinced the others, and me, to kick Dave out.'

'You did it?'

Benny smiled.

'I was happy to,' he replied. 'He was an insufferable prick and his past actions and attitude were killing the band. If he'd stayed, we wouldn't have lasted the millennium. We found proof he'd sourced the gun for Nick illegally and used this to activate the morality clause in his contract. He was out.'

'Wait,' De'Geer held up a hand. 'Dave Manford hated his brother, but still found him a gun?'

'Probably wanted him to get caught with it,' Benny shrugged. 'Or shoot himself. As it was, we didn't see the gun again after that Acton appearance.'

'Then what?' Monroe asked. 'Because so far I'm not seeing a reason for you to hide.'

'So once Marna took control, the band changed direction. I was being cut out,' Benny puffed on his cigar. 'I decided screw this, and I retired about twenty years back. Managed some other bands, put some money into companies, you know, kept my hand in, but I still watched *Alternator's* progress. I took a morbid delight that it was rapidly hurtling down the toilet. And then we reach about three years ago.'

'When you admitted yourself here?'

Benny shook his head.

'Before that,' he said. 'Bruce appeared on the scene again. Said he was sick of hiding, that he was coming clean. He was a producer by then, and he'd found out he was dying. One of the cancers, he never said which one. He knew they couldn't stop him with court cases and he could wait out the clock while letting them try to shut him up, and he hired Ray Cornwall, Lydia's husband, to represent him in interviews. He went to Andy and Marna and effectively told them to put their affairs in order.'

'And then he died.'

'Yeah,' a tear slid down Benny's cheek. 'Bloody fool. Told them I would back him up, even though I wasn't really sure. But Ray was the wrong choice. He'd already been used by Andy and Marna, back when the two girls started to mouth off after Nick's death. He'd gone in with lawyers; nowadays you'd call it *super-injunctions* but those days it was just threats. Solid bloody threats. And after speaking to Bruce, Ray told Andy and Marna, giving them a heads up. Next thing we know is the night Bruce meets them—'

'His car drives off a cliff,' Monroe said. 'He was seven times the legal limit.'

'That's bollocks. He never drank,' Benny replied. 'I mean, he did, back in the day, but he was about to start chemo. He'd gone dry for a good month. But they didn't know this.'

'You think someone did this?' De'Geer rose in surprise.

'I bloody know they did,' Benny snapped. 'Because the next day, I had Andy come and visit me at home. I had some advance knowledge though, so I pulled in a nurse friend and she played the part of my carer, saying I'd had a stroke a couple of days earlier, that I didn't know where I was or who anyone was. I played the fool for a good half hour. He was so convinced I was doo lally, he even called someone on the phone while there, saying I wasn't a threat, but he'd monitor me, and they'd watch Ray and Lydia for good measure.'

'Why didn't you go to the police?' Monroe asked.

'I was going to,' Benny shrugged. 'And then two weeks later, right before I called, Ray Cornwell has a heart attack and dies. Now it might be natural, and it could have been bad timing, but seeing both of them die in two weeks? I thought Andy and Marna were cleaning house. So, I bought an apartment here and put myself in. It's actually quite nice, you know. A real health spa.'

'And Dave Manford?'

Benny nodded.

'I was at the club because I'd been brought into the meetings with the finance guys,' he said. 'Sitting in the background and smiling vacantly, as if I'm giving my blessing to it all. I saw they were looking to create a final payout for the album, and I realised they were cutting David and Lydia out, lowballing him with a cheap offer of pennies on the pound. I decided that no matter how much of a prick he was, he didn't deserve that, so I was at the gig to offer my support. I saw there were photographers at the front, so I waited by the back door. And that's where I saw Nick walk past.'

'And Peter Suffolk,' De'Geer added.

Benny nodded.

'Although that was later.'

There was a *beep*, and Monroe pulled out his phone, his eyes widening.

'Sir?' De'Geer asked.

Monroe turned the phone to show him the message from Temple Inn.

'Apparently Andy Mears showed Peter Morris a blood covered metal straw on live TV, and was arrested immediately after,' he mused. 'We need to get back quickly.'

'What about me?' Benny asked. 'Am I about to be outed?'

Monroe looked sadly at him.

'I fair believe you are, Mister Simpson,' he replied. 'And to be honest? Because you kept the secret of Lorraine Warner's probable death quiet for thirty-five years? You bloody well should.'

He walked back to the house.

'Put your affairs in order,' he said. 'We'll come for you later.'

'Wait!' Benny shouted. 'What about a deal? Put me in witness protection! I have something else!'

'Tell it to me now and we'll ensure the court notices your help,' Monroe hissed, no longer even pretending to like the man in front of him.

'Peter,' Benny almost pleaded. 'I saw him after the gig.'

'We know that,' Monroe turned to leave again. 'He came out, saw you.'

'That's just it,' Benny said. 'He didn't come out. I was there for half an hour, and nobody went in or out of that door. And when Peter arrived and spoke to me, he came from down the street.'

Monroe stared at Benny.

'You're absolutely sure of that?' he asked.

Benny nodded.

'One hundred percent.'

Without replying, Monroe turned and stomped back through the nursing home, De'Geer matching his pace, knowing not to speak as Monroe pulled out his phone, dialling it.

'Anjli,' he said into it. 'You back at the Unit yet?'

'*No,*' Anjli replied down the line. '*I'm driving back to Temple Inn now.*'

'Good,' Monroe stopped, as if deciding before continuing.

'Change of plans. Use your connections to find out anything you can on the Randall family.'

There was a pause down the line.

'When you mean connections, do you mean...' Anjli left the sentence unfinished.

'I do, lassie,' Monroe nodded, even though she wouldn't see this. 'Go find the Twins, and see if they know anyone we can talk to. Criminal families like them must know each other.'

Before she could answer, or more accurately *protest* this, Monroe disconnected and, phone in his hand, stared out across the ornate driveway of the nursing home.

He was furious. They'd been played from the start. And Peter bloody Suffolk had been involved in it.

But *why?*

———

22

INFORMER

WHEN MONROE HAD EVENTUALLY MADE IT TO NEW SCOTLAND Yard, he'd found Bullman waiting for him. *Peter Morris in the pm* was filmed on the South Bank, and this was not only the nearest station with a cell but also the best place for such a high-profile case.

She was in the lobby when he arrived, having sent PC De'Geer back to the office to help Anjli and Declan when they returned. She was in conversation with a man in uniform, the white shirt and black tie of a police officer, but the diamonds on his black epaulettes giving him the rank of Chief Superintendent. He was tall, with short grey hair, whiter on the temples and under thin, black-rimmed glasses, and as he looked to Monroe, he smiled.

'About damn time,' he said. 'Press are having a feeding frenzy out there.'

Monroe shook Chief Superintendent David Bradbury's hand warmly. Bradbury controlled the City of London's police force and was Bullman's direct superior. He was also the officer that controlled the investigation into Monroe's attack a few months ago, working secretly with Billy to bring down a corrupt, privately run security company with delicate government contracts, an investigation that had also forced Declan Walsh to go on the run.

At no point had Bradbury truly believed that Declan was rogue, and for that, he had the *Last Chance Saloon's* loyalty for as long as he wanted it.

'Sir,' Monroe nodded. 'Traffic was a bugger from Guildford.'

'Guilford, eh?' Bradbury led them to the elevator. 'They filmed the church scene in *The Omen* there. You should have visited. Although you'd probably have been struck by lightning.'

'You're not wrong there,' Bullman smiled as they entered.

———

ANDY MEARS WAS ALREADY IN THE INTERVIEW ROOM WHEN they arrived, and a familiar face was by his side.

'Miss Woodstock,' Monroe nodded to the blonde solicitor as she looked up, nodding in return. 'We have to stop meeting like this. People will talk, and rumours will spread.'

'Funny,' Carrie Woodstock deadpanned. 'I've never heard that one before. Never.'

Bullman and Monroe sat facing Andy and Carrie, but Monroe paused before pressing the button on the recorder at the end of the desk.

'One quick thing,' he asked Carrie. 'Are you the solicitor for all of *Alternator?*'

'That's not relevant to this interview,' Carrie replied calmly.

Monroe nodded.

'Aye, I get that,' he said. 'But if you are, you might want to call in some help, lassie. You're about to have a busy day.'

'I'm nobody's *lassie*,' Carrie replied, as calm and collected as she'd been earlier. 'And I'd ask you to refrain from addressing me as such.'

Monroe smiled and pressed the recorder.

'Interview with Andrew Raymond Mears, his *lassie* Solicitor Carrie Woodstock present. Also in the room are Detective Chief Inspector Monroe and Detective Superintendent Bullman.'

He looked at his watch.

'The time is four fifty-two pm,' he added before looking back at Bullman. She was stone faced, but he knew that inside, this was killing her. She'd been a fan of the band since she was at university, and here she was interviewing one of them on charges of murder.

'Shall I take lead?' he asked. Bullman nodded, still straight faced.

'Please.'

'For the record, Detective Superintendent Bullman has given me lead,' Monroe said, as he looked across the table at Andy.

'Do you want to tell us your side of the story?' he asked. 'Before it gets uncomfortable?'

'I'm being framed,' Andy muttered. 'Everyone can see that.'

'Really?' Monroe raised an eyebrow. 'Because what we see is a man that, on live TV pulled out the blood-covered murder weapon of Lydia Cornwall and held it up.'

'There you go!' Andy exclaimed. 'Would I have done that if I did it?'

'You'd be surprised what the criminally insane do,' Monroe smiled.

'My client has not been charged, nor has he been classed as insane,' Carrie intervened. 'Please stick to the questions, DCI Monroe.'

Monroe nodded at this.

'Aye, fair do's,' he said. 'Mister Mears, can you explain to us how a blood-covered stainless steel drinking straw, one that is currently being checked against fatal wounds suffered to Lydia Cornwall, and one which is confirmed to have both her blood and your DNA on, was placed unknowingly in your pocket?'

'Wait, my DNA?' Andy was confused. 'How so?'

'The tip,' Monroe pointed at his lips. 'Where you put your lips to suck. The saliva traces left there match your DNA, taken when you were admitted.'

'That can't be,' Andy looked at his solicitor. 'That wasn't my straw. It couldn't be.'

'And why's that?'

'*Because I didn't ram it into Lydia's bloody neck!*' Andy shouted angrily. There was a motion at the door; an officer peeked in, but Bullman waved him off.

'Please, keep your voice down,' Monroe carried on. 'You're not on stage now. We're right here.'

'Look, let me rephrase this,' Andy muttered. 'It is my straw, but I had it on me all the time. I take it everywhere. And last night I took my grandchildren out for a milkshake and I used it when I was there, as it's better than the paper ones. And it sure as hell wasn't covered in blood then.'

'What time was this?' Monroe asked.

'Six, maybe seven.'

'And your grandchildren will confirm this?'

'I'm sure there's a security camera there that can. However, I'd ask that my children and their kids could be left out of this.'

Monroe nodded. They had information on file that Andy had a son and daughter, born in the early nineties, and that the daughter had given birth to twin girls six years ago. The story made sense.

'Where were you before that?'

'*Bear Studios.* You know I was, because your officers saw me there.'

'Bit of a journey for you, wasn't it?' Monroe pressed. 'North to West London? I mean Hayes is near Heathrow, and I've tried to get there at rush hour. Nightmare. And then to come back?'

'I had time, and I made it easy.'

'Did you have a lot of time?'

'Enough.'

'Enough to travel to Lydia Cornwall's address?'

Carrie went to speak, but Andy stopped her.

'No, I can answer this,' he said, looking back at Monroe. 'No, I didn't drive to her flat, no I didn't stab her in the neck with a drinking straw and no, I didn't then hang out with my family with her blood on the straw.'

Monroe nodded.

'Where did you go afterwards?'

'Home!' Andy exclaimed.

'Whose home?' Bullman spoke for the first time this interview. 'Yours or Marna Manford's?'

'Mine,' Andy replied. 'Although it's no secret that Marna and I have been partners. We have keys to each other's houses.'

'Did Marna have a problem with her sister?'

'Marna always had a problem with Lydia,' Andy muttered. 'Ever since she got a share of the album simply for shagging Dave.'

'You sure it's just that?' Monroe smiled. 'Not perhaps that she got the share because she was there the night that Lorraine Warner disappeared, or because she terrified some rape victims into keeping quiet on behalf of your band?'

Andy said nothing, glaring at Monroe.

'For the recording, Andrew Mears has refused to reply.'

'This is that nutter, Brookfield,' Andy hissed. 'He's been trying to destroy us for years.'

'And why would he do that?'

'It's well known he fancied Lorraine,' Andy snapped. 'Maybe he killed her after she left, put the blame on us.'

'How drunk were you that night?' Bullman asked.

'I'm sorry, but what does that have to do with the death of Lydia Cornwall?' Carrie asked.

'Leads to cause,' Bullman replied. 'What happened that night could have led to the murder. Both of them.'

There was a long moment of silence in the interview room.

'I didn't kill Dave Manford,' Andy said, shaking his head. 'The man was a prick and he was fleecing us, gaining work in his studios and loans from banks by claiming he'd written songs that I had, but he deserved to do that. He was a founder of the band.'

'That's a very generous opinion,' Monroe leaned back in his chair. 'And not one we've heard from anyone else we've interviewed.'

'Benny fired Davey, not us,' Andy snapped. 'Go ask him. If you can get a straight answer. He spends half his time with the fairies these days.'

'Had you spoken to Dave Manford before his death?'

'Christ, no,' Andy shook his head again. 'I hated him. He was toxic. You know for all this *oh, I saved my brother, I looked after my brother, I pulled him from drugs* shit he peddled for years? It was all bollocks. He made more money as Nick's dealer than he did from royalties in the mid-nineties.'

Monroe wrote this down in his notebook.

'So you got home,' he said. 'Then what?'

Andy thought for a moment.

'Peter came around,' he said. 'Around six, I think? We needed to talk about some tour things. Band stuff. He was there half an hour and then he left. After that I watched TV.'

'You sure it was 'band stuff'?' Monroe asked. 'You weren't ensuring that Peter had betrayed no band secrets when we spoke to him yesterday?'

'DCI Monroe,' Carrie was obviously tiring of this. 'This morning you had another of my clients arrested for the murder of Lydia Cornwall. This afternoon you've done it again. Unless you have—'

'We have a murder weapon with his DNA on it,' Monroe snapped back. 'So don't get on your high horse, lassie. We have him for murder and we'll be examining every aspect, thank you.'

There was a long moment of silence in the interview room.

'I wasn't drunk,' Andy muttered. 'I wasn't drunk because I wasn't there the night Lorraine disappeared.'

'Where were you?' Bullman snapped, tiring.

'I was at home,' Andy looked up at her. 'I wasn't part of the band at that point, I wasn't officially named as Bruce's replacement until the tour for the album. So I didn't get a room bought for me. I would commute there and back every day. And I spent my nights at home with my wife. We'd married a year earlier.'

'And will she confirm this?'

'Well, it's thirty-five years ago and we're obviously not talking these days, so I don't know,' Andy replied. 'I didn't drink back then. It was long-term exposure to Nick Manford that did that.'

'Did any of the band say anything about Lorraine Warner's death?' Bullman asked.

Andy shook his head.

'Honestly, all of them were a little freaked out, and convinced they'd had their drinks spiked,' he said. 'Lorraine had given Martin and Graham bottles of champagne, claiming it was an apology from the pub after they were attacked outside. But when the dust settled, they worked out that Martin had brought both bottles to the studios, and that's what they'd all been drinking.'

'What, so Lorraine had done this as revenge for what they had done to her friends, allegedly, at the party?' Monroe leaned back. 'If someone did that to me, I'd be angry.'

'Angry enough to kill,' Bullman added.

'Whether any of the others did this, it's irrelevant here,' Carrie repeated. 'My client has explained his whereabouts on that night. He wasn't anywhere near there.'

'This is your last chance, laddie,' Monroe leaned in close. 'We're close, I can smell it. And when we work out everything, when that last jigsaw piece falls in, Bruce Baker, Lydia Cornwall, Dave Manford, Lorraine Warner, maybe even Nick Manford will have their moment in the spotlight. And currently, you're in the lights beside every one of them.'

'How do you see that?' Andy asked, angry now. 'I wasn't anywhere near Bruce—'

'Yes, but he was driving to you, or maybe *from* you when he crashed, wasn't he?' Monroe pressed. 'He was going to tell you he'd decided to come clean about something. Maybe the events of that night. And then he's dead.'

Andy stared at Monroe.

'Who told you that?' he asked softly. 'I never told anyone we were supposed to meet with Bruce that night. Only Lydia and Raymond knew—and Benny...'

He chuckled.

'Oh, that sneaky little shit,' he said. 'Benny's been talking to you, hasn't he?'

'Bernard Simpson is suffering from dementia and is in a nursing home,' Monroe replied calmly. 'Are you saying you know something different?'

'What about Martin and Graham?' Andy was scrabbling now, the anger being replaced with desperation. 'They were the reason Lorraine was there. Maybe they did it, killed Bruce.'

'So now he *was* killed?' Monroe laughed. 'Make up your mind.'

Andy leaned back in the chair.

'What are my options?' he said to Carrie. 'Earn your money here.'

'They have a weapon, and they have your DNA on it,' she replied. 'You've given your alibi, and so it's up to them to work out whether or not it's true.'

She looked back at Monroe.

'To drive to Hackney, my client would have gone through countless areas with traffic cameras. I'm sure you can use some kind of automatic number plate recognition to see if he did. Or perhaps find me footage of him entering buses or trains? Because currently, although Lydia Cornwall's blood is on my client's straw, there's no proof yet that this was the weapon, and not another straw that was simply coated with the victim's blood.'

'You should hang out with our Divisional Surgeon,' Monroe muttered. 'You'd get on like a house on fire.'

Carrie pursed her lips, biting off a reply as Monroe glanced at Bullman. The solicitor was correct; the weapon was revealed in public, but they hadn't heard from Doctor Marcos on whether or not it was the actual weapon.

And if it wasn't, this would be the second time a suspect walked out of the door.

Monroe leaned across and turned off the recording.

'Interview paused, five oh-six pm,' he said, looking back at Andy.

'Don't think you're done yet, laddie,' he said, now moving from the desk, Bullman rising to join him. 'We're a long way from being done here.'

Walking out of the room, allowing the door to close fully before he spoke, Monroe looked at Bullman.

'Thoughts, Ma'am?'

'I think he's either superb at this, or he was framed,' she said. 'For this murder, that is. That sneaky bastard in there knows more than he's letting on.'

'Aye,' Monroe nodded. 'We just need to find a way to get it.'

23

FREEZE-FRAME

IN A STRANGE, TWISTED WAY, THIS CASE WAS THE BEST THING that had happened for Billy in a long time.

The reason for this was a battered old Mac computer, easily twenty-five years old, that seemed to be the only data-based record keeping system that *Bear Studios* had before the new millennium. It was so old that the Mac OS system opened with *MAC OS 7.1* on the screen when it booted up; a tall, boxy, yellowing device with a black-and-white screen and a 3.5 inch floppy drive underneath, a one-click mouse and keyboard plugged into the back. On the front, at the bottom right, was a multicoloured apple logo with the faded text *Macintosh Classic II* written next to it. This meant the computer was from somewhere between 1991 and 1993, and with the operating system released in Autumn 1992, the computer had arrived at least five years after *Alternator* had been there.

That said, there was no reason why the disks might not have anything useful on them, and so Billy gathered up all the disks he could find, placing them into a shoebox marked *MICROPHONES.*

'I could help you,' Errol offered, placing a cup of tea in front of Billy. 'I know the place like the back of my hand.'

Billy looked around the small, soundproofed room he was now in, currently piled high with boxes, files, and old computer disks.

'What was this room?' he asked. 'Before? Because it stinks.'

'This?' Errol smiled. 'This was the second recording booth, although for the last few years we've not needed two. Barely needed one, actually. More rehearsal space these days. And the smell's because we're by a refuse dump, and I reckon it seeps through the brickwork. Only gets terrible on hot days, and the extractor fans we installed usually remove it.'

He smiled apologetically.

'That's the other reason we've not used it. Sorry.'

Billy nodded, half listening as he found a writeable CD marked *1998 BOOKINGS.*

'This could be the one,' he said, putting it into the box. 'That must have the logs for Nick's solo work on it.'

He looked back at Errol.

'That reminds me,' he said with a slight, embarrassed smile. 'I need the songs he recorded put onto a drive, or a disk, whatever it would be. You know, for evidence.'

'Not your fangirl boss, then?' Errol grinned. 'The guy who came, the DI, told me she was a bit of a stalker back in the day.'

Billy shrugged. 'Girl likes what she likes,' he said as an answer, spying an A4 book under a pile of master tapes.

'That might be a problem,' Errol replied. 'I didn't say it at the time, because that rich prick was there, but we don't have the masters anymore. Haven't for years.'

'What do you mean?' Billy stopped, looking back at Errol who shrugged.

'I mean they were recorded here, but sometime in the millennium, they disappeared,' Errol pointed at the pile of boxes in the corner. 'Probably in one of those. Keith never really cared to look, as he knew Manford wasn't coming back any time soon.'

'Were you here when that happened?'

'Yup, I've been here since the early nineties,' Errol replied. 'Hired when my other work dried up.'

'What was your other work?' Billy was removing the master tapes now.

'I was a sparks, an electrician for a building contractor,' Errol explained. 'Keith lost his one right before New Year '89, and he needed someone who could keep the lights on.'

'That's when Shaun Williams died, right?' Billy picked up the book, wiping it down.

VISITORS BOOK

'Bingo,' he whispered, opening it up.

'That's who I replaced, God rest his soul,' Errol replied. 'I only ever met him once, when I was working on this.'

Billy looked from the book.

'Sorry, what do you mean by *this?*'

Errol waved around.

'*This.* I was one of the contractors building this whole studio in '86,' he replied. 'I put in all the electrics. That's why when the contractors folded, Keith took me on. I knew the electrics like the back of my hand, because I'd put it all in.'

Billy sat on a box, sipping at his tea.

'So you would have been here during the recording of *Secrets and Lies*,' he said.

'I was,' Errol nodded. 'Well, only in passing. We worked during the day and they mainly pissed about in here during the night. We couldn't build much while they were recording, although they did their best to accommodate, especially when they had the fight.'

'I heard about that,' Billy was intently listening now. 'Was there much damage?'

'Nah, barely any,' Errol shrugged. 'We were only half-built then, anyway. Finished in early August and by then, they were pretty much done. They even built some of it for us, and I wish they'd let us swap jobs and play something for them, 'cause we might have been able to get in on that profit share thing they did.'

Billy felt a shiver run down his spine.

'Explain what you mean by *they built?*'

'What I said,' Errol waved around the room. 'They used the other recording booth because this one was still being built. Then one night, after they had one of their benders, sorry, recording sessions, they built up part of the plasterboard, saving us a good hour or two the following day. Probably rammed a boot through one, so fixed it up rather than apologise again, and hoped we wouldn't notice.'

'Do you remember when this was?' Billy asked, now rising slowly, looking at the walls, as if expecting them to fall.

'Summer, sometime,' Errol replied. 'As I said, we didn't really talk to them. Hell, after the job I didn't come back until after Shaun died, and everyone was gone by then.'

'Clive the producer?'

'Oh, they hired him, not us.'

'Peanut, the sound engineer?'

'Gone to college, I think,' Errol shrugged. 'Didn't even hear his name again until Manford came back.'

'Why was his name mentioned then?' Billy was now at the wall, walking along it, tapping on it at various points.

'Because Peanut returned as his sound engineer,' Errol replied. 'Apparently they bumped into each other in *The Bear* when Nick came back.'

'Do you know Peanut's real name?' Billy stopped tapping the wall.

Errol shook his head.

'Only Keith would,' he said. 'But he died a few months back. It's why the land's being sold, because he never paid his bloody bills.'

He stopped.

'All I remember is that they called him peanut because he was a peanut, if that helps?'

Billy Stared at Errol for a moment, as if trying to work out what he meant.

'He was a peanut,' he replied, pulling out his phone. 'Cool, okay. Do you have anyone here more superior than you?'

'Keith left it to me, but his wife's still involved,' Errol considered. 'Why?'

'You might want to call her and get her here,' Billy walked up to Errol. 'Can you remember what part of the wall was magically added?'

'Ah, it's been decades—' Errol started.

'Think *harder* then,' Billy hissed.

Taken aback by the change of tone, Errol pointed at a section of soundproofing, around halfway along the back wall.

'There, I think,' he whispered. 'Why?'

'Because I think you might have the body of Lorraine Warner behind it,' Billy was dialling into his phone now. 'And I'm about to bring the whole damn police force into here to pull it apart.'

ANJLI HADN'T BEEN BACK AT THE GLOBE TOWN BOXING CLUB for a couple of months now, and to be honest, she hadn't missed it. The last time she'd been here, it had been a ruse to flush out the true killer of Reginald Troughton from the *Magpies*, and after this Johnny Lucas, one of the infamous 'Twins' of the East End had told her that all debts that she had with them were paid.

Anjli had hoped she'd never need to come back again, but here she was, pulling up outside the red-brick building.

The boxing club had recently been renovated, and now state-of-the-art equipment lined the walls, with shiny, new leather smelling heavy bags surrounding the boxing ring itself. The last time Anjli had been here, the club had been closed, and she'd arrived with Tessa Martinez only to find a gun aimed at her face. It had all been a pre-set plan, but the image was still strong as she looked around.

The club was busy; in the ring a man, built to fight and in his mid-forties was sparring with a trainer, while around the ring teenage wannabe boxers worked the heavy bags. Anjli didn't care about them though, and carried on towards the back door, where a man in his thirties, tall, well built and with a blond buzzcut, blocked her way.

'Busy,' he said, simply.

'He'll make time for me,' Anjli replied. She didn't recognise the man, and because of this she assumed that in return he didn't recognise her. To aid memory, she showed her warrant card.

'Is it Johnny or Jackie today?' she asked, and the guard knew exactly what she meant. Johnny and Jackie Lucas weren't twins, but one man with multiple personality disorder. 'Johnny' was the rational, helpful one, while 'Jackie' was chaos personified, a different, darker side to Johnny's psyche, and in all ways the *Hyde* to Johnny's *Jekyll*.

'Johnny,' the guard said. 'But he's—'

'Always happy to see an old friend,' a man interrupted, walking out of the back door. He was tanned, his salt and pepper hair styled into a loose quiff, his deep blue shirt covered by a black suit jacket, left open, a deep blue silk handkerchief in his pocket.

'Mister Lucas,' Anjli said respectfully. 'I'm glad to see it's you today.'

'Jackie had business up north,' Johnny lied, keeping the pretence. 'I'd offered to take it, but now I'm glad I didn't. What can we do for you, Detective Sergeant? Are we in trouble, or did that wily Scot send you?'

Anjli smiled.

'The Scot,' she replied. 'He was hoping you might help us with an enquiry. In particular, information on a West London gang in the eighties and nineties.'

'Might be a bit before my time, but I'll see what I can do,' Johnny nodded. 'Who?'

'The Randalls,' Anjli pulled out her notebook, reading from it. 'Controlled the area around Hillingdon, reaching out past Ealing. Mainly drugs, extortion, that sort of thing.'

'Randalls,' Johnny was tapping at his chin with his thumb as he thought. 'I don't recognise the name, as in I don't recall working with or against them, but I remember there was a gang of pikey travellers around Heathrow who were pricks around that time.'

He smiled.

'They weren't exactly my league,' he said. 'I was moving into Premiership Football League status while they were still Sunday kickabouts.'

'Do you know anyone I could speak to?'

'Actually, yes,' Johnny grinned widely. 'A more legitimate source, in fact.'

He walked over to the boxing ring, where the burly boxer was now leaning against the ropes, out of breath.

'This here is Jimmy Shaldon,' Johnny explained. 'They call him the *Gypsy Duke*. Been on the prize fighting circuit for twenty years. Traveller, born and bred.'

On hearing his name, Jimmy looked down at Anjli.

'Problem?' he asked. Johnny shook his head.

'Anjli here, or rather DS Kapoor is an old friend,' he explained. 'She needs information on the Randalls.'

'Christ, that's a name I haven't heard for a while,' Jimmy replied, clambering out of the ropes and sitting on the side apron. 'Used to run drugs and shite in Middlesex. Pricks, the lot of 'em.'

'Told you,' Johnny smiled. 'I'll leave you two together. I don't need to be a part of this.'

As Johnny walked back into his offices, Anjli looked at Jimmy.

'What can you tell me about them?' she asked.

'Lots,' Jimmy shrugged his shoulders. 'I mean, I didn't know 'em personal, like, but I beat the living shite out of a few of 'em over the years.'

Anjli raised an eyebrow, and Jimmy grinned.

'In the ring, like,' he continued. 'Bare knuckle, mainly.'

'I'm trying to find out about a couple of incidents,' Anjli replied. 'Mainly about a death threat in 1998.'

'Ah, they always mouthed off with death threats,' Jimmy shook his head. 'Didn't mean squat. They were all mouth, no trousers. Most they did was batter people around. They never went full *Sopranos*.'

He stopped, a small, cunning smile on his face, as he worked out where Anjli was going with this.

'You're talking about the rock star guy,' he said.

'What do you mean?' Anjli played innocent.

Jimmy shook his head.

'Everyone knew about that one,' he said. 'It was a month before that war movie, the one with Tom Hanks came out.'

'*Saving Private Ryan?*'

'Yeah, that's the one. I'd just been to see it when I heard the Randalls were mouthing off, saying it was an anniversary of a death and they were getting revenge on the killer, and then they said it was the guy, Nick something.'

'Nick Manford,' Anjli was writing. 'So they said he killed someone?'

'I think,' Jimmy shrugged. 'I mean, Christ, it was all Chinese whispers back then. They said he killed one of their own.'

'Did they give a name?'

'If they did, I didn't know it.'

'Lorraine Warner?' Anjli asked.

At the name, it was as if a light went on behind Jimmy's eyes.

'Yeah, that was the one.'

'You said 'one of their own.' Are you saying Lorraine Warner was a Randall?' Anjli asked.

Jimmy nodded.

'The Randalls aren't just a name,' he explained. 'Travellers marry, cousins enter and leave as they move on. Randalls, Warners, Kavanaghs, they were all part of the same tribe back then.'

'Jesus,' Anjli muttered.

'They never would have killed 'im, though,' Jimmy laughed. 'We all heard what happened back then. Manford was in a club near Acton and the Randalls heard. So they all rock down there in their clown cars and face him with Stanley blades. Box cutters, for Christ's sake.'

'What happened?'

'Nothing,' Jimmy was laughing harder now. 'Pricks brought tiny knives to a gunfight. Nick pulled a gun out, started aiming it at them while screaming and shooting at the ceiling and they fair pissed themselves as they ran 'ome.'

'So what happened to them?'

'Apathy,' Johnny replied as he left his office and returned to the ring. 'I just looked them up. Sons weren't as ambitious as the fathers, it seems. They rolled over and died about ten years back.'

Anjli had been typing into her phone as she listened.

'*Saving Private Ryan* came out in September 1998,' she said. 'That sound about right?'

Jimmy nodded.

'I'd say so.'

'Hey,' Johnny said as Jimmy clambered back into the ring. 'That Scot of yours, tell him to take a holiday for a couple of weeks, yeah?'

'Any reason?' Anjli put away her notebook as she faced the gangster.

'Let's just say his past is catching up to him,' Johnny

replied cryptically. 'People from Glasgow with a score to settle.'

'Is it a serious threat?' Anjli asked.

Johnny nodded.

'Serious enough to have Derek Sutton back in town, and I don't know why,' he said. 'Just tell him to be safe. And don't you be a stranger either.'

He turned, walking back to his office.

'And say hi to your mum for me,' he said. 'I hear they've given her a clean bill of health now.'

Now alone in the boxing club, Anjli stared at the door, deep in thought.

The Randalls had supplied Nick.

Graham and Martin had been soundly beaten by locals, who backed off when Lorraine appeared, something that a simple barmaid shouldn't have been able to chase off.

So what the hell was Lorraine Warner before she died?

———

DECLAN EVENTUALLY ARRIVED AT THE ADDRESS THAT HAD BEEN given to him around four in the afternoon, having spent the last hour and a half bitterly complaining to himself that *he really should have driven his own car to Hampstead, as this would have meant that he would have been here a good hour earlier.*

Looking at his phone, he typed a single word message.

Here.

Standing alone, he looked around.

It was an old power station in South East London, now condemned and most likely soon to be turned into exclusive apartment complexes, the fate of many of these old buildings. He didn't know why Francine Pearce wanted to meet here, but he couldn't fault her for the dramatic intent she'd given in considering this location.

He'd been standing in a large, open space, with brick pillars holding up a very high ceiling while twenty-foot tall windows lined the walls for almost an hour before he finally gave up waiting. For all he knew, Francine was watching him from some upper level, laughing at the idiot copper who was standing around like a fool.

'If you're in here, come and talk!' he cried out into the open space, hearing it echo around the walls. Some birds, suddenly woken by the noise, flew off, and the fluttering of their wings also echoed around the building.

'Sod this,' Declan muttered, pulling out his phone and dialling Francine's number. Waiting, he placed it by his ear as it rang.

He half-expected Francine to answer, laughing, again amused by the hoops she'd made him jump through, but all he heard was a buzzing from the corner of the open building, a rhythmic buzz that matched the rings on the phone.

'This is Fran—' an answerphone started, as the buzzing stopped. Declan disconnected the call, now walking to the corner where, still lit up, was a smartphone.

Picking it up, Declan saw the unread message on the screen.

Here.

'Christ,' he muttered aloud, looking around the open space. There was blood on the floor around the phone, and the phone itself was also dabbed in it, blood that was now on Declan's fingers.

This is a sick game you're playing, Francine, Declan thought to himself as he pulled out a forensics bag from his inside jacket pocket, placing the phone into it and shoving it into his inside pocket again. This done, he took one last look around the building before striding determinedly towards the entrance he'd walked through an hour earlier. He didn't know if this was real, but the one thing he didn't want right now was to be part of a separate murder enquiry.

Dialling his phone, he held it to his ear as he exited the building.

'Anjli, it's me,' he said. 'I'm on my way back but I was just checking in—' he stopped as he listened.

'Tell them I'll make my way there,' he said, now running as he ran towards a road thirty metres away, hoping to catch a cab to the closest railway station. He needed to get to *Bear Studios* as soon as possible, and now he *really* regretted not driving.

He was so focused on leaving, in fact, he neglected to notice the shadowed figure across the power station, watching him walk out with a smile on her face, before turning back into the shadows, her own exit planned out to the smallest detail.

Trisha Hawkins had snagged her prey, and soon it would be time to reel him in.

———

24

ANOTHER BRICK IN THE WALL

By the time Doctor Marcos had arrived at *Bear Studios*, they had already found the body.

It was wrapped in plastic and secured tightly with at least two rolls of gaffer tape, making it into a completely secured, air-tight mummy, left in the gap behind the wall for thirty-five years. Well, it was classed as a mummy until Doctor Marcos arrived, anyway. She quickly pointed out that wrapping a body up didn't actually *mummify* it in decomposition terms. To truly involve mummifying, the killer would have dehydrated the body, so putting it in plastic wrap, no matter how well taped up, just contained it.

She took an almost pathological delight in the queasy expressions on the young forensic team that had arrived from the nearby Uxbridge Command Unit as she explained this.

Billy was sitting outside the studios when she had arrived with DC Davey; he'd explained that the room was small, contained even, and that the smell, now the wall had been pulled open, was a little too strong to bear. And so now he sat on the passenger seat of his Mini Cooper, legs out the side as

he worked though a large, A4 sized visitors log while forensics walked past him.

With her grey PPE suit on, Doctor Marcos entered *Bear
Studios*, winding her way through to the back room where the
action was.

A section of the wall had been removed, and it was here
where the body had been found, brought out through the
roughly created hole in the plasterboard behind the plywood
layer that had held the soundproofing for the booth. The
body had been tightly wrapped in what looked like decora-
tor's plastic wrapping, the sort that covered floors to keep
them safe from damage, and had almost been covered from
top to bottom in gaffer tape, sealing it from all external
damage, although there was now a gash in the left arm, likely
from the removal of the wall, the wrapping torn and the
exposed, decomposed body poking out.

'What the hell happened?' Marcos had asked, and a
sheepish officer in full PPE had explained that as they didn't
know exactly where the body was, or even if there was a body
there in the first place, they'd had to start on a rough area of
the wall. And, when they punched through the plasterboard
with a sledgehammer, they'd caught the side of it. Which on
the one hand was a good first try on location finding, but on
the other was not the best of beginnings, as the booth now
reeked of decomposed body.

And no matter how many of these you smelled, you never
quite learnt how to ignore it.

A hastily erected tent had been placed next to the studio,
and they had brought the body out, mainly to gain more
space and light while examining it, but also to use the outside
air to ventilate the scene. Officers from Uxbridge had also

arrived, locking down the area and ensuring the local press couldn't get through.

Once on the table, the wrapping was carefully removed; the gaffer examined as they pulled it off in small sheets. Someone had wrapped the body, and the adhesive tape was a location for DNA from whoever did it, as the body was likely to be decayed past the point of help here.

Now, with the plastic and the gaffer tape removed, Doctor Marcos stared at the remains of what was most likely Lorraine Warner.

The body was almost skeletal, with the clothing mostly intact. It was dried, stiff and damaged, mainly from years of fluids leaking out all over it and eventually drying out, but mostly still there. There was a darker stain around the midsection, and a tear in the dress with flakes of dried fluids around it made a solid case for a stab wound. As Doctor Marcos adjusted her mask and leaned in, DC Davey appeared from the studio, where she'd been examining the location of the body.

'We have human hair trapped in the tape,' she said. 'We're looking into it now.'

'Nice catch,' Doctor Marcos waved at the body. 'Cause of death?'

Davey peered closer.

'Stab wound in the midsection,' she said, but then stopped, examining the skull. 'Although there's a brutal head wound here, too.'

'That's what I thought,' Doctor Marcos stepped back. 'So stabbed and then fell? Or fell and then stabbed?'

Davey shrugged.

'You tell me,' she said. 'They pay you the big bucks. That's why you get to look at bodies and I'm checking rodent poop.'

Doctor Marcos stared at the body. If this was Lorraine Warner, someone had certainly killed her. *The question was, which wound did it?*

———

DECLAN ARRIVED ABOUT THIRTY MINUTES AFTER DOCTOR Marcos and walked over to Billy, still sitting in the passenger seat.

'You took your time, Guv,' Billy smiled.

'Anjli had the car,' Declan replied, deciding not to mention the bloodstained phone in his pocket just yet. There were more important things going on. 'Ended up getting a tube to Uxbridge and cadging a lift with a squad car. What do we have?'

'Lorraine Warner's body,' Billy pointed at the tent outside the entrance. 'Identified by ID found on the body. Dumped in the wall space about thirty-five years ago.'

'Do we have a cause of death yet?' Declan asked. Doctor Marcos, emerging from the tent and pulling off her mask, replied.

'Two wounds, but it's too early to say. I think she was stabbed in the midsection and she fell, cracking her skull open, but until I can have a good look, I'm at a loss. We have some hair strands in the tape, and we're checking those, but they're degraded, so we'll need to really work on them, and it could take some time for an answer,' she said. 'Even though it's been wrapped up for decades, all that did was keep it contained. The body's in terrible shape, and we might get nothing from it.'

'Gotcha,' Declan nodded. 'Let me know if I can help in any way.'

'You'll be first to know, Deckers,' Doctor Marcos pulled her mask back on and entered the tent.

'Still not a fan of the names,' Declan muttered.

Billy smiled.

'Spend your days looking at bodies, you probably need a little fun in your life,' he said.

Declan glanced around.

'Where's De'Geer?' he asked. 'I thought he'd have been front and centre for this?'

Billy grimaced.

'He's watching the Peter Suffolk video,' he said. 'It was the only way Bullman would let me come here.'

'All two hours? Christ, he's going to hate you,' Declan laughed.

'No, he wouldn't be doing that,' Billy shook his head. 'He'd at least watch it at two times speed.'

'Did you tell him he could?' Declan asked.

Horrified, Billy shook his head.

'No,' he replied. 'I hadn't considered that. I should call—'

Declan looked at his watch.

'He's probably finishing around now,' he said. 'I'd probably suggest not telling him he's wasted an hour or more.'

Billy nodded.

'Actually, I'm glad you're here, I think I might have something,' he opened the book at a page, showing it to Declan. 'This is the visitors log for 1986. The entire summer section has been torn out.'

'Convenient,' Declan replied, picking up the book, reading the lines of names. 'So what am I looking at here?'

'The visitors log for the bands before *Alternator*,' Billy explained. 'It turns out the Manfords weren't the first band recording there, I checked and there'd been a solo singer and a small jazz quartet in there first. And they signed in, including the staff who worked the desks.'

He pointed at a name on the page.

'This is the sound engineer, Peanut,' he said. 'It has to be.'

Declan looked at the signature.

Andrew Peter Knytte. Otherwise known as Peter Suffolk.

'Errol, the guy here? He said that the nickname was *because he was a peanut*,' Billy continued. 'And if you read it aloud, remembering Suffolk's real surname is pronounced *nut*, 'A P Knytte' sounds a lot like *a peanut*. Also, the original album list has the initials AK.'

Declan stared at the name.

'Do you think I'm mad?' Billy added. 'Could it be him?'

'Christ, Peter Suffolk was the bloody sound engineer,' Declan muttered. 'He told us he didn't have a stake in the album as a member of the band, but he did as a member of the *studio*.'

He looked around the car park, seeing Doctor Marcos's Mercedes.

'Tell Monroe about this,' he said. 'And tell Doctor Marcos I'm sorry.'

'For what?'

Declan was already running.

'For stealing her car!'

MORTEN DE'GEER WAS BORED.

He wasn't usually, as there were many things he had on his plate that kept him occupied, but Bullman, before leaving had asked him to run through the video feed from the funeral one more time, to see if there was anything that could help. The problem with this was that De'Geer couldn't scroll through the video quickly, or he could miss something. Bullman had given him this job because she'd known he was dutiful and diligent, her own words when asking him to do this, and words that, an hour and a half into the video, De'Geer knew had been stated purely to get him to accept the job.

For most of the video, he'd been staring at Peter Suffolk's quiet, attentive face. Occasionally Peter would smile, or nod, or even laugh, maybe drink from a bottle of water on the table; there was no feed to show what Peter at the time was watching, and his ear buds kept the sound non-existent—this made the out of context reactions a little more creepy, as if Peter was staring quietly at a mirror.

'Hey,' DC Davey leaned in through the office door, about an hour into the viewing. 'Billy called from the recording studio. We think we might have a body. You want to tag along?'

De'Geer didn't even take his eyes from the screen as he replied.

'I'll follow you on the bike,' he said. 'I think I might have something here.'

Davey had nodded and then left, leaving De'Geer alone once more, watching the screen, and the almost standstill Peter Suffolk, staring back at him.

He'd disappeared once, for the time that the average man would take to go to the toilet, but apart from that, he'd stayed static, intently watching the funeral that was appearing on his screen. And, as De'Geer sighed, leaning back in his chair and silently screaming, Peter Suffolk got out of his chair and walked off.

Sitting up, De'Geer noted the time, but although Peter was away longer, it was still less than two minutes before Peter returned to the screen, a mug of either tea or coffee in his hand. The mug was black, with text written on the side, saying I'LL PAY YOU BACK WHEN I'M FAMOUS, although the right-hand side of the phrase wasn't visible, thanks to the mug being half-turned as he placed it down.

Over the next ten minutes Peter sat, drinking from the mug, ignoring the bottle of water now, watching the screen. And then the feed ended, as the memorial also ended.

De'Geer stared at the image of Peter sitting at his chair, bottle and mug on the screen.

Bottle and mug on the screen.

De'Geer leaned closer, looking at the black mug, the half written text on it. It was familiar, as if he'd seen it before.

Using the mouse, De'Geer took a screenshot of the image, opening it up and moving it to one of the side screens. This done, he returned to the beginning of the video footage, starting it again.

On the screen, the table was empty, a bottle and black mug already in the picture. Peter walked into shot, sitting down and smiling at the screen.

'Hi everyone,' Peter said. 'Let me sort my video out—yeah, hey Ali, it's good to see you too. Just give me a moment and I'll mute everything.'

He leaned forward, fiddling with the video camera on top of the laptop, his hand covering the camera, and the image went dark, returning a moment later as Peter sat back down.

'*That better?*' he asked, now putting in a pair of ear buds. '*Good, I can hear you. I'll mute now. Good luck, guys. All my love.*'

De'Geer paused the screen.

The mug that was there when Peter leaned forward was now missing.

De'Geer returned the video to the start again, looking at the mug and the bottle, glancing at the screenshot.

They were in the same position.

'Oh shit,' he muttered to himself. Peter had been live, he was sure of it, as he was talking to the other people on the call at the start, in particular someone called Ali. De'Geer knew that if he checked, he'd find a feed where someone named Ali welcomed Peter as he arrived.

But that was where the live feed ended. Peter had leaned forward, adjusted the camera...

And clicked to a different feed.

De'Geer was almost impressed. Peter Suffolk must have sat in front of the screen, mimicking attentiveness, smiling and nodding at random moments to show that he was more than just a static image. De'Geer had heard of people using video to pretend to be in office meetings, but this was the first time he'd seen anyone do it.

But he'd definitely done this. He'd spent over two hours sitting and pretending to watch, obviously stopping it mere minutes before the actual memorial started. Then, he came on live, logging in physically, saying hello to people on the feed and then, when claiming to adjust his camera, he disconnected the feed, and started the video.

He would have gotten away with it if he had just cleaned up the mug.

The footage had started minutes before three pm, when the memorial had officially started. *Recorded* Peter would have been in the background for another two and a half hours, with nobody the wise, while *live* Peter could leave his house as it started, without anyone knowing. And, more importantly, this meant that Peter Suffolk could have made it to Lydia Cornwall's apartment within the timeframe of her death.

De'Geer wanted to fist pump the air, bask in the glory as his superiors sat watching him, stunned and impressed at his detective skills.

The problem was, there was nobody there.

Rising from his chair, he almost ran to the door of the office. Most of the others were at *Bear Studios*, while Monroe and Bullman were still in Scotland Yard.

It looked like De'Geer was going to have to bring Peter Suffolk back in himself.

———

25

DON'T YOU (FORGET ABOUT ME)

ANDY MEARS LOOKED UP AT THE DOOR TO THE INTERVIEW room as Bullman and Monroe returned, Carrie Woodstock glaring at them as they sat back in the chairs that faced across the table.

'My client has been—' she angrily started, but Bullman raised up a hand to stop her.

'Shut it,' Bullman said, her voice ice cold and emotionless. 'Before I arrest you as an accessory to murder.'

Carrie opened and shut her mouth twice as Monroe leaned back to the recorder, turning it on.

'We've had something happen,' he started, conversationally. 'Some additional evidence has come to light.'

'What evidence?' Carrie asked cautiously, glancing at her client as she did so. Andy, meanwhile, had paled, sitting silently as Monroe looked directly at him.

'We found Lorraine Warner,' he said. 'That is, her body, wrapped in plastic and hidden away behind a wall in *Bear Studios*. Tell me, Mister Mears, is this why you were there yesterday? Is this why you needed the money quickly, to buy the land and ensure that nobody tore down the building and found her?'

After a moment, Bullman leaned forward.

'For the recording, Andrew Mears is refusing to talk,' she said. 'Andrew Mears is probably realising that once we link his DNA to the body, he's screwed.'

'We spoke to your ex-wife,' Monroe smiled. 'She really hates you, by the way. You weren't kidding. God, I mean, I don't like my ex-wife, and I swear like a squaddie, but even I wouldn't use the words she said. But you know what she did say? That you *weren't* at home. That you *were* at the studio, the one you claimed you weren't at the night Lorraine Warner died.'

'She's wrong,' Andy muttered.

Carrie went to reply, but Andy shook his head.

'Look, it wasn't like that,' he continued. 'I was at home, I swear, but I got called back in.'

'Why?'

Andy looked at Carrie, who leaned back, hands in the air.

'I don't endorse this decision,' she said. 'I think you need to stay silent.'

'And I think you need to tell us the truth, so that innocent wee lassie's family can finally lay her to rest,' Monroe continued.

'She wasn't innocent,' Andy snapped.

'Go on,' Bullman encouraged. 'You've held onto this for thirty-plus years. Let it off your chest.'

There was a long moment of silence before Andy spoke again.

'It was a few days after Martin and Graham raped the girls,' he said. 'We knew they did it, but nobody could prove it. But Lorraine, bloody Lorraine, was in their faces. She was a barmaid, but she was mob-connected, you know? Irish Mafia and all that. Told them to *come clean, or she'd do something herself.* Lydia kicks off back at her, telling her to *mind her own bloody business*, and then goes off and threatens the girls into silence, offering them money to shut up. A day later Hagen and Reilly are attacked outside the pub, battered by some teenagers who knew the girls personally, but Lorraine comes out and stops it.'

'Why?' Monroe asked.

Andy shrugged.

'We thought she was just keeping the peace, but then she gives the two of them champagne to apologise from the pub and then apologises to Lydia for her actions. We thought she'd been bollocked by the landlord, worried he was about to lose some major trade from the band, but with hindsight, I think this was all a setup to explain the drinks.'

'Again, why?' Monroe leaned back.

'Because I think she intended to spike them,' Andy replied. 'I learnt years later that she was part of the same family that Nick had been getting his drugs from. She was probably the bloody dealer, who knows. But that night, I wasn't there in the bar. I heard this all later.'

'Go on then,' Bullman nodded. 'Tell us your side.'

'So around midnight, I get a call from the studio,' Andy explained. 'Nick, frantic, called me, begging me to come in.'

'Did he say why?'

'Later, sure. Apparently, Nick had decided he wanted to work on a song and told the band to come back. However, Martin and Graham hadn't drunk the bottles they were given, and so Lorraine and a couple of girls invited themselves along. Lorraine never went there usually, so that was instantly strange.'

'You think she went to ensure the champagne was drunk?'

'I think she wanted Graham and Martin to suffer like the girls had,' Andy said. 'Although things went pear-shaped when they got there, as the band started sharing the bottles around. Everyone was drinking from them. And everyone was feeling the effects, you get me?'

He looked around the room, gathering his thoughts.

'So about this point, randomly, Bruce arrives with Tamara. They're old mates and she'd confided in him about her affair with Nick. He drags her to the studio to tell Nick that not only is she pregnant, but it's with his kid and he needs to step up, or something. Tamara enters to find Lorraine and Nick in the back room. Nothing was happening, but Tamara's angry, wants a fight, and Lorraine in't going to back down. There's an argument between them; Tamara pushes Lorraine, and she falls, hitting the edge of the recording desk hard, killing her.'

'So Tamara killed Lorraine Warner?'

'That's what I was told,' Andy replied. 'But I wasn't there. So Tamara freaks out and Bruce drags her out of the studio and home, while Nick says he'll sort things out. The girls had already gone and the rest of the crew were spaced out on whatever Lorraine had spiked the drinks with. Nick was the only one still standing, probably because of the amount of drugs he'd taken in the past, giving him a kind of resistance to it.'

'So he calls you, and you arrive. Then what?'

'I took my time,' Andy admitted. 'It pissed me off I was going back in, I wasn't a band member yet and I felt I was being used a little. But when I got there, I found everyone unconscious and Nick, covered in blood, with sheets of plastic around him. He explained all I've told you, and then tells me he wrapped up the body in plastic, taped it up and dumped it in the wall space.'

'And you just went with this?' Monroe was astonished.

Andy shook his head.

'No, I went and looked, but I didn't see anything there,' he explained. 'I learnt later that he'd put a piece of the plasterboard up already and blocked off the gap so the builders wouldn't see it. At the time, I thought Lorraine had spiked everyone's drinks with hallucinogens and had a bad fall, but had gotten up and gone after Tamara had left. And regaining consciousness and finding the body missing, Nick was having a really awful trip, fuelled partly by all the mescaline he took back then.'

'Where did you think she'd gone?' Bullman asked.

'No idea,' Andy admitted. 'I thought she'd fixed herself up back at home and was laughing herself stupid at what she'd done to the band. And then the next day Benny arrived and heard the whole thing from Nick. He believed Nick more than I did, and they kept it from everyone else. Only me, Nick and Benny knew what really happened. Well, and Bruce and Tamara, but they weren't admitting to anything anytime soon.'

'You didn't tell the police?'

'There was a copper around, Brookfield, but he was looking into some serial killer being in town the same time. I was happy to let the police think it was connected, as it got us off the hook. And we never heard anything again.'

'And you had a share of the album, and a place in the band by then,' Monroe muttered. 'Amazing what someone would do for a shot at the big time.'

'My client has given you the events of the night in good

faith,' Carrie said as she leaned in. 'He didn't see the incident, and all three people who were there at the time, Bruce Baker, Tamara Rothstead-Page and Nick Manford are all dead now, or at least believed to be dead in Mister Manford's case. He didn't see the body, nor did he believe it was really placed where Mister Manford had claimed to have hidden it. The only thing he is accessory to is the continued belief that something happened, something that even he didn't believe, because of the state of mind of all witnesses.'

She leaned back.

'You have nothing,' she said.

'We have hair,' Monroe smiled. 'Hair strands caught in the gaffer tape that secured the body, DNA that we can compare to the saliva we already have from Mister Mears's drinking straw. Hair that, if we prove it to be from Mister Mears, discredits this entire statement.'

'Well then, we'll have to wait for the DNA results to return,' Carrie said, rising from the table and looking at Andy. 'I need to speak to my client.'

'We'll leave you alone,' Monroe turned off the recording and rising, but Carrie shook her head.

'I mean the client that pays me,' she said. 'I need to speak to Mister Storm about where we intend to move on this.'

Carrie walked to the door, opening it and passing the surprised officer on the other side. The officer looked to Monroe, who nodded, and as they took Andy back to his cell, Monroe and Bullman sat alone in the interview room.

'Shite,' Monroe muttered. 'So, are they still your favourite band?'

'You said his ex-wife told you he came into the studio,' Bullman said softly. 'I heard that call. She told you to go eff yourself and disconnected the call.'

'Did she?' Monroe smiled. 'I must have misheard her.'

Bullman rose from the table now, stretching her back.

'If the DNA doesn't come back positive, we have nothing,' she said.

Monroe nodded.

'Let's hope we get a win,' he said as he looked at his phone. 'I had a call from Billy, it went to voicemail.'

He listened to his phone's messages for a moment, his eyes widening.

'I think we just hit the jackpot,' he said, disconnecting it. 'But I think it's just going to make you even more sad.'

'Why?' Bullman frowned.

'Because Peter Suffolk looks to have been the sound engineer on your favourite album,' Monroe finished. 'So let me ask you again, Ma'am, are *Alternator* still your favourite band?'

'Let's just say that I'm remembering that I loved *Suede* more,' Bullman replied as they left the interview room. 'Maybe even the *Manic Street Preachers* or *Pulp*. Come on, DNA will take a few hours. Let's get back to Temple Inn before the others do and work out what's next.'

Declan arrived at Peter Suffolk's Hampstead house moments after De'Geer and Cooper arrived in their squad car, both with the same plan in mind.

'How did you know?' Declan asked by introduction, walking up to the front door as De'Geer turned to greet him.

'The video,' De'Geer explained. 'The entire part where he watched the funeral was recorded beforehand. This gave him two hours to get to Hackney and back. You, Guv?'

'The log book for *Bear Studios* back in 1986 outs him as the sound engineer, Peanut,' Declan looked through a window. 'Which means he has a share of the album that grows every time someone dies.'

De'Geer whistled to himself as he turned to Cooper, still in the car.

'You think this is why he killed Lydia and Dave?'

Declan banged on the door.

'Andrew Knytte! Open up!' he yelled before looking back to De'Geer. 'Well, it gives motive, but at the same time this still feels personal.'

He backed down the street.

'Billy said that he was also the sound engineer for Nick in 1998, right before he disappeared. In fact, he was likely the last person to see him alive.'

'And maybe the person to end his life too, sir,' Cooper said, exiting out of the car. 'There's no movement, and he hasn't answered both of you, so I've put a call out for his car, as it's not in the driveway.'

Declan nodded at this, secretly annoyed at himself.

They had Peter Suffolk. They had him under lock and key. And they let him go.

'I should have seen this,' he muttered. 'I sat in this house and looked him in the eye. And he played me.'

'How so, Guv?' Cooper asked. Declan rubbed at his neck.

'He led me right to the straw,' he said. 'Told me exactly what I needed, so that when we realised Lydia was killed with one, we'd look straight at Andy. And when he was found with the murder weapon, we didn't even question it. Dammit, he even told us he went to Andy's. He told us everything, and we didn't work it out until he'd gone.'

Declan thought back to every conversation he'd had with Peter, and every conversation he'd had *about* him.

'If he's not here, we need to know where he is,' he said. 'And we need to work out who his next victim is.'

'I get he could be here in the timeframe it took to kill Lydia Cornwall, Guv,' De'Geer commented, 'but he wasn't in the room when Dave Manford was killed. And if he was the killer, who was the man who looked like Nick Manford?'

'Also, why would he leave alcohol and latex in the sink?' Declan mused.

'Alcohol and latex, sir?' Cooper asked. Declan realised that he'd forgotten that the young officer hadn't been in the briefing.

'DC Davey found SD Alcohol 35-A and latex in the apartment,' he said, reading from his notes.

Cooper's face broke into a smile.

'I know what that is,' she said. 'I do amateur dramatics, and SD Alcohol 35-A is a key component in spirit gum. I'm allergic to it, so have to use liquid latex instead, when applying prosthetics or fake hair.'

Declan stared at Cooper.

'I'll tour in productions as Roy Orbison or Buddy Holly, you know the type of thing. I've gotten really fast on the makeup side for those gigs.'

'Peter uses prosthetics for his tours,' he said. 'When he plays dead rock stars. So would you use spirit gum when adding a soul patch to your chin? If you were, say, making yourself look like Nick?'

'Yes sir,' Cooper answered. 'If he did those sorts of tributes, he'd definitely use it.'

'And it's portable?'

'Absolutely, it's a tiny bottle, the size of nail varnish remover.'

Declan nodded. The Nick Manford that had been seen tampering with the amp, and who had faced Dave on stage in *Eastcheap Albums* had worn a hoodie and glasses, as well as a chin beard. All of which could have been hidden in the leather messenger bag he wore. And he could have walked into Lydia's apartment as Peter, claiming he was checking up on her, and then changed into the costume before leaving, deliberately passing the large, obvious security camera at the end of the road, which would explain the traces in the bathroom as he affixed it to his face.

But how was Eden Storm connected to this, if at all? And how did it link to a murder, thirty-five years ago?

'The sound engineer. Never knew his real name, scrawny runt, working the summer holidays before going off to wherever. But he idolised Nick when he wasn't mooning over Lorraine in the pub.'

'Peter Suffolk was in love with Lorraine Warner,' Declan said aloud in realisation. 'He must have somehow learnt the truth, that Tamara killed her. Maybe even when he did the solo album—'

He stopped.

'Peter must have learnt beforehand that Nick was recording,' he said. 'He staked out the pub, waiting for Nick to arrive and book it, and then offered his services. And if he knew or believed that Tamara and Nick had conspired to hide Lorraine's body, after years of believing that he was to blame... he's looking to kill the whole bloody lot of them.'

ANJLI HAD ALMOST REACHED TOWER BRIDGE WHEN SHE noticed the SUV that had been tailing her.

Turning into Thomas More street, she pulled up on the double yellow lines to the left, exiting the car and walking towards the SUV that, parked up behind her, was now indicating to leave.

She'd expected to find some dodgy, black-hatted government employee emerge, or some legal representative of the band, but instead the driver's door opened and Eden Storm stepped out.

'Eden. This isn't the way to get in touch,' she said. 'Why exactly were you following me?'

'Not here, let's take a walk,' Eden said. 'Please.'

'No bodyguard?' Anjli smiled. 'They let you out on your own?'

Eden looked pained, as if this jibe had bitten a bit too deep.

'Nobody believes me,' he said. 'That my father might still be alive, that is. I think you're the only person who could give me a straight answer.'

He nodded towards the entrance gate to St Katherine's Docks.

'Please,' he added. 'Five minutes.'

Anjli sighed.

The trouble you get into over a pretty face, she thought to herself as she followed him through the gate.

MARNA WASN'T EXPECTING ANY MORE CALLS, BUT THE MAN AT the gate intrigued her.

'I'm not putting the dog aside for you,' she said as she opened the door, staring out onto the porch.

'That's fine,' Peter said, hands in his pockets, feeling the weapon hidden inside the left one, gripping it tightly. 'This is a quick visit, and then I'll be gone. I have something for you.'

'Leave it there and I'll pick it up,' Marna said cautiously.

Peter sighed.

'Come on, Marna, I'm the only one without a grudge here,' he said. 'The curse thing? You, me? We're not involved.'

Marna considered this and then shook her head.

'Sorry, but no,' she replied. 'I saw you talking to the police outside earlier. I don't want to know what's going on and I need to work. Come back tomorrow.'

And with this, she shut the door as Peter Suffolk stared balefully from the gate.

'Fine then, do it the hard way,' he muttered, pulling out a remote control and clicking it. The gate started to slowly swing open and Peter walked through. And, walking up to the front door, he pulled out a metal house key from his leather messenger bag, placing it into the lock, and turning.

This wasn't the first time Peter had been in the house.

But it'd definitely be the last.

26

MANIAC

DECLAN PACED AROUND THE OFFICE, FURIOUS.

'I can't believe I didn't see it,' he muttered to himself. 'The bloody clues were there from the start.'

'If the lawyers had given us the names of the people involved with the royalties, we would have,' Monroe muttered morosely. 'The bloody man's cooked us like royal kippers.'

While Doctor Marcos and DC Davey had stayed at *Bear Studios* to keep investigating, the new information on Peter Suffolk had brought everyone else back into the office, and in particular, the briefing room; Billy had returned with a message from Doctor Marcos, saying she'd ride share back with Davey, and that *Declan had better not have bloody dinged my Merc* shortly before Monroe and Bullman returned from Scotland Yard, having had to release Andy Mears based on this new evidence. Declan had been the last to arrive, De'Geer and Cooper having stayed to keep watch on Suffolk's house, in case he returned.

Of Anjli, there was no sign and so Monroe, assuming that

Johnny Lucas was probably giving one of his stupidly long anecdotes, started without her.

On the plasma screen were the images of Martin Reilly, Graham Hagen, Benny Simpson, Peter Suffolk and Andy Mears. Beneath them, and crossed out were images of Bruce Baker, Tamara Rothstead-Hyde, Nick and Dave Manford, Shaun Williams and Lydia Cornwall.

'So what's his motive here?' Monroe asked, staring up at it.

Declan shook his head.

'I contacted Brookfield and asked if Peanut could have been the secret boyfriend of Lorraine, and he said it was possible but never proven,' he said. 'But if he was in love with her, it could explain a lot of this.'

He rose, pointing at the first picture, that of Bruce Baker.

'Except for this one,' he muttered. 'Look at the hypothetical here. Peter is young, enthusiastic, but naïve. He's excited about working with *Alternator*, but it costs him his chance with Lorraine.'

'He lives in West Drayton, where the party was that Martin and Graham attended,' Bullman said, sitting in the room this time rather than hovering around the door. 'It makes sense that he takes them to the party, maybe to show off a little. Probably doesn't realise what they did until later. Maybe he's blamed for this by Lorraine, maybe even helps her.'

'No, he didn't know, or he wouldn't have drunk the champagne,' Monroe shook his head. 'But I think he was to blame for this. In a way his one action, bringing the rock stars to a party, started everything.'

'And that's my problem,' Declan continued. 'Peter believes he was involved with a terrible death, one that he effectively caused. I can see how he'd feel he needed to gain righteous vengeance. But Bruce was doing the same, about to come clean. Why kill him?'

'So we still have more than one murderer,' Monroe mused. 'Maybe even several if we consider Tamara Rothstead to be a victim too.'

'MY MOTHER WAS AN EXCEPTIONAL WOMAN,' EDEN MUTTERED as he walked through St Katherine's Docks, Anjli by his side, her notebook in her hand. To their right was a long, brown brick and five-storey building, the bottom floors mainly taken by bars and restaurants, while to the left was the Thames, built into a marina with a ton of expensive looking boats moored up.

'I'm sure she was, but I don't understand how that matters here,' Anjli replied.

Eden nodded.

'She made a mistake,' he said. 'Two, really. She slept with Nick Manford, and then she confronted Nick Manford.'

'The first created you,' Anjli offered. 'Are you that sure you're a mistake?'

Eden nodded.

'I was told from a very early age,' he said. 'My entire family thought so. Apart from mom. She fought against them, ensured I had the best life. And, when I was seven, she brought me to London for the first time, and I met Nick.'

'You met your father?'

Eden paused at a boat, staring at it curiously.

'I think I own that one,' he muttered before continuing. 'Sorry. I met Nick many times between the age of seven and eleven, when he died, but at the start I knew him as Uncle Nick.'

He stared off into the water.

'The Rothsteads didn't approve, and the Pages thought I was a bastard,' he snarled, the anger and hurt in his voice clear. 'They wanted the will changed, so that when mom died, I didn't inherit. It was a whole cluster bomb, you know?'

'I get the gist.'

'So I'm about ten years old, and I meet Uncle Nick right after Christmas,' Eden explained. 'He gives me presents, so I'm overjoyed, as he's the only one outside of mom who gives a shit. And, while I'm playing, mom and Nick are talking in the other room of the suite.'

'You met in hotels?' Anjli was surprised.

Eden shrugged.

'Suites become second homes when you hit that level of money,' he said. 'Anyway, I never usually listened, but this time I went to speak to mom because one of the toys needed batteries, and I stopped outside, hearing them argue. Now, I'm ten, not a toddler, so I'm pretty savvy with the world. And, as I listened, I heard mom tell Nick that she wouldn't state publicly that he was my father, even though Ethan, my dad, had recently learnt the truth. She said that her and dad were divorcing, and she needed to cleanse herself. She needed to do right by the *girl*.'

'What girl?' Anjli stopped. Eden turned to face her.

'She didn't say, but years later I worked out she meant Lorraine Warner, the girl that died at *Bear Studios*.'

'You say it as if you know that for a fact,' Anjli said, deciding not to mention the recently revealed body found there.

Eden nodded.

'When they argued, mom wanted to know what Nick did with the body. *Her* body. He said he couldn't remember. There was more of a fight and she then said she couldn't live with the fact that *she killed her*. Now, at this point mom's assistant caught me and asked what I was doing there. I explained about the battery, playing down what I heard and mom and Nick, who I now knew was my dad, stopped talking. Later that day, when we were leaving, I heard mom tell Nick, when she thought I wasn't listening, that she couldn't go on.'

'If you don't mind me asking,' Anjli started softly. 'How did your mother truly die? We had it marked as an accident while snorkelling—'

'My mom committed suicide,' Eden replied simply. 'She drowned herself, rather than live with what she did. And Nick, or dad, whatever you want to call him, he committed suicide the same way, walking into the sea so that he could be with her.'

'You don't know that,' Anjli replied.

'I do,' Eden countered. 'I heard from Benny Simpson a couple of years later, and he showed me lyrics from a song Nick was writing for a final album. He literally said in it *he lost his love in the sea and soon he would search for her*. I think the album was supposed to be his suicide note.'

Anjli considered this.

'But if Nick wanted to release this before he went and killed himself, why only do half an album?' she asked.

'I think it became too hard to stay on land,' Eden replied.

———

DECLAN WAS PACING NOW AS HE THOUGHT ALOUD.

'Shaun Williams dies in a freak accident,' he said. 'Maybe he decided to talk, and someone offed him? If so, who?'

'Any of them,' Monroe replied. Billy nodded, tapping on his keyboard.

'Shaun dies, then Tamara dies in a freak drowning accident.'

'Nick disappears after,' Declan added, 'while recording with Peter, in his guise of Peanut, which is the first time we see him again.'

'Peter kills Nick?' Monroe suggested. 'He was probably prime suspect in Peter's mind.'

'Maybe, but then we have a bunch of years where nothing happens,' Declan carried on pacing.

'Peter releases a couple of singles during that time with the band he was with before *Alternator*,' Billy suggested. 'One is called *Love Lost To The Sea* and could be about Nick's suicide?'

'Did he write it?' Declan asked. 'Or is this one of the missing masters that they can't find, repurposed by Suffolk?'

'That's a question we need to ask him,' Billy nodded. 'I've heard it on *YouTube*. It's very similar in style.'

Declan shook his head, already moving on. 'He could have taken them out one at a time, but decided to do it now. Why?'

'The album sale?'

'But that doesn't explain Bruce dying, or Benny being terrified for his life,' Monroe interjected.

'Maybe Marna and Andy killed Bruce?' Billy offered.

Monroe nodded.

'That'd fit, but there's no way we can prove that without a confession, and that wee lassie who keeps being sent to guard them won't allow that.'

'Why is Eden Storm funding that, anyway?' Declan asked.

The image of Carrie Woodstock appeared on the screen now.

'Maybe it's a *Clark Kent* scenario,' Billy suggested.

'Clark Kent?' Monroe was bemused.

'You know, Superman's other identity,' Billy explained. 'Publicly Eden looks like the good guy, while quietly his bulldog stops the case moving on.'

'Clark Kent,' Declan stared at the image of the blonde, bespectacled solicitor. 'Billy, do you have the photos I took at Peter's house?'

Billy tapped on the keyboard.

'Hold on,' he said, pressing return as the images of the photo frames appeared on the screen.

'Zoom in on the one with Peter and his partner,' Declan said, leaning closer as the image of a slightly younger Peter Suffolk and his blonde partner, taken at some event, appeared larger on the screen, the woman's face now clearly visible.

'That's Carrie Woodstock,' Bullman muttered. 'She's not wearing glasses.'

'So the solicitor that's been in with Peter and Andy, and who's working for Eden Storm has been hanging around with Peter Suffolk for years?' Monroe held his hands up. 'And we're only just learning this now?'

'WHEN DID PETER COME TO YOU?' ANJLI ASKED. 'HOW DID YOU both meet?'

'Company fundraiser on a cruise ship two years back,' Eden admitted. 'I'd never told anyone that I was Nick's kid, and the rumours never had proof. And there I was, at an event where Peter Suffolk was on stage singing Nick's songs. He'd been with *Alternator* for years by then, and been hired by someone in my company by pure chance to perform solo. I was impressed and met him.'

'When was the last time you saw him?'

'About seven months back, I think.'

'And you gave him *Edisun* tech?'

'No, I never did,' Eden replied, surprised at the question, his eyes widening in realisation as he reached a conclusion.

'You mean *my tech* killed Dave?'

Anjli watched Eden carefully.

'You didn't know?' she asked. 'That he'd taken anything?'

'No,' Eden said. 'Only my legal team dealt with R&D, mainly to fill out the patents.'

Anjli pulled out her phone, dialling Billy.

'Yeah, we need to chat about that,' she said.

'So it's Tamara's family trying to silence this,' Declan leaned against a desk. 'They must know what she did.'

'But what did Tamara do?' Monroe asked. 'Rosanna said that there was a stab wound, but also a vicious head wound to the body. Did she do one of these, or both? Because if she didn't do both, who *did* give the killing blow?'

'If you believe Andy, it was Nick,' Bullman rubbed her neck. 'He was the only one conscious.'

'Any news on the DNA found in the tape?' Monroe looked at Billy, who shook his head.

'No, but it has to be either Tamara, Nick, Bruce or Andy,'

he said, 'if we go on the basis that the others were too spaced to do anything.'

'Of which three are dead,' Monroe added.

'Okay, so let's say that Peter offs anyone involved in Lorraine's death whether implicit or not,' Declan rose from the desk, walking around the room once more. 'Maybe he realises that once they make their money, they're untouchable.'

'Or he decides that he should have the money,' Bullman suggested.

'So he kills Dave Manford, dressed as Nick,' Declan continued. 'Nick is possibly still out there, so it's a valid play. We know Peter can work his magic on makeup, and a hood shadows his face. He speaks to Lydia at the bar, gives her the ring that eventually connects the circuit using the excuse that it'll monitor Dave's heart rate, leaves, changes in a back room with no camera, returns to kill Dave, leaves again.'

'And then the next day he kills Lydia, ensuring she can't mention the ring, again making it look like this is Nick, avenging himself.'

Declan looked at the images on the wall.

'What about Martin and Graham, though?' he considered aloud. 'Surely he'd gain revenge on them. They're the ones that caused this.'

'Not if he thinks he's to blame for what they did,' Monroe replied. 'He might feel they need a more public trial. He knew that we'd learn of the attack, and that we'd end up investigating it when we found them. Or they were being left until last, kept somewhere he could go to whenever he needed.'

Declan nodded. 'Maybe he wants them and Benny and Andy and Marna to spend their lives looking over their shoulders, waiting for 'Nick' to appear and kill them while he takes his album share.'

'Aye,' Monroe muttered. 'Because Andy and bloody Marna have ensured that everyone believes Nick is alive.'

'And Marna at least believes that he is, because he takes the yearly money,' Declan nodded. 'Which leads us to the possibility that Nick was killed by Peter in 1998.'

Billy looked up from his phone, now ringing.

'It's Anjli,' he said, answering it. 'I'm putting you on the screen, so use your camera.'

On the screen, the image of Anjli, taken from her phone camera, appeared.

'You don't seem to be in Globe Town,' Monroe mused.

'*No, Guv,*' Anjli spoke through the speakers. '*I'm with Eden Storm.*' The camera moved to show what looked like a confused and nervous Eden.

'Not the time to have a date, lassie.'

'*He's happy to answer questions,*' Anjli replied. '*He's in the dark as much as we are.*'

'Then ask him why his solicitor is working double time for *Alternator*,' Bullman snapped. 'Carrie Woodstock.'

The image moved and now Eden Storm stared into the lens.

'*Carrie Woodstock is a patents solicitor,*' he said. '*She's on retainer, not a full-time employee.*'

'Know all your employees that well, do you?' Declan asked.

Eden laughed.

'*If only,*' he said. '*I only recognise the name because she was the one who introduced me to Peter Suffolk a few years back.*'

'Would she have had access to *Edisun* tech?' Billy asked.

Eden nodded.

'*She filed it for patents, so yeah, she'd have been the first to see it all,*' he said. '*You think she killed Dave?*'

'She's Peter Suffolk's partner, and we think he did it, so it's probable,' Declan was pacing. 'So you're Peter, you've killed Lydia and Dave, where do you go now?'

'*Martin, Graham or Andy,*' Anjli suggested. '*Has to be one of them, they're the only ones left.*'

'Andy's been here, so he's safe,' Billy replied.

'Yeah, but he's not here anymore,' Declan added. 'His solicitor will have driven him home the moment he was released.'

'Carrie Woodstock. Christ,' Monroe looked at Billy. 'Ping his bloody phone, laddie. He's in a car with a potential murderer's associate, one that heard him confess about Lorraine's death.'

Billy started typing as DC Davey, running through the office door, came hurtling into the room at speed.

'We have phones, lassie,' Monroe said as she almost clattered into the doorway in her haste to arrive.

'I know sir, but I got the news as I arrived and it seemed easier to come straight up,' Davey wheezed, out of breath. 'We have the DNA results on the hair trapped in the gaffer tape.'

'Nick Manford?' Declan asked. Davey shook her head.

'Andy Mears,' she said. 'Definite match.'

'So Mears was involved in the body's hiding,' Declan replied to this. 'Does Peter know? Has he known from the start?'

Monroe considered this.

'He wasn't at the house, so there's a chance he doesn't know we're on to him,' he said. 'But if he knows Andy killed

Lorraine, and he's been holding him until last, he's finishing up tonight.'

'He's not in London,' Billy said. 'The phone is pinging on cell towers off the M23, moving south past Gatwick.'

'South?' Bullman asked. 'What's down there that Peter knows? East Sussex, Brighton...'

'Christ, Andy's being taken to the Birling Gap!' Declan exclaimed. 'We need to stop him!'

'How?' Bullman rose now, angry. 'It's a good two hours there from here. He's got an hour's head start, too.'

'I've been to Birling Gap,' Eden said through the speaker. *'I went to pay my respects a few years back. It's mainly fields and flat campsites.'*

'And how does that help, exactly?' Monroe spat angrily. On the screen, Eden shrugged.

'I'm a billionaire who has a helicopter on call,' he replied. *'I can have it in Temple Gardens in three minutes and we can be there within thirty. There's space for two or three people in it.'*

'Do it, laddie,' Monroe ordered, looking at Declan.

'You okay with heights?' he asked. 'If you and the Guv go, we can follow by car.'

Declan was already grabbing his jacket, following Bullman out of the door.

As the helicopter landed in Temple Gardens, Declan kept his head down as he ran to the door, opening it. In the pilot's seat was Eden Storm, headphones on, while next to him was a grinning Anjli.

'This is the best case ever,' she exclaimed excitedly as Declan clambered inside, Bullman following.

'Where's the pilot?' Bullman asked.

'I have a helicopter parked up in London, but I don't have a pilot on retainer,' Eden explained. 'It would have taken another hour to find one at this time of night, so I did it myself. I am flight certified, after all.'

'Then let's go,' Declan said, already strapping himself in. 'The others will join us there.'

And, as the residents of Temple Gardens came out to stare at the helicopter that had landed there, Eden pulled on the throttle and it rose back into the sky, turning south across the Thames.

27

SUNSET CLIFFS

Eden hadn't overstated the helicopter's speed; having effectively free rein speed wise, he had really allowed the helicopter to open up, and there had been several points during the journey where Declan, even being used to such aerial antics, had felt airsick. And then, with a jarring lurch to a stop they'd arrived at the Birling Gap, which seemed empty.

They'd landed in the furthest car park, emerging from the helicopter as Eden powered it down.

'Do you have a gun?' Declan asked as Eden exited the helicopter.

'My bodyguard Wardler does. He has a permit, it's all above board.'

'And he's still in London, isn't he?' Declan almost hit the side of the helicopter in frustration.

Eden shrugged.

'I have three police detectives with me,' he replied. 'I didn't think I'd need one.'

There were lights approaching from down the road, and

Declan led the others to the café, pulling out his lockpick set as he reached the door.

'We're hiding?' Eden said, surprised. 'I thought you'd just stop the car and arrest them?'

'We don't know who *them* is yet,' Anjli replied as Declan opened the door, ushering them inside. 'And *them* probably has a gun.'

'We also want to let things play out a little,' Declan was removing his extendable baton, before thinking better of this and putting it away. 'And we don't know where Peter is, so we might have a bit of a gathering turning up here, especially if he's meeting Carrie.'

'And if he takes Andy to the beach and shoots him?' Eden was a little gun fixated. 'Before you get a chance to stop him?'

'I've seen Suffolk on stage half a dozen times,' Bullman shook her head. 'He's a born showman. He'll want his moment in the spotlight.'

'And they're easier to talk to, as well,' Declan said, but his face belayed the lie he was stating. As the lights grew brighter, he moved everyone deeper into the cafe, leaving the door open as an obvious location for whatever Peter planned, watching the vehicle pull in to the car park.

It was Marna Manford's car.

'On with the show,' he said.

ANDY MEARS HAD BEEN ANNOYED FOR MOST OF THE JOURNEY down to East Sussex, but had kept quiet. After all, Carrie Woodstock seemed to know what she was doing, and he knew Eden Storm was footing the bill for this; she'd explained this to him when she first arrived in the interview room.

'Why here?' he asked as they drove south through some narrow country lanes. At no answer, he pulled out his phone. 'I need to call Marna.'

'She's waiting for us there, Mister Mears,' Carrie replied with a smile. 'It's a council of war to decide what's next.'

'What's next is that we get Peter Suffolk locked away for being a mad, murdering bastard,' Andy muttered. 'Is that why we're here? To hide? Or is it to bring him out?'

'A bit of both,' Carrie responded, indicating left down another long country road. 'We felt it's best to keep you all safe until this blows over.'

'Good,' Andy leaned back in the chair. 'Yeah. Good.'

Carrie didn't respond. If she had, she might have given everything away. But she stayed calm, content in the fact that within a matter of minutes, everything would finally end.

IT WAS ALMOST NINE BY THE TIME THAT CARRIE WOODSTOCK pulled into the carpark. There was a one-storey café and bar to the right, but it looked closed for the day; the sun was setting, after all. And on the left was a row of old houses, although as Andy looked closer, he realised they were one extensive building, with a middle section painted a different colour to give the appearance of a row. There was one other vehicle parked at the far end, and Andy recognised it immediately as Marna's.

'The Gap is owned by the National Trust,' Carrie explained as they climbed out of her car. 'Everything closes at five, and once the sun sets this gets quite empty.'

She pointed to a field at the back.

'Some people camp here, but there's nothing for miles, so they often come for the day and then go elsewhere at night. It's quite secluded.'

'And we're here because?' Andy followed Carrie as she walked across the car park, towards the sea view.

'It's the last place he'll look,' Carrie replied. 'My client knows how to end this charade.'

'And your client is Eden Storm?'

Carrie didn't comment as she now turned towards the café, and Andy saw that the door to the side was left open, the lights off inside.

Andy went to reply as they entered the building, but stopped as he saw who was waiting for him.

Marna, her eyes smudged with tears, ran to Andy, embracing him tightly.

'I thought they'd killed you,' she moaned.

Andy looked up at the man in the tattered hoodie, the gun now aimed at him.

'You did this?' he asked. 'You killed all of them?'

'Not all of them,' Peter smiled. 'I mean, you did well with Bruce and Ray, didn't you?'

'But why?' Andy was thrown, staring around in confusion. 'You're just the singer!'

'Peter Suffolk's a singer,' Peter replied. 'But you knew me in another name, another job back then. A sound engineer named *Peanut*.'

Andy stared for a long moment at Peter, as if trying to get his head around this.

'Where did you get that gun?' he eventually asked, focusing on the pistol for the first time.

'Nick gave it to me,' Peter smiled. 'A long time ago.'

'So you're going to shoot us?' Marna said, looking back at Peter now. 'With my husband's gun?'

'That's the problem I'm weighing up right now,' Peter admitted. 'One part of me knows this would extend the whole *Nick is alive* fallacy, but having you both jump to your deaths off the cliff would be just as easy, and we can class it as you committing suicide rather than get caught. You know, *Thelma and Louise* without the car. Nick returned and you committed suicide rather than facing him.'

'You called it a fallacy. You don't think Nick's alive?' Marna asked and as a reply, Peter just laughed.

'If he is, then he's bloody good at *hide and seek*,' he raised the gun, aiming it at Marna. 'Let's see how good *you* are.'

'That probably isn't the best of ideas,' Declan said now as he emerged from the kitchen area. 'I mean, in a hostage situation, you need hostages.'

There was a moment of confusion as Carrie glared at Peter.

'You didn't check to see if we were *alone?*' she hissed.

'The helicopter out in the campsite's back field was a bit of a giveaway,' Declan smiled. 'But as it wasn't lit up and you both seemed so focused when you arrived, we thought it best to keep quiet. I'd suggest you put the gun down now.'

At this, Bullman, Anjli and Eden emerged from behind him.

'So we're all clear right now, Miss Woodstock, you're fired,' Eden snapped.

Peter didn't seem fazed by this, however and instead grabbed Andy, placing the gun to his head as he held him as a shield.

'Before you kill him, which by the way I'd rather you didn't, as we're arresting him too,' Declan moved closer. 'Can

I tell you how I think it came out? My boss is a big fan, and I want to ensure she goes home with closure.'

Peter shook his head, his gun still aimed at Andy's head.

'Nobody will get closure from this,' he muttered.

'This is all your fault, isn't it?' Declan asked, moving closer. 'I mean, you think it is, right?'

'I started it all,' Peter nodded. 'Lorraine died because of me.'

'You took Martin and Graham to the party, didn't you?' Declan asked. 'Where they spiked those girls' drinks?'

Peter nodded again.

'I wanted to look cool,' he said. 'I didn't know they'd do *that*. And I only realised what they did a couple of days later when Lorraine stopped the locals from bashing their heads in.'

'Were you seeing Lorraine at the time?'

'I was slowly winning her over,' Peter admitted. 'But as far as she was concerned, I now hung around with rapists.'

'So Lorraine spikes their drinks in return, and goes to the studios with you,' Anjli said now. 'While there you all drink, and you all pass out.'

'I don't even remember the girls going home,' Peter replied. 'When Benny arrived the next day, he had already spoken to Bruce, and he knew everything, although he kept it quiet. Said she'd left with a traveller clan that went off to Kent, needed a bit of space, had a secret fiancé and they were eloping. But because of Graham and Martin's antics, we needed to keep quiet.'

'But you remembered nothing.'

'Pretty much,' Peter replied. 'And I was never a hundred percent sold on the story, always convinced there was more, worried that I'd been to blame for her disappearance because of that party. I didn't do anything after drama school, became a bit of a failure, really. Doing part time work here and there, drinking in *The Bear* at night, pissing away the blood money I received every quarter from that album. And then one day, late in 1998, Nick bloody Manford returns. But it's not the same Nick I knew. This one doesn't drink, is off drugs, and he's grieving.'

'Tamara was dead.'

'Yeah,' Peter agreed. 'He wanted to make a new solo album, quiet and off grid, and when he'd booked the studio, Keith aimed him at me. Probably thought he was helping me, giving me a second chance. Which in a way, he was. And here and there we'd get together, usually after he did a gig, and record songs. He was a changed man, a haunted man. One night, after he sang a particular song, he told me that Tamara had committed suicide. She blamed herself for Lorraine's death that night, and felt she needed to atone by dying.'

'He said my mom killed Lorraine?' Eden asked.

'Blamed herself for the death,' Peter corrected. 'I learned later that's a different thing. But the conversation shook me. I didn't remember Tamara being there, and this was the first time someone had stated Lorraine was dead. I assumed he was just misremembering, but now I knew there was a conspiracy going on. And now and then, he'd look around the studios and mention he *couldn't remember where he put it*, and it wasn't until years later I realised he meant her body.'

'How did Nick die?' Declan asked.

Peter shrugged.

'He left his gun back at the studio and drove straight here that night,' he stated.

'And the money?' Declan asked. 'The fifty grand a year he was removing?'

'No idea,' Peter replied, frowning a little at this. 'He explained about his plan to get away one night. Maybe he managed it, and he's still out there, taking his yearly cut?'

Marna and Andy stared at each other, open mouthed.

'And then a few years later you joined *Alternator*,' Declan continued now. 'Did you arrange the accident for Jesse Morrison?'

'No,' Peter shook his head vehemently. 'Jesse wasn't to blame for any of this, so I wouldn't have hurt him. I'd made contact, as *Peter Suffolk, singer* with Martin and Graham, trying to find a way to expose them publicly. They didn't know that I was once the kid they knew called Peanut, it'd been a good twenty years or so since we'd last met, and I was stick thin back then with a skinhead cut. When the spot came up, they suggested I took the job.'

'Oh, this is bullshit—' Andy went to speak, but Declan stepped in.

'Don't,' he said. 'We've got DNA on the tape that matches you. We know you sealed the body up, and we also believe you were the one that gave Lorraine the second, fatal wound.'

There was a long, awkward moment as Peter, letting go of his hostage, now stared at Andy in surprise at this revelation.

'I was scared and confused!' Andy snapped back. 'I arrived as Bruce and Tamara left, and when I got in there, everyone was away with the faeries and Lorraine was bleeding out on the rug! I didn't know who else had seen this, or if the police were coming, so I did what I had to!'

'You killed her.'

'I was merciful!' Andy continued. 'The head wound was vicious. You could see broken skull, brain even. She wasn't going to survive. I put her out of her misery.'

'And then you hid her, letting Nick think that he did that,'

Anjli said. 'Is that why you had Dave fired? Because he'd guessed that there was more to this?'

Andy stayed silent, so Anjli looked at Peter again.

'At what point did you begin planning revenge?'

'When Bruce Baker died, three years ago,' Carrie spoke now. 'I was a junior associate at *Sutherland and Abnett*. I learned that Bruce wanted to break his *Secrets and Lies* NDA, and had mentioned confidentially that he wanted to come clean over what happened. But then he died. And Ray Cornwall died, and then Benny Simpson had a stroke the day after Andy and Marna visited him. I found Bruce's deposition and read it, saw the legal forms that Tamara filed back in the eighties, and the threats Ray made in the nineties on those poor girls. I saw the injustices that were pushed through to keep the deal quiet. It didn't sit well with me.'

'And then we met by chance at an event,' Peter added. 'We got talking, and somehow we end up discussing this. I wanted justice, and she knew I wouldn't get it. So I decided to go a different route. Revenge.'

'Bruce deserved what he got!' Marna protested. 'We didn't know he had cancer!'

'Shut up!' Andy snapped at her. 'You're damning us!'

'You were both damned a long time before this,' Declan said, before turning back to Peter. 'I'm guessing that Miss Woodstock here gained the *Edisun* tech?'

'We wanted to muddy the waters,' Peter said. 'Using Nick's son as a patsy, and dressing like Nick, it all gave everything plausible deniability when we finally acted. And, when the back catalogue deal was offered, I realised that now was the only chance I'd get as after the payouts were made, *Alternator* would probably disband.'

'The night of Dave's murder, you broke into Marna's

house, didn't you?' Declan was on a roll now. 'You placed the greyhound in the cellar so she couldn't raise an alarm by barking, and you went through his old things, taking a hoodie, glasses, even a necklace phial of blood.'

Peter nodded.

'I wanted to leave things around that gave the impression that Nick was returning from the grave,' he said. 'I wanted to leave Nick's blood with Martin and Graham when I eventually shot them in the caravan, but Lydia grabbed at it when we fought, and I didn't realise it was gone until I'd left.'

'You stole Marna's house keys when you swapped the straw,' Andy muttered. 'And what, swapped the bloody straw back into the pouch when you came to see me after you killed Lydia?'

'Pretty much,' Peter shrugged. 'Dave had a real fear of having another heart attack, so I had a ring made, and said to Lydia that if Dave wore it I could measure his heart rate from outside, call her if there was an issue. In actuality, I just needed him to wear it when we connected him to the mains. She believed it worked, and that made Dave believe it.'

He glanced out of the window, into the approaching night.

'I made a big thing about the argument with Lydia so you'd contact me first, allow me to misdirect from the start,' he explained. 'So I gave my performance for the CCTV at the bar, ducked into the loos, put on the hoodie, glasses and beard, plugged the device into the amp and then stood in front of Dave when I pressed the switch. I escaped out in the chaos, ducked into a side street, swapped clothes and then came back.'

'Where you bumped into Benny.'

Peter's expression darkened.

'Yeah, I didn't expect to get found out there,' he said. 'I genuinely didn't recognise him. I'd always heard that Benny was a vegetable in a chair, you know? And he didn't give me his name.'

'And then you killed Lydia.'

'She was complicit too, both her and her husband,' Peter shrugged. 'She deserved what she got, I killed her and changed quickly, getting the hell out.'

'Clever bit with the funeral,' Anjli added. 'You ruined it with the mug in the shot though.'

'Yeah, I realised that later,' Peter nodded. 'But by then I'd framed Andy on live TV, so I was hoping to run out the clock. And Carrie was keeping everything moving.'

'And why exactly are you doing this?' Declan looked at Carrie, who shrugged.

'It's amazing what a few zeros on an account will do, especially when your billionaire boss hasn't given you a bonus in years,' she said. 'And as I said, it didn't sit well with me.'

'I didn't mean for *Bear Studios* to go bust, and I didn't know Lorraine was there all this time,' Peter admitted. 'The plan was to kill these two tonight then go find Graham and Martin tomorrow, shooting them with this gun, the bullet matching one fired into an Acton club ceiling in 1998. Then, I'd simply disappear. People would never know if Nick returned from the dead or not, you would never solve the case and this would kill the back catalogue deal so that nobody made a penny. It'd leave the whole thing tied up like a bow.'

'So you'd escape onto a non-extradition beach?' Declan asked.

'Oh no,' Peter looked down at the gun in his hand. 'I'm guilty too. Everyone pays.'

'And what about Benny?' Bullman asked, slowly moving forward.

'He would have passed away quietly in his sleep, but that's out of the window now,' Peter sighed, looking through the glass panes into the night. 'Now the only one who can pay for their sins properly is me.'

And then, before anyone could stop him, he pulled the trigger, firing the gun, shattering one of the back windows before hurling himself bodily out of it, running into the night.

'No!' Carrie cried out. 'That's the—'

She stopped as they heard the scream, a horrifying noise made as Andrew Peter Knytte, otherwise known as Peter Suffolk, otherwise known as Peanut deliberately ran off the edge of the cliff, falling to the stone beach far below.

'Elvis has left the building,' Bullman muttered to nobody in particular.

EPILOGUE

After Peter committed suicide, the confrontation ended. Carrie Woodstock was arrested by Bullman as Anjli and Declan arrested both Andy Mears and Marna Manford for the murder of Bruce Baker three years earlier, adding the murder of Lorraine Warner in 1986 for Andy.

And, as they walked the three suspects out of the café, Declan could already see the blue flashing lights of the local force that had been sent to assist, amused that they'd arrived from London quicker than the local teams had.

Declan realised that Bullman had been correct; Peter Suffolk did want his moment in the spotlight.

And now Peter Suffolk was in the spotlight one last time, as forensics officers examined his broken body on the shore beneath the cliffs by torchlight.

'It really was a good plan,' Monroe said as they stood on the bridge that led to the steps down to the beach. 'And

Miss Woodstock's already talking, explaining that Peter had written a will naming her as beneficiary in the event of his death.'

'He didn't intend to survive this,' Declan realised. 'He was wiping every guilty party out, including himself. And by then we'd add him to the list, assuming it was Nick that had abducted him.'

'All killed by a dead man,' Monroe nodded. 'It'd be the ultimate cold case.'

Eden Storm walked over, Anjli beside him.

'Thank you,' he said. 'You've laid my father's memory to rest.'

'I've kinda destroyed it a little,' Declan admitted. 'I mean, now everyone's going to know he was involved in a murder conspiracy and a whole ton of God knows what.'

'Maybe it'll force him to come out of hiding, if he's still alive,' Eden smiled.

'What will you do?' Declan asked. 'Will you claim the back catalogue?'

'I will,' Eden nodded. 'I've just purchased the recording studio too.'

He looked out to the sea, dark against the evening sky.

'I'm going to set up a foundation in their names,' he said. 'Mom and dad. The *Alternator* songs, his solo ones once we find the masters, all the money they'll ever make will now go to those.'

'And the contract with *Secret and Lies?*' Anjli asked.

Eden shrugged.

'I think the only person still alive who isn't dead is Benny,' he said. 'And I feel he might be swapping his nursing home for a prison cell soon.'

Declan nodded.

'Especially as we can prove he doesn't have dementia, and spent two decades aware of what happened, I think Benny will be answering a lot of questions.'

'I'll be leaving now,' Eden looked back at the helicopter. 'I have an early meeting tomorrow.'

'Going anywhere nice?' Declan asked.

'Paris,' Eden replied, looking at Anjli. 'There's room for another if you want?'

'I'll pass,' Anjli said, glancing at Declan. 'My place is here.'

Eden nodded.

'If you ever need me, please let me know and I'll drop everything,' he said. 'Especially when you need more statements.'

And this said, Eden Storm walked back into the car park, climbed into his helicopter and, after a moment, rose up into the night, flying away.

'You should have gone with him,' Declan said. 'You could have had a life of luxury, and drink great coffee every day.'

'I already have great coffee,' Anjli punched Declan on the arm. 'I bought a machine, remember?'

'You should both get some rest,' Monroe said. 'It's been a busy few days.'

'How, Guv?' Declan asked. 'Our cars are in London.'

'There's a pub a mile or two up the road,' Monroe pointed northwards. 'They have half a dozen rooms, and I've requisitioned them for us all. Go grab some scoff, get some sleep, and we'll get a squad car to take you back tomorrow, when we'll start interviews again.'

He looked down at the beach.

'Let's leave tonight to the scientists.'

Declan nodded, glancing at Anjli.

'Dinner?' he asked.

'I could eat,' she replied as they left the bridge, walking across the car park. 'Vegan?'

As Declan started laughing, Monroe stared at them, no idea why this one statement was so funny.

Obviously, Anjli was an expert in telling jokes.

THEY FILLED THE NEXT COUPLE OF DAYS WITH INTERVIEWS AND confessions; Graham Hagen and Martin Reilly, terrified at the arrival of armed police at their caravan had quickly admitted to the assault on two girls over thirty years earlier, claiming Peanut, the sound engineer had done the spiking without their knowledge. Of course, with Peter Suffolk now dead, there was no way to discredit this, but even with a life of court cases and civil suits ahead of them, social media had already decided their fate, and as Graham slunk back to LA on economy class, Declan knew that neither of them would ever work in the industry again, their *profits* from *Alternator* now long gone.

Marna had admitted to conspiracy to murder Bruce Baker, claiming it was all Andy's idea to force feed him whisky and send him on his way, while Andy did the same, claiming that Marna had been the brains behind everything, even buying the whisky on Bruce's card. And Benny Simpson, now out of self-imposed exile and making deals by testifying against them, didn't know which of them was the worst one.

The one thing everyone could agree on though was that Andy Mears had killed Lorraine Warner; not only had he admitted it to Declan, Bullman and Anjli in the café, he'd also left his DNA on the body while gathering it into the plastic wrap. There was no way either of them would return to Hampstead soon, and Declan learned that Marna's assistant had apparently adopted the greyhound before quitting.

Carrie Woodstock's case was a little more difficult; not only was she an accessory to murder, she'd stolen proprietary tech, and the weight of the US judiciary system hit the Temple Inn Command Unit within hours of her arrest, demanding her extradition to California to face a variety of charges including attempted murder. Declan didn't know what would happen there, but he knew it wouldn't be pretty. Which suited him fine.

And Errol gained a hefty windfall from the sale of *Bear Studios* to Eden Storm, donating a percentage to Lorraine Warner's family, and splitting the rest between Keith's widow and himself. He even claimed to be considering opening a new studio, now he'd gained renewed interest.

Declan had suggested that he build the place *before* allowing people to record there, though.

A WEEK AFTER THE BIRLING GAP ADVENTURE, MONROE SAT IN a pub on Fleet Street. *The Olde Cheshire Cheese* was a traditional tourist fare, but he wasn't there as a tourist.

He wasn't there as a policeman, either.

In front of him, drinking a Newcastle Brown Ale and complaining about how it tasted was Derek Sutton. He'd appeared on Monroe's doorstep the previous day, telling Monroe in no uncertain terms that they needed to talk. And so this meeting had been arranged, and Monroe now sat opposite Sutton, mildly terrified as to what could be so important.

'There's a hit out,' Sutton half slurred. 'I've spent the last week quietly advising people not to take it.'

'Why a hit?' Monroe asked. 'Who's decided to have a pop? I mean, I've got a bit of a queue going on.'

'It's from home, old history,' Sutton replied, and Monroe nodded. Back in the day Monroe's family lived in a small, two up-two down terraced house on Stoneyhurst Street in Possil, a Glasgow suburb where his older brother Kenny had hung out with the *Hutchinsons*, the local crime family, meeting and working with Sutton over several years.

'Is it to do with my brother?' he asked carefully.

Sutton nodded. Kenny was dead, killed in a drive-by shooting on a Hutchinsons' bar in Blackhill when Monroe was still a teenager, but he'd been into a ton of dodgy things by then, and even though it was never proven Kenny Monroe had been the target, everyone had assumed that he was.

'So I'm now the target?' Monroe asked. Surprisingly, Sutton shook his head.

'It's your grandniece,' he said. 'Claire.'

Monroe stared at Sutton for a moment.

'I don't have a grandniece,' he said.

'Aye, you do,' Sutton finished the pint. 'Kenny had a kid with a wee lass named Sherie, back when you were still in short trousers. A daughter named Amy, your niece, and she birthed Claire about seventeen years back.'

'So it's one of them that the hit's on?' Monroe asked, feeling like he was drifting at sea, a *whooshing* noise in his ears.

He had a family he didn't know about.

'Aye,' Sutton replied. 'It's Claire. She's hanging out with a dangerous crowd in Edinburgh, and she's pissed off someone big.'

'Who?' Monroe felt his stomach fall.

He already knew who it was.

'It's the Wright Brothers, isn't it?' he asked. The Wright Brothers were the criminal family that had been rumoured to have killed Kenny. Sutton had shot two of the brothers in a Glasgow bar and left for London before the police could catch him. Years later, and now a police officer, Monroe had learnt that the gang that had killed Kenny ran workshopped arms from outside Leyton, in North East London.

By then Sutton was working for the Lucas Twins, and Monroe had told Sutton what he'd discovered. That night, Sutton burned the nightclub that the London firm worked from to the ground, killing all of them.

The matter of Kenny's death had finally been closed that night.

'I didn't get all the bastards back in Glasgow,' Sutton replied. 'And now the youngest, Lennie, he's cleaning house, proving he should be top dog again.'

Monroe nodded.

'So Lennie Wright is gunning for the Monroes, is he?' he said, finishing his pint and rising. 'What time's the next train to Edinburgh?'

DECLAN WAS AT HIS DESK WHEN THEY CAME FOR HIM.

'Declan Walsh?' A woman's voice spoke from the door to the Unit's office, and Declan turned to see a young woman, no older than thirty, leading a team of uniformed officers into the room. She was ginger, with long straight hair over a vintage olive green German army jacket and jumper. She also had a warrant card in the air, showing Declan as she walked towards him. 'Are you Detective Inspector Declan Walsh?'

'I am,' Declan rose to meet the officers, suspicious. 'What's this to do with?'

'I'm DC Ross, and I'm here in connection with the disappearance of Francine Pearce,' the woman explained. 'Can you tell me when you last saw her?'

'It was just over a week ago,' Declan replied. 'She was following my daughter. I told her not to.'

'And before that?'

'When I visited her while on the run from the police, a few months ago.'

Ross nodded, as if expecting this answer.

'Did you text or phone her? Or did she text or phone you?'

'You know she did,' Declan replied again, his tone becoming terser. 'I put her phone into forensics downstairs.'

He picked up his own phone, finding the message and showing it to Ross.

We need to meet. Now. End this once and for all. Alone, no cops, no subordinates. Say yes and I'll send a public location. FP

'And what did she say when you met her?'

'I didn't meet her,' Declan replied. 'As you already know, I waited an hour, called her number, and found it in a corner of the warehouse with blood on it. I bagged the phone—'

'Not before contaminating the evidence with your own fingerprints,' Ross interrupted.

'I bagged it and gave it to my divisional surgeon.'

'And when did you do that?'

'The following day, when I arrived back at the Unit.'

'Why didn't you place it immediately into a chain of—'

'I was hunting a murderer,' Declan snapped, angry now. 'I didn't have time, and besides, nobody was there to take it because they were hunting the same murderer too.'

He stopped.

'What's this truly about?' he said. 'I made a statement about this.'

'Miss Pearce is missing, and has been for over a week,' DC Ross explained. 'In fact, the last time anyone spoke to her seemed to be when she texted you, arranging a meeting.'

'And that's illegal?' Declan asked, realising that things weren't going the way he expected.

'No, but it is curious that you ensured you took public transport to meet her, considering you had a police issue car here,' Ross smiled. 'One that you know has a tracker on it, as with all police issue vehicles.'

'I was on a case and I'd shared the car with my DS,' Declan explained. 'Again, it's—'

'In the report,' Ross smiled again, and Declan could see that this wasn't one borne of humour, this was a smile of disdain, a feeling that was confirmed when she pulled out her own phone, scanning through the apps for the sound recorder. 'But you didn't put everything in the report, did you, Detective Inspector Walsh? You didn't, for example, put this into the report?'

She played a recording. It was rough, made on a phone, but the voices were clear.

'I get you have issues with me,' Declan's voice spoke. *'But Jess is off limits.'*

'I'm sure I don't know what you mean,' Francine's voice was

nervous, wavering. Declan had wondered about this at the time, but it had all been for show.

'You go near my daughter, you talk to my daughter, you even look at my daughter and I will kill you. I've been a copper for a long time. I know how to make you disappear. And my army training will ensure you know you're dying.'

'Is that a threat?'

'It's a prophecy.'

DC Ross turned off the recording.

'Was that you?' she asked.

'Yes,' Declan reluctantly admitted, realising now how much of a patsy he'd been played for that evening.

Francine Pearce had wanted him to see her. She had wanted him to get angry.

'You threatened, on tape, to ensure that she would disappear,' Ross continued. 'And the next day she did. You were in the same location, an abandoned warehouse for an hour with her—'

'I was not.'

'Then with her *phone* before you left, easily enough time off the grid to dispose of her body, and leave blood we now know is hers on a phone you held on your person for almost twenty-four hours. So let me ask you now, *did you kill Francine Pearce?'*

'I did not,' Declan repeated, the world feeling a little more off-kilter now.

'We examined your car,' Ross continued. 'As a police vehicle, we're allowed to do this without a warrant. In the boot of it, we found traces of blood. Francine Pearce's blood in fact, matching the blood samples on her phone. Did you put her body in there when you killed her?'

'I don't—' Declan was speechless. *How had blood been found there?* 'I mean, I can't—'

'Declan Walsh, I'm arresting you on suspicion of the disappearance and possible murder of Francine Pearce,' Ross said as, at a nod from her, one of the officers that had arrived with her walked over to Declan, turning him to face his desk as he handcuffed him. 'You do not have to say anything, but it may harm your defence if you do not mention when questioned something which you later rely on in court. Anything you do say may be given in evidence.'

'I know my rights, and this is bullshit,' Declan snapped as, on the desk, his phone started ringing. 'Can I at least get that? It might be my boss. And I don't want to get into trouble.'

'You don't think you're in trouble all ready?'

'As I said, this is bullshit.'

'Then it can go to voicemail,' Ross said, indicating for the officer to lead Declan out of the office. 'Get him out of here.'

With that, Declan was led out of the office, which was a shame, because it meant that Declan didn't hear the voicemail made by a frantic Trix Preston.

'Declan, it's Trix. Look, call me the moment you get this, yeah? And you need to get Liz and Jess somewhere safe, somewhere off the grid.'

'We were played. Karl Schnitter knew we'd move him once we'd broken his code, and he had people jump us while transferring him.'

'Dec, he's out there. He's free. I don't know who he had help him, but we reckon it was some of the old Rattlestone crew, and we're looking into it. But seriously, get Jess to safety. He might go after her.'

'And Dec? Get Monroe to call. Tom was driving the van.'

'*I think he's dead, Dec. I think they're all dead.*'

But Declan didn't hear the message. And neither would anyone else for a while.

Because Declan Walsh had been arrested for the abduction and possible murder of Francine Pearce.

And there wasn't a damn thing anyone could do about it.

DI Walsh and the team of the *Last Chance
Saloon* will return in their next thriller

A DINNER TO DIE FOR

Released 12th December 2021

Order Now at Amazon:

http://mybook.to/adinnertodiefor

ACKNOWLEDGEMENTS

When you write a series of books, you find that there are a ton of people out there who help you, sometimes without even realising, and so I wanted to do a little acknowledgement to some of them.

There are people I need to thank, and they know who they are. People like Andy Briggs, who started me on this path over a coffee during a pandemic literally a year ago to the day as I write this, people like Barry Hutchinson, who patiently zoom-called and gave advice back in 2020, the people on various Facebook groups who encouraged me when I didn't know if I could even do this, the designers who gave advice on cover design and on book formatting all the way to my friends and family, who saw what I was doing not as mad folly, but as something good, including my brother Chris Lee, who I truly believe could make a fortune as a post-retirement copy editor, if not a solid writing career of his own.

Also, I couldn't have done this without my growing army of ARC readers who not only show me where I falter, but also raise awareness of me in the social media world, ensuring that other people learn of my books, including (but not limited to) Maureen Webb, Maryam Paulsen, Edwina Townsend and especially Jacqueline Beard MBE, who has copyedited all eight books so far (including the prequel), line by line for me, and deserves *way more* than our agreed fee.

But mainly, I tip my hat and thank you. *The reader.* Who, five books ago took a chance on an unknown author in a pile of Kindle books, and thought you'd give them a go, and who has carried on this far with them.

I write Declan Walsh for you. He (and his team) solves crimes for you. And with luck, he'll keep on solving them for a very long time.

Jack Gatland / Tony Lee,
   London, September 2021

ABOUT THE AUTHOR

Jack Gatland is the pen name of #1 *New York Times Bestselling Author* Tony Lee, who has been writing in all media for over thirty years, including comics, graphic novels, middle grade books, audio drama, TV and film for *DC Comics, Marvel, BBC, ITV, Random House, Penguin USA, Hachette* and a ton of other publishers and broadcasters.

These have included licenses such as *Doctor Who, Spider Man, X-Men, Star Trek, Battlestar Galactica, MacGyver,* BBC's *Doctors, Wallace and Gromit* and *Shrek*, as well as work created with musicians such as *Ozzy Osbourne, Joe Satriani* and *Megadeth.*

As Tony, he's toured the world talking to reluctant readers with his 'Change The Channel' school tours, and lectures on screenwriting and comic scripting for *Raindance* in London.

An introvert West Londoner by heart, he lives with his wife Tracy and dog Fosco, just outside London.

Chapter Titles

This time, as the novel was music orientated, I've named each chapter after a relevant song. As several are names used by several bands, and a couple are quite obscure, I thought I'd name them below.

Prologue (Renaissance, 1972)
Jailhouse Rock (Elvis Presley, 1952)
Taking Care of Business (Bachman–Turner Overdrive, 1973)
Direct Action Briefing (999, 1978)
Abney Park (Abney Park, 1998)
Cross-Eyed Mary (Jethro Tull, 1971)
Money, Money, Money (ABBA, 1976)
Roadkill (The 1975, 2020)
I Am The Law (Anthrax, 1987)
Spies Like Us (Paul McCartney, 1985)
Under Your Thumb (Godley and Creme, 1981)
Live To Tell (Madonna, 1986)
Our House (Madness, 1983)
Meat Is Murder (The Smiths, 1985)
Every Breath You Take (The Police, 1983)
No Explanation (Peter Cetera, 1990)
Lifestyles Of The Rich & Famous (Good Charlotte, 2002)
Notes In The Margin (John Williams, 2008)
Hampstead Incident (Donovan, 1966)
My Generation (The Who, 1965)
Guns Don't Kill People, Rappers Do (Goldie Looking Chain, 2004)
Informer (Snow, 1992)
Freeze-Frame (J. Geils Band, 1981)
Don't You (Forget About Me) (Simple Minds, 1985)
Maniac (Michael Sembello, 1983)

Sunset Cliffs (Paul Wright, 2008)
Epilogue (Electric Light Orchestra, 1981)

Locations In The Book

The locations that I use in my books are real, if altered slightly for dramatic intent. Here's some more information about a few of them...

Bear Studios is a location fictionalised but based on a real place, the onetime *Ram Rehearsal Studios* on Dawley Road, named after *The Ram* pub opposite, sadly now demolished.

Ram Rehearsal Studios closed many years ago, but in the 80s and 90s it was the rehearsal space of many bands, often college students, and in 1987 it was where my short-lived hard-rock college band rehearsed before the college year ended and we all went our separate ways, forgetting our dreams of becoming rocks stars.

The name of our band back then was *Alternator*, by the way...

Abney Park is a real place and is found in Stoke Newington, in the London Borough of Hackney. It's a historic parkland originally laid out in the early 18th century by Lady Mary Abney and Dr. Isaac Watts, along with the neighbouring Hartopp family, and is named after Sir Thomas Abney, who served as Lord Mayor of London in 1700–1701.

In 1840 it became a non-denominational garden cemetery, a semi-public park arboretum, and an educational institute, which was widely celebrated as an example of its time. A total of 196,843 burials had taken place there up to the year 2000, including William and Catherine Booth, founders of *The Salvation Army*, who are buried in a prominent location close to Church Street.

It is now a Local Nature Reserve.

Billionaire's Row, more officially known as *The Bishop's Avenue* is classed as one of the wealthiest streets in the world. The 66-house street runs displays a variety of architectural styles and average property prices on the avenue surpassed one million pounds in the late 1980s. In 2006, the smallest houses in the street were selling for five million while a larger house, Turkish tycoon Halis Toprak's *Toprak Mansion*, sold amidst great secrecy to the president of Kazakhstan, Nursultan Nazarbayev, for fifty million in January 2008, making it one of the most expensive houses in the world, as listed by Forbes magazine.

However, *The Guardian* revealed in 2014 that in total 16 of the properties (an estimated worth of three hundred and fifty million) are derelict and have not been lived in for several decades. According to one resident, perhaps only three of the houses are occupied on a full-time basis. Most of the properties in the most expensive part of the avenue are registered to companies in tax havens including the British Virgin Islands, Curaçao, the Bahamas, Panama, and the Channel Islands, allowing international owners to avoid paying stamp duty on the purchase and to remain anonymous.

Birling Gap is a coastal hamlet situated on the Seven Sisters, not far from Beachy Head and is owned by the *National Trust*.

Coastal erosion has already removed some of the row of coastguard cottages built in 1878, but those that remain are still inhabited. There is a cafe, shop and visitor centre run by the *National Trust,* and a metal staircase leading down to the enclosed pebble beach and the Seven Sisters chalk cliffs. In time, the houses are likely to be demolished due to the severe coastal erosion; the Government has concluded that the commercial value of the houses does not justify the construction of sea defences.

If walkers are cut off at high tide, they can climb the ladder, which is replaced often, to Birling Gap.

Finally, Eastcheap Albums is another 'name-changed to protect the innocent' location, based on *Eastcheap Records*, part of the *Records Bar* family of clubs, live venues and bars. Near Monument tube station on the corner of Eastcheap and Lovat Lane, the real venue boasts two bars, two stages and live music every night.

To my knowledge, no performer has died on stage there.

If you're interested in seeing what the *real* locations look like, I post 'behind the scenes' location images on my Instagram feed. This will continue through all the books, and I suggest you follow it.

In fact, feel free to follow me on all my social media by clicking on the links below. They're new, but over time it can be a place where we can engage, discuss Declan and put the world to rights.

www.jackgatland.com

Want more books by Jack Gatland? Turn the page...

THE THEFT OF A **PRICELESS** PAINTING...
A GANGSTER WITH A **CRIPPLING DEBT**...
A **BODY COUNT** RISING BY THE HOUR...

AND ELLIE RECKLESS IS CAUGHT IN THE MIDDLE.

JACK GATLAND

PAINT
— THE —
DEAD

A 'COP FOR CRIMINALS' ELLIE RECKLESS NOVEL

A NEW PROCEDURAL CRIME SERIES WITH
A TWIST - FROM THE CREATOR OF THE
BESTSELLING 'DI DECLAN WALSH' SERIES

AVAILABLE ON AMAZON / KINDLE UNLIMITED

EIGHT PEOPLE. EIGHT SECRETS.
ONE SNIPER.

THE
B⊕ARD
ROOM

HOW FAR WOULD YOU GO TO GAIN JUSTICE?

NEW YORK TIMES #1 BESTSELLER TONY LEE WRITING AS
JACK GATLAND

A NEW STANDALONE THRILLER WITH
A TWIST - FROM THE CREATOR OF THE
BESTSELLING 'DI DECLAN WALSH' SERIES

AVAILABLE ON AMAZON / KINDLE UNLIMITED

THEY TRIED TO KILL HIM...
NOW HE'S OUT FOR **REVENGE.**

NEW YORK TIMES #1 BESTSELLER **TONY LEE** WRITING AS

JACK GATLAND

THE MURDER OF AN **MI5 AGENT**...
A BURNED SPY **ON THE RUN** FROM HIS OWN PEOPLE...
AN ENEMY OUT TO **STOP HIM** AT ANY COST...
AND A **PRESIDENT** ABOUT TO BE **ASSASSINATED**...

SLEEPING SOLDIERS

A **TOM MARLOWE** THRILLER

BOOK 1 IN A NEW SERIES OF THRILLERS IN THE STYLE OF
JASON BOURNE, JOHN MILTON OR **BURN NOTICE,** AND
SPINNING OUT OF THE **DECLAN WALSH** SERIES OF BOOKS
AVAILABLE ON AMAZON / KINDLE UNLIMITED

JACK GATLAND

THE LIONHEART CURSE

HUNT THE GREATEST TREASURES
PAY THE GREATEST PRICE

BOOK 1 IN A NEW SERIES OF ADVENTURES
IN THE STYLE OF 'THE DA VINCI CODE'
FROM THE CREATOR OF DECLAN WALSH

Printed in Great Britain
by Amazon

23132151R00202